Fall 1997 Vol. XVII, no. 3
ISSN: 0276-0045 ISBN: 1-56478-177-1

THE REVIEW OF CONTEMPORARY FICTION

 Address all correspondence to:
The Review of Contemporary Fiction,
ISU Campus Box 4241, Normal, IL 61790-4241 USA.

The Review of Contemporary Fiction is published three times a year (February, June, October) by The Review of Contemporary Fiction, Inc., a nonprofit organization located at ISU Campus Box 4241, Normal, IL 61790-4241. ISSN 0276-0045. Subscription prices are as follows:

Single volume (three issues):
Individuals: $17.00; foreign, add $3.50;
Institutions: $26.00; foreign, add $3.50.

DISTRIBUTION. Bookstores should send orders to:

University of Chicago Press Distribution Center, 11030 S. Langley Ave., Chicago, IL 60628. Phone 800-621-2736; fax 800-621-8476.

This issue is partially supported by grants from the Illinois Arts Council, a state agency.

Indexed in *American Humanities Index, International Bibliography of Periodical Literature, International Bibliography of Book Reviews, MLA Bibliography,* and *Book Review Index.* Abstracted in *Abstracts of English Studies.*

The Review of Contemporary Fiction is also available in 16mm microfilm, 35mm microfilm, and 105mm microfiche from University Microfilms International, 300 North Zeeb Road, Ann Arbor, MI 48106-1346.

The Review of Contemporary Fiction

Future issues devoted to: Rikki Ducornet, Curtis White, Milorad Pavić, Richard Powers, Ed Sanders, Latvian fiction, and postmodern Japanese fiction.

Back Issues

Back issues are still available for the following numbers of the *Review of Contemporary Fiction* ($8 each unless otherwise noted):

Douglas Woolf / Wallace Markfield
William Eastlake / Aidan Higgins
Alexander Theroux / Paul West
Camilo José Cela
Claude Simon ($15)
Chandler Brossard
Samuel Beckett
Claude Ollier / Carlos Fuentes
John Barth / David Markson
Donald Barthelme / Toby Olson
Paul Bowles / Coleman Dowell
Brigid Brophy / Robert Creeley / Osman Lins
William T. Vollmann / Susan Daitch / David Foster Wallace
William H. Gass / Manuel Puig
Robert Walser
José Donoso / Jerome Charyn
Georges Perec / Felipe Alfau
Joseph McElroy
Djuna Barnes
Angela Carter / Tadeusz Konwicki
Stanley Elkin / Alasdair Gray
Edmund White / Samuel R. Delany
Mario Vargas Llosa / Josef Skvorecky
Wilson Harris / Alan Burns

Special Fiction Issue: Fiction by Pinget, Bowles, Mathews, Markfield, Rower, Ríos, Tindall, Sorrentino, Goytisolo, McGonigle, Dukore, Dowell, McManus, Mosley, and Acker

Novelist as Critic: Essays by Garrett, Barth, Sorrentino, Wallace, Ollier, Brooke-Rose, Creeley, Mathews, Kelly, Abbott, West, McCourt, McGonigle, and McCarthy

New Finnish Fiction: Fiction by Eskelinen, Jäntti, Kontio, Krohn, Paltto, Sairanen, Selo, Siekkinen, Sund, Valkeapää

New Italian Fiction: Interviews and fiction by Malerba, Tabucchi, Zanotto, Ferrucci, Busi, Corti, Rasy, Cherchi, Balduino, Ceresa, Capriolo, Carrera, Valesio, and Gramigna

Grove Press Number: Contributions by Allen, Beckett, Corso, Ferlinghetti, Jordan, McClure, Rechy, Rosset, Selby, Sorrentino, and others

New Danish Fiction: Fiction by Brøgger, Høeg, Andersen, Grøndahl, Holst, Jensen, Thorup, Michael, Sibast, Ryum, Lynggaard, Grønfeldt, Willumsen, and Holm

The Future of Fiction: Essays by Birkerts, Caponegro, Franzen, Galloway, Maso, Morrow, Vollmann, White, and others

Individuals receive a 10% discount on orders of one issue and a 20% discount on any order of two or more issues. Postage for domestic shipments is $3.50 for the first issue and 75¢ for each additional issue. For foreign shipments, postage is $4.50 for the first issue and $1.00 for each additional issue. All orders must be paid in U.S. dollars. Send payment to:

Review of Contemporary Fiction, ISU Campus Box 4241,
Normal, IL 61790-4241, *tel* 309 438 7555, *fax* 309 438 7422

contents

"On the road to Ermenonville" (1928)
Courtesy of the Centre de Documentation Raymond Queneau

CANIS MAJOR:
Introducing Raymond Queneau

Mary Campbell-Sposito

> Yes, it could begin this way, right here, just like that [. . .] in this neutral place that belongs to all and to none . . .
>
> —Georges Perec

On 29 October 1976, one day after the funeral of his friend and mentor Raymond Queneau, Georges Perec wrote the opening lines of his masterpiece *Life A User's Manual,* dedicated to Queneau's memory.[1] The inscription signals Queneau's influence on writers of his and succeeding generations. As an editor, a novelist, a poet, an essayist, an "amateur" mathematician, a painter, and a screenwriter, Queneau was involved in many of the twentieth century's most intellectually dynamic years.

Raymond Auguste Queneau was born on 21 February 1903 in the port city of Le Havre, France, the only child of parents who owned and operated a haberdashery. A good student, he had a special gift for philosophy. During his school years he acquired habits that would remain a part of his life, frequenting local bookstores, reading voraciously (the Larousse dictionary included, "even the pink pages"), writing, studying Arabic, Hittite, and Hebrew on his own, and attending films, notably those of Charlie Chaplin.

In the fall of 1920 Queneau enrolled at the Sorbonne to study philosophy, and in 1926 he received his university degree. From 1924 to 1929 Queneau regularly haunted the surrealists' headquarters during their period of greatest ferment. There he met André Breton, Louis Aragon, and Robert Desnos, among others.

Called to military service in 1925, Queneau was a member of the 3rd Zouaves until early 1927, mostly in Algeria. His work there consisted of building roads, sweeping (an activity that figures as a leitmotiv in several novels), interminable night watches and "getting plastered." In the summer of 1928 he married Janine Kahn, whose sister Simone was married to André Breton. After his honorable discharge from the service, a break with Breton for "strictly personal reasons," and a trip to Portugal during which he read Joyce's *Ulysses* (a tremendous influence on his writings), he was at loose ends, lacking a permanent job. From 1930 to 1933 he took refuge in the National Library to study "literary madmen." He also worked at various times as a salesman of paper products, a bank clerk, and a tutor to a wealthy American. In 1932 Queneau and his wife made an "initiatory voyage" to Greece, which inspired his first novel, *The Bark Tree* (1933). Publishing regularly in the 1930s, Queneau's writing was certainly influenced both by Kojève's lectures on Hegel from 1933 to 1939 (Queneau's lecture notes were later published by Gallimard as *Introduction à la lecture de Hegel)* and by the analysis he underwent during that same period. These productive years saw the formation (and occasional rupture) of friendships with Henry Miller, Georges Bataille, Max Jacob, and Michel Leiris.

From 1936 to 1938 Queneau wrote a column in *L'Intransigeant* called "Connaissez-vous Paris?" and in 1937 he co-founded the review *Volontés.* By 1938 he was employed as an English reader for Editions Gallimard, a welcome source of support for his wife and young son, Jean-Marie. In 1941 he was named secretary-general of Gallimard and by 1945 he had become director of its *Encyclopédie de la Pléiade.*

For fifteen years after the Liberation in 1945, Queneau was a popular participant in the Saint-Germain-des-Prés scene. This was particularly so after he published *Exercises in Style* (1949) and "Si tu t'imagines," the poem-turned-song Juliette Gréco made famous in 1949, and after his election to the Académie Goncourt in 1951.

Queneau became a member of the Collège de 'Pataphysique in 1950, a "society of erudite and useless research" inspired by the work of Alfred Jarry to establish a "science of imaginary solutions." In the fall of 1960 Queneau and François Le Lionnais originated the Oulipo (Ouvroir de Littérature Potentielle, or Workshop of Potential Literature). Its first meeting was held in November 1960, with ten founding members, as a subcommittee of the Collège de 'Pataphysique. The Oulipo's members were a varied group made up of writers, mathematicians, professors, and 'pataphysicians. Their aims were to redeem ancient literary forms and constraints, to investigate the rapport between mathematics and literary creation, and to synthesize new structures. If it should happen that a structure thought to be new had already been invented in the past, the Oulipo simply qualified the text in question as "plagiarism by anticipation."[2] One example of an Oulipian product is "La Cantatrice sauve," composed of one hundred permutations of Monserrat Caballé's name, each preceded by a short explanatory paragraph. Another is the S + 7 Method: given a text, one replaces each substantive with the seventh one following it in a dictionary of choice. Queneau was very much a guiding light and a source of inspiration for the Oulipians. Gilbert Sorrentino's "Variations for Raymond Queneau" pays him homage in true Oulipian fashion.

Queneau's concerns as a writer remained relatively constant throughout his career, informing his novels and poetry and espoused in his essays. Of interest to him in his early years as a writer was the fact that formal written French and French as it was spoken in everyday life bore little resemblance to one another. Furthermore, during his stay in Greece in 1932, he learned that the Greeks make a formal distinction between the *Katharevusa* (pure language) and the *Demotic* (popular language). For a time Queneau called for reform of formal written French—not only its orthography but its syntax and morphology as well.

Another interest of Queneau's was mathematical structure, so vital in the first novels. Poetry, of course, already imposes a certain form on its content. His essay "Technique of the Novel" (1937) addresses this enthusiasm and the way in which it was used in several novels. As his daily life filled with more responsibilities, the novels required several years instead of just months to write, and they became freer of structural preoccupations than the earlier work. The first novels were "conditioned by a concern for . . . order and structure," part of which was "a game in which one invents the rules one then obeys." Language as a game with rules, a "game of reasoning, or a game of chance with a maximum of reasoning," remained a principal theme throughout his lifetime.[3]

Ever-present in Queneau's work is his tendency—within the strict rules he set himself for composition—to blur borders. As he put it, "I never saw essential differences between the novel, such as I wish to write it, and poetry."[4] This creative philosophy allowed him the freedom to explore form that his strict rules of composition would not. Claude Debon's essay, "Queneau and Poetic Illusion," probes Queneau's relationship to the novel-poem and the comic. Exploration of form extended to individual words: neologisms, portmanteau words, the macaronic, combinatorics, and permutations. These effects were used in the novels and poetry to temper serious topics and to encourage readers to see things in a new way.

Affiliated with structure, language as a game, and exploration of forms are humor and philosophical considerations. Queneau's humor, like Rabelais's, is the laughter of the carnival, "festive . . . universal in scope . . . ambivalent . . . mocking, deriding."[5] In an absurd universe one does as well to laugh as to despair. Queneau's use of laughter-provoking characters and language underscores the fact that man is always free to choose his reaction and to refuse to see things in absolute terms, an attitude that relates in turn to experiments with language and the forms of literature. The nature of being and nonbeing is a constant theme in Queneau's novels as well.

Queneau's fiction, poetry, and essays cover more than half a century. For the most part, our discussion is limited to his fiction. Queneau's first novel, *The Bark Tree,* was written in a relatively short period in 1932-33. Highly structured, mathematical, philosophical in nature, humorous, and experimental with regard to narrative techniques, *The Bark Tree* perceptively explores being and nonbeing using "spoken" French instead of formal written French. Begun as a translation of Descartes's *Discourse on Method* into spoken French, influenced by the Greeks' dual language system, by J. W. Dunne's *An Experiment in Time,* and by James Joyce, the novel's plot is an intricate one, circular in nature, predating Joyce's circular *Finnegans Wake* by several years. This highly plotted prismatic novel includes scenes in which a concierge delivers a soliloquy taken from Plato's "Parmenides," a funeral is described from a dog's perspective, a bank employee incarnates Descartes's *cogito,* a treasure hunt surrounds an old door, and characters at the book's end discover that they are fictional.[6] The French title, *Le Chiendent,* (crabgrass), contains the word *chien* (dog), probably Queneau's first autoreferential gesture, which, like Alfred Hitchcock, he never fails to provide us.

Gueule de Pierre (1934) was later combined with *Les Temps mêlés* (1941), considerably modified, and published in 1948 as *Saint Glinglin.* Gilbert Pestureau's essay, "The Art of the Novel in *Saint Glinglin,*" explores Queneau's integration of the full range of literature into the novel as well as his use of multiple thematic domains (psychoanalysis, ethnology, the philosophy of history, cinema, and science fiction). The novel's final version emphasizes myth and anthropology. Its title is part of the French expression "jusqu'à la saint-glinglin," which means roughly "until the cows come home."

Two more novels, *The Last Days* (1936) and *Odile* (1937), are very much autobiographical works covering Queneau's university days, his search for happiness, falling in love, and his years in the surrealist movement. *Oak and Dog* (1937) bears the subtitle "Novel in Verse" and details Queneau's life from birth through psychoanalysis. Its title links two words Queneau saw as dual sides of his own character: "oak and dog: these are my two names, delicate etymology" (81). In Norman dialect *quesne* is the word for *chêne* (oak) and *quenot* the word for *chien* (dog). He felt that his character was embodied by the oak, "noble and tall [. . .] strong and powerful" and by the dog, "cynical, indelicate [. . .] ferocious and impulsive" (81).[7]

Children of Clay (1938), excerpted in this issue, is the last of Queneau's novels to be translated into English. More than one-third of the text is the result of his research on literary madmen, represented as the headmaster Chambernac's *Encyclopedia of Inexact Sciences.* The novel's fictional portion details the story of the Limon (Clay) family in France from about 1914 to 1935. Queneau institutes a new technical device: use of the page's right half only for quoting biblical passages, "literary madmen," interior monologues, or for a character's thoughts. Queneau himself appears in one of his most overt cameos at the end of the novel as a young writer who agrees to take on Chambernac's *Encyclopedia.*

A Hard Winter (1939) is a short, well-fashioned novel, containing fewer experimental techniques than earlier works. The linear narrative details one man's psychological passage from bitter despair (after losing most of his family in a fire years earlier, coupled with an old war injury) to the ability to love another person again. Jacques Jouet's contribution, "Three 'Interludes' from *Raymond Queneau*" is in part an exploration of the novel's referencing of *Hamlet.*

Pierrot (1942) appears to be a light and humorous work, but its foundations are serious and philosophical. Pierrot is a simple and aimless young man (a "pinball wizard" nonetheless) who works at Uni-Park, a Parisian amusement park. He drifts through a series of events, unable to connect with anything, though he falls in love with the boss's daughter and meets the guardian of a "Poldevian" prince's mausoleum. The guardian wishes to make Pierrot his heir, but Pierrot does not materialize to sign legal papers, so the opportunity is lost. When Uni-Park mysteriously burns, he takes a job driving some animals to the south of France. His two passengers, Mésange and Pistolet, are eventually revealed to be respectively an ape and a wild boar, but not until Mésange has smoked a cigar, jumped on a hotel bed, and displayed atrocious table manners with Pistolet. Pierrot's final act at the novel's end is to burst out laughing. In his own way he realizes a profound truth: that laughter is humans' best defense against a vast, meaningless, and absurd universe which they cannot control.

The Skin of Dreams (1944), like *Pierrot,* appears to be a light novel lacking in seriousness, but Harry Mathews's essay, "Charity Begins at Home," reminds us that here again there is more to Queneau than meets the eye. The protagonist, Jacques L'Aumône, is a daydreamer who leaves his job for a singer and ends up in Hollywood as a movie star called James Charity. The line between Jacques's daydreams and his real life is so blurred that it is hard to tell when one leaves off and the other one begins. His greatest film is *The Skin of Dreams,* a retelling of his life story up to the point where he signs a contract for his next film . . . *The Skin of Dreams.* The cinema and its techniques are very much in evidence in this novel.

Queneau's next published work was unprecedented, neither a novel nor poetry. *Exercises in Style* (1949) had as its point of departure a banal argument on a bus. Queneau began by recounting the incident in twelve different ways. Several years later there were ninety-nine "exercises in style." Some of the titles give an idea of their variety: "Litotes," "Anagrams," "For ze Frrensh," "Back Slang," "Dream," "Permutations by Groups of 1,2,3 and 4 Words," and "Haiku." The idea was based on Bach's *The Art of Fugue,* the principle of which Queneau felt could be applied to writing as well as to music. Repetition of the commonplace theme with permutations lends the written text a comic quality. The sheer virtuousity of the variations is stunning.

Queneau's *We Always Treat Women Too Well* (1949) appeared under the pseudonym of Sally Mara. The story involves the occupation of a Dublin branch post office by Irish revolutionaries during the 1916 Easter uprising and is a parody of the graphically violent and erotic nature of some American detective fiction. Allusions to James Joyce abound. Queneau uses names of minor characters in *Ulysses,* duplicates many of its locations, and refers to Joyce himself. The revolutionaries' password is "Finnegans Wake!" (an anachronism that Queneau delights in pointing out in a footnote). This and *Journal intime* (1950), Sally Mara's supposed diary, represent his pseudonymous writings, later published as *The Complete Works of Sally Mara.*

The Sunday of Life (1952) features another simple protagonist-philosopher, Valentin Brû. He marries a woman much older than he who owns a haberdashery. Because expenses are tight, Valentin goes on their honeymoon alone. His wife Julia's sideline is fortune-telling, and when she has a stroke and is unable to continue the job, Valentin takes over for her, discovering his gift for prognostication. Even-tempered with saintly qualities, Brû tries for a while to observe time passing while thinking of nothing, because "it elevates the soul." Sweeping is another occupation Valentin enjoys. His greatest interest is in visiting the battlefield of Jena, the site of Napoleon's victory over the Prussians in 1806, an event Hegel viewed as the beginning of the end of the dialectic of history.[8] Just before war breaks out and Paris falls to the Germans, Valentin is able to make the journey. The novel's ending is similar to *Pierrot*'s: Julia bursts out laughing when she sees Valentin trying to help three young women through a train window. She realizes that for him it is an excuse to grope them. Besides the simpleton-philosopher theme, references to gnostic philosophy, and Hegel's presence in the epigraph, the title, and throughout the text, Queneau continues to elaborate his narrative techniques in this poetic novel and to use spoken French as a source of dialogue. A typical visual (and ontological) joke of Queneau's is a brother-in-law who has several dozen last names. The surname varies by as little as one letter each time (Bolucra, Botrula, Botugat, etc.), but it always begins with a "B."

Queneau's next novel, *Zazie* (1959), signaled popular fame for him in France, largely because of the novelty of using slangy spoken language and phonetic spelling throughout. Zazie is a young girl left for the weekend in Paris with her Uncle Gabriel. She belies her innocence by using rough language. Her standard response to nearly everything ("my ass") becomes a leitmotiv in the novel. Her Uncle Gabriel is a female impersonator in a nightclub whose companion, the gentle Marceline, proves to be a man in drag. Zazie has a multitude of wild adventures, though she wishes only to ride the métro, on strike that weekend. When her wish comes true, she is sound asleep, oblivious to the ride. *Zazie,* a best-seller, was made into a film directed by Louis Malle not long after the book appeared, thus assuring its even wider distribution among the French population.

As an experiment with constraints on language, Queneau had long planned to write ten sonnets which would serve as a basis for multiple combinations (10^{14} to be exact). This he accomplished in 1961 with *One Hundred Million Million Poems.* The book's layout is uniquely composed in that each line of each sonnet is cut into a strip and is thus separate or independent from all the others. The book illustrates perfectly one system of constraints Queneau imposed on himself for creative purposes. End rhymes had to be compatible and neither too banal nor too obscure; each sonnet had to have a theme or some continuity, and the grammatical structure had to be the same for each. He reckoned that if it took forty-five seconds to read a sonnet and fifteen seconds to reorganize the strips, by reading eight hours a day for 200 days each year there would be enough material for more than a million centuries of reading in all. Along these lines, André Blavier's essay, "Drôles de Drames," ponders the complex network of allusions involved in a single line of one of Queneau's sonnets, "L'Amer" from *Fendre les flots.*

The Blue Flowers (1965) followed. Queneau's focus in this novel is upon dreams and history with language very much a player. In French "bonnes fleurs bleues" means "sweet dreams," so the title *Les Fleurs bleues* announces a principal thematic preoccupation. The two main characters, the Duke of Auge and Cidrolin, are each the other's alter ego. When one is asleep, he dreams the other. Oddly enough, the Duke of Auge lives in 1264 at the novel's beginning, while Cidrolin is a modern (1964) Parisian barge-dweller. With each dream, the Duke leaps 175 years into the future toward Cidrolin. He arrives in 1964 with stops in 1439, 1614, and 1789. History is a definite theme in the novel, from its first words: "On the twenty-fifth of September, twelve hundred and sixty-four" (7). Characters debate seriously how to determine the moment when an event becomes history and are concerned about "world history in general and general history in particular" (30). However, language is never far away: " 'So much history,' said the Duke of Auge to the Duke of Auge, 'so much history just for a few puns and a few anachro-nisms' " (7). Puns, twisted proverbs, neologisms, anaphora, and erudite talking horses are frequent reminders of Queneau's underlying interests. At the end of the novel, a great flood covers the land and Cidrolin's barge, appropriately named "The Ark," comes to rest on the top of a castle keep. Mud covers the earth still, but a few little blue flowers have begun to blossom.

A final novel, *The Flight of Icarus,* appeared in 1968. The French title, *Le Vol d'Icare,* has a double meaning that does not translate to English, as Barbara Wright points out in her essay on the pleasures and pains of "Translating Queneau." The novel takes the form of a play with seventy-four scenes, dialogue, and stage directions, whose characters come to life. Set in Paris in 1895, Icarus, the story's main character, escapes from the pages of a novel by Hubert Lubert, who tries with a detective's help to get him back. Icarus attempts to fly, as did his mythological antecedent, and is likewise unsuccessful. Jacques Jouet's contribution explores the Icarian theme in Queneau's writings.

Queneau's final poetic work, *Morale élémentaire* (1975), is divided into three parts. The first of these is discussed in detail in Jacques Roubaud's essay, "The Birth of a Form: *Elementary Morality.*" The two remaining sections are prose poems influenced by the *I Ching.* The tone of the poetry overall is somber, serious, and reflective. Puns and spoken French are nowhere to be found. Claude Debon sees the volume "in all respects as a crowning achievement," and she remarks that the poems of this collection are extraordinarily dense because they "weave tightly the triple thread of Logos, Anthropos and Cosmos."[9]

Raymond Queneau's position in twentieth-century literature is a distinctive one because of the sheer variety of his novels and poetry and his nonstop experimentation with language. As an editor, he was influential in shaping literary trends while participating actively as a novelist. His work constantly questions literary conventions and cultural institutions with humor and irreverence. By subverting fossilized structures, he leads us ultimately to a literature ever aware of itself as a genre, guided by great works from the past, always evolving, and capable of incorporating the subversion into new combinations.

NOTES

[1]David Bellos, *Georges Perec: A Life in Words* (Boston: David R. Godine, 1993), 619-20. Bellos most ably translated Perec's *La Vie mode d'emploi* as *Life A User's Manual* (Boston: David R. Godine, 1987).

[2]Warren F. Motte Jr.'s *Oulipo: A Primer of Potential Literature* (Lincoln: Univ. of Nebraska Press, 1986) is an excellent source of information on the Oulipo and its members.

[3]Raymond Queneau, *Entretiens avec Georges Charbonnier* (Paris: Gallimard, 1962), 56.

[4]Queneau, 56.

[5]Mikhail Bakhtin, *Rabelais and His World* (Bloomington: Indiana Univ. Press, 1968), 11-12.

[6]The concierge's platonic soliloquy is a meditation on being: "Being is, nonbeing isn't,/Being isn't, nonbeing is,/Being is, nonbeing is,/Being isn't, nonbeing isn't" trans. Barbara Wright, (London: Calder and Boyars, 1968), 248.

[7]These are my translations from Queneau's *Chêne et chien* (Paris: Denoël, 1937), 56.

[8]Jane Alison Hale, *The Lyric Encyclopedia of Raymond Queneau* (Ann Arbor: Univ. of Michigan Press, 1989), 19.

[9]Claude Debon, ed. *Raymond Queneau: Oeuvres complètes* (Paris: Gallimard, 1989), 1457, 1455.

ACKNOWLEDGMENTS

We wish to thank the contributors, particularly Harry Mathews and Barbara Wright, Suzanne Bagoly of the Centre de Documentation Raymond Queneau, Jean-Marie Queneau, Madeleine Velguth, Chas Kestermeier, Warren Motte, Marcel Benabou, David Bellos, Luc Derrendinger, Nathalie Malengreau, Laurent Charlet, and most especially Gary Sposito, who makes everything possible. Thanks to the following publishers for their permission to reproduce and to translate copyrighted material: Editions Gallimard (Paris), La Manufacture (Paris), and Peter Lang Publishing, Inc. (New York).

Variations for Raymond Queneau

Gilbert Sorrentino

I

Robert and Manuel lingered, looking at imagery.
Are you not ashamed of having tried to lift up a young lady's dress?
You know what I said to your father?
Mind your own business—and lock up your sisters.
Oh, but I'm kidding. "You give me the shivers."
Near the soda fountain I saw a strange-looking Stone:
Did you see those breasts? I shall try and sit beside *her* next time.

"Quivers, near the morning star . . . the sea!"
Underground, the night's lit up,
Extant is a letter by Leibniz
Near the soda fountain: "I saw a strange-looking stone."
"Extant" is a letter? By Leibniz?
Are you not ashamed of having tried to lift up a young lady's dress
Underground? The night's lit up.

Cento acrostic

II

The young lady's father tried to see
The underground fountain, the fountain of stone.
The extant sisters of Manuel are lit up by the morning.
You lingered, ashamed, up near a strange-looking
Business, you saw a lady's lock.

"Give her the letter," I said, "night's near,
Oh! night's near, time quivers and shivers."
I'm having a soda: To young Robert Leibniz!
To your dress and those breasts! (You did not sit up.)
"Shall you try a soda next?"

You lift, lift your dress. You mind, I know,
But is kidding not up to me?—is
The "stone" ashamed? By your own extant letter,
You saw the strange-looking underground
Imagery.

You and your Leibniz are beside the sea,
Looking up at what? A lit star!

III

The lawyer's fiancée tried to see
The fandango, the "fandango of sin."
(The stories of Musil are lit up by the Muses.)

You lingered up near a brothel,
You saw a lawyer's lavaliere.
"Give *her* the lease!" I said. (Nobody's near,

Oh, nobody's near, tinsel quivers and
Shivers.) "I'm having a Scotch: To Rudy
Lewis! To your dream! And those breakfasts!

Shall you try a Scotch next?" You lift, lift
Your dream, you mind, I know, but
Is kidding not up to me? Is the *sin*

Ashamed? By your own leave, you saw
Underwater. Idiots! You and your Lewis
Are beside the seraglio, looking up

At what? A *sunset?*

Nominal substitution

IV

A nomad and Queen Rayon query
Rude Don Money: Do you undo day, man?
"No, do you?" Query: Do you dye a door red?

"No, and you?" Query: Do you read on yonder
Quay, do you need money? "No!"
Are you mad on Monday, moody?
"No, damn you, no, you queer, dead duo!"

Queen and nomad, mad dyad, moan
And damn Don Money; deem Don "Mary,"
Mary Money, a May moon-daemon.

"Query me no more: my moon, noon, yard, quay,
my dray, my red rood—are done! Me, *Mary?*
Mary Money, a demon madonna?
O no! No, no! O doom!" Dead. (END.)

Beau present

V

You know what I said to your father?
"Give her the letter," I said. "Night's near!"
You saw the strange-looking underground
Business, you saw a lady's lock,
You lingered up near a brothel—
the Fandango: the Fandango of sin.

There was a time when there *was* sin.
Back in the days of mother and father
When boys dreamed of bedroom and brothel,
Of garters and sweat, of dazed sex near
And far, prayed for a room with a lock
On the door, a sweet life with girls, underground.

When my mother died I was numbly underground
Much of the time. Trying to overlook sin:
Unsuccessfully. No dark venue to lock
Up the gloom. But maybe *your* father
Will lie to you of his unique, great, and near-
Spectacular feats, e.g., "I Wept in a Brothel."

Some geezers spend their rotting years in a brothel.
This teaches them that women in "underground"
Vocations lie and laugh and like to slouch near
Chumps' wallets. Well, not so much a sin
As a small-time con. While your fled father
Weeps and displays mother's silky golden lock.

When the days at last collapse, an open lock
On the barroom door of the Fandango fancy brothel
Tends to enrapture puritans such as Father
Christmas and Cotton Q. Divine. Underground
Passageways soon funnel them to subtlest sin.
How stupid their faces when pleasure is near.

"Subtlest sin," by the way, is a near-
Cliché. As is any line with the dim word "lock"
In it. Says Dad: "I'm gonna sin and sin
Big! Sin balls and bricks and brains and brothel
And a yard wide! And plenty deep underground!"
(It's surely time to say goodbye to father.)

In the army a wild brothel was near-
Ly as sweet as an underground saloon, a lock
On every door, a father innocent of sin.

Sestina

Interviews with Georges Charbonnier — No. 5

Raymond Queneau

GEORGES CHARBONNIER: Raymond Queneau, you said to me one day that two great currents exist in literature and that basically one could, if I understood you correctly, link most novels either to the *Iliad* or to the *Odyssey.*

RAYMOND QUENEAU: I think that those are in fact the two poles of Western novelistic activity since its creation, that is to say since Homer, and that one can easily classify all works of fiction either as descendants of the *Iliad* or of the *Odyssey.* I had the pleasure of hearing this idea of the Occidental novel as a continuation of the *Iliad* summarized recently by Butor during a conference [25 July 1961]. He said excellent things in this regard, but he didn't speak about the *Odyssey,* and it seems to me that the *Odyssey* represents the other pole of Western literature.

GC: When would you say there's an Iliad, and when would you say there's an Odyssey?

RQ: First of all, these two works have one thing in common: one finds in them nearly all the techniques of the novel. It doesn't seem to me that anyone has discovered much that's new since then.

The *Iliad* is already an extremely erudite work, with a very well-defined subject; it is, as you know, the story of Achilles' anger, that is, something very specific, placed in a very vast historical and mythological context. One incident projects in a way a glimmer of light on the historical world which surrounds it and vice versa, but it is the incident which makes the story; the rest contributes only to the "suspense" and to the development of the story.

Many novelists likewise take well-defined, precise characters, whose stories are sometimes of mediocre interest, and place them in an important historical context, which remains secondary in spite of everything.

The Charterhouse of Parma and *War and Peace* are novels of the Iliad genre, not because they tell of battles, like Homer (that counts, too), but because the important things are the characters plunged into history and the conflict between characters and history; for example, the work of Proust is also an Iliad. The battles take place in drawing rooms, but they are still battles, and the nucleus is the narrator's personality and the people who interest him.

Moreover, there is the *Odyssey*. The *Odyssey* is demonstrably much more personal; it is the story of someone who, in the course of diverse experiences, acquires a personality or, if you will, affirms and recovers his personality, like Ulysses, who finds himself unchanged, aside from his "experience," at the end of his odyssey.

So there the examples are extremely numerous: *Don Quixote, Moby-Dick, Ulysses,* naturally, but also a book like *Bouvard and Pécuchet,* for example, which is well-situated in this line of descent. The story of *Bouvard and Pécuchet* is an Odyssey through the sciences, the letters, and the arts. Bouvard and Pécuchet as well find themselves as they were at the beginning of the novel since the book's conclusion is that they start to copy again, just as Ulysses returns to be the king of his little island.

Rabelais also, certainly Rabelais is an Odyssey; *The Red and the Black* is an Odyssey, whereas *The Charterhouse of Parma* seems to me to be an Iliad. And in the *Odyssey* there are, as much as in the *Iliad,* technical refinements which are extremely remarkable, and I'm surprised they aren't mentioned more often. For example, when Ulysses hears his own story sung by an epic poet and then he reveals his identity and the poet wants to continue singing and Ulysses isn't interested any longer; that's very astonishing, modern, shall we say, because it's really a novel within a novel. To have one's own story told by a third party who doesn't know that the character in question is himself the hero of the story being told, that's a technical refinement which could date from the twentieth century. It's true that one finds this sophistication also in *Don Quixote.*

GC: *Jacques le fataliste?*

RQ: *Jacques le fataliste,* that's also an Odyssey. I wonder if there aren't more Odysseys than Iliads among the great novels.

GC: That's what I was going to ask you; are there not more Odysseys than Iliads?

RQ: Zola's work is an Iliad. There again is an example of a story centered on characters who are sometimes not even very interesting; and with a great tableau, a great historical ferment in the background.

GC: How can we classify these memoirs which touch so closely on the novel, like *The Confessions* of Rousseau, for example?

RQ: Ah! All confessions are Odysseys. *Wilhelm Meister* is an Odyssey; all autobiographical tales are Odysseys; all lives are Odysseys.

GC: So that we find ourselves in the presence of very few Iliads when all is said and done.

RQ: Yes, there are in fact very few, but I can come up with some, even so. Perhaps Sagan is linked to the *Iliad.*

GC: But then is literature devoted to these two currents: to compose an Iliad or to compose an Odyssey?

RQ: Until the beginning of the twentieth century, it is easy to classify all fictional works under one or the other rubric. But perhaps the total awareness of this dependence with respect to Homer and the Greek epic, achieved by Joyce in *Ulysses,* perhaps that dissipated this sort of ascendancy of Homer over all Occidental literature. Perhaps since then, in fact, we have gotten a little away from this double aspect of either putting the man, the character, back into historical events or of making a historical event of his very life.

One can say that fiction has consisted either of placing imaginary characters in a true story, which is the *Iliad,* or of presenting the story of an individual as having a general historical value, which is the *Odyssey.* But after the magical act accomplished by Joyce with *Ulysses,* perhaps we are getting away from it. It seems to me that an author who has determined very new domains in literature is Gertrude Stein and *The Making of Americans* is doubtless very meaningful in this regard, because there, there is an attempt to suppress all history. It is the history of the making of the Americans. It is a very great Iliad because it concerns the creation of a nation. It is a very great Odyssey because it concerns the Odyssey, which is the story of Americans up to the point where they are well-established, and even so it is detached from the historical side in a sort of present that Gertrude Stein called the "timeless present," in a sort of formal immobility which causes peoples' lives—one can't say that it is exemplary, because the lives of Bouvard and Pécuchet, the life of Don Quixote are exemplary—peoples' lives to be at the same time concrete and ideal. It's a kind of transformation of the individual to a type, a little in the sense of the Platonic ideal, and one which remains even so extremely concrete. Banality is elevated to the rank of a metaphysical value. It is a response to the question "Is there an 'idea' of each individual?"

GC: In all the attempts at the contemporary novel, do you see a will to situate oneself with respect to what you have just defined?

RQ: I didn't quite grasp . . .

GC: Does the recent novel try to get away from both the *Iliad* and the *Odyssey?* Or is it that on the contrary it belongs deliberately to one of these currents?

RQ: Well, I'll admit that I didn't quite grasp the final meaning, the conclusion of Butor's conference, but it seemed to me that he was more interested in the Iliad aspect of literature and that he spoke of it seeing himself in this same line of descent, even if he opposed it on certain points. He expressed himself more in terms of "society" than of "history," but all societies are historical; there have been only rare moments in history where individual histories were able to run their course without wars or revolutions. It was perhaps not until the nineteenth century, in the English novel, that we find people who are likely to spend a whole lifetime without being hit by bombs, who have a tranquil life in which history does not intervene. But, aside from this period, there have always been many things happening externally, and peoples' private lives are always thrown into disorder. The *Iliad* is the private lives of people thrown into disorder by history.

GC: So there would be nothing but Odysseys in the English novel of the nineteenth century?

RQ: I'm forced to admit that. There is a great novel likewise written at a time when history seemed to be immobilized, during the first century of the Roman Empire; I'm talking about the *Satyricon* of Petronius. It is an Odyssey obviously because people come and go, they are dragged from incident to incident, but one can say also that it is, potentially, the Odyssey of the Roman Empire itself. Outside of those who were busy with palace intrigue, the people, the "little people" above all, those of whom Petronius spoke, probably thought that it would always be that way, but one sees that he himself must not have considered this state of things as so long-lasting.

There were others who were not of this opinion either—those were the Christians, but that's another story!

One could wonder, moreover, if Petronius made allusion to Christianity in the *Satyricon*. It's a controversial question. The episode of the Matron of Ephesus and, in the last chapters, the story of the cadaver that the heirs have to consume anthropophagically seem really to me to be anti-Christian parodies.

GC: In a general way, would the *Iliad* and the *Odyssey* correspond to two realizations, two ways of apprehending things, two ways of conceiving them?

RQ: Yes. In one we think of giving importance to history, but it is the individual who is interesting, and in the other the individual is interesting and we want to give him a historical importance. In fact, it's the same point of view, that is to say the novelist's point of view, the creator of fiction's point of view. It is the character who interests him. Sometimes he wants to convince the reader that the story he is telling is as interesting as universal history, and sometimes he thinks that he will render this story interesting by slipping it into universal history. The story of Achilles could take place anywhere; that the all-powerful lord comes to take his favorite slave from him, it could happen in a completely different historical context from the Trojan War. It is obviously only the author's genius which persuades the reader that the story cannot be otherwise, that it must be accepted that way.

GC: Would the truth be a synthesis of these two?

RQ: Either a synthesis or a way out.

Translated by Mary Campbell-Sposito

"In a café," Jean-Marie Queneau (ca. 1965)
Courtesy of the Centre de Documentation Raymond Queneau

Technique of the Novel[1]

Raymond Queneau

> The rules (of the ancients) are good, but their method is not of our century, and whoever determines to walk only in their footsteps would doubtless make little progress and would entertain his audience poorly. We run, to tell the truth, some risk of going astray, and in fact we do go astray quite often, when we step off the beaten path, but we do not stray each time we step off. Some attain their aspirations, and anyone can take a chance.
>
> —Corneille

While poetry has been the hallowed ground of rhetoricians and rule makers, the novel, since its inception, has escaped all laws. Anyone can drive in front of him like a flock of geese an undetermined number of apparently real characters through a wasteland of an undetermined number of pages or chapters. The result, whatever it may be, will always be a novel. My intention here is not to impose, nor even to propose, laws for a genre which satisfies everyone as it is, writers and readers alike. But, for my own part, I cannot bow to such a lack of constraint. Though the ballad and the rondeau have perished, it seems to me that in resistance to this disaster, an increased rigor should be displayed in the exercise of prose. I would therefore like to show what a conscious technique of the novel can be, in the way that I myself have sought to practice it. But to begin with, I must take the double precaution, firstly, of apologizing for choosing as examples novels of which I am the author (but how can I do otherwise? "I'm explaining myself"); and secondly, to recognize my debt to the English and American novelists who taught me about the existence of a technique of the novel, most especially to Joyce. I should also name in this respect a rather illustrious older author, but I do not wish to alarm contemporaries. In any case, I am intent on assuring the French reader that I cannot claim originality in this domain.

The three novels I have chosen, *The Bark Tree, Gueule de Pierre,* and *The Last Days,* all express a single theme, or rather variations on a single theme, and consequently all three have the same structure: circular.[2] In the first, the circle closes on itself and rejoins exactly its point of departure, which is suggested, perhaps crudely, by the fact that the last sentence is identical to the first. In the second novel, the circular movement does not return to its point of departure, but to an equivalent point, and it forms a spiral. The final sign of the Zodiac, Pisces, is not situated on the same plane as the fish [*poisson,* in French, means both *Pisces* and *fish*]. Finally, in the third novel, the cycle is no more than seasonal, until the seasons disappear; the circle is broken in a catastrophe, which the central character states explicitly in the last chapter.

It was unbearable to me to leave to chance the business of determining the number of chapters in these novels. Thus it is that *The Bark Tree* is composed of 91 (7 x 13) sections, 91 being the sum of the first thirteen numbers and its "sum" being one. It is therefore at the same time the number of the death of beings and that of their return to existence, a return that I conceived then only as similar to the irresoluble perpetuity of hopeless unhappiness. At that time, I saw in thirteen a beneficial number because it denied happiness; as for seven, I took it, and still take it, as a numerical image of myself, since my last name and my first and middle names are each composed of seven letters and since I was born on the 21st (3 x 7) of the month. Even though in appearance it was not autobiographical, the form of this novel was thus fixed by completely egocentric motives, so it expressed what the content tried to disguise.

Reasons that were every bit as personal caused the zodiacal (and zoological) sign of *Gueule de Pierre* to be that of Pisces; I was born under this sign. As I stated above, this novel is not a completed circle like *The Bark Tree,* but open to the whole ontological point of view that separates animals from constellations, because the identification of the murderous son with the father is not a total identification. As we say in my birthplace, it is identification, without being so, while being so.

As for *The Last Days,* the autobiographical element there is so obvious that the numerical expression can claim to be more objective. Its number is 49 (=7 x 7, or rather 6 x 8 + 1). I'll get back to that later.

Each of the sections of *The Bark Tree* is a whole, with about two or three exceptions that I could justify. Each is a whole, first of all as a tragedy, meaning that each observes the rule of the three unities. Each is a whole, not only as to the time, the place, and the action, but as to the genre: purely narrative tale, tale interrupted with reported discourse, pure conversation (which tends toward theatrical expression), interior monologue with "I," omniscient narration (as if the author fathomed the slightest thoughts of his characters) or soliloquy (another equally theatrical mode), letters (of which some famous novels were entirely composed), journals (not diaries, but account books or newspaper clippings), or dream narratives (these must be used advisedly because the genre is in such disgrace).

Of these sections, every thirteenth one (the last of each chapter, consequently) is situated *outside* of the chapter, in another direction or dimension; these are pauses and their genre can be nothing but the monologue, the dream narrative, or a newspaper clipping. Naturally, the ninety-first breaks the rule and becomes narrative again to finish up the whole thing.

In *The Last Days,* each sixth chapter (see the qualifier farther on) is likewise a pause, the central character, Alfred, playing the role of chorus. It is also *with* him that the drama ends.

Gueule de Pierre, on the contrary, not having the structural inexorability of the two preceding novels, does not offer these rhythmic interruptions. It is composed quite simply of three parts, each of which is clearly individualized first of all as to the genre: the monologue of a solitary person in the first part, a tale and conversations when he returns to the people of Home Town in the second part, a poem finally in the third part when he rises up to become mayor. Next, as to the applications, to each part (more particularly to a given character) corresponds one of the kingdoms of nature, and naturally some sort of event to each sign of the Zodiac.

Therefore, *The Bark Tree* is comparable to a man who, after having walked for a long time, finds himself back where he started. *Gueule de Pierre* resembles a man who, reaching the top of a staircase, believes that there is one more step to climb when there is not. *The Last Days* is analogous to a man who sways perched on a scaffolding of chairs which will end up by collapsing. These are, one can see, three incidents suitable for provoking laughter—or an altogether different reaction in the opposite direction, according to one's level of agitation.

The distribution of characters must not be left to chance, anymore than anything else, because a whole part of their meaning depends on this distribution. I could not explain that of *The Bark Tree* without the aid of charts which could quite wrongfully give the illusion of a chessboard, a game which I admit having played a great deal at that time. To my way of thinking, it could no more be a question of allowing the characters in a novel to struggle like homunculi escaped from their broken jars than to consider them as chess pieces, the succession of moves constituting the sequence of chapters and the final checkmate the author's victory.

In *Gueule de Pierre,* all the characters are ordered according to lines of force created by these two poles: the "triplicity" of the sons (Paul, Pierre, and Jean) and the "triplicity" of nature's kingdoms. Their names are also partially determined as are their appearances.

Two characters or two groups, distinct but still autonomous, can express an equal reality, an equal tendency, an equal type; thus the echo or mirror chapters, such as II,3 and II,4 in *Gueule de Pierre* or XXIII and XXV in *The Last Days*. In this latter novel, behind four characters who correspond two by two, all the others are arranged, with the exception of the only one who is situated outside or centrally: Alfred the waiter, who plays here the role of chorus and well-oiled axis.[3]

I mentioned earlier that the number of *The Last Days* was 49, even though as it was published it includes only 38 chapters. That is because I removed the scaffolding and syncopated the rhythm; certain monologues of Alfred's, omitted from publication, form a "zero" time; Jules's monologue, unexpected, marks a dissonance before the final resolution.

Rules cease to exist once they have outlived their value, but forms live on eternally. There are forms of the novel which impose on the suggested topic all the virtues of the Number. Born of the very expression and of the diverse aspects of the tale, connected by nature with the guiding idea, daughter and mother of all the elements that it polarizes, a structure develops, which transmits to the works the last reflections of Universal Light and the last echoes of the Harmony of Worlds.

NOTES

[1]This essay first appeared in *Volontés* in December 1937 and was later published in *Bâtons, chiffres et lettres* (Paris: Gallimard, 1965).

[2]*Gueule de Pierre* was later revised and published as a part of *Saint Glinglin*. It has been translated into English, also as *Saint Glinglin,* by James Sallis (Dalkey Archive Press, 1993).

[3]In *The Last Days* the chapter in the book's center is also called "Alfred" instead of chapter 19. The book's last chapter is entitled "Alfred" as well (as are chapters 6, 10, and 14). See *The Last Days,* trans. Barbara Wright, Dalkey Archive Press, 1990.

Translated by Mary Campbell-Sposito

From Children of Clay[1]

Raymond Queneau

Damp and naked, Sire Chambernac, headmaster of the lycée of Mourmèche, heard a tap at the bathroom door where he was scrubbing himself for the second time that day, performing a considerable number of ablutions because of the intense oleoproduction of his dermis, an oleagination that he attributed to the profuse concentration of cervical moisture (not volatile but fixed and perlifying everywhere on the surface of his body), resulting from special research and studies that were difficult, singular and unusual.

Damp and naked, Sire Chambernac, headmaster of the lycée of Mourmèche, emerged from one of his daily baths, when he perceived, through the soapy drops of water bubbling in his ears, a knock.

"Don't come in," he yelled, unsure of not having closed his door.

"Would you be so kind as to repeat the second-to-the-last word of the sentence that you just uttered?" said the knocker from the other side (he is soon going to be on this side).

"What?"

"I was asking you to repeat."

"Who are you, for Chrissakes? The plumber?"

"No."

"Leave me alone, then."

"What? I can't hear you very well."

"I told you not to enter."

" 'Enter'—you did say the word 'enter'?"

And he entered.

Running into the drain, the gray water, before disappearing, left a thin layer of silt on the sides of the tub.

The new arrival closed the door behind him, and sized up his man, damp and naked, with an eye uncontaminated by any subjective judgment, emotionally sickened by the nudity of a paunchy, nonmuscled sexagenarian, or perhaps homosexually appreciative of an unknown anatomy.

"Well," the stranger said amiably, "at least one can say that your stomach isn't wrinkled."

However, the headmaster was lost in a maze of unholy terror and labyrinths of indignation. The former began to relax his visceral activity gently, the latter to reduce his pulmonary capacity.

"Me," continued the stranger less amiably, "I don't understand why you tell people to come into the bathroom when you are completely naked."

"Wha-what?" stutteruttered Chambernac.

"Well, it's simple," said the other, furious, "you told me to come in and you are naked. You must be perverted. I'm really revolted by such manners."

The victim wiped his face, now damp not with salubrious bathwater, but with the sweat of anxiety.

"Do you think it amuses me to see your pudenda? Definitely not! I'd rather not look."

And he turned around, but in the mirror attached to the door, he was able to watch the guinea pig's behavior, for it was the first time he had given himself over to this sport and he was not yet very sure of his technique.

The headmaster, taking advantage of this discretion, begins to get dressed again; he puts on his BVDs, he puts on his shirt, he puts on his underwear; is there anything he hasn't put on? His pants: they are in the next room. He explains this to the invader.

"Right, then, let's go next door."

He opens the door and shows the way.

"Really," the stranger said pensively, "what Mourmechian family man would ever think that the headmaster of the lycée devotes himself to nudist exhibitions in front of, I say, in front of men?"

Suddenly abandoning his impressive calm, he began to prance to and fro while shaking a handkerchief and hurling interjections considered faggy by people who know nothing about it except from caricaturists and cabaret singers. The patheadicmaster, seated on his bed, looked on, overwhelmed.

"Well," said the other, "aren't you going to say anything?"

"Get out," whined the tormented one.

"Come in, get out, that's all you know how to say."

"But I never told you to come in, after all! It was you who came in like that. And then, how did you get into my apartment? I'm going to call the police."

"I dare you."

"That's what we're going to see."

"When you told me to come in, you no doubt believed that it was one of your students."

"What atrocious slander," exclaimed the headmaster. "I'm going to put on my pants."

"That's not going to get you back your respectability."

"Ah, ah, ah, ah, you believe respectability is lost just like that?"

"I don't believe it, I know it."

Chambernac puts the upper part of his body in a suit coat and the lower part in pants.

"Now that I'm dressed, you are going to do me the favor of decamping."

The other doesn't budge at all.

"Count yourself lucky that I'm not calling the police to make you forget your liking for jokes of rather questionable taste."

"Say, you've changed your mind since a moment ago. Just now you wanted to call the police. I see that you've thought about it. You're doing the right thing. Now all we need is to do some serious talking."

"I would have liked you to come to that point sooner."

"Let's sum up what's happened. One: I enter; two: you engage in filthy behavior."

"Oh!"

"And three, you must make amends to me."

The intrudee breathed: *that's* all it was. With the single coin offered him, the intruder would see it was a farce. The intruder guessed it:

"But what do you want me to do with a 40-sou coin? Forty sous!"

With contempt he spat (for real) on the carpet.

"*I'm* not asking for charity. I don't live on alms. *I'm* not on a quest. *I'm* not a mental case. What *I* want is work."

"Work?" Repeated the headmaster, "you say *work?*"

"I said work, and I want work. You understand me, you filthy old man?"

"And what do you know how to do?" groaned the victim.

"It's not a question of what I know how to do, but of what I want to do."

"And what do you want to do?" oangred the victim.

"I want to be a teacher."

"Aaarrrggghhh," roared the victim.

"Pull yourself together."

"P.E. teacher?" jeered the victim, who found sufficient strength to emit some hiccups imbued with grim pleasure.

"Don't make fun of me."

"So you want to be a teacher, just like that?"

"Yes, it's a vocation. All I lack are the degrees. But how important are degrees?"

"Yes. How important are degrees?" repeated Chambernac in a sickly voice.

"I'm not malicious, I'll take the class which is the most convenient for you."

"Christ Almighty, there *is* the philosophy class. Bouvard just died suddenly."

"I like philosophy," said Purpulan.

"Christ Almighty, it's going to cause me trouble."

"Less than if you didn't want anything to do with me."

During the following months, Chambernac abandoned all hope of publishing the Encyclopedia, loathing besides to do it at his own expense or rather at Astolphe's or the baron's or anyone else's who was capable of lending him many thousands of francs, for he risked in this way placing in circulation a book which would be received indifferently, and of himself entering into the category of "literary madmen." The thick manuscript now lay in a drawer in his bedroom; as for him, lodged on the Boulevard Lefebvre, he made himself useful, as they say, and calmly waited to die, putting into this effort the most discretion of which he felt himself capable.

One day just like that around the month of March he had a chance encounter. A guy next to him, a four-eyed guy, about thirty, spoke to him.[2] By dint of having loitered around editors, Chambernac was recognized by people in the business.

"Mister Chambernac?" asked his neighbor.

"Yes, that's my name."

"We have met several times," said the stranger, "in the offices of the N.R.F., at Paulhan and in the offices of Denoël."

"I believe I remember that," said Chambernac indifferently.

"Excuse my indiscretion," said the anonymous one, "has your great work on literary madmen not appeared?"

"No. No editor would take it. Besides, they were right."

"And why is that?"

"Useless."

"Pardon me?"

"I said that it was a useless book. In any case it no longer interests me."

"No?"

"No. I have other things in mind. My manuscript is in a drawer and it will stay there until my death and even beyond. But does it interest you?"

"Uh, I'd be really curious to have a look at it."

"Truly? I don't know who you are but you are going to see how I am. If this manuscript presents the slightest interest to you, I'll give it to you. You can do what you like with it. I'm completely uninterested in it."

His listener was quite surprised. The following day at the agreed-upon hour Chambernac in fact brought the mass of paper which constituted the Encyclopedia of Inexact Sciences.

"Here it is," said Chambernac. "Keep all of this and sort it out. I'm making you a gift of it. But I warn you that it's not a gift of great value."

A few days later they saw each other again.

"Well?" asked Chambernac, smiling.

The other one said to him:

"You may feel some repugnance because I attribute your work to a character in a novel that I am in the process of writing."

"Not at all," said Chambernac, laughing. "I find the idea comical. You write novels?"

"Naturally your name would appear on the cover with mine."

"Useless," exclaimed Chambernac. "It's all the same to me. Don't do anything. I have no vanity."

"Still . . ."

"No, no. Attribute my work to one of your characters if it means something to you. As for me, I'm only too happy to be rid of this millstone. And it really matters very little to me whether my name survives. I'll tell you again: I have no more vanity. Rework these old papers into a new book if you feel the need; and if you're capable of it.[3] As for me I am quite satisfied to be divested of it: I shall be able to die happy. You are doing me a favor."

Chambernac continued:

"And this character, what's he like?"

"He's the headmaster of a small provincial school. He's married, with no children. One day a demon gets into his bathroom."

"Wait. The best thing would be for me to tell you the story of my life. Wait. I don't think it's extraordinary but it can give some realism to your book."

"I don't know how to thank you."

"But you're welcome I'm sure my dear Mister, Mister what?

"Queneau."

"You're welcome, my dear Mr. Queneau. I assure you, you're welcome."

NOTES

[1]We are indebted to Professor Madeleine Velguth, English translator of Queneau's *Les Enfants du limon,* to be published by Sun & Moon Press, for the title.

[2]Thanks to Jane Alison Hale for permission to use her translation of this sentence (see *The Lyric Encyclopedia of Raymond Queneau,* 12).

[3]See note 2.

Translated by Mary Campbell-Sposito

Charity Begins at Home

Harry Mathews

Each time I read a novel by Raymond Queneau I remind myself that I have yet to do my homework: the author's acknowledged spiritual masters—the Gnostics, Hegel, and Kojève (whose lectures on Hegel were compiled by Queneau himself)—remain on my shelves unread. Planning to read Hegel has in fact come to typify for me the well-meaning New Year's resolution that will never be fulfilled. My road to death, if not to hell, is decidedly paved with such good intentions, and I shall no doubt depart this world ignorant of Hegel and the Gnostics, self-deprived not only of what I might learn from them but also of the tools I need to penetrate to the kernel of Queneau's thought. In each of his books I sense mysteries, which I suspect to be Gnostic and Hegelian, nourishing each delicious mundanity. As I stare into the tantalizing background, the promising shadows vanish, and again I curse my sloth. If only I knew!

On the other hand, perhaps not. My fellow Oulipians, who are the Queneau enthusiasts I know best, had read Hegel before their majority and the Gnostics not much later. Strangely enough, they too find Queneau's novels mysterious. It seems that the main difference between us is that they have richer materials from which to concoct their mysteries. Even with their superior knowledge they speculate as unremittingly as I do in my ignorance.

The fact is that no one has ever completely deciphered any one of Queneau's novels, and my suspicion is that no one ever will. Perhaps that's part of their point. Perhaps novels, these no more than any other, aren't meant to be deciphered but to provide grist for endless deciphering, which suggests that the process of deciphering may be more rewarding than its completion. Certainly, when reading Queneau, unresolved residues of meaning do not detract from our pleasure, quite the contrary: they make us pay particular attention to what he does, since we know that explanations will not be served to us on a platter. The author himself wrote somewhere that only trivial literature provides answers, whereas serious literature raises questions.

The Skin of Dreams (Loin de Rueil), published in 1944, certainly qualifies as serious literature; it also exploits a quantity of trivia that would normally bore us beyond all patience and that instead induces only delighted curiosity. Body lice, to take one example, play a prominent role in the text. Countless references are devoted to them, as well as several pages of dialogue scattered here and there through the book. This dialogue is peculiar: when people talk about lice, whether at home, in cafés, or improper society, they always say more or less the same not very interesting things; and this variable litany, in addition to whatever it may tell us about the relationship between humanity and the louse, by its very recurrence comes to play a role in the book that can be called musical. We greet its reappearance with the same satisfaction we take in the return of a bizarre theme in, say, *Til Eulenspiegel* or *Petrushka;* we furthermore sense that merely by assuming this musical role the apparently trivial subject of lice has assumed at least formal significance.

It has another significance. The recurrence of the topic of lice suggests that it is a very concrete universal of human experience; more exactly, that it is treated as a universal at moments of small talk. But the use to which people in *The Skin of Dreams* put conversation suggests that there is little else, that all talk is small talk. Is this necessarily so, and if so, why?

An interesting feature of this novel is that it virtually concludes with its own summary. The story ends as it began in Rueil, a sleepy suburb of Paris, where a talking film starring and directed by James Charity is being shown. The film's opening is set in France, in the last years of the silent movie. A little boy called James Charity, who is watching a Western with William Hart, suddenly climbs out of the audience and into the film, where he assumes the remainder of the hero's role before at last returning to his seat. Growing older, James goes on living in similar fantasies. We see him in turn playing the part of explorer, inventor, artist, boxer, and thief. His dreams lead him at times into dubious situations.

In one farcical episode he joins a provincial touring company. By chance he goes on to play bit roles, including some in films. We see him gaining prominence. He is cast as an explorer, an inventor, an artist, a thief. He spends time among the Borgeiro Indians, a tribe noted for its savagery. In San Culebra del Porco he meets Lulu L'Aumône and goes with her to Hollywood to try their luck. Fame and success await them. They marry. In the final take, as he kisses Lulu on the mouth, he signs with his free hand a fabulous contract for a multilingual film called *The Skin of Dreams,* the very film now being shown.

And the very book we have just read. Readers know, as the spectators do not, that James Charity began life as Jacques L'Aumône (*aumône* = charity) and Lulu L'Aumône as Lulu Doumer; readers also recognize something familiar in "The Ramon Curnough Company presents . . ." of the production credits. We are aware of witnessing a double transformation: Jacques L'Aumône has turned his story and his identity into a movie, and Ramon Curnough has turned his book into an imaginary version of itself. Which of course it always was; but usually such facts are not advertised. Here the revelation is so satisfying it strikes us as not only right but inevitably so. To put it more simply, we feel that there can be no other way out.

The written summary of the cinematic summary of the written book attains a peculiar significance by appearing as an *event* in the narrative, indeed as a climactic one: the narrative from the start has been composed of tangible occurrences and the imaginary occurrences that proceed from them, the two sorts existing side by side with one another in a state of perpetual, unstable exchange. Two apparently incompatible worlds seem to be present in human activity, neatly contrasted in the title of the final film, *The Skin of Dreams,* and the name of a winning horse Jacques has played much earlier in the story, Skin of a Louse. The omnipresent louse infests the tangible world as dreams do the other. The tangible or louse world might be described as the world of materiality and our direct perception of it; the other world is the realm of dreams and fantasies. It would be convenient to say that the material world is real and the fantasy world illusory, but this turns out not to be the case: *both* are illusory—a fact that the fantasy world acknowledges and the material world does not.

On the face of it, the material world would seem to be anything but illusory. The mechanism of cause and effect, its sovereign law, governs its human subjects ruthlessly: in Jacques L'Aumône's life, his demonstration of a movie kiss to the immature Camille Magnin is paid for years later by a painful love affair with her; the pleasure of pinching Suzanne as she brushes against him leads to fatherhood and an unsatisfactory marriage. Furthermore, nothing, absolutely nothing, can become manifest in the world without acquiring a material form; even Jacques's fantasies only become "real" as a movie. Given this unyielding presence, how, in *The Skin of Dreams,* can the material world be considered an illusion?

For one thing, material forms are transient: everything we perceive is doomed to become something else and is as we perceive it already a prey to change. The memento mori emanating from Offroir's discussion of the agents of posthumous putrefaction only crystallizes what has been happening throughout the book: identities and appearances incessantly dissolve, nothing is left as it first so solidly appeared to be. Early on, Jacques chances upon the blabbering senile husband of his concierge, healthy several days before, whose gift of speech has now been reduced to a repeated

"Everything's okey-dokey-doke, everything's okey-doke": Jacques identifies himself at once, and intensely, with this image of the transience of flesh, bone, and brain.

But the illusory nature of materiality is revealed more tellingly in the plight of those who must cater to its laws; more exactly, of those who look to the material world for the satisfaction of their imaginary longings. *The Skin of Dreams* is essentially an account of Jacques L'Aumône's struggle to achieve a synthesis between two irreconcilable worlds.

Characters neither blessed nor afflicted with immaterial fantasies live comfortably enough within the bounds of materiality: Jacques's parents; the entomologist Offroir; Suzanne, Jacques's wife; and the veterinarian Baponot. It is the dreamers who suffer—Louis-Philippe des Cigales, Rueil's local poet; Lulu Doumer (later L'Aumône); and Jacques himself. There are also one or two interesting people who cannot be classified either as pure materialists or fantasists, such as the pharmacist Linaire and Camille Magnin, who reappears as Rojana Pontez (and also, perhaps, the appealing Martine; perhaps even Ramon Curnough himself).

Des Cigales, while poor, is satisfyingly appreciated in Rueil and its environs as a semi-official poet; he might live content if he did not suffer from ontalgia, the malady of existence itself. Its devastating seizures, both physical and metaphysical in their effect, are provoked by his awareness of the material confines of his life: the certainty of death, the pathetic restriction of his fame, and his passionate, ineradicable attachment to his wife, who has deserted him forever (her death will allow him to start a new life). Lulu Doumer's odyssey mainly occurs offstage. When we first meet her as an eleven-year-old, she is already a romantic dreamer, albeit a savvy one, and when Jacques's path crosses hers in San Culebra del Porco, the degradation of her hopes has not crushed her nature, and she can still say, "No, but tell me, joking aside, after all, what is more interesting than affairs with women for men, and affairs with men for women." But we can only imagine what has befallen her in the interval. Only with Jacques do we witness in detail what a dreamer's engagement with materiality involves.

Jacques begins life with endowments that enchant his sock-manufacturing father: physical dexterity, exceptional intellectual gifts, and a character of tranquil good nature. Jacques takes pains to conceal another attribute that might worry his parents: his prodigious talent for creating fantasies. This talent is nourished by moviegoing but not dependent on it. It is not, in fact, dependent on anything—certainly not on Jacques's volition—and simply pours through any chink that appears in the routine of his existence: a word, a sight, a fact is enough to release it. (His father's passing mention of des Cigales's noble origins turns Jacques instantaneously into a king.) Jacques's childish penchant for fantasy-making stays with him after he grows up, adapting itself to changing circumstances and hopes, in its intensity both inspiring and crippling him.

It isn't surprising that Jacques's fantasies disarm him for material success. His visions always bring him to the achieved status of king, pope, or inventor, never to the paths that might get him there. He is, for instance, a talented boxer; but when it is suggested he train for the championship, he soon quits because he has at once "experienced" not only being champion but the life that might follow such success. At one point he bitterly admits that, young as he is, his future is already behind him (as his father has so sententiously told him), and he thereupon recites a glorious page-long list of all the achievements he has "unrealized." He says that he has no use for specialization, and while he makes the remark contemptuously, it is a pertinent one. Specialization means submitting to the process of becoming, to materiality in its inextricable succession of illusory stages (the last of which is death). What Jacques wants is pure, unmediated being.

But in the material world no such thing as pure being exists. So Jacques must suffer, and suffer failure, as a dreamer as well. Either actively or through observation, he explores a variety of human activities that might bring him freedom, all of which sink him lower in his despair. After boxing, he dabbles in gambling and a pathetically low form of confidence racket. His indulgence in sexual pleasure leads him into a domestic prison in which he is an indifferent father and cuckolded husband. He endeavors to get his hands on a chemical invention that will make him rich; his own ill-prepared efforts produce eccentricities at best, and when he approaches the pharmacist Linaire, who has actually found a cure for ontalgia, he not only is turned away by him but learns that the capacity for making such an extraordinary discovery has not freed its possessor from the bonds of the sensuous world. Jacques then turns to love to make his own escape. He pursues in turn the two Magnin sisters he had known as a boy. Camille, now Rojana Pontez, throws him out after ridiculing his childhood dreams. Dominique, married to a tycoon, hypocritically indulges his idealized passion without yielding to him. Each woman exemplifies in her way the mediocrity that follows submission to the material life, Rojana by her more sympathetic but bitterly narrow-minded pursuit of theatrical career, Dominique by her voluntary confinement in the world of wealth that Jacques had once dreamed of and that now disgusts him.

This disgust fuels Jacques's ultimate attempt to transcend the world, although it is initiated by his frustrations in love. His aim, both ludicrous and touching, is to attain humility, sainthood, and "nothingness." He achieves only humiliation, absurdity, and more fantasies, which now of course center on the glories of ascesis. He still does not understand that, even through denial, materiality allows no way out of itself. Whether Jacques strives after fortune, love, or holiness, he can only find more transience and more unreality. The louse is everywhere.

It isn't that the louse represents the inexorable dominance of materiality in human life. That view is more the received opinion of those (virtually everyone) who discuss the subject. The louse may or may not be a universal of human experience; it unquestionably is one of human conversation; and this suggests a more interesting connection with materiality, that of language, that is to say, language as we currently use it *not* to say anything to one another. (The author on one occasion mentions the pitfalls to which "knowledge of human language" can lead.) It would seem that people are condemned not so much to abide the louse as to talk about it, forever repeating a round of clichés (the women complaining that louse ointment makes for dirty pillows, the men recalling the incursions of lice in army life). The conversational louse extends the intractability of the material world beyond such unsurprising domains as money and ambition into the realm of speech and consequently of thought, where it contaminates the abstract topics we resort to in our contemplation of the human condition, not excluding such grandiose ones as love and death.

It is des Cigales's comparison of the death of the louse with that of the individual that brings on his first ontological seizure, during which he reflects, as he struggles for survival, that man is no greater than a louse—an image that occurs to Jacques L'Aumône at the start of his first movie fantasy (much later, in his ascetic period, he will associate the dissection of a louse with that of his own body); it is in speaking to Jacques that des Cigales vividly connects the doom of true love to this fragile mortality: "That is not love. You shall see later. One day. It squeezes your heart like a vice and it tears it for you crrac! and afterwards it bleeds, it bleeds. A whole lifetime." Less nobly, the louse also infiltrates the nest of love in the guise of *phthyrium pubis,* vulgarly known as the crab: Linaire in the blindness of his obsession with the adolescent Pierrette cannot refrain from mentioning it to her, and Jacques provocatively refers to it just before his illusions concerning Dominique's chastity are rudely shattered.

Jacques, it should be said, takes an interest in the louse that verges on affection. He declines filling the parental socks so as to do research on lice; he knocks a man down for saying only a fool could bet on a horse called Skin of a Louse (he confesses to an actual fondness for the name); and while working in Baponot's laboratory, he devotes time to developing a strain of giant lice. Jacques (it should also be said) is more than an ineffectual dreamer, and throughout his misadventures he displays considerable wit, originality, and a great if confused enthusiasm for life. It therefore hardly surprises us that he plans to raise giant lice, nor does the choice seem haphazard: it rather suggests that he is aware of the absurdity of the task of reconciling boundless imagination with the constraints of the tangible world. His "dream" lice would have embodied his quandary in aptly grotesque form.

The giant lice, even had they existed, would clearly have been a "reconciliation" of the two worlds that belonged less to the material than to the imaginary one: the potential giant-louse circus that seems to excite the interest of *le Tonton* (rediscovered in San Culebra) is already theater: that is, halfway to the absolute dream-domains of poetry, where des Cigales modestly flourishes, and film, where Jacques will ultimately triumph. The point to be made is this: there is no escape from materiality except one, which is to accept that there is no escape, that contingency and transience are the stuff of the world and of our lives. It then becomes possible to choose to imagine—to dream—exactly such a world, and in imagining it to transform it into an object of play. You declare yourself the world's inventor—an inventor on a scale that even Jacques had never contemplated—and do what you like with your invention. If you cannot materially be the pope without going through the process of becoming the pope, you can play being pope or anyone else anytime you feel like it. For this it is not necessary to be an actor: any one of the lively arts will provide the terrain and rules for such games. It is not even necessary to be a lunatic; being a lover or poet will do—such inspired folk all make things up, assign them names of their choosing, and call them true. This is not how schools teach us to behave; but neither are we taught that we have been born into a world where a dutiful pursuit of reasonableness promises nothing but a deluded struggle for survival.

This in any event is the path Jacques chooses for his way out, or in. Even before he comes to San Culebra del Porco, the battering he has undergone (mostly self-inflicted) has so diminished his resources that things can hardly get worse, and his lively nature has begun to reassert itself. Almost involuntarily he recovers his pugnacity; he experiences some professional success; he takes up with Martine, who is smart and affectionate. One evening his frustration with the virtuous Dominique abruptly impels him to leave town. On the train to the coast he meets a boyhood chum. This man, who has also rediscovered Dominique, has found her not only attractive but available. His enlightening statement, "And so, that's the way it turned out: she got layed," concludes the chapter and middle section of the book. We skip straight to Jacques's arrival in San Culebra del Porco. The documentary on the Borgeiro Indians that he had just filmed has subjected him to extraordinary hardship, and disreputable San Culebra is the last stop at the end of all lines. It can be assumed that the material world has no illusions left for him. It is here, among other fugitives from Rueil, that Jacques meets Lulu Doumer and sets off with her to Hollywood. Interestingly enough, we learn of his subsequent life only through a newspaper interview read out loud by des Cigales to Jacques's parents, wife, and son, who have no inkling who "James Charity" might be. The interview is written in a systematically inflated style that sounds neither like Jacques nor anyone else of this world, and this is quite appropriate, since the "real" Jacques and Lulu have disappeared. The final paragraph of the San Culebra chapter contains one sentence, "They go out together," and not only from the Saint James Infirmary Bar but from the book and from the material world. They have been translated into purest stardom. The question of their happiness is left unresolved; happiness belongs to the reader. Jacques's disappearance from the world of lice into the world of dreams may or may not bring his ascesis to a desirable end, but it resolves another ascesis, which is the one we have experienced as witnesses of his story, now transformed into what might be called the "Parable of the Skins."

The spirit of this conclusion—light-heartedness informing a radically pessimistic view of human life—is wittily, beautifully, and captivatingly reflected in the structure and texture of the novel. An apparently whimsical collage of inane dialogue and inconsequential events (all given pith, however, by the author's debonair linguistic sleight-of-hand) is invested with a dramatic relevance to Jacques's progress that becomes apparent only after each episode is behind us. The collage is firmly ordered according to discreet, simple structures. The action is presented in clearly demarcated "acts": they can be reckoned as five if one considers the sequence of chapters in terms of time (1-2: childhood; 3-4: youth; 5-6: domesticity; 7-8: flight; 9-10: apotheosis) and three, corresponding to the sections of the book, in terms of the protagonist's evolution (1-4: exploration; 5-8: struggle; 9-10: realization). The chapters themselves—except for the last, which follows Jacques's withdrawal, a "real-life" epilogue stuffed with surprises—scarcely vary in length by more than a page or two, a fact worth mentioning since Queneau cared about such things and no doubt imposed this symmetry on his wackily eclectic narrative. (The novel was written long before the Oulipo's founding, but two details at least should be pointed out to the group's afficionados. They are Jacques's monovocalic statement near the beginning of chapter 1, and in chapter 6 a wonderfully apposite palindrome of sentences about his wife uttered by the confounded Linaire: "She is well. Thanks. She is in bed. She goes to bed early. It's a habit of hers. She goes to bed early. Thanks. She is well.")

Among the multitude of narrative devices used in *The Skin of Dreams,* a certain number are taken from film. Movies obviously play a central role in the story itself. Aside from Jacques's filmgoer's fantasies, there are detailed accounts of ritual evenings at the movies before and after the introduction of talkies. Lesser references abound; the inconclusive end of the first section, for example, breaks off thus: "[Jacques] followed the quays. People were going home. They had been to the cinema." The unusually flat expression "had been" raises the question of what, in these circumstances, "being" may signify. Still within the domain of subject matter, Jacques's penchant for identifying himself with others, "less in order to discover the other than to put him on for a few minutes," suggests the extension of moviegoing habits to everyday life. But the presence of film is most telling in its visual and dramatic use. The very opening of the book is cinematographic: a close-up of garbage tumbling out of a can, the camera dollying backward to reveal the can and the arm holding it (it belongs to des Cigales) and then panning to include the arrival of Lulu Doumer. At the end of the first chapter, dialogue from the next scene intrudes unexpectedly into a conversation des Cigales is having at a café: the effect strikingly resembles that of sound track and image overlapping (its conspicuousness is fully justified; it is at this moment that Jacques enters the scene). There are many similar straight cuts, and they never fail to bewilder and then delight. My favorite occurs when Jacques, returning by riverboat from Rueil to Paris, unfolds the latest *Paris-Sport* (a racing paper). One line later we hear an acquaintance saying he'd never have put money on a horse with a name like that. We thus know how Jacques has found out that, much advice to the contrary, in Skin of a Louse he has backed a winner.

Although less demonstrably cinematic, other moments appear to be at least partially derived from film. At the Saint James Infirmary Bar, Jacques, after talking to one of the B-girls for a while, asks what her name is: "Lulu Doumer" is the reply, which means nothing to Jacques, who has never laid eyes on her, but for us rings a loudly familiar bell; and to accommodate, as it were, its reverberation, a striking (a *visually* striking) event ensues: one of the nightclub performers devours a live lobster, shell and all. This seems rather like showing fireworks in the wake of a movie embrace (of course it's a lot less corny). The incident also suggests less atmospheric meanings, such as the dissolution of the tangible in the "impossible." If this were the case, the eating of the lobster would not only reflect the significance of Jacques's and Lulu's encounter but point forward to Jacques's final "appearance" in which he, with Lulu at his side, disappears like the lobster into his own story—one which the Ramon Curnough Film Company has now made ours.

There is, I should add, a "happy" coda to the happy epilogue. Des Cigales, with whom in his affliction the novel began, and who from the start has shown himself to be an expert movie fantasist, now starts finding contentment in his poetic oeuvre. As we leave him, he is about to go to bed with Suzanne, Jacques's first and most-material wife. He is leading her toward *the bedding,* which is, fittingly, the last word and the last object in the book—the original and incomparable field of dreams. At this moment I am looking forward to my very own bed, and looking forward to dreaming in it, perhaps hoping that I may some day even manage to dream about Hegel and the mysterious Gnostics. Last night, curiously enough, just after finishing a draft of this article, I was visited in my sleep by a man called Valentine—but surely he is a character from another novel?—and was solemnly asked this question by him: To which class of mankind did I think I rightly belonged, the material, the psychic, or the spiritual? He no less solemnly warned me that all matter is evil, that only the spirit is good. He told me that salvation can only be attained through the possession of esoteric knowledge, and that such knowledge cannot be learned: it must be revealed. I then inquired of him if he might not pronounce a few first words to start me on the path toward illumination. He acquiesced at once, saying with perfect gravity, "And so, that's the way it turned out: she got layed."

The Art of the Novel in Saint Glinglin

Gilbert Pestureau

A complex and ambitious work whose composition and writing were spread over nearly fifteen years *(Gueule de Pierre* [1934]; *Les Temps mêlés* [1941]; *Saint Glinglin* [1948]), *Saint Glinglin* provokes in readers and critics alike contrasting reactions. Some appraise it as one of Queneau's masterpieces, a learned and original novel, full of meaning and richness, serious and comic at the same time; others see in it a strange heteroclite compound too full of symbols.[1]

At the intersection of the author's autobiographical period (1933-1941), with *The Bark Tree, The Last Days, Odile, Oak and Dog, A Hard Winter,* and of a creative time largely free of family and personal tensions, *Saint Glinglin* bears witness above all to an artistic composition which explores multiple technical and stylistic devices as well as a varied set of themes. It seems to me particularly to be an homage to one of Queneau's masters, James Joyce, whom Queneau admired without reservation and to whom he refers in this novel as well as in those signed with the pseudonym "Sally Mara" in 1947 and in 1950.

What interests me here are some aspects of a technique that tends to integrate into the art of the novel the entire means of literature—therefore including poetics, dramatic arts, contemporary techniques—in relation to a thematic opening into multiple domains: psychoanalysis, ethnology, philosophy of history, cinemas and science fiction. Thus this composite work presents itself as a provisional evaluation foretelling an easier-to-read novel but one also that defies hermeneutics: *The Blue Flowers* (1965).

Structure and Genres

Queneau has always attached great value to a firm, precise, and conscious construction of the novel. As he was, moreover, an "arithmomaniac," this composition often has to do with numbers, in particular the prime numbers, and, among them, three and seven which, with their product of twenty-one, are the "personal" numbers of the author: his name, formed of three names of seven letters each—Raymond Auguste Queneau—and his birthdate, 21 February 1903. Thus one finds these two prime numbers again in *Saint*

Glinglin; the two original novels, *Gueule de Pierre* and *Les Temps mêlés* were each comprised of three parts.[2] Once integrated into the final novel and completed with a new part, we have the famous seven, a number as sacred as three, itself thematically illustrated by the three hero sons and by the three kingdoms of nature, the animal, the vegetable and the mineral.[3] Numerology, already praised and illustrated in *The Bark Tree* and in numerous aesthetic and theoretical writings of Queneau, finds here again its illustration. The third part of the novel consists of ten poems, a common round number.

In addition to this essential numerical architecture, the novel illustrated a desire for harmony and rhythm by alternating long or relatively short parts: 1, a long monologue by Pierre, the eldest son; 2, a long classical narration with dialogues; 3, a lyrico-epic monologue in ten brief cantos by Jean, the third son; 4, a rather short monologue by Paul, the youngest; 5, a long narration with dialogues; 6, a short interior monologue by Helen, the daughter; 7, the longest narration with dialogue added to it. The variations of length and above all the alternation of monologues and narratives introduce variety and rhythm. The three narrative parts (2, 5, 7) are emphasized by the various inserted monologues: Pierre's metaphysical and Joycean monologue, the pseudo-Claudelian lyricism of Jean, the sarcastic and passionate monologue of Paul, and the Faulknerian monologue of Helen. Queneau even succeeds in inserting an epic parodic poem (3), and he obtains, it seems to me, an original and balanced ensemble.[4]

With *Saint Glinglin,* Queneau gives us also a humorous lesson in literary history: implanting this poetic text in the third part, he reminds us that the novel is born of the epic in "langue romane"—the ancestor of the French language at the dawn of the Middle Ages—and illustrates his credo that verse and prose are no more than variations on form from the same inspiration. The whole novel, moreover, attests to the transition from the mythic to the prosaic carried out between the Middle Ages and the seventeenth century through the development of the romance. Even though it is very modern in form—language, style, and so forth—and substance, it is also a return to the source and, after the manner of Joyce, an homage (both serious and parodic) to the origins of occidental literature.

The first state of the text *(Les Temps mêlés,* 3) shows that the author wished to integrate not only poetic art but also theatrical art into the novel. Queneau's entire work demonstrates his penchant, if not his passion, for such theatrical forms as farce, vaudeville, melodrama, and popular drama. Thus *Saint Glinglin* is strewn with situations and comic—if not burlesque—dialogues, with astonishing recognitions, with providential meetings and encounters, with moments of suspense and of unexpected reversals of situation. The art of the spectacle is also represented therein by the village's spring fair—the Festival, a sort of carnival-potlatch with sexual connotations, the carnival booths and the people's banquet, the ritual murder of the father, whose corpse immersed in a mineral spring is erected as a statue which, once dissolved by heavy rains, is replaced by sculpted marble, the essential role of the cinema and of the star as a theme, myth and dream as reality, nautical amusements, the eel-basket/tethered balloon (a fictional invention of Queneau's akin to an inverted eel-basket used to trap clouds) and the final festivities. Previous novels of Queneau *(Pierrot mon ami,* for example [1942], or later ones, *The Flight of Icarus* [1968]—the latter written entirely in dialogue) attest to how much the taste for amusement and theater impregnate his artistic creation.

Technique of the Monologue

As did many of his contemporaries, Queneau found in James Joyce a revelation and a model from the beginning to the end of his life, particularly so because of his passionate fondness for literary technique.[5] He discovered *Ulysses* in French in 1929, at the moment of the publication of the translation, then he read the English text in 1932; it is obvious that he leafed endlessly through this novel that he considered at the outset a masterpiece, and he also did much reading on Joyce and his work. Introducing *Saint Glinglin* in 1948, he emphasized this aspect of "work in progress" finally completed.[6] Admittedly, it is a very different novel from *Ulysses,* but Queneau gained from the research and discoveries of his master. One interesting technical aspect is the method of exposition; like Joyce, Queneau, from an enigmatic presentation, chooses progressive revelation, particularly as far as the family drama and the confinement of the daughter are concerned.

Study of the composition also revealed what an essential role the monologue plays in different ways in the economy of Queneau's novel. Midway between the interior monologue and the diary, part 1 offers the dilemma and the existential meditations of Pierre, the eldest son, sent from "Home Town" to "Foreign Town"; this latter city is very likely inspired by London, but realistic reference is effaced in favor of symbolic value—exile, noncommunication, strange customs—according to an aesthetic dear to Joyce as well. This discourse intertwines the philosophical reflections suggested by the contemplation of fish, crustaceans, and other primitive creatures of our universe (our ancestors; sometimes it is even the fish that speaks through Pierre!) with the examination of his conscience: the anguish of failure because of an incapacity to learn the language and thus to justify the "Honorary Scholarship," family relations and remembrances of childhood, solitude. But it is the monologue taken as a whole that is marked by spontaneous cries of anguish or of revolt.

The third part, a poetic account in the first person, forms a striking stylistic contrast. This monologue offers another side of the enigma that it clarifies little by little, but it is also, as I said, an exercise in parody which leads us back to the sources of literature and the epic, more biblical than Homeric. It contrasts as well with part 4, which is the counterpart or the respondent in the first monologue: on both sides of the mystical and vengeful son Jean, the brothers Pierre and Paul, the unsuccessful student and his younger brother, converse in symmetry, as in a mirror image; Paul in his turn expresses his revolt, cursing the country where he must live and where his solitude is as great as that of Pierre's in a foreign land, while his meditations rely on another spectacle, no longer the aquarium at the Zoological Garden, but the movie theater of Home Town, and above all the extraordinary dreams born of the "films in a foreign language"—obviously from Hollywood!—for which Paul develops an irrepressible passion, similar to that of his creator.

This triple monologue of a family triad illustrates three forms of adolescent lyricism and testifies in three different tones to life's unhappiness in days of youth, its anxieties, its passions, its desire to live and to act, and its efforts to articulate its vivacity, to find a form adequate to each person's character. There is the metaphysico-naturalist lyricism of Pierre, which is Queneau's voice devoted to the sciences and to philosophy. There is the biblical lyricism of Jean, between mysticism and the ritual murder of the father, the echo of a temptation dominated, perhaps mocked here, but certainly recurring. Finally there is the drunkenness of distaste experienced by Paul, who is shaken with violent sensual passion, that of "mouvizes" (the best phonetic French equivalent of "movies") and, through them, sublimated sensual drunkenness, transcended for a blonde star come from beyond the world.[7] As the monologues of Stephen Daedalus give us back his reflection on his dependence with regard to the world and his quest of the known toward the desired unknown, so (and differently, admittedly) the voices of the Nabonidus sons form the triptych of an education and of a voluntary birth into the world. Very Joycean also is the inclination for lyrical flights at the end of the interior discourse, like a triumph of the effusion produced by the word liberating itself; this is very much the character of the end of parts 1 and 4.

But the most Joycean of the monologues of *Saint Glinglin* appears to be that of part 6. Joycean or Faulknerian? One cannot prevent oneself from thinking of Benjy in hearing the voice of Helen, a mentally handicapped girl confined by her father.[8] But we know that since the wonderful confidences stammered out by Molly Bloom, the "stream of subconsciousness" has assumed a feminine gender. As for Queneau, he delivers to us the falsely naive babblings of Helen, a variation on the technique of the monologue and on the individualized vision of a reality less certain than the imaginary. A small female, imprisoned and quasi-mute, hesitatingly formulates her "innocent," partial, and original world vision. Queneau then takes up the staccato style of Edouard Dujardin in order to show better the fragmentation of consciousness and the return of poignant obsessions. In point of fact, this monologue leads back more to Joyce than to Faulkner by the humor that is deployed. While offering a reflection of Helen's uncertain consciousness, nods and winks to earlier authors mix with the flow of thought. We find coded references to hypertexts (Shakespeare, for example) as well as comic definition of daily realities as if they were observed by a foreigner. The latter is very much a literary process, as La Bruyère used it in describing the Versailles court or Montesquieu throughout the *Lettres persanes.*

Originality of Language

It is suitable to complete these few remarks on the art of the novel in *Saint Glinglin* by speaking of the originality of the language and particularly of the elaboration of vocabulary. Two procedures together emerge from this work as from others of Queneau's: first, the appetite for popular language linked to that of ludic phonetic spelling (less established than the customary language), second, the imitation of Joycean language and the creation of multiple neologisms. It is there that the translator's work is the most arduous, the most risky, the most disappointing at times for the Queneau fan.

Queneau says he retains his taste for spoken language from the days of his military service and from reading Louis-Ferdinand Céline.[10] Moreover, the monologues of *Saint Glinglin* are also at the intersection between Joyce and Céline; familiar or slangy language and approximate phonetics are sprinkled through the text with a picturesque vocabulary, elisions of orality, deviations of sound, or grammatical slippages. More than a desire for realism, it is obviously a question of ludic and comic operations. Thus "jamais gniavait dboue," ("never wuzthere inny mud"), "qu'elle se révélassassât" ("that she revealededed"), "Dédicacélemeuh!" ("Inscribeitome!"), "i montra du doigt kékchose dans lciel" ("And 'e raised 'is hand and pointd a finger to sumthing in thsky"), or of the very concentrated "Imélamin'hocudlastar!" ("Heput'ishandonthstarsass!"). Speaking of phonetics, let us recall the author's fondness for the amusing naturalization of English words; he assimilates joyously the "faseur" (father), the "mozeure" (mother), "sisteure," "coquetèle" (cocktail), "chorte" (shorts) or "ouateurproufe" (waterproof [i.e. raincoat]), and "mouvizes." Moreover, he mischievously displaces Hollywood to "Holy Wood," translating it as "le Bois Sacré." What a beautiful and fruitful way to defend French against the danger of Anglo-American invasion: let's naturalize as hard as we can; this will be funnier and more effective than impotent rules to govern spoken language!

But Queneau proves to be above all an emulator of Joyce by imitating him straightforwardly, for example in Pierre's first monologue and with the multiple variations on "existence": "aiguesistence," "eggsistence," "ogresistence," "eksistence," "hainesistence," "alguesistence," "âcresistence," "aigresistence," "haecsistence." Besides the French, to which he attaches a new semantic value ("turpin" and "ganelon," for example, which, derived from heroes of chansons de geste, become names of coins), Queneau invents numerous words, by derivation ("urbinatalian" [from Ville Natale], "hipipourassements" [hiphiphoorayments], and "houlouloulements" [ulululuations]) or by composition ("chasse-nuages" [Cloud-Chaser]) or by pure creations ("fifrequet" [an alcoholic drink], "brouchtoucaille" [a fantastic meal], "trénuclie" [an illness], all invented by Queneau). Finally, he privileges the portmanteau procedure dear to Lewis Carroll: "vertigénial" (vertiginous + genial), "Obscar" (Oscar + obscure), "méthodethnologiquement" (methodically + ethnology), "désirativement" (desire + hastily), "foultitudin-(er)" (foule [crowd] + multitude), "faïencée" (fiancee + faïence), "fammpouse" (femme + épouse), "callipilaire" (capillary + calli-), "se profilocher" (profile + effilocher [to shred]), etc.

Here is a writer who is eager to enrich the novel with all the resources of verbal material, levels of language, phonetic games, gallicizing, association, fusion, or pure invention.

Conclusion

By means of soliloquies, dialogues, and narrations, Queneau composes in *Saint Glinglin* an allegory of human history, from fish—our wet forebears—to weather control, from tribal traditions to the all-powerful cinema—a new form of the imaginary, of delirium, of sensuality, and of passion—from myth to science fiction. This novel is a characteristic example of a work elaborated in stages, where the author, profiting from brilliant examples, directs his own original creation.

Constructing a complete microcosm—"All space in a nutshell"—geographical, ethnological, and mythical, completely disengaged from the tensions of history in the thirties as well as in the forties, Queneau, escaping his time and stylish dogmas, shows himself to be a disciple of a theory of art such as that conceived of by Joyce: far from dated engagement and from an ephemeral politico-social message, to give an account of man poetically and novelistically, of his anxieties, of his gropings, of his passions, and of his dreams.

NOTES

[1]Cf. J. M. Catonné, *Queneau* (Paris: Belfond, 1992), 192. The references to *Saint Glinglin* involve the French edition of 1948 (Gallimard) and the English edition of 1993 (Dalkey Archive Press).

[2]The title *Gueule de Pierre* means something like "Pierre's Mug" (or "Muzzle"). *Temps mêlés* means "Mixed Weather" as well as "Mixed Times."

[3]Cf. Queneau, *Bâtons, chiffres et lettres* (Paris: Gallimard, 1965), 29-33.

[4]For those who are interested in genetics, here is a rapid résumé of textual transformations from the two first novels to *Saint Glinglin.* In part 3 of *Gueule de Pierre,* the first twelve cantos linked to the signs of the zodiac become ten and the zodiacal names disappear: Is this a desire to erase coded references which appeared excessive or artificial in 1948? Moreover, this parodic epic in the third person is transposed to the first person. The transformation of *Les Temps mêlés* is even more profound: part 1 disappears completely, an ensemble of poems of which eight had already been integrated into the collection *Bucoliques* in 1947; also, part 3, which was a kind of play in five tableaux—uniquely dialogues and didascalia—loses its precise theatrical form and is rewritten in dialogued narration with important basic changes; parts 2 and 3 become therefore 4 and 5 in the new novel, to which are added two new texts, 6 and 7.

[5]In the review *Volontés,* in 1938, Queneau praises the "continuous and transcended inspiration," "this freedom in necessity, this grace in constraint, this joy in creation dominated" proper to Joyce, whom he considers a classic the equal of Homer or Rabelais. (Queneau, *Voyage en Grèce* [Paris: Gallimard, 1973], 133-34, 141, 207).

[6]*Saint Glinglin* (Paris: Gallimard), 7. The 1948 preface is not picked up in the English edition.

[7]The American star who provided this symbolic transposition is Alice Faye, "Phaye" in this novel, whose Parisian screen appearances Queneau followed avidly and faithfully in the thirties and forties, going so far as to

see certain films five or six times.

[8]Queneau was certainly interested, as were Gide, Simone de Beauvoir and Sartre, in the legal proceedings of the "Hidden-Away Girl of Poitiers" in 1930, Mélanie Bastian, daughter of eminent citizens, locked away in her room for years and neglected.

[9]It should be recognized, however, that the usual translator of Queneau, Barbara Wright, is worthy of admiration for her talented equivalencies. I regret that she refused the translation of *Saint Glinglin* because of other work.

[10]Queneau, *Bâtons,* 15, 17.

Translated by Mary Campbell-Sposito

"Interludes" from Raymond Queneau[1]

Jacques Jouet

Second Interlude: *A Hard Winter*

More than a mere temptation, there is in Raymond Queneau a will to classicism. To approach this ideal, it seems to me that the instrumental rigor characterizing his entire body of work needs to be accompanied by various innovations with a centrifugal power, that when all is said and done the most objective and clearest productions need a breath of fresh air that could be called baroque, provided that we consider, as does Francis Ponge in his *Pour un Malherbe,* that classicism is "the most tautly stretched rope of the baroque."

That is how I read *A Hard Winter,* for example, a novel of 1939, published one year after *Children of Clay* and two years before *Les Temps mêlés.* These are Queneau's two most abundant, if not to say most confused, novels, those most weighted by a symbolic jumble. The reader will have understood that I have a weakness for *A Hard Winter* and that for me it is the novel with which to begin navigation of the Queneau archipelago, if one has never read his work.

In the story a man is overcoming his hate of the world. The scene is Le Havre, in the middle of World War I. Bernard Lehameau has been wounded in the war (a leg was injured by shrapnel) and wounded by a news item, a harsh news item: the fire at the Grandes Galeries Normandes during the showing of a film, a disastrous entertainment, 21 February 1903, the date of Raymond Queneau's birth, as the first line of *Oak and Dog* informs us:

> I was born one Feb'ry twenty-first,
> Le Havre, nineteen o three.
> My parents fair for joy did burst
> in their haberdashery.
> Inexplicably things got worse,
> injustice struck my nest:
> they placed me with a greedy nurse
> who offered me her breast.
>
> *Oak and Dog,* trans. Madeleine Velguth

The catastrophic event of the novel is not a birth, but three cremations, perhaps four, which affected Lehameau deeply: those of his mother, his sister-in-law, and his wife who was perhaps pregnant. Lehameau is affected by three losses: physical (his leg), affective (thirteen years after the fact, he remains in mourning: he has not touched a woman), ideological (Lehameau is a grumpy, malevolent, bitter reactionary, not far from declaring himself pro-German).[2] In the eyes of those around him, misfortune explains his bitterness and the leg excuses him.

The healing will be triple, in its turn, as surely as the three wounds are linked together. It takes place at the end of a short novel which cleverly discloses little by little the signs of improvement, by means of repetitive and slightly changing layers, of mirror situations and of slightly gradated words. "He whose soul gasps for breath" (in French this is rendered "Dont l'âme halète" [i.e. Hamlet]). It is thus that Michel Leiris defines Hamlet in his *Glossaire.* Lehameau's recovery itself gasps for breath, as he periodically whispers his "Helenas." Little by little, his leg begins to heal, he denounces a false Swiss spy of the Germans (perhaps not by patriotic conviction, but it has the desired result), he finds the love of Annette, an adorable little nymphet, after many amorous tentative gropings, listed here in ascending order of conviction: Mrs. DuTertre, the bookseller; Thérèse, the sister-in-law; Miss Helena Weeds, the flirtatious friend; Madeleine, the courtesan who finally restores his potency.

With Queneau the novelist, the theme of the rite of passage to being is central. It has already been encountered with respect to literary madmen, just as it will be found again many times over from *The Bark Tree* to *The Flight of Icarus.* Etienne, in *The Bark Tree:* "It isn't happiness I'm concerned with, but existence" (trans. Wright 95). It is as if this fire has excluded Lehameau from time. In a single blaze he has no more past (the mother), no more present (the wife), no more future (the wife who was perhaps pregnant). What was Lehameau between 1903 and 1914 then? It took a noble war for History to seize him back and heal him, return to him his *being,* indisputably, finally authorizing him to raise again the question of happiness. However, contrary to official discourses, Lehameau does not see the end of this war, Lehameau champion of all categories of demoralization.

Certainly, all the commentators of *A Hard Winter* have pointed out the references to the story of Hamlet, from the name Lehameau, which is its literal translation (as Jacques l'Aumône in *The Skin of Dreams* is transformed into James Charity) to the scene of the gravediggers in which Yorick is Ducouillon (in English, the name could be rendered as "Numbnuts"), and including Monsieur

Frederic, vaguely Polonius, and Miss Helena Weeds, vaguely Ophelia, who disappears into the liquid element, a specter.

This is an opportunity to emphasize the referential nature of Queneau's work and how much it mirrors literature, in that it utilizes literary reference as a compulsory lens conditioning all perception or representation of its objects. A question consequently arises: How can we read *A Hard Winter* with respect to this reference? Is its location necessary to the reading? And if this location is real, to what extent can it act legitimately?

We know that Raymond Queneau defended the idea that a book (his own) could give rise to several levels of reading. Just as an onion is formed of successive layers, to each layer corresponds a particular reading. The reader is free to remain at the periphery or to hollow out the bulb. The more one reads Queneau, and the more one reads his commentators, the more obvious it is that the dialogue with others' books, with the lines of poetry that precede him, with the characters of previous stories, constitutes an autonomous mode of reading. I do not believe that the reference to Hamlet, here in *A Hard Winter,* is gratuitous, as Claude Simonnet says. That *Hamlet* is not a structural key to the novel, in the sense that the *Odyssey* is a structural key to Joyce's *Ulysses,* granted; that it is not a symbolic key either is understood. Lehameau is not Hamlet; but what if he were a possible Hamlet? A Hamlet to whom something else happens starting from the same premises? To put it another way, I believe that once Hamlet's axiom is postulated, there are other possible adventures, other destinies. This is why I see a profound necessity for reference that functions as a backboard, perhaps in the writing itself, certainly in the reading. There is dialogue with a strong work, a rival fiction which has the benefit of age and glosses, and with which, the length of his work, Queneau attempts to arm wrestle. There again, Queneau is a *faber.* He does not write the *n*th exegesis of *Hamlet,* but he uses this material at regular intervals: Chapter 30 of *The Last Days,* a poem from *Battre la campagne,* "To Be or Not to Be," two poems from *Fendre les flots,* "My Ancestors" and "Ophelius," the monologue of Gabriel in *Zazie*. I don't know if the list is complete. Hamlet is a backboard against which the work bounces, and this backboard is not exchangeable with any other.

A Norman, Queneau sees himself as a descendant of the Vikings who came perhaps from Elsinore: "Between them and me towers Hamlet's famous face" ("My Ancestors"). In this case, what does the hamletic rebound mean in the match that constitutes *A Hard Winter?* Hamlet, Lehameau, same worsening of the world. All is black and rotten. Lehameau "harvested hate," "Lehameau gorged himself with contempt and horror and his soul leaped exalted." "Haime," in the mouth of the gravedigger who sings as Ducouillon did, is rather a lovely portmanteau word (combining "aime(r)" ["to love"] and "haine" ["hate"]) in Bernard Lehaineux's (the Malevolent) store of knowledge.

But, contrary to Hamlet, who does not make the omelette of his mourning without breaking eggs (a pun [Hamlet/omelette] that Queneau does not spare us in "My Ancestors"; one finds it also in Lacan) and who does it a bit late over Ophelia's body, Lehameau is, in the end, helped more, and his reconciliation with the world is achieved by the very thing Hamlet detested in women: the possibility of childbearing, that is, the perpetuation of a detestable world.

"My child, my child, my little my little friend" becomes simply, at the end of the novel: "Annette, my life, my life, my life" (128). It is the very relief that bled through at the end of *Children of Clay,* the tenderness of the end of *Odile.*

It is not a question of rationalizing Queneau by way of Hamlet. Reference is not a closed order; it is in perpetual mutation, in perpetual trial, eventually contradictory: "We'll never say who played at madness or who was mad" ("Ophelius").[3]

However, reference helps to reveal, from the novel that fights it, uniqueness. Lehameau's reconciliation illustrates a type of situation very rare in Queneau's novels. Compared to all the others, and compared to "Hamlet," *A Hard Winter* constitutes in this work the exception of happiness.

Third Interlude: *Icarus, or the "Rhetorical Trace"*

in nature or elsewhere even
more or less everywhere grow
the sophisms of error
all of which we don't even know
—"An Unending Cold" *(Battre la campagne)*

A wrong note and the pigeons fly in all directions. Wandering about to consume the sparse crumbs, they roundly devoured this charitable pittance when the error occurred, changing the satisfaction of a customary harmony into a depraved screeching, then into the sort of sonorous explosion in between boom and vroom. The wrecked instrument no longer produced satisfaction. In complete ignorance, simply by the report of their hearing, the colomboids disappeared in rectilinear but varied trajectories. Debris from the group were found on the edges of roofs, on tree branches, on the arms of statues. A few feathers fell back, useless testimony to a divergeance already written. (*Morale élémentaire,* 141)

Error, always error . . . error is in nature or it is the melody's false note, the dissonance that smashes a fragile order to pieces. The feathers that fall back down are perhaps those of Icarus, discretely indicated in Breughel's tableau, the consequence of an error in calculation as to the resistance of materials.

To what is the Icarian theme linked in Queneau's work? I believe it to be central and particularly contradictory. Icarus is one who tastes emancipation, independence, the drunkenness of the exploit. He is the naive other side of the free-thinking Hamlet. He proves (but not for long) that the law is not the law. He is one who repeats the experiment of falling bodies, picturing himself as a pigeon, as Queneau dreamed in *Lorsque l'esprit.*[4]

Drunkenness and fatal fall: these could be ingredients of a romantic treatment of the poet's function. The exercise of art distances the practitioner from the world, isolates him, confers on him the marginality of unhappy genius. If he should chance to approach beauty, truth, love, the straps of his wings melt. He participates in infinity without having its nature. It is Antonia d'Hoffmann *(Le Conseiller Crespel)* who dies for singing like no one else; it is Leverkühn of Thomas Mann's *Doctor Faustus* for whom the fall is destined by a pact with the devil, an obligatory counterpart to the creative spirit.

The Quenellian Icarus is not tragic except in a superficial way. In the novel *The Flight of Icarus,* the author Hubert Lubert, noticing the disappearance of his hero, at first believed it was a theft-kidnapping, when it was actually a theft-flight and escape. Whereas Madame Cloche or Jacques l'Aumône do fear metamorphosis, whereas Aroun Arachide of *Zazie* is seen to be by turns Pédro-Surplus, then a nameless-ageless person, then Trouscaillon, then the Inspector Bertin Poirée, Icarus is never anyone but Icarus. His escape is, one could say, programmed by Lubert-the-author who keeps him on a short leash, since it is he who named him. Only Morcol's error (" 'I shan't be able to write a word until the mystery's solved and Icarus comes back' [. . .] He [Morcol] writes Dicky Ruscombe in his notebook" [trans. Wright 17]), which echoes that of the sapper Camember (he looks for a certain *Six Mules,* because of "someone who called himself [se dit] Six Mules" [se dissimule (dissimulate)]), leaves a little space for the fugitive and makes the novel possible. "The only thing I don't like about kites is the string that curbs them . . ." says Icarus in chapter 69 (trans. Wright 181). Even so, the character is always tied down.

When Icarus crashes to earth (he who could not miss fulfilling his destiny as a pioneer of aviation), the last word goes to the fictive author, who admits his duplicity, but it is also the *explicit* of Queneau's novel which admits its triplicity: Hubert, *closing his manuscript on Icarus.* "All happened as was anticipated: my novel is finished" (192). Icarus is the figure of the poet in the sense that the poet is fundamentally "of this earth" (that is to say of clay, of dirt, of dung, all at the same time), as Queneau states in *Chansons d'écrivains* and that his flight compulsion is naive and maladjusted. "And man who has no wings/talks, talks and talks of it" *(Petite Cosmogonie portative,* IV, line 225). But Icarus is not the figure of the poet for at least two reasons. First, because of the historical relativity of the reference: Pilâtre de Rozier (failure), but also "Vilburvrichte" (i.e. Wilbur Wright, fortunate pioneer of aviation, who—well, well!—began by making bicycles, as did Icarus) will be contradictorily present in the *Petite Cosmogonie,* an Icarus and an anti-Icarus.[5] Second, and above all, because an allegory presupposes an author of the allegory. The distinction author/character obviously places the second under the control of the first. Oh! These coquettish novelists who claim to be the slaves of their characters, you know "they came to life and I can do no more than watch them act, than follow their ramblings." No, the author, according to Queneau ("There is no literature unless it is voluntary" would be his motto), the author displays the serenity of a very modest creator. He constructs a microcosmic world. And decidedly, for Queneau that is not tragic. Icarus is instead moving in his incompetence and naïveté.

> Icarus had tallow in the hollow of his armpit
>   and not steel
> he fell in the water, losing his straps
>   miserable montgolfier
> and here am I departing to other universes
>   leaving behind me
> the rhetorical trace and investment in a few lines
>   of this troubling exploit.
>   "Un troublant exploit" (*Le Chien à la mandoline*)

The rhetorical trace remains. The fact of putting into verse and into a novel Icarus' failure signals a small success. A poem is just a small thing, but it is a fragment of order. The world is what one makes of it.

Fourth Interlude: *Laughter*

We must linger for a moment on the image of a laughing Queneau, Queneau the amusing, Queneau the schoolboy, Queneau who pleases because he makes us laugh.

One of the most striking things upon reading the *Journal* (I mean the only year published: 5 July 1939 – 24 July 1940[6]) is the total absence of buffoonery, of irony, of humor–or of comedy. Certainly, the reader accustomed to Queneau will not fail to bring to the table the salivating impressions of his conditioned reflexes, in which case, wetting the bed, wanking, a pile of shit, or constipation during evening prayers will provoke laughter. However, it is a laughter of those who have already read Queneau, of those who project on the events recounted the characteristic literary treatment of his different works. Queneau himself, in an article in *Volontés,* "L'Humour et ses victimes" (1938, reprinted in *Le Voyage en Grèce*), crossed swords with humor. He visibly does not wish to allow himself to be trapped in a current of derision (dada revisited by cabaret singers), an "automatic negativism" of which humor is nothing more than a veneer to try to hide ignorance, to excuse all the easy options, a humor of intellectual cover-up or of concealing despair. An empty-shelled empty-boned humor, Rabelais could have said, and in fact Queneau reproaches these espousers of humorism for excluding Rabelais from their Pantheon.

We find there again this grievance against destruction which has so often stuck to Queneau's coattails (destruction of language, of literature). To the extent that the function of laughter, in its modern conception, is held to be denigrating, Queneau sees himself naturally as a member of this cohort. Mikhail Bakhtin, who underlines this modern function, opposes it to that of the Renaissance where, he says, "laughter has a positive significance, regenerative, creative" (in *Rabelais and His World*). What is it about Queneau's laughter, about his comedy? The reply of Gabriel in *Zazie* is often cited: " 'We've had a simply *wonderful* time. Meussieu is so amusing.'/'Thank you,' says Gabriel. 'Don't forget the art in it though. It's not only fun and games, it's art as well' " (184). I believe that for Queneau laughter is not spontaneous, but that it is a voluntary product of art. That would explain why in the *Journal,* where the writing is the least elaborated, the least corrected of all, comedy almost does not appear. Missing are a certain number of ingredients that are at the source of Quenouillard comedy.[7] Logic, for example, when, because of poverty, Julia lets Valentin leave alone on their honeymoon *(The Sunday of Life).* The art of contrast:

"But *I* am alive, and there ends my knowledge, for of the taximann, fled in his locatory jalopy, or of my niece, suspended a thousand feet up in the atmosphere, or of my spouse the gentle Marceline, left guarding the household gods, I know nothing at this precise moment, here and now. I know nothing but this, alexandrinarily: that they are almost dead because they are not here. But what do I see above the hairy noddles of the good people who surround me?" (*Zazie* 100)

The extreme contrast here between the levels of language, hypertrophied poetic inversion followed by an alexandrine hindered by "hairy noddles" (i.e. "noggins"), is decisive in its comic effect, but it is a technique that requires mastery and finesse in its handling. Another very frequent procedure is the rapidity of association which creates surprise. *Petite Cosmogonie portative* provides a veritable feast of it. Related to that is accumulation, the cascade of possibles, which drags the reader along in the torrent:

> Near the meadows near the waters a naive people
> struggles incongruously farm animals or winged creatures
> the turkey hen the turkey cock the horse the mare
> becuz a calendar says it is springtime
> Man in his cities jealous of his fate
> man fucks in the evening and fucks in the morning
> he fucks at Christmas at Easter at Halloween
> the fourteenth of July and the eleventh of November
> he fucks when it rains he fucks when the wind blows
> without wishing that the sun, not a very cunning sphere
> dictate the ups and downs of the prepucial member.
>
> (*IV,* lines 140-150)

We can never overstate that the comic needs speed of expression. Laughter is provoked by dynamics, it plunges into running water . . . unless it is a fracture, a leap from a moving freight, a coitus interruptus breaking up the dynamics. It is thus that Queneau seems permanently to defy a too-serious or too-lengthy sentimental tone and sounds the death knell with an astounding mildness:

> If life goes away
> goodbye tomorrow
> if life goes away goes flowing away
> you have to ask if it's worth it
> all that alarm clock and toothbrush.
>
> "If Life Goes Away" (*Fatal Moment*)

This completely incongruous toothbrush makes me laugh. I would not be surprised if it produced a sinister effect in another reader. This "cold shower" procedure is so systematic with Queneau that sometimes it becomes annoying.

Another thing, in principle related: as a good Hellenist, Queneau completely assimilated the practice of satyr plays, which, since Aeschylus, have brought the tragic trilogy to a close by developing catharsis in comic fashion. And the idea that the *Batrachomyomachy* (war of frogs and rats) was attributed to the same author as the *Iliad* doubtless pleased Queneau. Scarron made Virgil respectable; Queneau sinks Lucretius to the depth of daisies (alexandrine), and representing the artist, he chooses a ballerina [*un danseuse*].[8] I'll admit that what made me laugh most in *Exercises in Style* is the fact that the story told is the Quenellian novel reduced to its simplest expression: an encounter; the programmed chance of a second encounter where the fiction is provoked by an error (in taste): the button is Old Taupe's door.[9]

We see that Queneau's comedy is not particularly satirical or moralistic; he does not have the habit of bringing down the character who bears the brunt, even if it is Queneau himself when he serves as his own target: "to the biped cosmogonist fate makes sparks fly" *(Petite Cosmogonie portative, V,* line 107). It is a comedy of jubilation, in which, obviously, the body, a rather vulgar body, occupies a large place. If the death's head causes anxiety, there are still filth, excrement, secretions, and sexual organs (this last point approached in a particularly allusive fashion) which all cause laughter and in which Queneau's text is especially fond of rubbing its nose.

This comedy is first of all an emancipation, the affirmation of a freedom (not to say that it is the only way). It is, fundamentally, a privileged place of the human being in conflict with history, a weapon which the human subject has at his disposal in the unfolding of his miseries, and notably as to the final unhappiness, the dominant unhappiness: "XV. The comic novel/When the narrator smiles and spurns death, we/call his tale a comic novel" *(Une Histoire modèle).* For Zazie, Paris is a parenthesis which should be without history (if one is to believe what she recounts of her family adventures at Saint-Montron, she is in need of a little break), and her refrain "[something] . . . my ass!" is more than the linguistic emblem of Queneau the joker. It is well and truly his best defense against history, that is to say against others, until the point where history is, in the end, the strongest, because the novel *does not end* with the following dialogue:

"Well, did you enjoy yourself?"
"All right."
"Did you see the métro?"
"No."
"What *have* you done, then?"
"(Whadja do my [ass]!)"[10]

NOTES

[1]Unless otherwise noted, all translations are my own.

[2]In French the expression "pro-boche" is akin to "pro-Hun."

[3]The alliterative effect of this line is lost in translation: "On ne dire jamais qui fit le fol et qui fut fou."

[4]Raymond Queneau, *Lorsque l'esprit,* Edition de Collège de 'Pataphysique, collection Queneau 1 (Paris, 1955), rpt. *Contes et propos* (Paris: Gallimard, 1981).

[5]Pilâtre de Rozier (1756-1785) was a French chemist and aeronaut. He made the first balloon voyage in 1783 with the Marquis d'Arlandes. He died while attempting to cross the English Channel by balloon.

[6]A new volume of *Journaux,* covering the years 1914 to 1965, has just been published by Gallimard.

[7]*Quenouillard* is a word modeled on *La Famille Fenouillard* by Christophe. The Oulipo is the "Quenouillard Family" to Jouet.

[8]In the English translation, Gabriel is asked what kind of artist he is: " 'Ballerina,' he replies." In French this incongruity can be expressed by using a masculine indefinite article with a feminine noun: *"un* dan*seuse."*

[9]The sense here is that the button acts as a thematic generator, as does Old Taupe's door in *The Bark Tree.*

[10]In the novel the final words actually are "I've aged" ("J'ai vieilli"). See *Zazie,* trans. Wright (London: John Calder, 1982).

Translated by Mary Campbell-Sposito

Queneau and Poetic Illusion

Claude Debon

When readers approach Queneau's works, in particular his novels, one well-established idea is very likely in their minds: these novels are poems. The reason for this is simple: Queneau himself placed it there.

In 1950, in the celebrated and frequently cited essay in *Bâtons, chiffres et lettres,* "Conversation avec Georges Ribemont-Dessaignes," Queneau declares, speaking of his novelistic creation: "I laid down for myself rules as strict as those of the sonnet. . . . I wrote other novels with the idea of rhythm, the intention of making a sort of poem of the novel." These rules, which had escaped the first readers, had been unveiled much earlier, in 1937, in the no-less-celebrated article from the same work, "Technique of the Novel."

This relationship of the novel to the poem reappears in another formulation in the *Interviews with Georges Charbonnier* in 1962, when Queneau assimilates "literature" and "poetry": "as far as I'm concerned I see no difference between the two. As you well know, literature has been called into question; poetry has been placed in the leading position and removed from 'literary' criticism; but for me, it is the same thing; let's say 'poetry' if that makes people happy." Here one sees poetry annexing the whole field of literature.

By virtue of a reverential procedure rendered traditional in critical practice, the idiolect of the *auctor* establishes authority and goes perhaps even beyond his wishes. All Queneau criticism, beginning with Claude Simonnet's masterly *Queneau déchiffré,* has followed its master's voice: "An epic poem which is enhanced by a determined and completely classical esthetic, *The Bark Tree* has no other meaning than to exist as a gratuitous monument, as a close work, rigorously closed on itself. But at the same time and with no contradiction, this poem must read itself, must decipher itself." And on the concluding page: "it concerns a poem whose content cannot be isolated from its form." This begging of the question is found nearly everywhere, including in my own introduction to the *Oeuvres poétiques* in the Pléiade.

However, there is another obvious fact that imposes itself on the readers of most of Queneau's novels: their comic quality. This quality is in its turn so linked to the author's name that some of the novels which today may appear to us if not as poems, at least as poetic novels, were appraised as comic novels at the moment of their publication. Here are, among other examples, passages from an article by Maurice Saillet, to whom we owe Jarry's *La Chandelle verte,* an article taking into account both *A Hard Winter* and *Les Temps mêlés:* "This story (that of *A Hard Winter),* one suspects, belongs to a rare genre. Both denser and more agile than the better part of our funny novels (I am thinking of *La Jument verte,* of *Clochemerle,* of *Fesse-Matthieu l'inconnu)* it sometimes recalls the pugnacious vein of American storytellers, from Mark Twain to William Saroyan." As for *Les Temps mêlés,* here is how Maurice Saillet appraises it: "These strange episodes, as we see, link the modern 'practical joke' to ancient and solemn myths. But one obviously should question the merit of such a work. It hits you right between the eyes. It has the necessity of true fantasy. Next to epic fragments, lines of doggerel and advertising slogans whose gimmicks and spirit are irresistible, one also encounters pages of incomparable realism. The whole is pleasing, passionate, always intelligent—and what a trip to Fantasyland!"

Other more recent signs seem to shake up the conventional wisdom according to which Queneau's novels are considered poems. In a recent study of *Zazie,* for example, Michel and Stéphane Bigot write, "If Queneau does not differentiate, in his creative work, between novel and poetry, it does not, for all that, tend toward the festoons and garlands of the so-called 'poetic' novel." Proceeding by an examination of the metaphors in the novel, they conclude the chapter, "By its strangeness this novel seems an illusion, but it does not suggest a dream." We can see how this opinion enters directly into the framework of Queneau's formulations.

This tension between the dream and the comic is at the heart of Queneau's creative activity. The problem before us could be considered a simple question of words. It seems, however, to be much more important, to the extent that it involves the reception of texts, their study, and furthermore, the idea that we have today of poetry. The problem concerns also the idea that the novelist developed of poetry and the consequences that it provoked.

I admit that my desire to attack such a problem was emotionally influenced. While determining a program for students, a colleague and I decided to discuss the poetic novel. My colleague, after having suggested to me some titles with which I agreed, wished to include as the last work on the program a text by Georges Perec, *Quel petit vélo à guidon chromé au fond de la cour?* I took a dim view of this. Could one really consider this little book a poetic novel? We had a hard-fought conversation, from which I emerged victorious, but very upset, because a fourth of the dust jacket, in a parodistic transport, placed the *Petit vélo* in the field of poetry: "From time to time, it is good that a poet, not fearful of the rarified air of the summits, dares to elevate himself above the vulgar in an epic inspiration, to exalt us in the here and now."

How can we approach this problem?

Queneau's formulation implies a certain representation of the poem and of poetry that must first be stated clearly. We shall see that it does not exclude another representation, apparently contradictory to the first.

These representations are not separable from a contemporary debate on the genre of poetry, an amply theorized debate, but one still open. It is, moreover, naturally coupled with that of the comic genre and the question of the compatibility of the two genres.

It is doubtful that I can approach here the whole of the problem in all its complexity. Therefore, I shall first accent the Jakobsonian representation of Queneau's novel-poem to show that it enters into tension with a perceptible apprehension of poetry far removed from the purely formal approach. This duality is emblematic of the tension present in the debate described above.

The rational choice present in the discourse of the *écrivant* remains grounded in reality, as I shall try to show, by impulses of another category. Queneau desires the form so forcefully that this desire becomes suspect, judged only by the yardstick of rationality. The writer himself is moved by other impulses flowing out of him. He creates a new object, for himself and for others. Can this object be poetic and comic at the same time? Can one laugh and experience a poetic emotion simultaneously, laugh and dream?

In order not to entangle these questions even more, I shall leave to one side the extension of the notion of poetry to all of literature. It is in fact a matter of a historical debate whose details can be found in an article of Queneau's dating from 1940, "Naissance et avenir de la littérature" *(Le Voyage en Grèce)*. This article is a response to a book by Guastalla, which as it happens places poetry and literature in opposition.

I shall keep to the idea of the poem, within the limits of its suitability to novelistic creation. For Queneau, the common denominator between the poem and the novel is the rhythm. This rhythm is nothing other than a certain quantity of formal recurrences arranged in advance: return to the beginning, and there one finds a circular form, recurrence of the same numbers of chapters, recurrence of characters in twos. Whence the notion of rhymes, described in the "Conversation avec Georges Ribemont-Dessaignes." This repetition, which structures most of Queneau's novels, including sometimes even refrains ("Talk, talk, talk, that's all you can do . . . ," "Another fucking fiasco," etc.), is the exact equivalent of *versus,* which turns back, as opposed to *prorsus,* which goes ahead. It is a great temptation, therefore, to speak of poetic structure. However, it is evident that recurrence in the novels is not accompanied by the *perception* of recurrence, which alone would permit the understanding of equivalencies and render them meaningful. This perception is never immediate; it is not mastered except after many readings and rereadings. Would perception of recurrence suffice to render the novel poetic? No more than a line is poetic because it is composed of twelve syllables. In other words Queneau clings voluntarily to a purely formal conception of poetry, connecting it in extremis in "Technique of the Novel" to a Pythagorian theory of the cosmos: "Rules cease to exist once they have outlived their value, but forms live on eternally. There are forms of the novel which impose on the suggested topic all the virtues of the Number. Born of the very expression and of diverse aspects of the tale, connected by nature with the guiding idea, daughter and mother of all the elements that it polarized, a structure develops, which transmits to the works the last reflections of Universal Light and the last echoes of the Harmony of Worlds." So be it. But the poetic virtues of pure mathematics remain to be proven for ordinary people.

This position, which currently governs most studies on Queneau's novels, was developed in 1937, at a time when, imbued with the thought of Guénon, in favor of transcendental metaphysics, Queneau was settling accounts, most particularly with surrealism. It is easy to show to what extent his position is polemical and cannot be understood except in this double context. Without entering into the details of an exegesis of "Technique of the Novel," one only has to listen to the text's tone to be persuaded that it does not obey rational forces, but is moved by disgust. Whence the perceptible contempt in expressions such as: "Anyone can drive in front of him an undetermined number of apparently real characters through a wasteland of an undetermined number of pages or chapters. The result, whatever it may be, will always be a novel." The emphasis with which Queneau rejects this type of novel is none other than that of rejection of the surrealists: "But, for my part, I cannot bow to such a lack of constraint." And farther on: "It was unbearable to me to leave to chance the business of determining the number of chapters in these novels."

The manuscript of this text, which has been preserved, bears witness to an even greater violence and to a foregone conclusion. The first version of the sentence quoted above was as follows: "Nothing, to my mind, seems more alien to the art of the novel than a narrative fragment in which the author, full of himself and unaware of being so, pushes limping along before him [like a flock of geese: *insertion*] a gaggle of apparently real characters." All of this first draft, far removed from the definitive version, merits an attentive reading. I shall give only a few passages. Here is the beginning: "No one remains unaware that the liberation of poetry, a favorite topic [*jument de bataille* in French; "war horse" is the closest English rendering] of Arthur Rimbaud, was killed under him in the battle of Charleville in 1873. Since then poets have done no more than inhabit its carcass; prose, intoxicated by romanticism, collapsed at the first real shelling; with the same blow the survivors of another age died: the sonnet, the ode, the ballad and the rondeau." There follows a virulent critique of the metaphor and an encomium of the Anglo-Saxon technique of the novel: "I do not wish to describe here the various stages spanned by the technique of the novel; it must be recalled, however, that after serial novels *(Gil Blas)* and novels composed of unconnected episodes *(Don Quixote),* the first to possess a rhythmic structure was *Tom Jones.* To pursue another path, the research of Henry James on the narrative itself must be pointed out [passage erased]." Then comes praise for *Remembrance of Things Past.* This text, an interesting one, develops an enlightening comparison with respect to the characters, which has disappeared from the definitive text: "For me, the characters form an orchestra, sometimes one plays and another is quiet, sometimes those [a blank] sometimes [a blank]. And, as in a jazz orchestra, another devotes himself to an improvisation where his freedom is affirmed."

It is curious to see, moreover, that the epigraph of "Technique of the Novel," in *Volontés* and in *Bâtons, chiffres et lettres,* does not figure in the manuscript. This text of Corneille seems to contradict the traditional formalism expressed in the article since it appeals to a liberation regarding the rules of the ancients, a liberation which carries risks, but which can also be positive.

Reread in this context, "Technique of the Novel" would wrongly be considered as the whole of Queneau's thought on the poem and on poetry. In the same text several commentators had already noted the gap emphasized by Queneau himself between the rationalism of numbers and their symbolic exploitation, both universal and autobiographical, a mixture of objectivity and admitted subjectivity. But above all, the author develops elsewhere other theories far removed from this mathematical formalism. In particular in the *Entretiens avec Georges Charbonnier,* produced in 1961 and published in 1962, Queneau introduces new ideas such as the opposition between information and communication ("it [poetry] transmits hardly any information . . . it transmits a lot of communication"); he evokes repeatedly the mystery of poetry, its moving character, and he is reduced to saying nearly the opposite of what he wrote in 1937: "there is [in the realm of poetry] a vocabulary, there is syntax, and there are problems of information and even of communication; and then all of a sudden one emerges from all that, and it is poetry." We know otherwise that the poet expressed as a poet this "poetic mystery":

Well placed well chosen
a few words make poetry
words—it's enough to love them
to write a poem
one doesn't always know what one's enunciated
when poetry is created
one must then seek again the theme
to title the poem
but other times one cries one laughs merrily
in writing poetry
it always has somethin' extreme
a poem

(*L 'Instant fatal*)

This poem is exactly contrary to the theories of the novel-poem described earlier. The affective values (love of words, emotions like laughter or tears), the poet's ignorance, the recognition of that which cannot be formulated inherent in poetry ("somethin' extreme") are the exact opposite of harmony and of the use of numbers as guarantors of a reflection of "Universal Light."

Many other texts and arguments could be brought in to lend credence to this irrationalist conception of poetry, such as the poetic anthology of Queneau, his judgments of other poets (Apollinaire, for example), and his recognition of the poetic phenomenon as radically *other.*

It seems difficult, upon reading such texts, to credit Queneau's novels with this "somethin' extreme" to which the author was so sensitive. But perhaps it is more suitable to indict readers than Queneau himself. After all, he never said that his novels were poems or even that they were poetic. He only proposed analogies—"like a sonnet," "a sort of poem"—at a time when his polemical commitment provoked him to put his thought in relief.

Hereafter, it remained true that the reference to fixed forms of poetry and to rules decreed by the classical writers (the rule of the three unities, for example) was in a position to serve as an alibi to the formalists, supplied as they were with statements such as Queneau's. It must be recalled that for classical writers, forms were never separable from the content: the ode was destined for lyric poetry, "which expresses acutely the feelings which stir him [the poet]," the epigram and the madrigal, which belong to the genre of "fugitive poetry," are defined by their content. Their canonic definitions still figured in the manual of literature in use at the end of the nineteenth century and at the beginning of the twentieth. Even the sonnet, defined by Boileau in a purely formal manner, is a small poem which "lends itself best to the development of a feeling or of a thought." The reduction of forms (such as the ballad, which evolved from the lighthearted song to the development of a fantastic or legendary tale or from a tragic adventure) to pure formal arrangement opened the way to the aberrations of severe formalism and had to be illustrated by the overrated example of Jakobson: "I like Ike," confusing phonetic recurrence and poetry. Queneau's intelligence had moreover quite correctly grasped the problem since, in the article quoted above on Guastalla's book, he poses the question, "Would rhythm be of use henceforth only to sing 'Dubo, Dubon, Dubonnet?' Du beau, du bien, du vrai [the beautiful, the good, the true] seemed ridiculous. These have been replaced by Dubo, Dubon, Dubonnet. That's how it is." Upon which he proves that the rhythm is not separable for him from a representation of the world and of values, as the allusion to Plato shows.

Thus the idea of empty form in Queneau is an antisurrealist reaction impregnated with the guénonism of this period and enlightened by the reflections of idealist thought, but it marks also a thrust of the formalism that would dominate in the sixties (and in this Queneau plays an important role as a precursor).

I cannot, within the limitations of this article, touch upon all the questions provoked by the preceding remarks. I shall say only that the modern conception of poetry, since the romantics, then Baudelaire, Mallarmé, and Rimbaud, requires a rethinking of the categories that previously had a different relationship to one another. Poetry and the comic were not mutually exclusive, to the extent that the comic was transgeneric. Ever since poetry has had metaphysical ambitions, it has not harmonized so well with laughter (see Baudelaire: "There is therefore, according to the Sage, a certain secret contradiction between his character of Sage and the primordial character of laughter").

However, since the analyses of Jakobson, the poetic has been restrained to the self-centered message, to the forms of language, a restriction which would lead to an assimilation of the highest linguistic technical nature with the highest degree of "poeticity." The other functions, as Jakobson says himself, are not absent from the poem, but they are secondary. It is this assertion that causes a problem in the present debate and that, modified, could clarify it. The expressive function, in other words the voice, relayed by that of the reader, plays not a secondary role in poetic communication, but a major role, relegating the message and its form to one role among the others. Or rather poetry is not completely realized except when all the functions are combined, including the referential function. The poetic voice, suitable for poetic expression, can then be heard, a displaced voice in slow motion, as if it were coming from another world.

To show that this poetic voice does not let itself be heard in most of Queneau's novels, I shall give an example taken from *The Bark Tree.* At the end of the novel, Missize Aulini, the Etruscan queen, alias the concierge Madame Cloche, unveils her real personality:

"Well, I am, I'm the rain! The rain that dissolves the constellations and upsets kingdoms, the rain that inundates empires and macerates republics, the rain that makes your shoes stick in the mud and runs down your neck, the rain that trickles down dirty windowpanes and rolls down to the gutter, the rain that shits everybody up and makes no sense. And I am also, pay attention now, the sun that defecates onto the heads of harvesters, that skins naked women, that scorches trees, that pulverizes roads. And I am also the icy patches on the roads, that cause accidents, and the ice on the ponds, that cracks under the feet of the obese, and the snow that sends a chill down your spine, and the hail that splits your skull, and the fog that macerates your lungs. Yo soy also the summer months, the spring months that breed venereal diseases, bring faces out in pimples and cause stomachs to swell. Zhur swee the spring, that sells a sprig of lily of the valley for a franc, and the summer that kills people off because they live too intensely: I'm the autumn, that causes all the fruit to rot, and the winter that sells its boxwood on Parmesan Day. Ich bin the storm that howls with the wolves, the tempestuous tempest, the blizzard that blitzes the lizards, the hurricane that hurries you into your coffin, the gale with its hail, the cyclone on its bicycle, the thunder with its icicles, and the lightning that lights life. Eyeamme . . ."

Let's attempt a transcription of this text into a poem for the eyes and for the ears:

Well I am
I am the rain
The rain that dissolves the constellations
and upsets kingdoms
the rain that inundates empires,
the rain that macerates republics
the rains that makes your shoes stick in the mud
and runs down your neck
the rain that trickles down dirty windowpanes
and rolls down to the gutter
the rain that shits everybody up

and makes no sense.
And I am also, pay attention now,
the sun
that defecates onto the heads of harvesters
that skins naked women
that scorches trees
that pulverizes roads
And I am also the icy patches on the roads
that cause accidents
and the ice on the ponds
that cracks under the feet of the obese
and the snow that sends a chill down your spine
and the hail that splits your skull
and the fog that macerates your lungs.
Yo soy also the summer months
the spring months
that breed venereal diseases
bring faces out in pimples
and cause stomachs to swell.
Zhur swee the spring
that sells
a sprig of lily of the valley for a franc,
and the summer
that kills people off
because they live too intensely:
I'm the autumn
that causes all fruit to rot
and the winter
that sells its boxwood
on Parmesan Day
Ich bin the storm
that howls with the wolves
the blizzard
that blitzes
the lizards
the hurricane
that hurries you into your coffin
the gale
with its hail
the cyclone
on its bicycle
the thunder
with its icicles
and the lightning
that lights
life
Eyeamme

All the formal ingredients of a poem are there. Anaphora, parallelisms, rhymes, assonances, rhythm (and even, at the cost of an elision, an alexandrine). The signifiers conclude by engendering the text on their own, on the model of the song: "J'ai la rate/qui s'dilate" ("I have a spleen/That's expanding"; "se dilater la rate" means idiomatically "to kill oneself laughing") The "poem" designates itself as a "poem" by: "qui ne rime à rien" ("and makes no sense") immediately moreover contradicted by "tenez-vous bien" ("pay attention now"), which rhymes with "rien." The content itself belongs to the great myths: Missize Aulini embodies malevolent cosmic forces, and joined together here are the components anthropos, cosmos, and logos, which, if you believe Group Mu of Liege, are the conditions of poetic discourse.

And yet what poetic voice could bear this text? I imagine someone like the actress Maria Casarès beginning a reading of it and filling listeners with dread. The rift would be produced from the verb "moisten" placed side by side with "republics," the antitheses "inundate" and "moisten" implying either a certain respect of the rain for a regime to which it accords its benevolence or the insignificance of republics that are not even equal to an inundation. In every case there is a satiric trait, which comes in to break the solemnity of the preceding affirmations. Retrospectively, "upsets" would be felt as a stylistic fall. What follows would do no more than amplify the phenomenon, and I wager that "The rain that makes your shoes stick in the mud" would trigger if not laughter, at least a smile. It is unnecessary to pursue the demonstration. The tone here is burlesque, that of laughter. The poem or the burlesque epic was a real poetic genre, which dealt with a serious subject in a trivial form. It does not, however, correspond to what we call poetry today because it breaks down all the oneiric possibilities of the text.

To recapitulate, Queneau's novels are neither poems nor poetic novels, such as we understand them today. This statement must be moderated, if one thinks of certain novels, like *Odile* or *A Hard Winter* (then it would be a question of "poetic passages" very different from the insertion of pseudopoems, on the whole rather antipoetic [such as the "poems" inserted in *Children of Clay* and even of those in *Temps mêlés*]). But it would be an aberration to say that *Zazie* or *The Blue Flowers* are novel-poems. These blue flowers, with their romantic connotation, are the emblematic image of the ambiguous that we are trying to abolish, because they could pass for an antiphrasis, even if the whole of the novel rests on the border between dream and reality and gives hope of opening onto the dream. In reality, the novel's tone is burlesque from one end to the other, and the dream designated as such has nothing to do with poetry.

Why did Queneau provoke such ambiguity, he who was also a

poet, as no one can doubt after having read his poetic work? The response is, as we have seen, in part historical. But it probably has more secret roots, which go back to the origins of Queneau's literary vocation—a poet from his childhood and adolescence, he was first preoccupied with philosophico-linguistic problems. The idea that led him to write his first great text, a masterpiece, was of linguistic origin: it was a matter of adapting philosophical texts written in obsolete French to the language understood and spoken in our time. In this case the text was *The Discourse on Method* of Descartes. When Queneau, influenced by his discovery of the demotic in Greece, undertook this adaptation, he discovered simultaneously its comic virtues. And he was the first to be astonished. Chance put him on the path to a discovery that would create his success and unleash the creative expression of the later novels. Can it be said that he never recovered? He had never wished to be a comic author. All his philosophical and spiritual preoccupations, linked to an era when humor was predominantly black, distracted him from a comic apprehension of the world, but language imposed it on him. He had, with difficulty, publicly to assume this quality that he had not really wished for. The revendication of the novel-poem was a way of reconciling his poetic commitment and his comic genius. But it torments us in turn. Let us assume what he could not assume: Queneau's genius is comic. He knew also how to be a poet, according to the idea of poetic emotion we have developed today. But it would add nothing to his reputation to be determined to reunite at any price in his work the two aspects of his creation.

Translated by Mary Campbell-Sposito

Translating Queneau

Barbara Wright

Everyone who knows Queneau's work knows that he was a unique writer, a polymath with a vast range of interests and talents, a man who put into practice his profound belief that prose is no different from poetry. His poetic prose is composed of what seems like an infinity of elements: erudition and farce, philosophy and wit, literary and other allusions, rhythm and "internal rhymes," and humor. He also enjoyed treating serious matters lightheartedly and lighthearted matters seriously. So such a man should be fiendishly difficult to translate. Well, yes; he is.

Nevertheless, given that all translation without exception is difficult, I sometimes tend to ask myself the heretical question, "What's the difference between translating Queneau and translating anyone else?" This leads on to another question: "What *is* translation, anyway, and how should we approach it?"

Before I try to answer these two questions, though, I should say something about how I came to be translating Queneau in the first place. It was by pure chance. Some friends, Stefan and Franciszka Themerson, had started a tiny avant-garde publishing house, Gaberbocchus Press, and I had translated Alfred Jarry's *Ubu roi* for them. (That too was pure chance. I was supposed to be a musician at the time, but one day the Themersons asked me whether I would like to translate *Ubu roi* and I said, "Why not?" So, with much help and advice from them, I did. At least I had lived in France as a music student.)

Stefan and Franciszka then met Queneau in Paris, and he gave them his two short stories "The Trojan Horse" and "At the Edge of the Forest" to publish, and they gave them to me to translate. Queneau had had very little published in other languages at the time and he was very much interested to see how I was translating them. (He himself translated books from English, among them Amos Tutuola's *The Palm Wine Drinkard.)* He was not only interested; he was very helpful. We had quite a long correspondence, and it was at his suggestion that the first paragraph of *Le Cheval troyen,* "Un homme entra dans le bistrot, ce qui fit de la buée," became "A man came into the café, and there was a mist."

Some time later I too met Queneau, and, as he was reputed to be shy (which I certainly also was at the time), we didn't know what to say to each other. So I seized on the first thing that came into my head and asked him which of his books he would most like to see translated. Without hesitation he replied, *"Les Exercices de style."* After which, no doubt, there was another embarrassed silence.

I was flabbergasted. I had thought the *Exercices* was one book that was totally untranslatable. When I got home, though, just to amuse myself and out of curiosity, I started to translate it. I didn't tell anyone, and naturally I tackled the easier of the ninety-nine variations first. After a year (!), however (although certainly not working full time), I began to see daylight and wrote to Queneau asking his permission to continue. He was more than enthusiastic, wanted to see what I had done so far, asked me to send him each new exercise as I did it, made wonderfully helpful comments, agreed that seven of the exercises really were untranslatable, and approved the seven I invented to take their place.

When *Zazie dans le métro* was published in French, I thought that it too was untranslatable. Nevertheless, after a few months I plucked up courage and wrote to Queneau to ask him whether I might try it. What I should have known, but didn't, was that in the meantime *Zazie* had become a best-seller in France and that all sorts of translatory shenanigans had been going on. It just so happened, though, that at the precise moment when I wrote to Queneau both the Bodley Head in England and Harpers in the United States were looking for a different translator for *Zazie.* I did a sample for them, and they accepted it.

Next came *Les Fleurs bleues,* for the Bodley Head again, and for Atheneum in the U.S. *The Blue Flowers* is a superb book, marvelously lighthearted and extraordinarily funny. (Queneau somehow seems to incite one to hyperbole.) Writing about this book, Vivian Kogan has pointed out "the multiplicity of reading the text makes possible, readings which evoke questions about history and the unconscious, origins and ends, time and space, the subject and language, literary codes and their decoding." Phew. Yet with all this, *Les Fleurs bleues* really is easy and enjoyable to read. And, as with all of Queneau's books, each subsequent reading reveals different layers of meaning.

Almost the whole of the first page of *The Blue Flowers* flaunts a bravura display of puns, good or bad (Queneau frequently amused himself by perpetrating the most dreadful puns imaginable). About twenty pages farther on, there is a fanfaronade of phony and comically deformed proverbs. I suppose the mere fact of having to brave such challenges really does make translating Queneau somewhat different from translating anyone else; it certainly involves infinite time and much agonizing, although when things seem to be coming right it is deeply satisfying.

Titles are always one of the most vital—and difficult—parts of any translation. For *Les Fleurs bleues* both Queneau and I were of the opinion that just to translate these three words literally wouldn't do justice to the multiple meanings and harmonics they carry in French. Finally I came up with *Between Blue and Blue,* which I had found somewhere and which in its original context did have plenty of harmonics, and we settled on that for the English edition. Oddly enough, I can no longer remember where *Between Blue and Blue* came from, nor can I find it in the quotation book. (I rather think it was from George Eliot.) In the meantime, however, Atheneum in the U.S. had simply gone ahead and called the book *The Blue Flowers.* Whereupon we all agreed that, after all, this was the best title!

After *The Blue Flowers,* I tried to persuade the Bodley Head to let me translate Queneau's first novel, *Le Chiendent* (1933), but they weren't interested. John Calder was, though, and he published it, and then *Le Vol d'Icare,* and then *Le Dimanche de la vie,* and then *On est toujours trop bon avec les femmes* (all of which were published in the U. S. by New Directions).

For *Le Vol d'Icare,* I can still see myself sitting opposite Queneau in his minute office chez Gallimard and saying, like a half-wit: "At least we won't have any problems with the title this time." I took it for granted that *The Flight of Icarus* would be good, faithful, and adequate. Queneau looked up at me gently and quizzically, and of course I immediately recognized that to be absolutely faithful the book should be called *The Flight and the Theft of Icarus.* Some title!

There really was no problem with the title of *Le Dimanche de la vie,* straightforward French translation of Hegel's *Sonntag des Lebens,* and it goes very nicely into English as *The Sunday of Life.* My main remembrance of this translation is of the wonderful few days I spent with James and Ann Laughlin at their Connecticut home while we "Americanized" my English version. Neither JL nor I saw anything amiss with this procedure at the time, but I have since come to the firm conclusion that to change the odd word here or there in any piece of writing, whether original or translated, in order to suit the presumed tastes of either the English or the Americans, can only produce a bastard text that destroys its inner unity and betrays the author. What confirmed me in this conviction was my recent reading of the English version of Erik Orsenna's *Love and Empire.* This American translation, by Jeremy Leggatt, was published in England without (I presume) a word being changed, and it read splendidly as a homogeneous and faithful interpretation of the French original. It contained a few American words that I didn't know, but what are dictionaries for? I believe that by now, readers on both sides of the Atlantic are mature enough to accept either an American English or an English English text without beefing and without thinking that it matters how you spell *color* or *grey*.

The last two Queneau novels I translated were *Pierrot mon ami* and *The Last Days*, both of which I could again become hyperbolic about and both of which were published by Dalkey Archive Press. Asked to translate *Saint Glinglin* and *Les Enfants du limon*, though, I had to say no, and the reason for my reluctant refusal is fundamental to my "philosophy" of translating. I am perfectly certain that one should only agree to translate books that at the very least one *likes* and feels on the wavelength of. How, otherwise, can one do justice to an author? I think I have clearly described my unbounded admiration for Queneau, but I don't at all feel on the wavelength of *Saint Glinglin*, however many times I read it, because the Freudian/Oedipal angle goes right over my head. The same applies to *Les Enfants du limon*, which is a book I greatly admire, with the exception of the frequent interpolations of the *fous littéraires* sections. The reason I don't admire these is that I don't understand them. Queneau seemed to be interested in and to understand *everything*, and as a young man he did a lot of enthusiastic research on many scientists and inventors who were called crazy in their time because of their weird and way-out theories which their contemporaries certainly did not understand. Queneau collected their writings in an early book which Gallimard rejected without qualm.

When he was more established, though, Queneau got his revenge by simply smuggling these *fous littéraires* into *Les Enfants du limon*, his fifth novel (1938). I'd love to know what, if anything, was said at Gallimard about this subterfuge, whether anyone protested but then thought, "Oh, what the hell."

So in my translating "career" I started from the top, and this somewhat unorthodox beginning had the advantage that it gave me an infinite respect for the art of translation. Randolph Quirk has said, "Translation is one of the most difficult things that a writer can take upon himself." Ronald Knox said, "Translation is an actual sharing in the experience of artistic creation, an insight into the purposes of the writer." Michael Ignatieff said, "The translator is the writer's soul-mate." (I make a list of these pronouncements whenever I come across them and could easily provide many more examples.)

It was through translating Queneau that I gradually came to acquire my firm convictions on what literary translation is. The translator must not only respect his trade; he must also, as I have said, respect and like his authors and their works. He must soak himself in the book he is to translate, *feel* his way into it, and he must also have made a comprehensive study of the author's other books. It has been said a million times but it remains true: the translator must aim at producing the book the author would have written if he had been writing it in the translator's language. The vital thing is to reproduce the author's *tone* as faithfully as possible.

Sadly, a lot of critics seem never even to have considered these problems. They often ignore the translator altogether and, for instance, quote with admiration whole chunks of his words as if they were the original ones. Or they will condescend and, taking it for granted that no translation can ever be good, will say that "even in translation" a book makes a favorable impression. They don't seem to realize that a large part of everyone's cultural heritage is directly dependent on translators. Just a casual glance through the *Oxford Companion to English Literature*—to *English* literature—shows the names of such writers as Anacreon, Cervantes, Croce, Dostoyevsky, Hegel, Ibsen, Ovid, Racine . . .

I haven't seen the latest edition of this invaluable reference book, but I hope it includes the name of Queneau.

Drôles de Drames

André Blavier

I

One can't, in any case, think of everything . . .

It is by a dire consequence of this lability of the mind that my *Notes,* or rather "modest proposals" *(Temps Mêlés Documents Queneau,* no. 150 + 45-46, 1990: 40) were purged of a bit of jubilantly superfluous gloss. They were nonetheless fraught, as we shall see, with multiple and nagging questions, in their turn devoid of the slightest usefulness, public or private.

Thus, as regards the poem "L'Amer" ["Seamark"] from *Fendre les flots,* I had pinpointed the famous Sugarloaf rising up "at the end of the boulevard" (which is not this Boulevard Bourdon at the starting point of "a sort of farcical encyclopedia" (and what a farce; at the same time, what a masterpiece!)).

Like anyone, and like Queneau himself, I compared it (an elementary and an inevitable symbolism: but was the architect conscious of it?) to a phallus, or, I added, a tube of lipstick.[1]

I went so far as to reproduce a postcard representing it, which, moreover, was more pudgy than spindle-shaped, in the frontispiece of the *TMDQ* no. 150 + 41-44, 1990: *A Hard Winter,* edited by Claude Debon.

One fine morning when I was breakfasting on a beheaded boiled egg in its eggcup (of white faïence finely edged in gilt) the providential anamnesia occurred. Like a hiccup of anaphoric[2] contrition I remembered a "current event" of the College [of 'Pataphysique] in its Being and in its Works, *intra* as *extra muros* (could it be enclosed in boundaries other than administrative?) published on page 31 of *Subsidia 'Pataphysica,* no. 11 of 8 gueules 98 (E.P.). The reporter, probably Paul Gayot, one of the main characters in the expedition to Sainte-Adresse, had, well before me, although in an inverse reaction, quoted the beginning of the sonnet in questions with respect to this promontory that Marcel Duchamp might have called "malish," this candle-phallus upon which "a woman had placed her finger—by chance"; even going so far, the chronicler, not the woman, as to treat it, the candle, as a " 'pataphysical suppository."

But, and it is here that the drama takes shape [an allusion to Desnouettes is lost in translation: "se noue" ("takes shape") is the opposite of "dénouement"], he indicated in a smooth-tongued way that this sugarloaf-candle-phallus-lipstick tube (a retracted foreskin rising up from its condom case)-suppository, that this Pain de sucre "was dedicated to her husband by Madame *Lefèvre* des Noettes" (my italics).[3]

Another problem (as stated in Pléiade; I, 754 [*pro blême* in French, with *blême* meaning pale or ashen]): was the wife in question, that of the Major (of retreating artillery—the Major not the artillery) *Lefebvre* des *Noëttes,* author of *L'Attelage: Le Cheval de selle à travers les âges* [*The Harness: The Saddle Horse through the Ages*] (Paris: Picard, in-8, 312 pp. and an album of 457 pictures), probably published in 1932?[4] The work, in fact, does not figure in the list of Queneau's reading established alphabetically by Florence Géhéniau, and I do not have the Bibliothèque Nationale's catalog on my nightstand.[5]

Queneau devoted a very favorable review to it in *La Critique sociale* 7 (January 1933: 39-40), a review picked up again in *Le Voyage en Grèce* (Paris, Gallimard, 1973: 33-39). Therein, he acknowledges, hardly ironically, after having stated his intention, following the author's example, that it was a matter of a *contribution,* not of a *comprehensive explanation* of the phenomenon of slavery in Antiquity, "the only important theoretical contribution that would have been made in France to the materialist interpretation of history."

In addition, in the preface to *Le Voyage en Grèce* (11), he confides that this (chief) gunner was, with Vernadsky and Pavlov, one of the "only authors chosen by (him)self" for his critical collaboration on Boris Souvarine's journal.

If my reading of the *Subsidia* is correct, *Lefèvre des Noettes* is a spelling that the subsequent *Errata* do not rectify.

A new question, hardly ancillary: if it is a matter of the same and particulated patronymic [i.e. nobiliary particle, such as "de" or "des"], why the contraction of "ebv" into "ev"? Why eliminate the diaerisis [in French, the word is "tréma"]: a *point,* literally a *hole,* according to my old nineteenth-century Larousse?

Above all, what is the link, or not, with Desnouettes Square where the Queneaus settled in November 1928?

And this Desnouettes? In the notes taken with a view toward his collaboration on the *Intran (Connaissez-vous Paris?),* Queneau grants only three lines to a Desnouettes *Street:*

"2-4 old houses
32. Paving-stone Warehouse (!)
74-84 Old houses"

but he ignores the *square* of the same name. The two places coexist, however, peacefully, even though they are not far apart: the square is served by the métro station *Porte de Versailles* (a small green space right next to the boulevard Victor), the street next to the *Convention* station. Now, Vincent Tuquedenne [*The Last Days*] lived for a time on *rue de la Convention* . . .

Lacking a good *Dictionary of the Streets of Paris,* I resolve to ignore completely this allegedly respectable Desnouettes. Who was he: a little-known doughboy from World War I, a city council member from some arrondissement or other, a minor patron of the arts? "Any acceptable solution to this awkward question is welcome. We'll publish it."[7]

Well, what muddles, questions, "mysteries and even, as you might say, enigmas" [". . . de mystères, et même, pour dire le mot juste, de cachotteries . . ." *(Le Chiendent,* 78)] are brought up, if not resolved, in the course of [reading] a single line of Queneau . . .

NOTES

[1]An interpretive maniac would not fail to support this: the sugarloaf drowsing *whitish* at the service entrance of the *neighboring lighthouse* and these *narcissistic* landowners, when others hardly see farther than the end of their docks . . .

[2]*Anaphora,* in the medical sense rather than the rhetorical one.

[3]Doubtless an autochthonous and popular appellation (or nonindigenous: a disdainful British tourist?), correct as to a *decent* morphology, but perhaps disrespectful as to the possible purpose of the edifice: vault, mausoleum, vacant cenotaph, as the "tranquil repository" of the fourth verse of the second quatrain seems to suggest. (This protective purpose will soon happen to be vouched for formally.) Let us note here that this curious monument (which does not seem to appear in *A Hard Winter,* nor to transpose itself into the Bouville of *La Nausée*) is provided with a little door—for interior maintenance and/or meditation (inside)—and surrounded by a self-opening fence with two hinged sections. See also note 4.

[4]A new and cruel enigma (as Paul Bourget said): the lady had to break forcibly through the fencing to put "her finger there," even if it were "by chance"; unless the said laying on (of the finger) took place before the encirclement. In what capacity was she so authorized? Or was she acting clandestinely? See here note 5.

[5]The wife (and widow) should not be confused with the lady ("a lady") who left an imprint of her finger (which one?) in still-fresh material, cement or concrete. And why this gesture, inadvertent or intentional, and what was the intention? Perhaps nostalgic, or vengeful? The poet does not tell us. We can from then on imagine anything, or invent.

[6]Still a mystery. Of the books or articles read on behalf of *La Critique*

Sociale, Queneau did not record any but the following on ad hoc dates: Jean Grave (read 15 May 1931); the two Allendys; the *Impressions d'Afrique* and the *Nouvelles impressions,* the first starting in June 1925, but the second only in November 1972; and finally Jacques Baron, treated quite cavalierly.

He notes the reading, in February 1932, of Pavlov's *Leçons sur l'activité du cortex cérébral,* published in French in 1929 and to which he refers, moreover, in his review. He would have read nothing of Paul Nizan (if we stick to his "registers"). I have, however, retained quite a good memory of his *Antoine Bloyé* and above all of *La Conspiration,* which doubtless at the time flattered my young instincts. He read four works by Benda, but not (still according to the same source) the *Discours à la nation européenne.* He notes in 1949 the reading of *La Biosphère* of Vernadsky, though he had already cited it in his review of 1932. Of Ferrero, he read only Volume II, *Julius Caesar,* in 1921 and only in 1937 the whole six volumes. More strangely still, no reading of Koyré is mentioned before 1945.

[7]This quote, which could have concluded each of my moments of indecision (nodal with Epicure, mine being only relative, equal to that of modern microphysics . . . modern for how long?), concludes the translation, by J. C. Cuzin and, objective chance?, in the same no. 11 of the *Subsidia* (56) of *A Hemospherical Problem,* an excerpt from *The Rectory Umbrella* (written in 1850 but first published in 1898). Well, this solicitous conclusion, which has a touch of Allais [Alphonse Allais (1854-1905)—a humorist of the nineties] by anticipation, does not appear in my edition of the *Complete (?) Works of Lewis Carroll* (Spring Books, 1968)! I do not possess, in my modest boondocks library, the Nonesuch Press Edition.[8]

[8]Ravaged by so many acute botherations ("turlupinations," as Mme Hachamoth said in *Children of Clay),* I set about consulting the Le Havre Association of Diverse Studies, from which Queneau received a medal in 1920. Here again was the copious and exemplary documentation of Jacques Birnberg (cf. *A Hard Winter*).[9] Just then a *Guide Bleu de la Normandie* fell into my hands, which (232) delivers me from some of these botherations. The Sugarloaf, which—a question I had neglected to ask myself—is "a conical signal (skillful evasion) serving as a landmark for sailors. It is a monument (ha! ha! See my note 3) erected by the widow of General Lefebvre-Des-Nouettes (in two words) in memory of her husband, who died in a shipwreck off the Irish Coast, 22 April 1822." Whew! The author of *L 'Attelage* is not thus at best but a descendant (in a direct or related line) of the "nice general" of whom the biographers tell us that he "shined" at the debacle of Waterloo.

But what about the Desnouettes of the Square and of the Street?

[9]I take advantage of the sunshine to make hay, or in this case two trifling observations. First, I always thought that the often-quoted sentence of Matthieu Galey in *Arts,* cited yet again by Christopher Shorley and Jacques Birnberg, should be read, in the original, too: "to change everything radically in *derision* or the unusual" and not: in *division.* Secundo: by what typographical quirk in the 1946 reprint of *A Hard Winter* (the one embellished with a binding by Mario Prassinos) is chapter 6 (and it alone) headed by an intermediate title in capital letters? "Any solution, etc . . ."

II

This palinode (if you like) because

"Queneau. On Queneau I have nothing MORE to say . . ."

It is just that, laying bare for a time the unperturbability which would be appropriate (an ideal of which one can only strive to be the asymptote), I am *irritated* by the "they-says," the unsaid, the too-much-said and the "countersaid," which make cracks in what formerly pleased me very much to call the Quenien community.

Why should I opt FOR a criticism "of proximity," of the "buddy" genre, a companion for (part of) the way, a critic who was a little bit of a "lout," as one could reckon the epistemology of a Feyerabend to be a bit loutish, for example, AGAINST sometimes pointed analyses, of varied methods or modes (among which are those of *kuas* . . . [see the *I Ching*] and of *couacs* ["wrong notes" in French])?

Opt *FOR* reader-amateurs of long standing *AGAINST* professionals, professors or other, often simultaneously ingénue-ingenious, knowledgeable and hard-working, or even boring or enlightening?

NEITHER RECIPROCALLY nor *VICE VERSA*. *Resurgo eadem mutata*. The 'Pataphysica includes and surpasses all ways of approach and above all of pleasure to Queneau, *with whom I lived*. Surpassing: is it not one of the most tintinnabulating rattles of Progress; if not its definition?

NOTE

[10]And the Philosophers, in all that. Zay laffe . . . !

Translated by Mary Campbell-Sposito

The Birth of a Form: Elementary Morality[1]

Jacques Roubaud

@1 I shall begin by speaking of a poetic form which is called **elementary morality.**

@2 Beginning is not without its problems. One needs to know where and with what? Above all, what should be the form of the beginning?

@3 I really cannot say, "What I know best is my beginning."

@8 The principal problem of beginning is what there is or is not beforehand, especially what there is before everything, the problem called "jadis et naguère" ("in the past and formerly").

@21 There are good reasons to think that at the beginning was the *substantive.*

@22 Let's look at it quickly. Initially man sees things, singular things, singulars. These things merit names, proper names. These are substantives, or nouns. The nouns, the substantives, are proper nouns, the names of singulars. Gertrude Stein reminded us of that.

@23 And what deals mainly with the proper name of things? Poetry.

@24 Poetry, as Gertrude Stein more or less tells us, deals with caressing, loving, revering, adoring, idolizing, and let's add insulting, raving on, transforming, removing, inventing . . . the nouns.

@26 To think calls for the verb, and consequently the infinitive.

@27 Poetry does not prohibit the verb (after all, the poet is part of the tribe, he uses its words, even impure ones). We know besides that the "Grand-Singe" poetry, in part transcribed by Jacques Jouet of the Oulipo, remaining close to its origins, itself uses verbs already, but it treats the verb as a substantive, as a perhaps slightly restive noun, which must be rendered poetically suitable.[2]

@28 The privileged form of the verb in poetry is doubtless still the infinitive, but one must not believe that it is a thinking infinitive. It is an infinitive of poetry, doubtless better named a *definitive.*

@29 Besides, and for the same reasons, if the substantive in poetry is a proper noun, what can we call the proper noun? It should be named the *sur-proper noun.* Laura, in the *Canzoniere* of Petrarch, is an excellent example of this.

@30 But we aren't here to do grammar. We are here to begin.

@31 Since it is a matter of poetry here, of a poetic form, we shall keep the substantive at the beginning.

@32 How does poetry deal with the substantive in the most natural way possible? By means of the *list,* the basic poetic form of poetry, its *forma fondamentale,* as Veronese calls it (it has to do with a sequential form whose geometric model should be looked into in the theoretical work of the Italian mathematician Veronese (1894)—explanatory parenthesis).

@37 In modern times, the poetic list-form has a tendency to be hidden. But we can flush it out without too much trouble, if we wish. Consider, in the diaries of poets, that the erudites lovingly publish for our pleasure and our instruction shopping lists; consider their beautiful and inspired laundry lists . . .

@42 The most primitive form (and consequently the most poetically charged) of the substantive's gloss is doubtless the **epithet** (even though this point is controversial among linguists, it is indisputable in the case of poetry). Before honoring (or fighting) the noun, poets direct epithets to it.

@45 The first poets, foxes, squirrels, badgers, dormice, otters, hedgehogs, humans or primates met, and identifying in their eyes a singular, they immediately named it a poem of one line, which then was called a word. It is probable besides that together they produced, in pronouncing the same word, a dialogue-poem in what was the first form of the distich.

For example:

MAMMOTH!!!
MAMMOTH!!!!

@46 Linguistic note: epithets are sometimes called adjectives.

@51 Let's jump quickly over several millennia, and turn toward a rough draft of Mallarmé's:

Forgotten woods	somber winter lack only	solitary captive
heavy bouquets	vain number supreme firebrand	old armchair
who often wishes		

to have
the visit
must not
with too many
flowers load the stone

lost strength light hearth
murmured name

@52 attention: the status of this piece of writing is uncertain: the free verse is not really established. To see this as a poem is doubtless an anachronism.

@53 Let's retain this text and pass on to the birth certificate of the poetic form that absorbs us now.

@54 In opening number 253 of the *Nouvelle Revue Française* dated January 1974, the attentive reader would not have failed to notice therein some of Raymond Queneau's poems (under the title, in fact, of "Poems"), accompanied by the following explanatory note:

@55 "The reader will have noticed that the topic concerns poems of fixed form. First of all, three times three plus a substantive group plus adjective (or participle) with some repetitions, rhymes, alliterations, echoes *ad libitum;* then a sort of interlude of seven lines of from one to five syllables; finally a conclusion of three plus a substantive group plus adjective (or participle) more or less resuming some of the twenty-four words used in the first part.

@56 Purely internal 'reasons' determined this form which was not preceded by any mathematical research or explicable rhythmics. The first of the poems thus written was properly 'inspired'; some reflection and a certain practical experience provoked modifications giving the form finally adopted. That the body of the poem (minus the interlude) includes thirty-two words and that the whole presents fifteen lines (one more than the sonnet) does not result from any prior decision."

@57 This text is both mysterious and provocative with regard to Quenellians. Provocation: "no mathematical or explicable rhythmics"; or "thirty-two words," "fifteen lines (one more than the sonnet)"; this is what calls for investigation.

@59 still a mystery: the inspiration. On this point we turn to the Pléiade edition and Claude Debon's "Note" (1451-52).

@60 (in 1972) "Queneau resumed the writing of his journal . . . each morning he practices mathematics . . . he takes long walks with his dog, Taï-Taï . . . The first part of *Elementary Morality* was written from April-May 1973 to 14 April 1974, Easter Sunday . . . The genesis of *Elementary Morality* is clarified by a preparatory file consisting of eight pages.

@61 "A completely inspired poem without erasures (May or April)/Then about two months after, I find its pleasing structure. And I use it with flexibility for many other poems until I succeed in setting down a form.

A	B	C
	D	
E	F	G
	H	
	(5 or 6 pentasyllabic lines at most)	
A'	B'	C'
	D'	
	or	
I	J	K
	L	

Musical rhythm. The letters designating a bi-word (Substantive + Adjective) A to H must be punctuated with strikes of a gong or a large drum. Then comes a sort of ritornello. The end resumes in general with variants of the elements from A to H or continues from I to L still with strikes of a gong or large drum." (to retain for implementations)

@62 A note should have completed the presentation in the *NRF:* "the musical accompaniment (if desired) seems obvious to me: a strike of the gong (or of any other percussive instrument) after each substantive plus adjective group. And with the ritornello, I see (I hear) a small air of the flute or reed-pipe."

@63 All that does not enlighten me much, however.

@64 I am not going to do a critical study of these poems. I would be most incapable of it. Here is the first one:

@65:

Dark Isis	Green fruit	Spotted animal
	Clear neologisms	
Red flower	Transparent attitude	Orangy star
	Clear springs	
Brown forest	Russet boar	Bleating flock
	Clear tree	

A boat
on the water
aloneruin
follows the current
A crocodile
bites the gam
in vain

Ochre Isis	Furniture statue	Apricot totem
	Clear neologisms	

@66 Remarks: the substantive = adjective groups are provided with capital letters, whereas in the "free" part the beginnings of the lines, in accordance with a rather steadfast habit of Queneau's, are not marked (except to indicate, which the punctuation does not do, that it is the beginning of a sentence). They receive a privileged status, that of internal sur-lines.

@67 Each of these lines is such in the sense of the poetry of origins, a bi-word (as Queneau calls it) composed of a proper noun, a poetic substantive, and of its gloss, the epithet that, if the substantive is a name, must be regarded as a first name (postpositive, as in school roll calls in the past).

@68 There are then, in the first publication, nineteen of these "poems."

@69 The fixed form introduced thus has no name.

@70 In the Pléiade edition we learn that Queneau, in his journal, gives it the name "Lipolepse," but he does not maintain this term in the *NRF.*

@71 Considerably augmented, the "lipolepses" appear in 1975 as the first part of a book entitled *Elementary Morality,* the last book of Queneau's poems, certainly one of the most beautiful, above all in the prose poems of parts 2 and 3.

@72 There are then fifty-one (having almost been fifty only, because the total number of poems in the book was supposed to be 131, "a suitable enough prime number," writes Queneau [it is not only prime, but palindromic and satisfies the condition of the n-ine; thus it is a "Perecian number"]).

@73 But the form is still nameless.

@74 And yet all fixed forms pose problems of aesthetic acceptance. The absence of designation does not facilitate things.

@75 The Oulipo intervenes.

@76 Remark: in his definition, Queneau points out that "his" form has one line more than the sonnet, which, he says, "does not result from any prior decision." Without placing this assertion in doubt, we can nonetheless recall that the sonnet has always deeply preoccupied Queneau, who composed many of them and finished by implementing a quantity largely exceeding the efforts of his predecessors. (These are the famous "one hundred million million.") Speaking of and to the Oulipo he often compared the forms born of new constraints to the sonnet, offering it as perspective and model. His assertion concerning the new "fixed form" that he presents in *Elementary Morality* may thus appear in part as a denial.

@77 It is not, however, in anyone's power to "create" a new poetic form. The "notaro" of Frederick II, Giacomo da Lentini, cannot be said to be creator of the sonnet form except by anachronism. It is because others, and many others, composed poems constructed on the same model as that proposed by Giacomo da Lentini that this model has become that of a form, which was then named *sonetto*.

@78 In inventing these "lipolepses," Queneau could be certain of one thing only: he had proposed the possibility of a new poetic form, a form which would be "fixed" (we know that the "fixity" of the sonnet is totally relative), and which would achieve this status if it were employed "sufficiently" and significantly. He could not know if these conditions would be fulfilled.

@79 According to the most plausible hypotheses, the "sonnet" first circulated as the money of poetic exchanges, of Provençal "tensos," among the inventor's friends.

@80 We shall not be surprised to learn that it is inside the Oulipo that the Quenellian form began to spread.

@81 Everything begins (here again is a beginning), if I'm not mistaken, on the next-to-the-last page of the fourth fascicule of the Oulipian Library, a volume of homage (posthumous) by the Oulipo, entitled "To Raymond Queneau." Jean Queval gives to his contribution the following title

Elementary Morality (with a clinamen)

lousy sex   twisted guys   crazy hookers
big spenders cut off
big-lipped pussies   melted queers   chucked-out destitutes
out of it suckers
thunderass   stuffed chicks   dry twats
terminal jerk johns

y'all
yours truly
at the niers ball
word of honor
I'm your shepherdess
don't be stuck up
hands on ass

wandering pricks   youse out-of-date   not nice snatch
shackled slit

@82 In this rather esoteric poem, we cannot help being struck by the fact (but not surprised knowing Jean Queval) that the heralded clinamen (an intentional violation of the constraint) is produced from the supposed first pair made of a substantive and an adjective, but above all that there are at least two and doubtless four other violations in the rest of the poem (in writing "pair" and "violations," I wonder if that is not the meaning, completely Quevallian, of the text).

@83 Some time afterward (the fascicules of the Oulipian Library, or O.L., have the unfortunate habit of being undated), Paul Fournel, under the title of *Moral Elementary* (is it a matter of a group of S-adjectives or of adjectives-S?), publishes (it is no. 8 of the O.L.) twenty-one, that is to say 3 x 7 of these poems in a still-nameless form. He presents them thusly:

@84 The following texts owe to Raymond Queneau:

1-Their structure: it is that of the poems of the first part of *Elementary Morality,* such as it is described on page 20 of Number 253 of the *Nouvelle Revue Française.*

2-The words that compose them:

-The substantive-adjective groups were drawn from various of Raymond Queneau's books (cf. table of contents). When the two elements were inverted we took the liberty of putting them back in the order substantive-adjective. When they were separated we put them back together, but in all cases, they were dependent.

-The central part of the texts is extracted from the same textual fragment, but no liberty is taken with the word order.

-Seven being a key number for Raymond Queneau we drew from the vocabulary of each poem in a group of seven pages. Because Queneau died at the age of 73, we took as our point of departure page 73.

@85 example

Indefinite quantity	Empty day	Unconscious problems
	Difficult day	
Disgusted air	Devastated day	Turned-in papers
	Extreme severity	
Amateur mathematician	Dialectical problem	Powerful protectors
	Mysterious sentences	

To fill up my solitude
by giving me back
something
comical
place de la
République

Famous genius	Recurring series Serious questions	Personal papers

@86 Contrary to his predecessor and to many of his successors Paul Fournel respects Queneau's mode of presentation.

@87 The form for him still has no name. If Queval's "title" represented a proposed name for the form, it is still not being used.

@88 And yet, to give a name indicated the intention of form. No form without form's name. The name is what identifies it as formal, singular, perceptible as such. The sestina of Arnaut Daniel is not yet a sestina when it is composed. It will be a long time until a form of this name "exists."

@89 In the same manner, a book has a title, which (Gertrude Stein again tells us is its proper name. Books begin to have titles when people begin to have names and civil status; the book, in being printed, takes on a civil state.

@90 As I indicated, the name is one of the conditions of existence of the form, its poetic civil status; it is not the only one because there must also be examples.

@92 After years of work the Oulipo collected, in its volume 55.29 (or 32, depending on how one counts) examples more or less in agreement with the definition; and the title given to this work indicates that a name had been chosen for the form, that of the book in which it would appear: *Elementary Morality.*

@93 The title being *Other Elementary Moralities,* one notices that the Oulipo appends to this form the texts previously written under constraint (or claiming to be). Queneau thus composed 51 elementary moralities, Queval one (!), Fournel twenty-one.

@109 In most of the poems in the form of *elementary moralities* composed by Oulipiens, the Oulipian treatment functions as a decoration of the existing form (that of Queneau).

@110 There is there a strong analogy with the Oulipian treatment of the sonnet as an experimental site of constraint.

@112 - examples (I am citing only fragments: of the beginnings and a middle, which builds an elementary morality in a patchwork of patchworks):

today virgin	today vivacious drunken wing	today handsome
deprived cicadas	north wind come neighboring ant	little piece
dark prince	widower prince abolished tower	inconsolable prince

one was coming
from the Bastille
the other from the
Jardin des Plantes
the biggest dressed in cloth
the smallest
with lowered head

naked sword terrified century strange voice
vile burst

@118 The case of no. 03 of the O.L. 55, without a title but not without an author (Jacques Jouet):

white bonnet white bonnet white bonnet
white bonnet
white bonnet white bonnet white bonnet
white bonnet
white bonnet white bonnet white bonnet

if the not same
matches
the same
we say then
what it is
it is
from the similar to the same

white bonnet white bonnet white bonnet
bonnet white

@125 Jouet's "White Bonnet" poses in a spectacular manner the tormenting problem of the poetry of substantives with gloss of epithets: Should the adjective be put before or after?

@126 I confronted this problem in 1941, at the time of my first encounter with the English language (and thus with its poetry). I composed the following "elementary morality" to evoke this memory:

Moral elementary

Morning good Board black Chalk white
Sheep ba ba black
Riding Hood red Daffodils yellow Sky blue

	Sea green	
Father grand	Mother grand	Bo Peep little
	Grass green	

"The more it snows
tiddely-pom
the more it goes
on snowing
and nobody knows
how cold my toes
are growing"

Air Force Royal	Night good	Bye good
	Goodbye	

@127 Now we must go a little farther back. I recall for those who do not know them, certain facts:

@128 In August 1939 Vincent Degraël, a young professor of letters, invited to the home of his colleague Denis Borrade's parents, discovered in the library a book by one Hugo Vernier, *Le Voyage d'hiver* (The Winter Journey), dated 1864.[3] He realized Vernier had been pillaged by most poets at the end of the nineteenth century. After this discovery, they may no longer be considered except as the "copyists of a brilliant and poorly-known poet who in a unique work had known how to pull together the very substance upon which three or four generations of writers would be nourished."

@129 A sensational discovery if ever there was one. Alas, the war arose and in 1944 Degraël was unable to find a trace of Vernier's work. He died insane.

@130 In 1980, without indicating his sources, Georges Perec, in a text entitled precisely *Le Voyage d'hiver,* recounts this incredible and distressing adventure.

@131 A short time later, Perec's text falls by chance into the hands of Denis Borrade Jr., son of Vincent Degraël's friend, in the Norman villa of the parents where the fateful discovery had been made. Invited to Australia where he meets Perec, Borrade has the luck to find his father's young sister, Virginie, a Wedderburn by marriage, who had lived in Brisbane since the end of the war and possessed the only surviving copy of Hugo Vernier's work, as well as other valuable family papers of the genius. These documents prove irrefutably that the plagiarism of Vernier by the moderns begins in fact much earlier than Degraël had believed, who had had on hand only the printed volume of Vernier (and that for only one night). In fact, it appears that *The Flowers of Evil* attributed to Charles

Baudelaire is an absolutely brazen marking down of Vernier's first work, of which the real title was *Le Voyage d'hier* (Yesterday's Voyage). All this is related, as exactly as possible by me according to the information furnished by Professor Borrade in a volume of the Oulipian Library, no. 53, under Vernier's authentic title, finally re-established, *Le Voyage d 'hier.*

@132 This slim volume, of an inevitably limited scope, did not take into account all the elements contained in the file handed over by Virginie Wedderburn née Borrade to her nephew Denis. It is given to me today to be in a position to furnish you some complements. They are not without relation to our subject.

@133 In the preparatory notebook to *Le Voyage d'hier,* one can read, among others, two poems. I deliver them to you without comment. They speak for themselves:

@134 The first:

Ancestor academy	Dowager academy	alarmed tropes
	red bonnet	
Old square alexandrines	revolutionary wind	dictionary
	red bonnet	
senator word	common word	white swarm
	red bonnet	
	I say	
	to the nostril	
	ah	
	but you	
	are nothing	
	but a	
	nose	
equal words	free words	major words
	bonnet red!	

@135 The second:

today virgin	today vivacious	today beautiful
	drunken wing	
hard lake	forgotten lake	transparent glacier
	flight fled	
magnificent swan	sterile winter	
	the region sung	

where to live
the bird will shake
its collar
the
plumage
is taken

white agony — inflicted agony — pure brightness
cold dream
useless exile

@138 A flock of questions arises. Haphazardly,

@139 Was Perec in fact aware of the whole file? Did he hold back new revelations?

@140 Could Perec have met the Wedderburns before his stay in Brisbane?

@141 Could Denis Borrade Jr. have plagiarized Perec?

@142 Is not Perec's text much earlier than the date of its supposed composition?

@143 Would not a first version, an ur-version, date from Perec's high school years, from confidences of his old professor in his last year at Etampes, Vincent Degraël?

@144 Could Queneau have read *Le Voyage d'hiver? Le Voyage d'hier?*

@145 Had Hugo Vernier read Hugo Victor, or Hugo Victor Vernier Hugo?

@146 Did not both of them "copy" an earlier author?

@147 Much much earlier?

@150 It is clear first of all that Mallarmé had copied Vernier in an even more profound manner than we could have thought.

@151 But was not Vernier himself reviving an even more ancient and secret tradition, like the one Saussure brought to light earlier, that of the anagrams of saturnine poetry and of paragrams (revealed by Julia Kristeva) which are everywhere and above all in the newspapers?

@152 But wouldn't this secret, venerable and antique tradition be that which, by means of *Le Voyage d 'hier* (in a version certainly more complete than the unique edition carefully destroyed by its beneficiaries) was handed down by unknown paths to certain privileged authors such as Queneau, of course, then Perec?

@153 And is that not what Queneau intimates when, deciding to render visible the tradition of what we now call *elementary morality,* he takes as the first work of his first poem in this form Isis, a sur-proper name if ever there was one? Isis the mother, matriarchal divinity of ancient Egypt, does she not represent, as one may think in reading a sonnet of Scève (surely a link in this long chain of initiated poets of whom doubtless the *fedeli d'amore* invoked by Dante in the *Vita Nuova* were a part), the obscure secret of poetic forms? Is it not for this reason that she is called "dark"?

@154 In the notes of her edition Claude Debon offers us a "biographical" explanation (admittedly perfectly legitimate) but one which does not contradict the one we offer now (it reinforces that one, rather):

-Variant C ("black cemetery"), the presence of Isis, the image of the crocodile (Odile, in Queneau's novel of the same name, incarnates the beloved woman), finally the boat "aloneruin," so many indices which seem to be references to Janine Queneau, who died 18 July 1972.

@158 François Caradec's contribution to the Oulipo's volume of *Elementary Morality* is, in this context, essential. Let us read no. 27:

Hobbling along	Giddyup Clip clop	Hop to
Quack quack	Whee whew Woof woof	Tweet tweet
Meow meow	Click! Purr purr	Glug glug
	A glance sufficed A sniff sniff followed a fox ran in the night	
Buzz buzz	Blah blah Click!	Beep beep

Beautiful elementary morality, actually!

@166 We are experiencing a crisis of language, after the crisis of poetry diagnosed by Mallarmé, which was its premonition. There was wooden language and there is now muesli language, marshmallow language, mushy language, TV language, which reigns alone. We have had a mouthful and an earful.

@167 We must (it is our republican duty) do something. And who can do something? Poetry, by the intervention of poets (they are there for that). The time is past to renovate language, the time is past to reconstruct it, the time is past to recast it. We must make it re-be. We must re-singularize words, restore to them their pristine splendor (I see with horror that the word *pristine* is not in the dictionary; could it be an English word? I don't dare believe it).

@168 One must therefore place words in a form, place them in a poetic form. We must plumb the geologic layers of language, do the paleontology of language. We must reconstitute these fossils that are the oldest witnesses of the oldest poetic monuments of humanity. We must clone the linguistic mammoths imprisoned in the permafrost of fixed traditions. (I'nnit byootiful!)

@169 For this long and heavy task (that we must accomplish courageously before, like Mr. Vigny's wolf, suffering and dying speechless), we are not entirely helpless, we are not leaving without provisions: we have the list form which deals with substantives; we have, thanks to Queneau, who exhumes it, who makes it blossom again, in an "inspired" manner, the classic elementary morality which takes charge of the substantive-adjective groups. But that does not suffice; we must also deal with adjective-substantive groups (see Jouet's "White Bonnet"). (A great effort is needed to exchange the order of groupings.)

@170 It is to this task that I invite you.

@189 It is finished.

NOTES

[1]Thanks to Harry Mathews for his suggestion of an English title for this untranslated work of Queneau's.

[2]Thanks to Warren Motte for making me aware of Jacques Jouet's "Le Chant d'amour grand-singe" ("The Ape's Love Song") in *La Bibliothèque oulipienne* 62 (Paris, 1993).

[3]Translated into American by David Bellos (*Conjunctions* 12 [Fall 1988]).

Translated by Mary Campbell-Sposito

Selected Bibliography

Campbell-Sposito, Mary. " 'Ça, c'est causer': Dialogue and Storytelling in Raymond Queneau's Novels." *French Forum* 11 (1986): 59-69.

———. "Onomastics as a Defamiliarizing Device in Raymond Queneau's Novels." *French Review* 61 (1988): 724-33.

———. "Raymond Queneau Novelist: 'Quel diable de *langaige* est-ce là?' " *Paroles Gelées* 2-3 (1984-85): 23-33.

Cobb, Richard. "Queneau's Itineraries." *Promenades: A Historian's Appreciation of Modern French Literature.* Oxford: Oxford Univ. Press, 1980. 61-77.

———. *Raymond Queneau.* Oxford: Clarendon Press, 1976.

Coleman, Dorothy Gabe. "Polyphonic Poets: Rabelais and Queneau." *Words of Power: Essays in Honor of Alison Fairlie.* Ed. Dorothy Gabe Coleman and Gillian Gendorf. Glasgow: Glasgow Univ. Printing Department, 1987. 43-68.

Esslin, Martin. "Raymond Queneau." *The Novelist as Philosopher: Studies in French Fiction 1935-1960.* Ed. John Cruickshank. London: Oxford Univ. Press, 1962. 79-101.

Gobert, David L. "The Essential Character in Queneau's *Zazie dans le métro.*" *Symposium* 40.2 (1986): 91-106.

Gray, Stanley E. "Beckett and Queneau as Formalists." *James Joyce Quarterly* 8 (1971): 392-404.

Guicharnaud, Jacques. *Raymond Queneau.* New York: Columbia Univ. Press, 1965.

———. "Raymond Queneau's Universe." *Yale French Studies* 8 (1951): 38-47.

Hale, Jane Alison. *The Lyric Encyclopedia of Raymond Queneau.* Ann Arbor: Univ. of Michigan Press, 1989.

Hall, K. E. "Zazie and the Tigers." *Hispanofila* 105 (1992): 45-53.

Keffer, Charles Kenneth, Jr. "Raymond Queneau's Encyclopedic Energy: A Defense of Youth." *Kentucky Philological Association Bulletin* 8 (1981): 37-44.

Knapp, Bettina. "Raymond Queneau." *French Novelists Speak Out.* Troy: Whitston, 1976. 41-47.

Kogan, Vivian. "The Fiction of History in Raymond Queneau's *Les Fleurs bleues.*" *Studies in the Humanities* 11 (1984): 7-11.

———. *Flowers of Fiction: Time and Space in Raymond Queneau's* Les fleurs bleues. Lexington: French Forum, 1982.

———. "Raymond Queneau (1903-1976)." *French Novelists 1930-1976.* Ed. Catherine Savage Brosman. Vol. 72 of *Dictionary of Lit-*

erary Biography. Detroit: Gale, 1988. 300-313.
Mercier, Vivian. "Raymond Queneau: The Creator as Destroyer." *The New Novel from Queneau to Pinget*. New York: Farrar, Straus and Giroux, 1971. 43-103.
———. "Raymond Queneau: The First New Novelist?" *L 'Esprit Créateur* 7 (1967): 102-12.
Morey, Philip. "The Treatment of English Words in Queneau." *Modern Language Review* 76 (1981): 823-38.
Motte, Warren F., Jr., trans. and ed. *Oulipo: A Primer of Potential Literature*. Lincoln: Univ. of Nebraska Press, 1986.
———. "Raymond Queneau and the Aesthetic of Formal Constraint." *Romanic Review* 82 (1991): 193-209.
Prospice. Special issue on Queneau. 8 (1978).
Redfern, Walter D. *Queneau: "Zazie dans le métro."* London: Grant and Cutler, 1980.
Shattuck, Roger, and Simon Watson Taylor, eds. *What Is 'Pataphysics?* Special issue of *Evergreen Review* 4 (1960).
Sheringham, Michael. "Discreetly Tangential." *Times Literary Supplement* 27 April 1990: 455.
———. "Raymond Queneau: The Lure of the Spiritual." *Literature and Spirituality*. Ed. David Bevan. Amsterdam: Rodopi (1992): 33-47.
Shorley, Christopher. " 'L'Irruption de l'histoire': 6 February 1934 in the French Novel." *Nottingham French Studies* 30.1 (1991): 56-71.
———. " 'Joindre le geste à la parole': Raymond Queneau and the Uses of Non-Verbal Communication." *French Studies* 35 (1981): 409-20.
———. *Queneau's Fiction: An Introductory Study*. Cambridge: Cambridge Univ. Press, 1985.
Struebig, Patricia. "Transvestites and Transformations: Or, Take It Off and Get Real: Queneau's *Zazie dans le métro*." *Journal of the Fantastic in the Arts* 1 (1988): 49-64.
Stump, Jordan. "Naming and Forgetting in Queneau's *Pierrot mon ami*." *International Fiction Review* 20 (1993): 112-19.
Swigger, Ronald T. "Reflections on Language in Raymond Queneau's Novels." *Contemporary Literature* 12 (1972): 491-506.
Thiher, Allen. *Raymond Queneau*. Boston: Twayne, 1985.
Toludis, Constantin. "Disjunction and Repetition in Queneau's Fiction." *International Fiction Review* 15 (1988): 103-09.
———. "The Impulse for the Ludic in the Poetics of Raymond Queneau." *Twentieth Century Literature* 35 (1989): 147-60.
———. *Rewriting Greece: Queneau and the Agony of Presence*. Collection "American University Studies," series 2, no. 211. New

York: Peter Lang, 1995.

Velguth, Madeleine. *The Representation of Women in the Autobiographical Novels of Raymond Queneau*. New York: Peter Lang, 1990.

Winspur, Steven. "Queneau's Contexts of Irony." *Romanic Review* 82 (1991): 70-75.

Numerous Ph.D. dissertations have been written on Queneau, and extensive critical work in the form of articles and books is available in French (see, for example, *L'Herne Raymond Queneau,* 1975). Special thanks to Chas Kestermeier for his help with this bibliography. Bibliographical questions may be e-mailed to him at this address: chaskest@creighton.edu

"Reunion of the Oulipo" (23 September 1975)
Seated, left to right: Italo Calvino, Harry Mathews, Françios Le Lionnais, Raymond Queneau, Jean Queval, Claude Berge; standing: Jacques Roubaud, Paul Fournel, Michèle Metail, Luc Etienne, Georges Perec, Marcel Benabou, Jacques Bens, Paul Braffort, Jean Lescure, Jacques Duchateau, Noël Arnaud. On table: André Blavier.

Selected Translations of Queneau's Works into English

The Bark Tree. Trans. Barbara Wright. New York: New Directions, 1971. Originally published as *Le Chiendent.*

The Blue Flowers. Trans. Barbara Wright. New York: Atheneum, 1967. Originally published as *Les Fleurs bleues.*

"A Blue Funk." Trans. Barbara Wright and ed. Simon Watson Taylor. *French Writing Today.* London: Penguin, 1968. 32-34. Originally published as "Une trouille verte" in *Contes et propos.*

Children of Clay. Trans. Madeleine Velguth. Forthcoming.

"Dino." Trans. Barbara Wright and ed. Simon Watson Taylor. *French Writing Today.* London: Penguin, 1968. 25-28. Originally published as "Din" in *Contes et propos.*

Exercises in Style. Trans. Barbara Wright. New York: New Directions, 1981. Originally published as *Exercices de style.*

The Flight of Icarus. Trans. Barbara Wright. New York: New Directions, 1973. Originally published as *Le vol d'Icare.*

A Hard Winter. Trans. Betty Askwith. London: John Lehman, 1948. Originally published as *Un rude hiver.*

Introduction to the Reading of Hegel: Lectures on the Phenomenology of Spirit *Assembled by Raymond Queneau.* Ed. Allan Bloom, and trans. James H. Nichols, Jr. New York: Basic Books, 1969. Portions of originally published *Introduction à la lecture de Hegel.*

The Last Days. Trans. Barbara Wright. Elmwood Park, IL: Dalkey Archive Press, 1990. Originally published as *Les derniers jours.*

Oak and Dog. Trans. Madeleine Velguth. New York: Peter Lang, 1995. Originally published as *Chêne et chien.*

Odile. Trans. Carol Sanders. Elmwood Park, IL: Dalkey Archive Press, 1988. Originally published as *Odile.*

One Hundred Million Million Poems. Trans. John Crombie. Paris: Kickshaws, 1983. Originally published as *Cent mille milliards de poèmes.*

"Panic." Trans. Barbara Wright and ed. Simon Watson Taylor. *French Writing Today.* London: Penguin, 1968. 28-32. Originally published as "Panique" in *Contes et propos.*

Pataphysical Poems. Trans. Teo Savory. Greensboro, NC: Unicorn Press, 1985. Translations of poems originally published as *Les ziaux; L 'instant fatal; Petite suite; Courir les rues; Battre la campagne.*

Pierrot Mon Ami. Trans. Barbara Wright. Elmwood Park, IL: Dalkey Archive Press, 1987. Originally published as *Pierrot mon ami*.

Saint Glinglin. Trans. James Sallis. Normal, IL: Dalkey Archive Press, 1993. Originally published as *Saint Glinglin*.

The Skin of Dreams. Trans. H. J. Kaplan. Norfolk, CT: New Directions, 1948 Originally published as *Loin de Rueil*.

The Sunday of Life. Trans. Barbara Wright. New York: New Directions, 1977. Originally published as *Le dimanche de la vie*.

The Trojan Horse and At the Edge of the Forest. Trans. Barbara Wright. London: Gaberbocchus, 1954. Originally published as "Le cheval troyen" and "A la limite de la forêt" in *Contes et propos*.

We Always Treat Women Too Well. Trans. Barbara Wright. New York: New Directions, 1981. Originally published as *On est toujours trop bon avec les femmes*.

Yours for the Telling. Trans. John Crombie. Paris: Kickshaws, 1982. Originally published as "Un conte à votre façon" in *Contes et propos*.

Zazie. Trans. Barbara Wright. New York: Harper, 1960. Originally published as *Zazie dans le métro*.

Carole Maso

photograph by Helen Lang

Carole Maso: An Introduction and an Interpellated Interview[1]

Victoria Frenkel Harris

> a woman trying to translate pulsations into images for the relief of the body and the reconstruction of the mind
> —Adrienne Rich, "Planetarium"

Carole Maso came late both to writing and to the teaching of writing. Although she has directed one of the nation's premier creative writing programs since 1995, when she accepted her current position at Brown University, Maso herself never enrolled in an MFA program. Indeed, she taught the first creative writing workshop she ever participated in—at Illinois State University, where Maso served as Distinguished Writer-in-Residence during the 1991-92 academic year. Maso, who says she "was not a huge reader as a kid" (Cooley 32), didn't begin to write creatively until her final year at Vassar, when she submitted about fifty pages of prose poems as her Senior Honors Thesis. From that point on, however, Maso knew that she wanted to be a writer.

Following the advice of the professor who directed her thesis, Maso decided not to attend graduate school (she accepted a generous graduate fellowship from Boston University, only to change her mind at the last minute). Instead, after graduating from Vassar in 1977, she dedicated the next nine years of her life to what she has called her apprenticeship, learning to write by writing. During this period, Maso supported herself by working six months of each year at odd jobs (as a waitress, an artist's model, a fencing instructor); the rest of the year, she devoted to writing, living at artists' colonies or taking such jobs as house- or cat-sitting which provided ample time to practice her art. In the process, Maso invented assignments and exercises for herself which she now uses in her creative writing

---

[1]Many of the biographical details in this essay are found in the two major interviews with Maso: Nicole Cooley, "Carole Maso: An Interview by Nicole Cooley," *American Poetry Review* 24.2 (March-April 1995): 32-35; and Joyce Hackett, "Carole Maso," *Poets & Writers* 24.3 (May-June 1996): 64-73. My own interview with Maso took place over a period of several months in 1996-97 and was conducted by telephone, e-mail, letters, and in person.

classes. The result of this near-decade-long immersion in the craft of fiction was *Ghost Dance* (1986), Maso's first novel.

Because of their unconventional nature, Maso's novels have often been described as experimental. According to Maso, however, her books seem transgressive, not because she deliberately flaunts the orthodoxies of traditional fiction, but because her models are not drawn from the novelistic tradition at all. The primary influences on her work, rather, come from the visual arts, from dance and music, from film, and from poetry (Maso and Vladimir Nabokov are the only fiction writers ever to be featured on the cover of *American Poetry Review*). Because of its perceived strangeness, *Ghost Dance* had difficulty attracting a publisher (since no agent would touch it, Maso had to send the manuscript out herself). After almost a year of futility, Maso submitted the book to North Point Press, a small independent literary press in San Francisco that had published Michael Palmer, a poet Maso admires. After keeping Maso's mansucript for ten months, North Point finally agreed to publish it.

A critical if not a commercial success, *Ghost Dance* established Maso as an emerging writer of rare promise. Shortly after its publication, she was awarded in quick succession a $25,000 NEA fellowship, a $15,000 Rose Fellowship for Vassar alumnae-artists, and a residency at the Provincetown Fine Arts Work Center. For the first time since graduation, Maso was able to quit working and devote all of her time to writing. In its early stages Maso's next book, *The Art Lover* (1990), resembled *Ghost Dance* in its focus on a fictive family (the family that, in the novel's final version, are the main characters in the novel-within-the-novel written by Maso's protagonist Caroline). When Maso's friend Gary Falk fell fatally ill with AIDS, however, Maso began to write a different book, one whose textual strategies are even "stranger" than *Ghost Dance*'s. Balking at its unconventionality, North Point insisted that Maso delete the graphics from her text as well as the transgressively straightforward autobiographical fifth section of the novel. Only when Maso threatened to withdraw the manuscript did the publisher agree to go ahead with the book's publication as Maso had written it. Unfortunately, North Point declared bankruptcy just as the book was being released. Without promotion, *The Art Lover* failed to attract either the reviews or the readership of Maso's first novel.

Still living off of the NEA fellowship, Maso spent the next two years in southern France, writing *The American Woman in the Chinese Hat* (1994) while staying at the Karolyi Foundation, an international artist's colony. Typically, Maso chose an unconventional narrative form for *American Woman*, which may be her riskiest book. "For me," she told Nicole Cooley, "the ultimate risk was not to do anything that I knew how to do and not to provide any escape through memory or imagination or sex, not to exploit the potential of language, not to exploit the potential of narrative, and a conventional narrative at that, it's about breaking down, falling apart, and language unable to do anything about it" (33). When she returned to the United States in 1991 to teach at Illinois State University, she still had been unable to place her new novel with a publisher.

In the meantime Maso had also begun work on a fourth novel, which she saw as the first book in a projected trilogy of novels about "the history of oppression versus the desire for freedom" (Hackett 67). It was this novel, entitled *AVA* (1993), that she gave to John O'Brien, founding editor of Dalkey Archive Press, whom she met at a dinner in Normal where O'Brien had come to negotiate the relocation of his press from a Chicago suburb to Illinois State University. O'Brien decided to move his press to Normal and to publish *AVA*, which in many respects represents Maso's breakthrough novel, attracting enthusiastic reviews in most of the major review media and being chosen as one of the ten finalists for the 1993 National Book Critics Circle Award for fiction.

Since the publication of *AVA*, Maso's career has continued to flourish. In 1993 Dalkey Archive published *The American Woman in the Chinese Hat*, and Maso won another major literary prize, a $50,000 Lannan Foundation Fellowship. This time, however, Maso did not quit her job—she had become a tenured member of the creative writing faculty at Columbia Graduate School of the Arts after having spent 1992-93 as the Jenny McKeon Moor Writer-in-Residence at George Washington University in Washington, DC—in order to devote all of her time to writing. Instead, she used the money to buy a house in Germantown, New York, not only continuing to teach but opting to leave Columbia in 1995 to administer the creative writing program at Brown.

"Eventually," Maso told Joyce Hackett, "I think that teaching and buying a house, rather than doing the traveling I feel I need to do for my work, will take its toll" (73). So far, however, that seems not to have happened. All of Maso's books are now in print: in 1995, Ecco published *Ghost Dance* and *The Art Lover* in paperback, Dalkey Archive released *AVA* in paperback, and Plume issued a paperback edition of *American Woman*. Last year, Ecco published *Aureole* (1996), Maso's collection of "erotic études," and in 1998 Dutton—Maso's first mainstream publisher—will publish *Defiance*, a "murder mystery" Maso says she wrote during the academic year, while she was teaching. Classroom and program administration demands on Maso's time and concentration prevent her from working during the academic year on her more ambitious project, a novel called *The Bay of Angels*, which was initially conceived of as the second book in her projected trilogy and a sequel of sorts to *AVA*. Exerpts from this work-in-progress have appeared in *Common Knowledge* (Winter 1994: 178-90) and the anthology *Tasting Life Twice: Literary Lesbian Fiction by New American Writers*, edited by E.J. Levy (Avon, 1995, 320-37). A portion from the novel also appears in this issue of *RCF*.

Carole Maso's writing is somatic, her world a world in which matter matters. When I asked about how she sees her writing as making an intervention into traditional narrative, Maso underscored the physical imperative in her writing, how important it is to her to inscribe the implicatedness of the female body for the female mind. "The mark of the hand," Maso responded, "the breath, the pulse, the tremblings, the pressures, the intrusions of the lived life in the world, the press and the waywardness and intensity of desire—its less than orderly or linear progression—seem to be at work in my fictional 'interventions' as you call them. The inability to believe in points on the ordinary trajectory anymore—the unstable, beautiful, flawed, gorgeous happenstances—seems now to me to be more the 'story.' The motions of the mind, alive—the motions of consciousness, the longings and yearnings of language, mind, body. The desire for freedom, the desire for wings, for flight, cannot be approximated without 'intervention.' Without deep forays into the silent, the wild, the unknown."

Unlike the French feminists who theorize writing the body as a gender issue, Maso reveals her lyrical bent in her attachment to more traditional notions of subjectivity and voice. "I am in the process constantly of trying to forge a credible voice for myself and my material, with all that is available to me, and including, hopefully, all that matters most. The more conventional structures simply fail to near or address or satisfy my visions or even concerns. As Ava says, 'and if not the real story, then what the story was for me.' The longing and the falling and the distractions, the way the soul in darkness gropes in darkness toward light, the way the darkness lessens (slightly, momentarily), or the way the light gives way. All the lingerings . . . all the vulnerabilities. In short, to restore to fiction, to our world, what it is to be human, the motions of human thought—and all that is mysterious, impossible to grasp, outside the ordinary reach or grasp. And yet to still try, even now, the impulse to reach, to yearn there—to create a document of longings: hopes, regrets, fears, joys. (A preface to my erotic book, published by Ecco, addresses some of this in more detail.)"

Maso maintains the expressivist paradigm that figures so prominently in the romantic sensibility, while resisting genre definitions.

When I asked about what counts for her as valuable fiction today, Maso responded: "I think it's terribly important to continually revise what counts as fiction—or more accurately, I am most interested in using whatever formal device serves my expressive end. This of course means that writing in prose or poetry, in fiction or nonfiction, becomes a moot point. In my new book, *Aureole*, work becomes suddenly (or not so suddenly) unclassifiable. I've worked hard to get there. And I am pleased to be writing outside of constrictions more and more, outside of enclosures."

In much of her fiction Maso's characters flex against closure, against constraints that are ideological, as well as against physical impositions. In *AVA* Maso rejects, for example, a man who had committed a "sin of language" when he suggests that Ava is "into kinky sex." Maso asserts, "For me writing is a means to become free; most of my books are about freedom on some level. Personally, writing has been about freeing myself from preconception, from breaking out of the prefabricated molds, definitions. To find a way to live with uncertainty, ambivalence. I never could have dreamed I'd even get this far along in that journey toward freedom, with a handful of words, twenty-six figures on fire [re *Aureole*]. How wonderful really, and odd."

When I asked who she would imagine to be her faithful reader, Maso explained: "As for readers—I'm not sure I've got a 'faithful reader.' What I do know though is that there are many serious, smart, and curious readers out there, and readers who are really starving for alternatives to what the mainstream tries to force feed them. There's been on the part of publishers and writers, I think, a real tendency to condescend to the reader, instead of trusting him or her."

Maso's an activist in her rationale for writing—asserting that a text should *do* something—but she stops short of objectively describing what precisely it should do. Attention must be paid, Maso asserts, to "imagining mutual transcendence between reader and writer, partnership, intimacy, freedoms, allowances, trust. I think it's important not to dictate or legislate what the reading experience should be, not to make the old assumptions. It seems an important and little considered part ot the literary endeavor. A place of creativity and spaciousness and possibility is what I hope to afford any reader and it's become more and more what I need from a reading experience. But a genuine experience and not just the record of an experience. I think in this TV passive age, the desires are very great to make and to have a place where there might still be interaction: exchanges of thoughts, shapes, emotional weights, bodily fluids—sounds a little dangerous doesn't it? Living texts." The responses to the work of Carole Maso in this issue attest to the success with which she resists closure and objectivity and coaxes a wide variety of responses, of where and how, even, to locate the issues raised by the text.

It is clear that Maso has high expectations regarding her readers, while typically resisting prescriptions. "While I have no intentions really, certainly I do not intend as part of my project to awaken the 'desensitized.' I think it may be something that might happen, no? I guess if there's engagement at all with a text, and not just dismissal, then yes, it seems to be a by-product of this kind of work. I have no mission or agenda however. While I believe language is capable of anything—and I do mean anything—even changing the world—it's certainly not what I want to do."

Maso's description of her writing aligns her with some essentialist notions of *écriture feminin,* intermingling the implications of language and body. "The body to me," Maso states, "is interchangeable with language. It's that immediate and wild and mysterious. Both have weight, emit heat and light, carry great emotion, are capable of extraordinary passion, are the place of desire, pleasure, pain. In *Aureole* I am investigating in a very physical and also I'd say spiritual way the relationship between desire and language. Body and word. I feel like I've only just begun to explore the syntax of passion. While the body has been present in the very fiber, I'd say, of all my work, never have I done such a systematic and formal investigation as I am now doing in my series of erotic études, as I like to call them. I feel this is an area that is almost completely yet to be explored—it's really quite exciting. Particularly for women. While many younger writers in particular are writing about sex, it does not seem to me that they are writing particularly sexually. I've only just begun my experiments with all this. Suffice it to say, I feel thrilled to have a chance to go on this flight. Fluid, shifting points of view, deranged language, speechlessness—and so much more—seem like a starting off place for a new kind of composition written according to desire's demands—and the body—which for me is always both squarely at the center of my work and my life."

If there's a formal mimesis in Maso's intentions, it's that the rhythms of the lines in her prose echo the pulsations of the body. "That there is finally no circumventing the body, as there, while writing, is no circumventing the mind, is something that I must come to terms with over and over again," Maso says. "Where and why do we breathe in a text? Where are the harbors, the clearings—these are physical qualities. Why and how does the line break—and what does that have to do with the body, the heart? When the heart breaks, how does language reflect it? The head spinning. Everything suddenly soaking. The ways of escape. Or the blur—how to capture the sexual blur? And outside the sexual—the body in pain, the body at rest, the body in its inexorable movement toward death. The body as spiritual, transcendent vessel, as light. The passions of the mind. Now there's another enormous, extraordinary amazing desire. Philosophical passion. Another subject though."

Maso's writing seems so intertextually marked that I asked her whether or not she felt there were similarities in the body of her texts to the concept of the cyborg body. She responded, "I don't pretend to understand the cyborg mentality well enough to know where we may converge and diverge, but yes, it certainly seems that we're on many levels quite different. I tend though these days to judge far less quickly than I once did. Perhaps I am just getting older. I feel less capable of assessing. But the sensuality of language, the body of the text as erotic, the textures of perception—these seem quite far from my cyborg pals. Where we are more similar it seems is in the notion of fragility, of all that is shifting, fleeting, disappearing, whirling, changing. I write a bit about the electronic in a recent *Review of Contemporary Fiction* essay about the future of fiction" (Spring1996, 54-75).

When asked about the major influences on her work, Maso responded: "Early on Woolf was the great presence and in fact I've had to work fairly hard to break away from her. Stein is an influence. Barnes to some degree. Beckett. I have read intensely and passionately all the great poets from Sappho on. Film has been an enormous influence. Antonioni, Godard, Tarkovsky."

The interview concluded with a question about Maso's current work-in-progress. "I am moving toward a more abstract fiction—emotionally felt, a fiction of vibrancy, shape, and pressures, freedoms and expanses, tremblings, allowing a different literary experience—one less interested in meaning as conventionally defined, and eschewing the accepted notions of narrative, character, and plot. Informed by the music of the mind and body and heart, my next work, to be called *The Bay of Angels*, shall be a continuation of my investigations of passion and freedom, history and imagination through form, but it shall also be a departure into utterly new, unknown territory for me. A kind of visionary fiction—one that excites, frightens, and humbles me as I begin composition."

Except Joy: *On* Aureole

Carole Maso

Aureole celebrates the resplendence of language and desire. It is a work of reverie and ruin. Pleasure. Oblivion. Joy. A place where we are for a little while endlessly possible, capable of anything, it seems: fluid, changing, ephemeral, renewable, intensely alive, close to death, clairvoyant, fearless, luminous, passionate, strange even to ourselves.

It was written in a kind of waking dream, an erotic hallucination in which I was only semiconscious and yet utterly lucid. I abandoned myself to the pressure, the touch of language, its sexual slur, the trance of it. The motions of the alphabet. I have tried to be attentive to its needs—its positions and shifts, its murmurings. The word's attraction for the word.

I write these after words now in Paris, city of light, in sweet breeze, in first heat, *golden square devour me*—after a winter so vast and white. *Aureole* was written in a blizzard of emotion, in a blur of want, in an audacity of trust. I was knowing and unknowing, conscious and unconscious, freezing and fevered. Passion pressing these pieces into shapes like the press of animal tracks in the snow. The heat of the living body. The hope was for a language as ancient as memory, as direct as a moan, as gorgeous as song, as imperfect as utterance. It is in love with beauty and abandon and excess, unapologetically. The desire all winter was for transformation, transcendence. Now when I lift my dreaming head all of a sudden spring has come, *golden square,* and it is Paris; I marvel as the Seine turns into the Ganges, or the Hudson River glistening, flowing through us on a white bed, on our pleasure river bed. The river being pulled through me like a miraculous, golden thread.

Aureole was shaped by desire's magical and subversive qualities. It imposed its swellings, its ruptures, its erasures, its motions. Sometimes wild, sometimes elusive, playful, wayward—it was driven by pleasure and forged in passion. I have tried to feel the sexual intoxication of the line or the page or the narrative—language overcome or desperate or greedy. The story staggered. The phrase gasping or begging or sighing.

With some dismay I realize that I am content in these pages to be, as Yeats said, "for the song's sake, a fool." I have overexposed myself in this work. I have gone too far and also not far enough, I have wandered off hoping to get close to that translucent, ephemeral thing. That impossible thing. Escaping. And the white page whispered back, continues to whisper back, *look, you're no match for it.*

Aureole resists categorization. My desire is far messier, more voracious, stranger than any existing or prescribed shape could accommodate. In fact I felt exiled, alien among those options. I could not recognize myself there. Desire pressing itself into odd shapes insistently, urgently, in a way I did not dare second guess. The impulse in these pieces is to free myself from constraint from preconception. The flight is from boundaries—linguistic, sexual, intellectual. The longing is for freedom.

Desire has made it possible for me to write into my greatest vulnerabilities, uncertainties. It has made it possible to not worry so much about the consequences, to let go a little. Desire has allowed me to write into its danger, its bliss, its silence, its abyss. To not care about failing. Whether these pieces were any "good" or not seemed hardly to enter it. I chose not to rely on facility. If I felt I was doing something I already knew how to do well, the rule was to start again in an attempt to break habitual patterns of mind and expression. I've tried to write into the heart of longing, regret, unsure once I was there how I would get back or if I'd get back. I have practiced courage a long time. I think of *The Art Lover.* Feigned it even when I did not have it, waiting for it to come. I've tried to write into reluctance—to actually feel the pull forward and back simultaneously, an erotic motion in itself. In this time of witness, of storytelling, I've tried to allow myself to walk into forgetfulness, dissolution. To give up a little. To let the earth go, and the ones I love most. To let a new logic take over. To live at the heart of the unknown, without explanation. Desire has allowed me to stray, to wander away from the familiar, to move far off into the landscape of passion or addiction—oblivion—snow or hope—the trance of our days here. . . .

Language for me has always been a profoundly sensual experience. Language *is* emotion, language *is* feeling, language *is* body. It is not merely the sign for something, but rather also a thing in itself. It has weight and heat; it emits light. Its meaning is inseparable from its sound, its rhythms, the way it is arranged on the page. It is primitive, charmed, charged, affective. Only secondarily is it conceptual and derivative. From a different angle, and through a different process, the philosopher Maurice Merleau-Ponty knew this thing, and I would recommend anyone who cares about such matters to read his amazing *Phenomenolgy of Perception.* I myself have arrived at such convictions simply through years of devotion to its untapped capacities for expressiveness, its recalcitrance, its elusiveness. Its incredible beauty has kept me, keeps me, completely under its spell. I believe like Maurice Blanchot that "language is possible because it strives for the impossible." And "the poet is nothing but the existence of this impossibility, just as the poem is nothing but the retention, the transmission of its own impossibility." There is a way of conveying meaning beneath the level of the meaning of the words themselves and this for me is where the true capacities and powers and charms and seductions of language reside. Language works on one in some of the same ways music does. It shapes silence. Through an arrangement of tones and rhythms, against a shimmering backdrop of silence, music can produce subliminal, physiological, psychological, emotional and sometimes mystical responses. The effect of key, the press of syllable, the modulation of tone, the vowel's drawl, the rhythm of hip and word and world, the flick of the tongue or the heat of the hand can create sublime and profound states. I am hoping in a series of books like this one to explore the erotic through the thoroughly incarnate medium of language. I am hoping to get closer to my own desire. I am imagining free. Free some day.

In this preliminary work desire has informed and shaped diction and syntax. It has shown me how to determine the line, the paragraph. It has intimately influenced not only the trajectory of the narrative but its very definition. Desire insisted at times on a kind of formlessness, indeterminacy, excess. A series of intensities without objective. Plans are abandoned, resolutions are broken, preconceptions fall away. Desire does not follow but rather distorts and warps the usual unities and coherencies, and some of the stabilized notions of self and other. I have let it determine my notion of "character" and the treatment of time. It is responsible for the various swellings and verges and delays and elongations and collapses—it has brought a certain wildness, vibrancy, immediacy, I have found somewhat lacking in my work. This book begins, but only begins, to explore writing as another kind of lovemaking, and lovemaking as another kind of writing.

Language is emotion. For a long time now, perhaps even twenty years, I have held in my body a single sentence. This sentence written by Virginia Woolf and placed at the heart of her great novel *To the Lighthouse* has haunted me. I believe I can trace my early belief that language was capable of great physical and emotional feats that had barely been tapped into to this one line of prose. Oh that fiction, of all things, might do something other than be descriptive! Here is the sentence: "Mr. Ramsay, stumbling along a passage one dark morning, stretched his arms out, but Mrs. Ramsay having died rather suddenly the night before, his arms, though stretched out, remained empty."

Feel how wounded this line is, how it limps with grief, how it is barely intelligible by the usual standards—as if the ordinary structures could not possibly hold this level of emotion, this weight. It remains broken, filled with confusion and yearning. The intelligence and intuition and true bravery on Woolf's part are really remarkable. The trust necessary to let go to the power of the emotion and then somehow believe utterly in the language's ability to express it, this essentially inexpressible thing, seemed to me above all what to strive for. A language capable of not only recording experience but of being an experience. I believe that there might be ways in language to express the things that exist at the extreme peripheries of speech. A form that might embrace content, after all. Each enlarging the other.

Line by line I have tried to get closer to an erotic language, a language that might function more bodily, more physically, more passionately. Enjambment, flux, fragmentation, the elision of the object, the detached clause, the use of arpeggios, a changing dynamics, dangling participles, various aphasias—the unfinished sentence, or the melting of one sentence into another, the melting of corporeal boundaries, the dissolving of a subjective cohesion—these are some of the strategies I have attempted here. For the most part they were done intuitively as I tried to surrender and enter a sexual reverie on the level of language. Blurrings, changes in focus, and contradictions abounded. The oxymoronic, the parabolic appeared, serving as—well, who knew?—perhaps as fortification against the dissolution, or a warning, of what might happen if one strayed too far from story. I have tried to explore a little the zones of speechlessness one sometimes enters during sex, the field of silence, the tug of it, the language voids and vacuums, the weird filling in with words. This called up Stein for me and her particular brand of playfulness—her baby talk, her repetitions, her abstractions, her songs. Her sense, her senselessness. The small codes, hopes, love letters she embedded in her texts.

In the strangeness of that emptying, then empty space, odd things came to the fore or swirled around that weird vortex I tried to fill up with nonsense, odd fragments of memory, with games from childhood (You are as light as a feather/As stiff as a board), hurtful games (she loves you not), with grand pronouncements, lies, small intimacies, with playfulness (violet-breasted, Poodle Basket), and other linguistic hijinks (She lifts her hips to her thirst and vice versa).

I have wanted a little of the way lovers sound, their sputterings, their hopeless stutterings, their confessions, what is most precious to them, the specific ways they are intimate—their ability to answer questions that have not been asked ("a lot of practice"). The direct plea asserting itself, the interruptions, the intervention of thought with sensation. This sentence from "Exquisite Hour" starts as a meditation and ends as a kind of urgent instruction: "The effect of key don't change it." I have played with changes in tense within a paragraph and sometimes within a sentence in order to capture that warped sense of time. I have worked with imprecision and with abstraction in order to mimic the varying tempos of perception, consciousness, lucidity as we sometimes near the sacred. A slow coming to marks the beginning of "Anju flying." Sleep and sex-drugged, dream-ridden, the images are kept deliberately fuzzy or vague as they come and go into focus.

There are point of view changes within paragraphs and sometimes sentences. Quick shifts in subject occur, as invariably one lover will call up a past love or experience, or fantasy will intermingle with reality, disrupting the more usual ways of thinking. The enlargement of a small detail which results in the loss of the whole, the blurring of the greater picture, the strange erasures of self, of place, and that other thing—is that you snow ghost?—which remains. Changes in perspective. How small and how far off the world seems all of a sudden. The trees like smoke. . . . The attendant sadnesses, insights, dizziness, revelations. I've become more and more interested in trying to near the most ambiguous and ephemeral and fleeting states—"Anju giggling hope elusive stay awhile."

I have experimented with using language at a slight remove from its literal meaning—setting words free to act on each other in different ways. I have delighted in the pleasuring of the image by repetition or recurrence: "good girl's knot." The reiteration of the odd phrase ("some jumper cables") that asserts itself and floats, existing mysteriously and autonomously in a text or above a bed. "In the liminal space." The image culled from hallucination: "a line of girls in communion clothes." The trust in the outlandish or off image. The creation of a place for "ovoid, opalescent, lunate," in these pages. Such words stay with me much in the same way sensation remains in my body long after the lover has departed. The prolonged pleasure of language. "Clavicle" or "striped shirt" will set me to shudder long after because of the mark it's made on the mind. "Bleary chalice." I may relive this language experience later—"the way lip clings. . . ."

I've tried to work closely with sound: the texture and friction of dissonance, the lull, the consolations of rhyme—or the sinister and constraining qualities of rhyme in a piece like "Dreaming Steven."

The derangement of syntax—to get closer to that tumult and disarray and disorientation. One of the greatest pleasures so far has been exploring the sexual energy of the sentence: "As bleary, delirious, the sound of bells, they make their way to the end of the long beach and sentence, far." I have begun to feel the erotic surge of the phrase, and have started to think more and more about how those insistences and urgencies might dictate the shape of a line. Poets, of course, are quite adept at such things, but it has taken me, the prose writer, a long time to get here. I love the ability to create new logics, a logic of passion, a logic of the body dramatized by where the line breaks, or the paragraph, a logic of passion created in the caesuras, in the gaps, where unexpected tensions or emphases can produce effects which are, to me at any rate, quite startling. A physical gathering of linguistic force might send the reader upward where finally all the pressure is brought to bear on an unlikely and startling word or phrase. Sounds pretty sexy, don't you think? Faltering, one stumbles perhaps, regains a kind of equilibrium and in the process enters a different realm. A realm where physical actions replace, or erase, thought ("downward stroke"). In an attempt to capture some of these swells I've tried to begin using punctuation to syncopate, much like a jazz musician, confident in her craft, conversant, in the hopes of bringing new pressures to bear, and also new places of release—so that a piece might tremble or shimmer or languish, surprise. I have wanted to reclaim punctuation from the prose writers a little. Liberate it, and myself. Have it make sense again. When the last double periods are placed on the lightkeeper's last matins I want to try to feel that finality, that force. To understand that there may be an instance where the parenthesis can never close. I want one day to get that right—to feel that vulnerable on the page, that bed of language, that world. Use of the upper and lower case too are meant to try to capture erotic surges, the press of the sexual, or the flow of emotion. The sentence staggered, breathless, lapsed or desperate. The sentence insistent or lingering. The sentence reinvented—dear Gertrude. The sentence as incantation.

As for the larger motions within the pieces, desire has been the inspiration and guide there as well. Many attempts have been made to try and get closer to that yearning, that longing through narrative decisions. In "Sappho Sings" I have tried to ride the crests and swells of delirious language making, the excess of it, the surfeit of language, visions, ideas, wishes. To simply get lost in the sensuousness of language, just to enjoy it, feel it in one's mouth—to relish its gorgeousness. Insatiable. To enjoy the fluidity of one getting lost in the other. I have tried to stay near to the kinds of audacities and recklessness and strange rigors that desire creates—the dizziness.

As if hurling myself off a precipice. In "Exquisite Hour" waywardness, disorientation becomes the narrative imperative. I am extremely interested in the incoherencies of desire, and this piece is incoherent, it wanders off—going far afield, shifting point of view and place without preparation. Images are strange and heightened; lines drop off or melt into one another to produce a lapsed, dissipated quality. There is an eerie and for me heartbreaking holding on and letting go simultaneously. I stumble here in this blizzard of language and narrative unable to know exactly what's going on in the blur—"Is that you snow ghost? Is that you candy gram? Strange visitations." This I am certain of: desire does not make a well-made short story.

In "Dreaming Steven" erotic fantasy informs the motions. Quick changes of position: physical position, language positions, positions of the mind are the given. The constant need for novelty, replacement, substitution, multiplicity, simultaneity, the desperate lust for more or different images, the loopy, complex needs: "fish in their mouths." The dark hilarity I have only begun to explore that often inadvertently exists in sexual fantasy. The elaborate and often comedic stagings in the theater of the mind. The artifice: the props, the funny colored lights, the costumes, the makeup. The flirtations with death, the jovial rehearsals for it—its seductive proximity and our desire for it. The thousand resurrections and reinventions. The demented jingles—its sweet, sweet music. Replenishments. Reinforcements. The refreshment. The courage afforded. It makes you rethink closure, that's for sure.

I love the insistence and tenacity of desire, the reiterations and rephrasings, the eternal returnings. The obsessiveness of the erotic imagination. The press and relentlessness of the vision: "the pier collapsing." The aching dissonances. The constant pushing of the voice up a notch, forcing the tone, changing the pitch, forcing the repetitions in a kind of extraordinary need, want, desperation. I am thinking specifically here of the "You Were Dazzle" pieces. And the shift in the construction of the recurring phrase "You were flowers in a barrel" to "You were flower petals floating in a barrel" which signals the move away, through the linguistic gesture as much as anything that is understood on the literal level. In fact, to my ear the literal statements, "you were never again," etc., sound like the kind of grand statement indicating that the obsession is far from over. But in the quieter "you were flower petals floating," the subtle shift carries makes me think that just perhaps. . . . A slight letting go of the obsession in a line like that begins to happen. The unconscious shift there tells me that just maybe. . . . Not to say on another day the lover will not have returned at the height of the obsession one more time. In a way the two "Dazzle" pieces are meant to be read on a kind of eternal loop. And in "Her Ink-Stained Hands" what interests me is the holding back, the taking away, the terrible truncated shapes left without any real means to complete or resolve themselves. The fear that has calcifed and assumes a kind of permanent stance.

Time as conventionally conceived in much fiction loses its meaning when placed in desire's crucible. Desire's temporality is not that generally of development, direction or movement. Often the erotic stops or suppresses time, and this is one of the notions I try to explore. Sometimes it warps time, sexual consciousness seeming to inhabit an odd hanging space. "In the passage between day and night. The transition. In the uncertain hour. In the time, you who are French speak, and I am able to attach a meaning to what you've whispered, as you approach me for the first time at the airport." That odd kind of tripped-up time where threads of thought, memory, sensation are all combined, dissolving the ordinary distinctions and boundaries in a kind of perceptual synesthesia. Only later can things be sorted out—and it is at this later point I believe that most writing, with its sense making, begins. But narrative here is far more diffuse; it's an altogether different kind of energy field. I have tried to enter the continuous present of the erotic experience—a present which is constantly unfolding and includes past and future in its fluid hold. Time is experienced, to borrow from Heidegger, as a "sequence of nows." That the past or future is autonomous seems not quite believable in this hanging, eroticized state. How to distinguish where the past leaves off and a present begins? When have we begun the future? In "Make Me Dazzle" there is the intermingling of time that allows the longing woman on the beach to converse in two time periods simultaneously to two different people in the simple: "you're right here." Other questions arise. Where do the lovers leave off and I, the writer, begin? Where does the life begin and the writing stop? But I am getting a little ahead of myself. What seems evident to me when thinking about time—and sexual desire pushes the issue—is that the now-routine way of calling up the past through the use of the flashback is disassembled here and rejected as a viable and truthful stategy. All formulas are suspect. Desire is not formulaic, lust is not formulaic, only pornography is. For me, many highly accepted and completely integrated and "cherished" devices, including the flashback, resemble nothing as much as themselves: accepted and recognizable storytelling devices of literary fiction and now staples as well of mainstream filmmaking. An agreed-upon way to shape reality. It reminds me of those traveling players in "Anju Flying Streamers After" who try to cobble together a bit of a scaffolding, jerry-build a clunky, makeshift structure so as to impose a bit of order on the disorderly, uncontrollable erotic life and death force.

I think of Lautreamont and his radical project in *Maldoror,* as he tried to expose and destroy simile and analogy. I think of his flagrant parodying of the novel at the end of that work. His irreverence. His dark joy. I take courage there.

I have given up any conventional notions of the novel in *Aureole.* I have tried to respect and indeed encourage the longing and the genuine mystery which exist between the discrete pieces. The hope is that this desire might augment, echo and speak to the other motions of longing in this work. The figures from piece to piece are connected peripherally. An erotic consciousness of abundance and allowance, a kind of gorgeous promoscuity, seems to allow them to move back and forth between space and time more readily than might otherwise be the case. Linguistic relationships seem freely transferable as well—floating through texts more as light comes and goes with its gleaming and ephemeral touch. As in electronic writing, which I find a highly charged and essentially erotic space, I have, from time to time, here attempted the splitting off of narrative or linguistic instants to both accentuate and dramatize the nearness and the farness of the various language and narrative constructions, with the hope of refining those proximities and creating new forms of yearning. Desires I was not even aware I had surfaced during the writing of these pieces. The true miracle of form.

I have chosen with some deliberateness the moments at which to hold each piece on the page. I have thought it most effective to allow them to exist in the hovering place—"in the night and glisten and holy water basin." In moments of arousal and suspension and vulnerability. Open. That Tantric state when the intertwined couple captures the moment right before *jouissance* and extends it into forever. To my mind, this work is a novel at the very moment of its forming, before the images and transitions and other kinds of ordinary assignments are made, and with those assignments a necessary imposition of design, authority, dissimulation and distance. I have tried, not entirely successfully I think, to keep the material nearest to its longing. At the place where there is no fixed central figure, no plot in the ordinary sense, temporality without chronology; the place of all potential. At the place where there is only mystery, uncertainty, wonder, fear, tremblings—our mortal gorgeous lives. The place of mergings, collisions, veerings, near misses, swervings, passages in the night, slurs and bleak repetitions—hesitations, magnifications, overlappings, multiplications and erasures and recurrences. The book is in a state of ravel and unravel to me, forming before our eyes, grouping and regrouping, gathering and dissolving. At the periphery of the more expected book lies this one, at the edge of the more obvious and stable book. On the horizon of story, before the shapes are made manifest, and the connections lose their tenuous, mysterious, human hold. I have tried to leave this work at the most erotic moment, the most vulnerable and open. *Aureole* for me exists forever on the verge, on the edge of a slightly heightened and unhinged world, just before the narrative strands coalesce. Ordinary story seems rather false, and indeed a bit preposterous under the circumstances. It is derailed, detonated, overwhelmed by the intensity of sexual desire, the force of desire. Plot cannot be contained given the subversiveness and potential extremity of the subject. Content insists on its form here. It is my hope that at the book's threshold the reader and the writer might be allowed to inhabit an extended moment of suspended sexuality where anything might still be possible. In the moment "before the woman in Paris becomes anything she wants to be yet." In the moment before "whatever will happen next will happen." In "the liminal space, in the gap. . . ." To float like the couple in the changing room, that unreal, crystalline chamber, "in some of their clothes," "in the just March."

Who has conjured whom here? One more time I begin to question my notions of the real. Some part of me is still in Paris and I look up to the beautiful floating window written in wrought iron, the astounding calligraphy of its balcony, to where the woman, when she is French, opens *The Fourth Book of Desire* or *The Book of Good-bye* once more. Set into a delirious language motion, sex motion, in the uncertain, hovering, luminous afternoon. Today it seems from her all else has been spun. On another day, based on my reading, or my mood, or my desire for the text, it might be Sappho, beached on that lilting nymph who dreams the rest of *Aureole*'s cast into creation. What do we know of what she wrote or saw in the place where the papyrus tore? Or of the woman who writes on the sheets. Who has conjured little Anna, trembling in the fire garden—walking away from almost everything—and then finally from everything. . . . Are these aspects of the unfolding self? Shall they ever find each other? Or is that not it at all? Where do I, Carole, exist in all of this? I cannot tell you the longing these figures bring up in me—each of us rising out of the other's want, each in dialogue with the other—as I attempt to live a little more through the openness and fluidity of the form. To be set a little free, rather than constrained by, reined in by it. Do the women on the winter beach dream Steven? Or has he in his solitude and need created them? Will he ever know the opium addict who has left her bleary snow globe on his mantle? And Anju through veils . . . Stay awhile. The woman with the child in her arms. Where has she come from? Where has she gone?

". . . streamers flying after."

True, there is no central character moving through conflict making its more or less linear journey here; but rather a pageant of consciousness, refracted, escaping and elusive, casting light and shadow in all directions. The potential in us, and the extraordinary, awesome potentials still asleep in the language. *Aureole* to my mind is the story of a woman who wants. A woman, free, before the author's final prescriptions. In the erotic, the notion of a stable, static being developing in the traditional ways makes little sense except as some kind of agreed-upon convention of legibility. I have only begun in this book to look for the places in the text where passion might yield another kind of logic, offer a different way of proceeding. *Aureole* remains a mysterious book to me. And the woman.

How will I find her—without a recognizable plot? How will I find her—as she changes shape and place, without warning? How will I recognize her as she wanders through every genre—that passionate terrain? Where will I garner enough trust, enough faith? How will I ever locate her without the usual landmarks? How will I find her as she blithely moves in and out of obscurity, of shadow and light. Again, the writing asks me to be a better, a braver person than the one I know how to be. None of the usual landmarks to hold onto. I am interested in how different as a process this work has been from the way I once worked. In my earliest novel, *Ghost Dance,* I followed a vision of an utterly mysterious woman into a kind of comprehensibility. But in *Aureole* the tables have turned. Who is that woman on the bridge who in different places and guises continually reappears? In the beginning of this project, I thought I knew; by the end I have no idea. A woman moving along the relentless trajectory of her desire, transformed over and over by it. I see works that will be called novels in the future with a notion of charater that is much more mutable. I believe notions of plot as well will be radically reimagined—and become much more open again. This is what art does for me: it opens new places, it afford glimpses not glimpsed before. Without it I not only fail to live fully, but I begin to die. All too aware of the loss, I become a mourning thing.

I have tried to create a vibrant, spacious landscape where I might live. A space that is generous in its allowances. A room of my own—part prose fiction, part prose poem, part journal, part notebook, part memoir, part song, sometimes part biography. None of these forms alone quite meets the dimensions or urgencies I have begun to feel. No one shape quite meets the requirements of my desire. I have needed, I have wanted everything—probably too much.

Desire has forced me into odd contortions, new constructions, a more unarticulated and primal space, filled with primitive recollections—notions of light and dark, hot and cold, birth and death, danger, fire, flood—memories of clearings, of harbors, tremor, convulsions as they press their way into language. Tracks in the snow. . . . When you came to visit me that night you left your enormous footprint in the ice. By the morning it had dissolved—and you. Shapes and forms that far from constricting or defining will be evocative, calling up the history of this ancient place, the memory of, survive, the immediacy of hand, pulse of blood, the heat of the intellect, all that is beautiful, all that is still possible (intimations more and more often now of the South of France that sun-drenched . . .).

Without apology, I have tried to create something of a feminine space. New kinds of intimacies. I do not believe in the myth of ungendered writing. Luce Irigaray is much better than I am on this. She says: "Only those who are still in a state of verbal automatism or mimic already existing meaning can maintain such a scission or split between she who is a woman and she who writes. The whole of my body is sexuate. My sexuality isn't restricted to my sex and the sexual act (in a narrow sense). I think the effects of repression and especially the lack of sexual culture—civil and religious—are still so powerful that they enable such strange statements to be upheld as 'I am a woman' and 'I do not write as a woman.' In these protestations there's a secret allegiance to the between-men cultures." It is essential, I believe, for women to make their own shapes and sounds, to enact in prose and poetry and all other genres, and in all other mediums, their own desire, and not just mimic the dominant forms. We must refuse to emerge already constructed. "The master mouthing masterpiece." Obviously this is a lot easier said than done. First because it is difficult and still largely theoretical, and second, because it asks us once again to marginalize ourselves, return to the periphery, just as we are acquiring a recognizable speaking voice (theirs) and being rewarded for doing it so well. Just as we are being embraced—even if it is a conditional embrace. And yet . . . I like to think of Hélène Cixous at times like this. She writes: "We must work. The earth of writing. To the point of becoming the earth. Humble work. Without reward. Except joy."

Except joy.

I have tried to make a place where pleasures and arousals spread in a lateral radiance, in a kind of prolonged ecstatic. In an aureole of desire. At once diffuse, specific and inclusive. A place where what is often discarded as unusable will be kept. A place at once interested in the abstract, distant, and also the utterly urgent, personal, even confessional. A place where we do not have to apologize. A place of forgiveness. I have incorporated, taken into the body of this book, my own past work. That there might be a place where we wouldn't have to disown ourselves, loathe ourselves in that mild, insidious way, feel ashamed of who we are, or who we were—ashamed by the one who was younger, played it more safely perhaps, made even more mistakes. To embrace our own texts, our written texts, and the texts of our lives. To risk the thing they love to call us most: self-indulgent, histrionic, irrational. Indulgent, excessive, pleasure texts—unconcerned with getting to the point. In love with freedom. To walk out of the constraints of perfection, or modesty, or approval, or taste, or integrity as integrity has too often been defined. To escape the burden of the already-constructed and received forms—like the props and scaffolding those traveling players cobble together in hopes of staging the story of the bursting, uncontainable Anju—their efforts, slightly funny, kind of wonderful, a little pathetic, sweet, naive, creaking and ultimately useless. And this is how I regard the old fictions. I want something else. I want there to be space enough for all sorts of accidents of beauty, revelations, kindnesses, small surprises. A space that encourages new identity constructions for the reader as well as the writer. New patterns of thought and ways of perceiving. New visions of world, renewed hope.

I have tried to create a space neither fictive nor autobiographical where I am allowed to exist in an utterly different way. Not as a character or through character, and yet not as author either. "Once again sadness has caught you off guard," a voice says in "Exquisite Hour." I have no idea who is speaking, it might be the drugs, or the desire, or the fencing master or a party guest—but I do know who is being spoken to—alas. It is me. Once again sadness.

In a piece I am working on now which shall appear in the next book, I have allowed my mind and body to exist at such an angle to the subject that I am allowed to inhabit the material in a way that allows me a new place in the text. The question arises, painfully, acutely, through the text, and not in the voice of the character and not in my own voice, and not in an "authorial" voice, it persists. A question I in any other guise would not have the courage or ability to pose. *Where does your life go?* The piece somehow has allowed me to ask the essential, unbearable question at the center of my fear. Because of the time it takes to make money I may not get to where I need to go. Overwhelmed, panicked, utterly dispirited by my day job. There has been no way to approach such a thing. But the text has allowed me to face it. This is perhaps the most difficult thing of all to describe. Through the urgency and force of my desire and through the open place desire has created in me I may enter my work and be engaged in ways that up until now have been off-limits. There is a different engagement—and the stakes finally start to make a little bit of sense.

Another interesting thing: for me there is less and less of a distinction between writing and living and this work has clarified that. But that does not quite say it. Let me ask Woolf once again for help here. She says, "The test of a book (to a writer) is if it makes a space in which quite naturally, you can say what you want to say. . . . This proves that a book is alive: because it has not crushed the thing I wanted to say, but allowed me to slip it in, without any compression or alteration." As I was finishing *Aureole* I happened to hear on the radio that Marguerite Duras, one of the presiding angels of this text, had died. If there had not been room enough in the body of my work to honor her, I would have considered this work to be a failure, a book that failed to live on the most basic level. What would my writing be worth then? If on that March day completing "In the Last Village," there had not been made a place for her? The creation of an inclusive place—a viable and flexible internal and external space, much like sexual space, at once immediate and remote, completely mundane and utterly sublime—that is what I am after.

(I want to go as far as we went that afternoon in that room in the trees, our bodies filtering leaves and sunlight—the shapes on the wall—that odd, tripped-up time, the hum of early summer—to let in that kind of pleasure, that kind of light. A line of girls appears—you were always such a child—then disappears. You are long gone—except here. Right here. And then you are gone again. But I will not close the parenthesis yet . . .

The tenacity of the erotic.

I am on a train, as I always seem to be these days, and walking down the aisle I stop to look at someone lying stretched out on two seats, who must have looked like you because standing over this innocent figure I whisper, *wake up now.* What has brought you here to me? The motion of the train? The desire in these pages, as I finish up the last revisions to *Aureole?* What has provoked such emotion, such delusion? Who has brought you here? Could it really be you? The movement of the train, does that have something to do with this delusion, this emotion? And the fact that I know you are afraid to fly and that you must be doing a lot of traveling lately and that you travel by train whenever you can, and because you are tired—sleeping in fact, as I stand over you in motion, scribbling, whispering—I try not to think of myself this way . . .

My desire to awaken you, and us, retrieve you again, and us, seeing you now as I do before me. You are in the midst of your fifteen minutes of fame and there is not a place, quite suddenly, I can turn without seeing your face—a face I have not seen in years now; there is not a mouth who is not saying your name—or so it seems. And as I write over someone quite asleep, desiring, longing to have you with me (that Amtrak bathroom), to keep you with me—even this sleeping version of you—though you have gone for what is probably forever—trying even here, in the most inappropriate places, an essay for God's sake—the elongation of the sentence, to keep you here—not allowing the pen to lift from the paper—to make the words, run on and on, in the terrible, too small—and yes of course, I notice as I stand there that I try in language, using every resource, every strategy to have you with me again. I dreamt that floating train carried us and the narrative. And those words, once broken off with some violence, resumed. At least for a minute.

I want to get closer to sexual abandon in language, erotic wonder, spiritual awe. I want to be pressed up close to the speechlessness—as we form our first words after making love, having come back from that amazing and sacred place. I want to live next to the impossible, next to that which forever escapes us, eludes us. *Aureole* is small progress. But the book I love is the book it suggests—and it sends me back again into my own desire and want. This, all this too, and why not this and more and yes. That is the kind of book I wish for. Always more.

More. I'd like fountains in the text, gardens, reflecting ponds, zones of peace. Deep space. Fleeting, unlikely moments. A place where a clock sounds. A woman sings in French. Her voice caresses the overcast. A child presses her hand against the glass. I see her breath on the pane. She draws a heart. I'd like more weather. The press of cypress against stone, rain at the lip of the rose, she sings, listen, something about the snow. . . . Charcoal gray graffiti and erasures on ancient stone. Prayers. Intimacies. What they whisper to each other on the rue Christine. The touch of sunlight, the way the hope comes and goes. The Seine running through me still—clinging still. I'd like there to be more swellings, more flooding in the texts. Abundances. More glances and glimpses, more tremblings. I want more hilarity, more bawdiness, more lust, pieces that are rougher around the edges. I'd like, as Cixous would say, more earth. More bloodstorm and sea ache, more bird song, small warblings. More shimmer and lull. More electricity, fever. Many hotels and boats. I'd like there to be more silence, more darkness. More magic. Made up languages perhaps; a place of babble. More memory of the sort that the body stores, and the memory that lives in the language. I'd like to pleasure the language for a long time yet, venerate, adore it. Worship the visionary, mystical, ecstatic alphabet—I'd like to get a little closer to what that might mean. So much desire. . . . Between the night and the night. Between the god and the light—before we are asked to say good-bye. Must be an angel, I think . . . or Paris . . . or maybe Paradise. . . . I'd like a lot of things. This is early work, I know. And I'm still a long way off. I recite a line by René Char to myself: *bring the ship nearer to its longing.* This book was written in offering to the book just out of reach—radiant, waiting.

May 1996

Traveling Light
from The Bay of Angels

Carole Maso

Flying. Flying not falling anymore and starlings. Rising. Larkspurs in the parlor. Rising not falling, floating, one wish. So many birds up here. Angels. A blur of wings. Listen: a distant music.

If you could make one wish Ava Klein.

Flying. Look, oh look! If not angels then what are these winged last hopes, last things? The Madame and Sophie. They're rising and hoping all buoyancy, ascendancy, yes. If not angels—

Turn over on your side the morning nurse is whispering now. Turn over on your side Ava Klein.

One wish.

Ava! Sophie cries, rising, waving. We're up here!

Lift your arm Ava Klein. This shouldn't hurt too much. There.

We're up here! If not angels—

Diminishing shape, fading stripe. Rising. Bliss in her darkening eye.

Ava! Sophie cries. Butterflies.

All is motion and lifting and upward. Madame takes the sails. Mad aerialist, mad last hope, we're in the air all right! Lifting, there.

The balloon rising higher. I hope you're satisfied now Ava Klein, rising, one wish, higher, higher. One wish. I hope you're satisfied.

Ava Klein, turn over. Yes. And now—

Having thrown all caution to the wind the balloon shifts, and the Madame having thrown, yells, do you happen to know—what's your name again?

Sophie.

Oh for God's sake. Do you happen to know how to steer this thing?

Ava, Sophie whispers, her arms outstretched in the thin air. We're over here. We're up here. Her arms reaching—holding—

If you could make one wish.

Do you happen to know how to steer this thing? One wish in her diminishing—

I think it's time, she says out loud, to learn to fly. Dreamily, drifting, it's as if—reaching—

Get a grip, get a clue the Madame screams. The balloon threatening to crash. You pick an odd time, Ava Klein, to feel like a bird. Then higher.

Madame is an aspirant: rising, hoping, all buoyancy, round the world, round the century voyager, traveler. If you could make one wish. I'd wish for this. Listen: a distant music.

The children's orchestra. The children's philharmonic. A flock of butterflies. Madame smiles. Why they're rather good!

And the children look up pointing at flying things. Beautiful balloon in the blue sky. Last hope, last wish. A distant salvation, music. Rising.

How are you feeling Ava Klein?

What answer would you be interested in other than the truth? Do you happen to know how to steer this thing?

And they're up and they're down, they're comme çi, they're comme ça, they're horses, they're tigers, *we're sinking!!!* Madame screams. Do you happen to know, *we're falling!* Put another corpse on the fire would you? To keep us afloat, up, and full of hot air. They're full of hot air but then they're not. Put another corpse. Saving the living with the dead. Burning the friends, yes, they were once her friends, so that they may fly. Not helpless. Put another log would you Miss

Prim, on the fire? The dead—

The hurt of the century. Put another corpse.

Sophie closes her ears to it.

The dead, Madame shrieks, are not any more dead after they are burned stupid, than before. Hear her out. The dead are not deader—do you get it, do you get it yet? Do you comprends, do you capiche? Put another corpse. Having burned all the available straw and sheep's wool and what have you. Last hopes. The dead aren't any more or less dead. And they rise. In the heat of the sun and the dead. Higher now. Full of hot air. There. And they float above the century for a while.

The children point to the sky. Ava smiles. Reaching out—and the landscape passes and no sadness, the precious, disappearing things and Madame whispers not yet.

On the distant radio, a radio that can't be turned up again. A small music in your ear. The hum and burn—the hurt of the century—from this distance witness the saluting man, an odd jerking motion, what a silly thing. From this distance.

A far music that now can't be turned up. Madame hands her a tiny ear megaphone. Straining to hear. The almost silence—imposed by that stupid saluting man—the rule now. Madame whispers, not yet. Madame whispers, please no. The teeny tiny violin of the end. The grand crescendo making almost no impact. Not yet.

But I remember music, Ava smiles. Stereophonic. I remember.

And they play a bit of Mendelssohn, what's that? The sleeping saluting one scratches his ear. What was that sound? Small annoyance. The children's orchestra.

Get some rest why don't you Gerhardt?

Er liebt mich, er liebt mich nicht, er—liebt mich—

The sleeping oaf who negates, who subtracts, who takes away.

Music.

The whispering man saluting, what did you say you big paluka? From this distance, can't quite decipher it my little Love Death.

But I'm afraid of the man who counts strangely in his sleep and whispers, Sophie says.

Yes, but he can't hurt us here.

With red, but he can't hurt us, what's he saying, with that smudge of moustache and shiny boot and bleak, bleak—All the bodies piling up. The hurt of the century.

If we could stay up here forever. Witness the counting man from this distance—o harmlessness—safe, floating, rising. And they watch the century pass and butterflies. If I'm not mistaken that's Amelia Earhart over there. If I'm not mistaken, Orville and Wilbur Wright. Samuel Beckett in a tree. Feeling . . .

Ava Klein, how are you feeling?

She reaches for her cat. Gray zeppelins pass. Danger is near. Foolish. Foolishness. Why did I think if I loved you I'd be safe. How did we think safe? Who did we think we could hide from up here? Madame adjusts the sails. She eyes the zeppelin. There goes the neighborhood!!

And she reaches for the gray cat that she loves but it blurs in her eye—come back—anxiety—gray zeppelin and she remembers Aunt Sophie's trembling look—are we near or are we far? Gray zeppelin, the soul floating off—Are we still alive then? In the soft and purr—where is the place it is safe? Warm and purr, blur in the eye you thought warm and safe up there (no grave) vase of music flowers in the parlor. Music once.

Larkspurs in the parlor, Sophie writes. A book for children. Blue bells and birds in the parlor. Beautiful things. Flying things. Starlings like music. Larks.

"He became our all in all. He did everything for us, he cleaned our house, he cleaned our chimneys, he got us in and he got us out and on dark nights when zeppelins came it was comfortable to know that he was outside."

Oh God are we still alive?

Gerhardt counts and turns, drenched in his sleep.

They find themselves tiny.

Pain. Some pain.

Ava Klein, give me your good arm. The morning nurse looks for a vein.

They find themselves tiny, why us up here, helpless floating in a cylinder of blood—falling. They find themselves grieving on a red field already. Not yet.

Read to me Francesco, even the hard parts. Read to me. Don't leave anything out. And he reads grieving already. Give us your good arm.

They find themselves on a red desert.

J'ai soif, she says.

As she comes in and out of consciousness now. The century falling.

You have thirst?

The troubled German in fever turns in his sleep. Salutes in his sleep. Again and again. His arm rising and falling. And we're up and we're down and we're tiny against a blood drenched field—that jerking motion. I don't know what would make one person do that to another. And we're dizzy, sick now on that saluting and brutal arm—red—read to me even now on a red backdrop dizzy, the perspective constantly changing and Madame screams. A kind of pumping motion. He's losing count. The fevered sky. They find themselves tiny. Silence. Music sucked from the room. Don't let go of the ropes, Madame yells. The sky on fire they find j'ai soif she says in fever blood drenched sky. Everything dangerous up here. How near and how far. How far off and up close at the same time. How are you feeling, Ava Klein?

How strange this feeling of flying and floating and falling all at once.

We're going nowhere fast!!! the Madame yells. But it is as if she is whispering now. And music drowned by counting. A child blows into a last tin whistle.

A child—

Let's stay like this. Before night. Unbearable that forward trajectory, narrative, to go any further. Because where is there to get to after all? Let's stay here for a moment. Before night falls . . .

Stay.

What's that? Thundering loud coming from offstage red what's that? It's called sadness idiot. It's called pain. Swatting away (he's losing count) little elbows, arms, knees. Last hopes. So minute, so faint. What's that? It's called fear. And yet.

Still a little music. Still, the children's orchestra. What's that?

Oh have a little schnapps would you and shut up.

Having made every attempt to turn down the cello the child played. Having made every attempt to take away roses. To leave only a small cup of thorns. To shut off the roses.

Pain, some pain.

Having made every attempt to silence the timpani, the cymbals. The small French horn, the child's song. He turns again in restlessness and weeps. Having made every attempt to turn down the feeling, he weeps.

Poor you Gerhardt! Madame shrieks.

Swatting away music in his sleep. Little arms, legs, faces, games. It's as if . . .

Poor you!

And he whispers kindergarten. Children are flying. Frau Schiller who taught him counting, he lines them up (over six million?) and weeps in his sleep.

Poor you!

Read to me even the hard parts, even the sad parts.

Too many birds, Madame yells, angels, getting caught in the sails.

He reads against a blood-drenched screen. Against that up and down. The page trembling. He holds it up to see the fine print. The darkness coming on. The silence. She inches closer.

Read to me. Never stop.

You walk among the ancient olives once more and they turn into a gray mist. Adding water to the pastis it turns into a cloud in your glass and you reach for, you reach—

I'm thirsty.

What did you think was beautiful there?

The way the hand hovers, the cat come home after—Blurring stripe.

Shine a little spotlight in her eye. Going blind. The night coming on (but not yet). Never die. The print dissolves and the world ends. Not yet. Gerhardt gathers the children. You bring the bone china cup to your lips. You walk once more among the ancient olives until—and the narrative stops. In that grove of mist. Right here. Like that don't move. Don't do anything any differently. Read every single word.

And the balloon hovers the way the hand—suspended—

We're going nowhere fast, Madame sighs.

Sophie writing, Sophie scribbling. A child's book. A child's guide. A flock of birds, larkspurs, butterflies.

They shine a spotlight in her eyes. Tiny white parachutes opening in her last eye. Unaccounting dark all of a sudden. It appears suddenly to be getting dark inside. And the film begins.

Against a field of extraordinary pain and music. The titles appear. Against a setting century. The rockets' red glare, the bombs bursting in air. Good God! Look! O look! The 747. The Concorde whizzes by. Hold onto your hats. In the ever darkening theater of the absurd. So many things up here!

Weather satellites, Orville and Wilbur Wright! Apollo 13, Apollo 7. Man on the moon! MTV. Samuel Beckett in a tree. Primo Levi at the top of the dark staircase.

I can't believe your wingspan! Madame says.

Siecle ô siecle des images.

What's that? A cloud mushrooms. What's that? Florescent wreckage washes up on the shore. That is the future, Madame whispers. The golden arches. Over six million souls.

What's that? Thousands of tiny parachutes opening before our eyes and falling on the Normandy coast. Saving o sweet. Saving o sweet yet to come. But not for us. An infinite amount of hope someone says in voice-over—but not for us.

Shine a spotlight: tiny white parachutes descend.

What's that? A small plane passes trailing its banners. Its glib messages. Eat at Joe's, and Entrée Libre and Visit the Children's Museum, the once was, the might have been.

He turns in his tortured sleep. The black banner. Six million and counting. Get a fucking life Gerhardt.

They're adrift. They're adrift all right. Over the sadness that is Europe and the century to the Suite for Unaccompanied Cello and the Madame whispers not yet, to the cloud about to mushroom, not yet, to 10,000 Chinese in a square not yet, to SIDA not yet; that's AIDS, not yet. Not quite yet. To Primo Levi on the dark staircase, not yet. Rare blood disease—not yet.

Father would do his funny walk that would make us laugh so hard we fell in the grass.

I'm glad you're back Ava Klein. I thought you were gone forever.

Fill my eyes with enough images to last.

I can't believe your wingspan.

Sophie sees a stork go by. Then another, another. Dropping babies another, another (how lovely) on the Normandy coast.

Sophie thinks the child. The child might have. The child might have pointed to the sky and said starling, larkspur, lark. She writes it down. She takes out her box of paints, thinks: the child. A flock of extinct birds pass. Sophie thinks the child. Against a setting century. Against a terrible and extraordinary music. She takes the child's hand. Make a mountain peak, then cross it. A. They draw an A. And the world begins again. I'm glad you're back Ava Klein.

And Sophie having washed the page in rose (before night) writes larkspurs (she loved flowers) a book for children. And the melancholy German turns—what's that?

She washes the page in spring (where children play) green from up here green how much I want you green. No, don't go, not yet.
What did you think was beautiful there?

She points to the turn of music and the century. Blaring. Diatonic harmony. The German loses count. A fitful sleep then Fritz? Undermining of major and minor. How about that Heinz? Sibelius, Stravinsky, Schoenberg, Ives. John Cage!!! Against a field of extraordinary (12 tones) possibility, what's that? What's that?

Night.

Not yet. Not yet.

The sun kept us buoyant but in the night. The sun offered its heat but in the night. The sun kept up half afloat. But now. Sinking now.

Put another corpse on the fire.

Birds sing near a black cypress. Birds sing in a black cypress. Birds (night now, nearly night) sing still as we sink and darkness falls.

We wanted a way but the winds were against us.

We wanted safe but the stars were against us.

We never hurt anyone. We never asked for anything. We thought we might open a little kosher deli or a picture museum. Start a children's philharmonic. We wanted a room up there. So what was our crime? What was our crime then remind me.

She washes the page in good-bye. She washes the page in not yet. She washes the fragile page in robin's egg blue (night, not yet . . .) Writes S. S is for her sister—she sang like a bird.

The night swallows are swooping and diving.

It's a Sunday afternoon in New York long ago. We were still alive then. That is all. What just the words Sunday afternoon, New York, can conjure. As night falls. Ava Klein we're glad you're back. We thought—

The lepidopterist tiptoes toward the unknown species.

Go to sleep now. Night.

Madame massages her wing bones. Not quite yet. Not yet.

If not angels then what? Sophie takes the child's hand. The night nurses whisper, close your eyes.

She rummages through her basket of consonants and vowels. Writing (night they say) scribbling (is falling now) notes to an unborn child (yes, night). What did you think was beautiful there? (The air blackening) Her pen poised.

S is for the way your sister sang. She sang like a B is for a bird. She used the vowels, remember, to live? R is for the roses.

She washes the page in rose under the title Night. Hopes.

Welcome to the Children's Museum. The once was, the might have been, the never was. Under glass or in a locked box preserved: what they loved, what they wanted, the games they played.

A silver cup, a xylophone, a seesaw, a sliding pond. Three types of seeds—Columbine, Bluebell, Larkspur. A tinker toy. A jump rope. A pink blanket. The rhyming alphabet.

Triple stars on the end of term exam.

Their songs:

> One I love, two I love,
> Three I love, I say,
> Four I love with all my heart
> Five I cast away—

Child's divination rhyme usually recited when plucking daisy petals, counting the seeds of the dogtail grass, or extracting pips from an apple core.

Some like it hot
Some like it cold
Some like it in the pot
Nine days old.

Infant amusement, also employed by school children for hand warming.

One's none;
Two's some
Three's many
Four's a penny;
Five's a little hundred.

Variously employed for infantile mathematics, for counting the hits at shuttlecock, and for underlining generosity when presenting sweets to a small companion.

A is for apple and B is for boat and so on. L is for larkspur, Sophie writes. Like her father, she loved flowers.

Larks in the parlor. The pale birds swoop. Madame grimaces, shoos them away. More and more now every day. Code word (if we ever get there) "too many larkspurs in the parlor." Angels in the parlor. The way the hand hovers, the way—Halley's comet falls. What's that? The births and deaths of stars. What did you think was beautiful? And how we could not make it work, Francesco, despite love, despite everything we had going. The way you looked that night, the way—

Traveling Light

Light leaves a star tonight that will reach a child's eye in two million years.

In two million years that child looking up at the night sky might say starling, balloon, lark.

Tinker toy, Treblinka, in fever.

The 107 virtuosos of the philharmonic fall silent. Children are flying. Strange vortex of silence and birds. What was our crime?

I will wait for you in the Fortezza for as long as it takes.

Light leaves. I looked up and you were gone. Light leaves a star to-night.

I will wait for you for as long as it takes.

You are so absorbed in your work, like a child drawing, that looking up you barely see or recognize me.

It's not unpleasant waiting here. Under this beautiful, striped para-sol. With a glass of the local wine.

The sun kept us buoyant—but in the night. How are you feeling Ava Klein?

We're sinking!! Madame screams slugging back her eau de vie. Help us we're sinking!!!

The crows maintain that

Madame shrieks. Who speaks? Who's there? What's that?

"The crows maintain that a single crow could destroy the heavens, for heaven simply means: the impossibility of crows."

What is that supposed to mean? She's three sheets to the wind. She's horrified by the night, its violent stars, its fireworks and bombs. The night nurses are swooping and diving. The sun kept us buoyant, but

Traveling Light

She throws things now madly from the balloon to lighten the load. She throw out all kinds of fangs: molars, incisors, baby teeth. Bones out the window to lighten the load, tibulas, fibulas, femurs. She hurls out the lead heart, the throbbing rose of the skull—The dark bloom of brain, all memory: April in Paris, the way you looked that night (Zoltan you were paradise, Madam whispers, out!!). She chucks the complete works of Shakespeare, Michelangelo's David, the Schubert string quartets, to be or not to be—oh for God's sake Madame screams! Empty bottles of eau de vie. And the skull sings a boating song and she heaves it, the skull says oh but when the horse chestnut is in bloom and she begs please no and she hurls it. And the skull says that someone is hurting her and the Madame says I'm sorry but. And the skull breaks into a little interpretive dance and she throws it far. She throws all caution to the wind. Chucks the eggs from her one basket. Discards the quadratic formula (useless) throwing

A strange old man—he had wings

Oh God, not you again! Can't you see I'm busy? Can't you see I'm just trying to steer this thing. Keep us afloat. Another corpse please.

"We all have wings, but they have not been of any avail to us and if we could tear them off, we would do so."

Why don't you fly away?

"Fly away out of our city? Leave home? Leave the dead and the gods?"

Oh for Christ's sake. She throws the Sistine Chapel ceiling, the Arena Chapel frescoes and all the other frescoes up there—Good God! And they're falling. Madame chatters and babbles. I do not like thee Doctor Fell, the reason why I cannot tell; But this I know and know full well, I do not like thee Doctor Fell.

F is for falling, not yet. S is for the way your sister sang. R is for the roses. Rest if you can in the place of past tense. F was for the way to the flower folded. Or the way you looked that night Francesco. W. We wanted everyone and everything in the world, remember?

I remember.

I will wait for you.

I'm glad you're back.

They sink. And the heart breaks again.

Where we could have gone together. And where I can't go alone.

And it's almost morning but not quite. A child in fever says tinker toys. Tinker. Treblinka. A child says I'm thirsty. J'ai soif. And he puts a cool cloth on her head. Someone named you Gerhardt as the century turned dreaming. Someone named you.

And the little cat Schnitzel come home, come back—the last thing she sees.

It's almost morning but not quite. Just before the rose of day where they might. Might have. They fall and they're falling in the almost sunlight. In the roses. Croix rouge français and the heart breaks. Rue des rosiers and the heart breaks again—what to remember if not angels.

> Ring-a-ring o' roses,
> A pocket full of posies,
> A-tishoo! A-tishoo!
> We all fall down.

The invariable sneezing and falling down in English versions of this little ring song give us the opportunity to say that the rhyme dates back to the days of the Great Plague. A rosy rash was a symptom of the plague, posies of herbs were carried as protection, sneezing was a final symptom and "all fall down" was exactly what happened.

If not angels . . .

Butterflies. Children pointing at flying things. Ashes. Ashes.

Read the Apollonaire one more time. Love me just once, just once more. He opens the book. As we fall.

Read me every word tonight.

She hears a bit of the Apollonaire and the century opens again and the world begins again. As they fall.

"You are in the garden of an inn on the outskirts of Prague
You feel completely happy a rose is on the table
And instead of writing your story in prose you watch
The rosebug which is sleeping in the heart of the rose."

C is for the cistern filled with tears. The columbine. The cat come back. Someone named her Carole at mid-century dreaming. Someone gave her a box of A's & B's & C's—a child's alphabet. Making something out of thin air with her beginner's set of letters and numbers and stars. Thank you in every possible language.

And it's almost morning but not quite—almost rose but not yet. And in the almost we fall.

In the beloved city of P where we wept, told stories, sang songs, feared death.

Falling not flying anymore.

Six kinds of dissonance resolve and he wakes up and he gets up and he puts on his perfectly pressed uniform with slash of red. The man who's lost count—no music—all the bodies piling up.

Light leaves a child's eye.

Starlings.

Guten tag. Hans, Horst, Frans. Had a bad night then Gerhardt?

No, not really. Exterminating, liquidating, laughing. Not really.

Morning. All the stars going out.

If you could make one wish.

It's an ordinary Sunday afternoon. The gingko trees. A walk in the park.

As we go down, down (but gently). Larkspur: a child's revery.

Pigeons on the grass, alas, Madame says.

Sophie guides the child's hand. What is this ache deep within for something I do not directly remember but which was mine?
If not an angel, then what?

A.

You have come a long way in the night to be by my side. Thank you in every possible way.

Diminishing shape. Fading stripe.

I want you never to die Ava Klein, the Madame whispers, as they touch earth.

The child draws the letter A.

I want you never to die.

Assisi, Italy
City of silence and birds
21 June 97

"We Will Speak and Bear Witness": Storytelling as Testimony and Healing in Ghost Dance

Louise DeSalvo

Virginia Woolf published her novel *To the Lighthouse,* containing that landmark complex portrait of a Victorian mother, Mrs. Ramsay, based upon her mother, Julia Stephen, on the thirty-second anniversary of her mother's death.[1] The primary emotional task Woolf faced in writing *Lighthouse* was, according to her testimony, ridding herself of her obsession with her mother. As she put it, "when it was written, I ceased to be obsessed by my mother. I no longer hear her voice; I do not see her."[2]

Just as Virginia Woolf's writing *To the Lighthouse* grew from her need to heal herself, so too does the narrator Vanessa Turin's celebratory and tortured portrait of her dead mother, Christine Wing, the gifted and disturbed poet in Carole Maso's *Ghost Dance,* emerge from a daughter's obsession with understanding her dead mother, from her need to care for herself in the wake of her mother's tragic and untimely death. Vanessa's most significant emotional work is to see her mother clearly, realistically—not as her mother wanted her to see her, but, rather, as she really was. Vanessa Turin's story, then, is told so that she can cease being a captive of her mother's vision, so that she can develop a view of her mother and of the world that is hers. This necessary work of separating from her mother is made especially difficult because her mother is dead.

Vanessa Wing's self-appointed task, then, is to understand the meaning of her mother's painful yet immensely creative and fulfilling life and the meaning of her early death. Her mother (like most mothers) is an enigma, a riddle Vanessa believes she is compelled to unravel if she is to thrive and flourish. Yet she knows her mother has given her few clues, little information, perhaps because Christine Wing does not see herself as someone her daughter needs to understand if she is to become an independent woman, for understanding requires interaction; instead, what Christine Wing requires of her daughter is that she be what her mother then needs—a playmate, a mute and undemanding inhabitant of the house they share, a helper, a child who makes no demands. In Christine Wing's cosmology the world and people are not things to understand but, rather, to marvel at or to be terrified by. The source of this lies in Christine Wing's childhood—a childhood about which Vanessa conjectures, for, as with everything else, her mother has given her only snippets of stories and parables to interpret. This is, perhaps, because Christine Wing's past is unavailable to her in memory.

Christine Wing believes that the reason people are what they are is part miracle, part mystery. The answer to her character, she tells her daughter, is to be found in legend, in story, and not in memory or in rational discourse. But because her mother so clearly often suffers from madness, Vanessa does not immediately understand which of her mother's stories can help her, which can harm her, for she cannot sort out what is truth, what parable, and what delusion. Vanessa does not immediately know that she cannot look to her mother for the causes of her suffering, for her mother does not herself know. Rather, she seems to accept her mother's explanation that she is a gifted poet, that she is mad, because she has been visited by the legendary Topaz Bird. Yet Vanessa's sense of stability initially depends upon her believing what her mother says no matter how absurd or unhelpful or harmful it may be. Better to have such a mother than to have no mother at all. But if Vanessa is to grow beyond the world of her mother and beyond her tortured life of drugs and abusive sex to a creative life, to a fulfilling sexual life (like the one her mother has had for years with her lover Sabine), She will have to manage the very difficult task of separating what can be useful to her in the example of her mother's life and what is potentially harmful, perhaps even lethal. And she must do this with very few guidelines from her mother, and she must do this alone.

Christine's only advice to her daughter is to face what you see, to trust yourself, "to live dangerously, to take risks."[3] The first two admonitions are impossible for Vanessa, for Christine has not helped her daughter to build the ego strength that will enable her to live in this way. Vanessa wants her own "point of view . . . a way to respond to the world that would be distinctly my own" (81), but because her mother occupies such a central position in her consciousness, this is difficult for her. The last two pieces of advice are dangerous, and these, unfortunately, Vanessa follows: she is heedless of her own well-being and continually places herself at physical and emotional risk, through her drug use and through her sexual relationships.

At the beginning of *Ghost Dance,* Vanessa imagines her mother standing under the great clock in Grand Central Station. In effect, *Ghost Dance* is a series of stories that Vanessa tells herself and the reader about her mother, some of which have occurred, some of which might have occurred, some of which Vanessa invents. In this narrative (which is repeated, with changes, elsewhere) Christine seems "calm, peaceful, at ease," and, to Vanessa, this can only mean that her mother is contemplating a poem she has been "struggling to finish for days," that she is "a little closer" (5) to the solution of the poem, which cannot be rushed or forced, which can only come in its own good time. Whatever Christine has been unable to give her daughter, we know, immediately from her fantasy, that she has taught Vanessa what doing creative work entails.

And as Vanessa imagines her mother thinking about her work, she also sees her witnessing her safe arrival at their meeting place. When Vanessa "step[s] safely, in her mind, from the taxi onto the street," Christine is "overwhelmed by an immense, inexplicable joy," and "quite suddenly the poem is complete" (5). In Vanessa's imagination her mother's knowledge of her own safety enables Christine to finish her poem. This is Vanessa's way of saying that her mother cares about her safety; it is also her way of insinuating herself into her mother's life as a poet, for her mother's creative life so often takes her away, both emotionally (in her preoccupation with her work) and physically (as she travels around the world to give readings). What Vanessa hopes is that she has something to do with her mother's talent. In fact, this is an enabling fantasy on Vanessa's part. For Vanessa cannot emotionally comprehend what is made obvious throughout the narrative: that her mother's work, her mother's madness, are the most compelling features of her life and that her mother is so self-involved that she could not realistically assess whether her daughter in fact was safe. Indeed, she is incapable of protecting her daughter, of preventing her daughter from being harmed. Theirs is what Vanessa aptly calls a "dark love" (11). Yet trying to understand it, Vanessa believes, is her only way to establish her own identity, to rewrite the sadness and hopelessness in her life.

When Christine arrives in Grand Central, though, we see how removed from reality is Vanessa's fantasy mother. For instead of the calm poet Vanessa imagines, Christine Wing is "in deep trouble" (7): she doesn't recognize her daughter; she is garishly made up, wearing rings on every finger, a cacophony of bracelets, and layers and layers of clothing, "her protection from the world" (7). Though Vanessa doesn't acknowledge that her mother's taking her for a stranger is painful, she indicates this when she describes how she imagines that the "sharp arms of the great clock" at Grand Central Station "slice into the back of her [mother's] neck" (7). Like her mother, Vanessa can communicate her anger only through the making of images. Her mother's madness enrages her, and in fantasy only, she exacts this gory retribution.

But Vanessa realizes that she must not comfort herself with images. Instead, she must put aside her fantasies of her mother; this time, she must try not to flinch at her mother's madness: she must "see her this time" (7). Vanessa's work is to *apprehend* her mother, to see her as she really is. Only then can she establish the emotional basis for a mature womanhood.

The most useful, the most dangerous thing Vanessa has learned from her mother is how to use the gift of her imagination, rather than a change in her behavior, to heal her wounds. Although in one sense this skill serves Vanessa well, in another sense it presents its own problems. It drives Vanessa deep into herself each time she encounters trouble, thereby causing a painful and lonely isolation. And it uses story, rather than substantive behavior changes, as a fundamental way of handling life's traumas.

The central image in *Ghost Dance*, used by Vanessa and Christine to explain both Christine's genius and her madness, is that of the Topaz Bird. Christine's family has used this self-created myth of the Topaz Bird as an explanatory principle to explain why some members of the family are creative (and crazy) and others aren't. This myth provides Christine with some comfort, for it enables her to understand the source of her power and pain. Still, in suggesting that it is the Topaz Bird and not Christine herself that is the source of her poetic gift, it robs her of the power she might have felt at seeing herself as the agent of her work, rather than as a medium through which the power of the Topaz Bird manifests itself. And it robs her daughter of an image of her mother as a creative woman, responsible for her art. This is the myth's most disastrous consequence: both mother and daughter believe that the creation of Christine's poems don't come through her effort, through her painstaking work. Rather, they come because of a visitation from the Topaz Bird, the "wild, brilliant Bird of Imagination," the "Bird of Great Invention," the "Bird of Genius" (16).

The Topaz Bird has been Vanessa's imaginary companion through childhood. After her mother's nightly storytelling ritual, just as she was falling off to sleep, Christine would remind Vanessa that she must never forget that the Topaz Bird "means us no harm" (10). Though meant as reassurance, this instead delineates the world as a quixotic place where harm and genius are visitations of the Topaz Bird; they are uncaused, unconnected to human acts, rationally inexplicable.

That this seductive yet captivating view of the world has its shortcomings is demonstrated by Christine Wing's death in a fiery automobile crash caused by the deliberate action of an automobile company to continue to manufacture a car they knew to be unsafe in certain situations. Vanessa's difficulty in coming to terms with her mother's death is, in part, the result of her mother's nightly mantra of the harmlessness of the Topaz Bird. Vanessa's lifelong challenge will be to understand that there are people who are harmful and that, in knowing this, rather than in believing her mother's infantile explanation of the world, one can begin to protect oneself, as one cannot when one is a disciple of Christine Wing's worldview.

How to live deliberately and responsibly in the world when you have been taught that there are unseen forces controlling sanity and creativity becomes the core of Vanessa's challenge in *Ghost Dance,* one that she does not altogether meet? As her anonymous lover (whose name she does not know, but whom she calls Jack) tells her (after telling her she is "one of the saddest people" he has ever seen): "what you don't know, is that you can change the ending" (33).

Her mother's poems, her stories, are no real solace for Vanessa when she needs solace most, though she pretends her mother satisfies her. In a story repeated throughout the novel, Vanessa indicates that Christine most often uses her imagination, not to help her daughter (as Vanessa tells herself), but, instead, to make herself the center of her daughter's consciousness.

One day, Vanessa hurts herself: she falls off her bicycle, shreds her knee, gets bits of the driveway's pavement embedded in the wound. When her mother comes ostensibly to help, instead of recognizing her daughter's pain and providing appropriate care, she tells Vanessa, "Your dress is magnificent." Vanessa then tells her mother, "*Your* dress is magnificent," and she consoles herself by telling herself that her mother is "inventing just for me" (52). The story becomes embellished; Vanessa is invited to forget her pain and enter the glittering, seductive invented world of her mother. So, Christine requires that Vanessa becomes her collaborator so that she can do what she does best—make up stories—rather than what the situation and Vanessa's needs require. But the story does not debride or disinfect the wound; it does not staunch the blood; it does not bandage the injury. Rather, as the blood flows down Vanessa's leg, her mother invites her to dance at the imaginary ball. It is no wonder, then, that Vanessa will be unable to recognize when she is hurt, to give her pain the attention that it deserves. There are limits to the curative potential of pretense.

But it is not only Christine who harms Vanessa. When Vanessa feels her father's impenetrable distance, his incapacity to answer one of her direct questions, she explains his behavior by enlisting a metaphor. He is a subaqueous creature who lives his life in the deep, in "tangled plants, in dim light," who must "travel a great distance to the surface" (19) for each encounter with his daughter. She responds to his unavailability by telling herself that she wants to rescue him. In her imagination she becomes a lifeguard: she saves him as he is drowning; she pushes "water from his lungs" (19). In her fantasies of both her mother and father, Vanessa is the caregiver. She tries to see her mother in "a safe place, where a small woman brushes your beautiful hair and sings you songs" (31).

In Vanessa's love affair with her mysterious lover, we see the damaging consequences of her upbringing, for this lover is as unreliable and unknowable and as unknown as her mother, as mysterious and as undependable as her father, and as toxic as both her parents. Vanessa does her best to turn their romance into something "mythic, far away" (18), unconnected to daily life. He is a phantom, a ghost-lover, a perfect, though dangerous, partner for her, for he is like her distant and distracted father and like her perpetually leave-taking mother.

It is no mystery why Vanessa chooses an abusive, anonymous lover, one who remains a mystery to her, a man without attachment to her, who comes and goes when he chooses. This is the lover that Vanessa's life in her parents' household has prepared her for. A lover who crushes her in his arms, who beats her until she is "covered with blood" (190).

Within this bizarre relationship, Vanessa acts out the murderous impulses that form the core of her parents' treatment of her. For they treat her as if she weren't there, as if she didn't exist. And so, as a young woman, she tries her best to please them: through drugs and brutal sex, she tries to eliminate herself. Once, she imagines her father walking—he has left the house to escape his children's questions—and she sees him picking up leaves, which remind him of children's hands: "he closes his own hand around them and crushes them" (29).

The truth of Vanessa's narrative, though she cannot understand this, is that neither her mother nor her father wants her or cares for her or considers her well-being important. Whenever her mother drags out her suitcases to go to her lover or to a poetry reading, Vanessa feels as if her breath was being taken away—the smell of them makes her feel as if she is suffocating. For though Christine Wing has her art and her lover Sabine and her family and her Topaz Bird, Vanessa does not feel as if she has a center to her life that will keep her stable in the absence of her mother.

Although she hopes for a caring mother, Vanessa provides herself with an abusive lover who beats her up, with a friend with whom she shoots heroin. Because she has been taught to concern herself with the wellness of her parents and because her parents have never concerned themselves with hers, she neither knows how to care for herself nor how to ask for comfort when she requires it. At the most distressing and pivotal points in her life, she is driven back into herself and her stories, and though these, in some sense, console her, still, they cannot altogether allay the pain that comes from a behavior that continually puts her at risk.

For Vanessa Turin is what Hope Edelman has called a "motherless daughter"[4]; she is an emotional orphan. Throughout her childhood, because of her mother's madness and her solipsism, Vanessa has put her mother's emotional needs first. It is Vanessa who is responsible for consoling her mother, for worrying about her whether she is appropriately dressed when the weather turns cold. And what Vanessa carries is the guilt that she wasn't a good-enough parent to her mother: "I would never be, as some children are capable of being, the grown-up my mother needed." It is not Christine who is at fault for requiring a parent in her daughter; it is Vanessa who is at fault for being such an inadequate caregiver.

Instead of being enraged at her mother's constant departures, Vanessa finds fault with herself for not helping her mother pack. Vanessa can't or won't understand that the heart of her tragedy is that her mother could never see her daughter as a person who required comfort and care; she knows that even when her mother looked at her, she "was not really seeing me" (41). In one of her most desperate moments, Vanessa whispers, "Help me, someone" (210), but there is no one who has ever helped her with her pain.

The imaginary mother whom Vanessa Turin conjures in *Ghost Dance* is a fantasy mother, a mother who is "*more* beautiful than Grace Kelly" (26), but she is the mother Vanessa never had. "In my house," Vanessa tells the reader, "she is always there, next to me" (17). In reality, Christine is rarely there. Yet rather than see her mother as a hopelessly troubled woman, who, because of her illness, couldn't meet the needs of her children, Vanessa idealizes and romanticizes her. It is too dangerous for Vanessa to see how unable her mother was to parent her; though she charges herself to see her mother clearly, there is little room in this portrait for her mother's failings. Vanessa reports, instead, how her mother has dedicated a book to her, *To Vanessa,* and how she has told her, "I have loved you my whole life. . . . Even when I was a little girl" (42). But Vanessa is unable to understand the absurdity of the last part of this remark and that ardent words and book dedications are no substitute for genuine, ongoing care. But if Vanessa were to admit her mother's inadequacy, her grief would be disabling, for Christine has tethered her daughter to her so tightly that Vanessa's existence depends upon keeping an idealistic representation of her mother foremost in her consciousness, for she has never been permitted to develop an independent self, a self beyond the family. She attends her mother's college; lives in her mother's dorm; she even sleeps with her mother's lover.

Vanessa uses her mother's madness and her poetic gift as an explanatory principle for the choices her mother has made. Mad or not, genius or not, these choices do not include her children's care: once, when Vanessa awakens from a nightmare and calls her mother and her mother doesn't come, Vanessa tells herself, "She must have been working" (52).

As a woman of supreme accomplishments, ones that Vanessa can't possibly match, Christine diminishes her daughter; she does not permit her to grow into a healthy young woman: "I would never be as good at inventing as my mother" (30), Vanessa tells us.

There are, Christine Wing believes, ghosts that haunt her house. And in a striking sequence, she joins with her children to find them. But she doesn't permit her children to be equal players in the game and though they welcome the opportunity to reach "the depths of our mother's heart," still, she is the "genius," they, "the servants," the "captives of her vision" (53).

Vanessa and her brother Fletcher unearth the story of Ted and Evonne Osbourne, and how they abuse and neglect their child (55). Though there is a question about whether the narrative is authentic, this is a story that parallels that of Fletcher and Vanessa and their parents' neglect (and, perhaps, abuse) of them. As Vanessa's parental grandmother remarks, "Children do not grow better by themselves" (81), and "Their own mother goes away for months and months at a time and [their father] ignores them. . . . It's not right" (89).

In an elusive scene Vanessa describes an enigmatic lover, a "musician [who] glides up the stairs to my bedroom in three-four time after everyone is asleep" (53). This can only be Vanessa's father, who is associated with music—he and Vanessa list the names of composers; he sits "in some dark room with the music on" (89); he is also a sleepwalker, who wanders the house at night. "His hands," Vanessa tells us, "rise and fall over my body; when he touches me, I make an exquisite sound" (53). Still, this is an act of love that obliterates her—"I know how I will disappear in the crescendo" (53). It is Vanessa's father, then, who haunts their house at night, who contributes to the "long, troubled life of our house" (56). And perhaps the "broken trust" (59) in the house, to which Vanessa refers, is her father's incestuous behavior. But the closest Vanessa comes to sensing that her musical lover is her father is her remark, "I am deeply disturbed by the longings of ghosts" (57).

Judith Lewis Herman's *Father-Daughter Incest* and *Trauma and*

Recovery[5] provide a useful context for understanding this elusive strand of meaning in *Ghost Dance.* Like other incest survivors' stories Vanessa's story is reported elliptically—it is simultaneously revealed and concealed—images are used to explore yet withhold information about what has happened; this form of reporting is more likely if the abuse occurs during sleep, as Vanessa suggests. And the entire structure of Vanessa's narrative represents how incest survivors report their stories—in fractured, repetitious sequences that double back over the material; that jumpcut from general discourse about violence to a seemingly unrelated event within the family (Vanessa describes the blood flowing down her leg from a bicycle fall; this is juxtaposed against the scene with the musician lover); by innuendo; by changing the content and meaning of the story to conceal or to reveal, to excuse or to blame, as compelling emotional needs dictate. Vanessa's story, too, reports feelings of profound and utter powerlessness, a world in which terror is pervasive, one in which happy endings seem impossible.[6] Like other survivors, Vanessa feels pity for her father and his shortcomings; he is presented as pathetic, helpless, and confused. Like other survivors, Vanessa longs for the aid of her virtually absent mother (Vanessa lacks "any internal representation of an adequate, satisfactory mother," and can only "imagine either the ideal mother" she wishes she had or "the neglectful mother" of her childhood[7]). (One could, perhaps, read Christine's madness as a response to what she knows happens in her household; her search for the ghosts that haunt the house can, in this context, be seen as her search for a way of explaining the trouble she knows exists there. "There's evil in there" [216], Christine says of her house.) Like other incest survivors, Vanessa reports feeling dominated and overwhelmed; in young adulthood, she finds a man who abuses her, and she gives him the power to dominate her completely. Like others, she fears losing her very identity and she is a drug addict. Like many survivors, she idealizes her parents. Like many others, she does not really know what has happened to her. Sexual abuse in childhood has tainted the quality of her life, has caused her overwhelming sorrow, mental anguish, self-destructive and self-abusive behavior, feelings of emptiness and detachment. But, like other survivors, Vanessa doesn't connect her bad feelings with childhood abuse.

The self-destructiveness of which Vanessa is capable is cued in one year's preparations for Christmas. Vanessa, unable to join in the good cheer of the holiday, knowing that her mother will soon leave, mangles her flesh as she helps prepare food: "my fingers caught in the sharp grids of the metal grater, my flesh becoming more and more mangled and bloodied. . . . What was I trying to feel?

Whom was I punishing?" (234). Vanessa takes her anger out on herself, yet, in fantasy, her fury unleashes an all-consuming fire of devastation. "I destroy everything," she says. "It all turns to ash as I watch, and I know I am responsible for this" (237). Among the objects Vanessa burns is her father's piano.

Christine Wing understands that her "children are not safe" (214) in her home. Once, she calls the Department of the Interior in Washington to tell them so. She shepherds her children to the middle of a bed, grabs a ball of string, and circles it "again and again until we were completely fenced in" (215). Christine's gesture passes for madness, but it is telling. For Christine is trying to fence off the bed, trying to prevent anyone from reaching them there. This reveals the child's bed to be the most dangerous place in this house. Yet Christine is unable to ensure that her daughter, especially, will not be harmed.

There are indeed many, many harmful forces in the outside world that are examined in *Ghost Dance:* "DES, asbestos, Agent Orange; Lilly, Johns-Manville, Dow Chemical" (209), and, of course, the Ford Motor Company, builder of the Pinto, the car in which Christine Wing meets her early and fiery death.[8] Still, Christine Wing's crazy call to the Department of the Interior shows that she knows that harm comes to her children primarily from the interior of her home. Yet she remains unable to confront her husband, perhaps because she only senses, but does not know, he is to blame.

Vanessa's incestuous history is not singular; rather, it is one that she shares with her mother; it is a pattern of their family's history. In recounting the story of her mother's life, Vanessa reports that Christine, too, was an unprotected, uncared for daughter, a motherless daughter—her mother died, after a long illness, before her daughter's adolescence. Like many other motherless daughters, Christine tried to quell her pain by becoming a wild teenager. She learned, too, that she could "Escape it with words; change it with words" (114), and that she could reclaim her mother through her writing.

But in trying to understand the cause of her mother's sadness, a "sadness with no explanation, your life of solitude, your retreats" (183), Vanessa invents a story, based upon a picture of her mother as an adolescent, wearing dark, horn-rimmed glasses, in which Christine's father asks her why she's covering up her beautiful eyes, and she responds, "to keep men away . . . men like your friends, men like you" (184). To Vanessa, the cause of her mother's sadness is that she has become the target of her father's and his friends' unwanted attentions. This is the only truly plausible explanation that Vanessa gives for the fact of her mother's madness; but it is an explanation that Vanessa discovers after her mother's death, and it is an explanation that makes no mention of the Topaz Bird. It indicates, too, that Vanessa understands the link between all-too-attentive fathers and depression, madness, and self-abuse in daughters.

Christine's gift as a poet is connected, not to visitations of the Topaz Bird, but to the abuse she has suffered as a child. Her art, then, is testimony, a way for her to tell her story and to transform her pain into something beautiful, something enduring. Vanessa's drive to tell her and her mother's story, too, proceeds from the same cause.[9]

Early in the novel, Vanessa tells us, "When I eventually learned of Virginia Woolf's death by water, I began to fear for my mother" (83). Vanessa believes that her mother, like Woolf, might end her life by drowning. But Virginia Woolf was an incest survivor; she was sexually abused by her half-brothers, Gerald and George Duckworth, from when she was six years old through her early twenties (Gerald, she remembers abusing her as a child; George, she remembers abusing her as a young woman). And her suicide—by walking into the River Ouse in 1941 with rocks in her pockets to weigh her body down—can surely be connected with her having been an incest survivor.[10]

I believe that Carole Maso's reference to Woolf indicates that we can read Christine Wing's life against the experience of Virginia Woolf's and the specter of incest that haunts both narratives. Nor is it coincidental that Maso has chosen the name Vanessa—Virginia Woolf's sister's name—as the name for her storytelling, surviving heroine, for Virginia's sister Vanessa, too, was, an incest survivor, and, though her lifelong battle with depression is clearly rooted in that early experience, unlike her sister, she did not kill herself. Both Vanessa and Christine, then, as incest survivors, are the emotional counterparts of Virginia Woolf and her sister Vanessa.

At the end of the novel, in an immensely complex scene, Vanessa has sex with her lover Jack, or imagines she is having sex with him. She perceives it as a violent, cannibalistic rape, and her description of it echoes the description of her mother's death. Like her mother's death, it occurs in the snow; like her mother's death, it is described as a violent impact: "I screamed and screamed, feeling some excruciating force enter me again and again in the snow. I was being slammed over and over. . . . 'Live,' he said, 'or die!' " (266-67).

Ultimately, though, the novel ends not with catastrophe but with the importance of bearing witness to catastrophe. This ability to speak about what has harmed her permits Vanessa to separate herself from her mother, to begin healing. "We will speak and bear witness," Vanessa says. "We will never stop speaking" (267).

In the closing words of the novel, in imagination, Vanessa lifts herself from her mother's body with which she has formerly been merged. The pain of doing this, Vanessa admits, has been "terrible" (267).

NOTES

[1]Mark Hussey, *Virginia Woolf A to Z* (New York: Facts on File, 1995), 301.

[2]Virginia Woolf, *Moments of Being* (New York: Harcourt Brace Jovanovich, 1985), 81.

[3]Carole Maso, *Ghost Dance* (Hopewell: Ecco, 1995), 82; hereafter cited parenthetically.

[4]Hope Edelman, *Motherless Daughters* (New York: Dell, 1994). Edelman's work illuminates Vanessa Turin's emotional conflict as the daughter of a mother who ignores her.

[5]Judith Lewis Herman, *Father-Daughter Incest* (Cambridge: Harvard Univ. Press, 1981); *Trauma and Recovery* (New York: Basic, 1992).

[6]Louise DeSalvo, *Virginia Woolf: The Impact of Childhood Sexual Abuse on Her Life and Work* (New York: Ballantine, 1989), xii, 12.

[7]Herman, *Father-Daughter Incest* 88, 107; DeSalvo 9.

[8]Of the scores of articles on the landmark Ford Pinto legal case, see especially Larry Kramer, "Fire Hazard Seen in 2 Million Pintos" (which reported thirty-eight fires, with twenty-seven fatalities, resulting from Pinto rear-end collisions), the *Washington Post,* 9 May 1978, D9; Larry Kramer, "Jury Indicts Ford in Indiana Pinto Crash" (describing how the Ford Motor Company was charged with three counts of reckless homicide in connection with the fiery death of three women riding in a Ford Pinto that exploded when it was rear-ended on a road in Elkart County, Indiana), the *Washington Post,* 14 September 1978, C1; Larry Kramer, "Ford to Turn Over Pinto Papers" (describing how Ford Motor Company executives knew of the Pinto's gastank design flaw, which made them particularly susceptible to fires from fuel leaks in crashes, yet decided to go ahead with their production) the *Washington Post,* 26 December 1979, D8. I would like to thank Julia Raynor, who provided me with these details about the Ford Pinto court cases.

[9]See Arnold M. Ludwig, *The Price of Greatness: Resolving the Creativity and Madness Controversy* (New York: Guilford, 1995). See also, "Madness and Creativity Revisited," *Science,* 2 December 1994, 1483, describing Ludwig's study, reported in the November 1994 issue of the *American Journal of Psychiatry,* comparing fifty-nine women writers with a group of nonwriters, matched "on social, demographic, and family variables"; Ludwig reported that "twice as many writers as nonwriters had some form of mental disorder" and that the pattern differed from that found in males; in women writers, he discovered that "many of the writers had histories of physical or sexual abuse."

[10]See DeSalvo 99-133. An early account of Virginia Woolf's incestuous experience was provided in Quentin Bell, *Virginia Woolf* (New York:

Harcourt Brace Jovanovich, 1972), though Bell wrote that he believed Woolf's response to her experience indicated that she was neurotic. Woolf's own account first appeared posthumously in *Moments of Being*.

The Dead Fathers: The Rejection of Modernist Distance in The Art Lover

Charles B. Harris

"The emotion of art is impersonal."
—T.S. Eliot, "Tradition and the Individual Talent"

"I do not believe in any of the fathers."
—Candace, *The Art Lover*

Giotto's *Noli Me Tangere* ("Don't touch me") is one of twenty-two paintings from which Carole Maso selected details for graphic reproduction within the text of her 1990 novel *The Art Lover*. That Maso also chose a detail from this particular painting as the jacket illustration for the original North Point Press edition of her novel suggests that Giotto's fresco may contain clues to Maso's thematic and aesthetic intentions. Perhaps to assist the reader in deciphering these clues, early in her text Maso interposes a portion of a page containing art historian James H. Stubblebine's interpretation of the fresco:[1]

> Christ, in his first appearance after resurrection, meets the Magdalen, who reaches out to touch Him. Kneeling and stretching out her arms toward Christ, her entire figure conveys a sense of almost unbearable yearning and emotion. . . . The very idea that she cannot, must not, touch Him is used by Giotto to suggest the idea of not only the transcendent nature of Christ but the very human tragedy of two people at a fateful and final moment, separated by an enormous gulf although they are close enough to touch. (27)

Details from the fresco recur four times in Maso's novel, and the nature of each detail as well as the order of its placement in the novel bear significance. In the initial detail (17), the figures of both Jesus and the Magdalen are displayed, the latter reaching out beseechingly to the transfigured Christ, whose hand extends backward to the kneeling woman as though pushing her away: "Don't touch me." In the second detail (24), which was reproduced as the novel's jacket illustration, we again see the poignantly outstretched figure of Mary Magdalen, but Jesus appears to have walked almost entirely out of the picture, with only his averting hand still visible in the frame. The third detail from the fresco (49) seems to reverse the relationship of the second detail, with the entire right flank and arm of Jesus, but only the Magdalen's hands, visible. Whereas the second detail evokes the Magdalen's sense of forlornness, the third accents the untouchable father, who appears to be warding off the woman's imploring hands, which seem to clutch at Jesus's robe. The fourth and final detail from Giotto's fresco appears almost 200 pages later, near the novel's conclusion. Jesus is displayed from the waist up, his left hand hoisting a victorious flag that had not been visible in any of the other details. Although this detail occurs in a cluster of graphics referred to as "the hieroglyphs of hope" (238), at this point in the novel the portrait of the triumphantly transfigured Christ, for reasons I hope to make clear, cannot be viewed without irony. Suffice it to say for now that the woman, Mary Magdalen, is totally absent from the picture.

As represented in four different details and viewed through the lens of Stubblebine's analysis, Giotto's fresco resonates at various levels throughout the novel. In a most obvious sense, the feelings attributed to the painting by Stubblebine recall the "almost unbearable yearning and emotion" Maso must have experienced as she awaited the "fateful and final moment" in the life of her friend Gary Falk, whose death from AIDS is described in the novel's harrowing—and remarkably transgressive—fifth section. In a less obvious sense, Giotto's painting also intimates what may be the novel's most significant motif: the abandonment of women by men. Max's sudden aneurysm, Christ's crucifixion, the untimely deaths of Steven and, of course, Gary Falk, Henry's desertion of his wife and daughters, even Joseph's defection from the holy family contribute to the novel's dominant mood of loss, a mood further reinforced by the accumulation of imagined and, given Maso's use of graphics, actual sensory impressions—lost pet posters, a passage from Roethke's "The Lost Son," lists of things missing, a stolen piano—that, taken together, constitute a formula for the *particular* emotion of forlornness.[2]

At its most subtle level, however, Giotto's fresco, especially the fourth detail, implies a more fundamental betrayal, of which the novel's various desertions and losses may be seen as refractions: art's betrayal of its lovers. More precisely, not art per se but art as defined by modernist criticism—which, Alan Wilde suggests, achieved such hegemonic proportions that modernist art became "virtually inextricable from the shape modernist criticism has impressed upon it" (20)—seems either to forsake the novel's art lovers, most of whom—Caroline, Candace, Maggie, Maso herself—are women, or, as in the case of the tragic Veronica, renders them its victims. This modernist view of art, with its false assurances of orderliness and transcendence, must itself be forsaken, the novel's final two sections make clear, before these lovers can get on with their lives.

In the modernist view, art's consolations exist in direct proportion to the artist's success in transmuting emotion into objective form. The impersonal theory of art resonates widely through modernist criticism and art, but its most influential formulation probably occurs in Eliot's 1917 essay "Tradition and the Individual Talent." "Poetry," Eliot writes in a famous passage, "is not a turning loose of emotion, but an escape from emotion; it is not the expression of personality, but an escape from personality" (58). Poets, Eliot is quick to proclaim, possess emotions and personality; indeed, he implies, they may suffer more deeply than most: "only those who have personality and emotions know what it means to want to escape from those things" (58). But it is poetry's singular function to *distance* these emotions, containing chaotic experience in the analgesic symmetries of art. The "more perfect the artist," Eliot maintains, "the more completely separate in him will be the man who suffers and the mind which creates; the more perfectly will the mind digest and transmute the passions which are its materials" (54). Artists unable to objectify their emotions, Eliot argues, must inevitably fail, as Shakespeare failed in writing *Hamlet*. In adducing "the grounds of *Hamlet*'s failure" (99) in his 1919 essay "Hamlet and His Problems," Eliot formulates the idea of the objective correlative, to which I earlier alluded. In Eliot's reading, Hamlet's realization that his mother is not "an adequate equivalent" (101) for his sense of disgust figures Shakespeare's own inability to find an external equivalent for the emotion he struggles unsuccessfully to express in *Hamlet*. That emotion, Eliot concludes, must have been "inexpressibly horrible" (102). And the consequence of an unobjectified emotion is that "it remains to poison life and obstruct action" (101).

Perhaps it is what we've learned in recent years about the powerful feelings impelling Eliot's creation of *The Waste Land* that allows us to perceive beneath the self-possessed cadences of his essay on *Hamlet* a profound fear of the engulfing complexities of modern experience or to read that fear into the familiar variations on the modernist themes of impersonality, aesthetic distance, and transcendence: the intentional and affective fallacies of modernist criticism, Yeats's timeless Byzantium, that frozen leopard on Kilimanjaro's summit, Faulkner's obsession with the lovers eternally transfixed on Keats's urn, Woolf's "moments of being," the Joycean epiphany. These images reflect the second of two primary models of modernism described by Alan Wilde. The first model, which Wilde associates with Cleanth Brooks, celebrates the poem's unique ability to recover for modern consciousness an organic unity inherent in the very nature of things. Practitioners of the second, far more characteristic model of modernism, however, express what they perceive to be an irreconcilable disjunction between the artist's rage for order and an irredeemably chaotic experience. In the second model, Wilde writes, "the writer stands not only above but, as it were, against experience, his poem or novel indicating not a mastery of the world but a defensive maneuver prompted by it, a tacit admission of failure to come to terms with its complexity" (25). Faced with "a world threatening incoherence," modernists of the second mode "first stabilized and then distanced" that world in their artistic constructions (40). Detachment and objectivity thus become "signs . . . of a failure to engage the world: a standing apart from experience" (26). The modernist legacy, Wilde concludes, is a "series of self-sustaining or organic constructs distantly proclaiming their inherent superiority to the messiness of life" (19).

Don't touch me.

In *The Art Lover* the character most clearly embodying the modernist view of art is Max Chrysler, Caroline's art historian father. "You tried to teach us something about art," Caroline tells Max in one of her imaginary conversations with her dead father, "its consoling nature, its transcendent nature, its ability to help distance" (185). For Max, modernism is more than an aesthetic; it's a personal ethos. Gourmet, connoisseur of art and film, music and poetry, the epicurean Max attempts to gather his family into something like Yeats's artifice of eternity. "We both agreed," he says of his and Veronica's three children, "*they shall not live unlovely lives*. There is so much that is crass, brutish, ugly. We shall show them what pleasure is. What beauty is" (47, Maso's italics). Like the true modernist he is, Max distances himself from the messiness of experience. "Why were they always invisible to you?" (36), Caroline asks her late father of his attitude toward the homeless; "why didn't you ever mention that everywhere around you young men were dying?" (165), she asks him of the AIDS crisis.

Unfortunately, Max's tendency to aestheticize experience extends to those closest to him. In one of the novel's key scenes, Caroline reflects on the art books in her dead father's library while listening, significantly, to Liszt's *Transcendental Etudes*. She realizes that the "cool, soothing appraisals of painting, sculpture, architecture" found in those books reveal something of the nature of Max's love for his wife and children: "It was a way to love too. It was the way, I see now, you loved us, a bit removed—but it was love nonetheless" (45). While Caroline gives her father the benefit of the doubt, Max's affection for his children is clearly evasive, self-protective, in the same sense that Eliot's escape from emotion is best understood as a fear of emotion. "What were you afraid of," Caroline demands of her distant and distancing father; "Did you think I'd betray you too, Max?" (190).

Although Caroline tries hard to remain nonjudgmental and though she clearly continues to love and admire her late father, she comes to understand that Max's aestheticizing coolness is "a little monstrous" (9), especially as it influenced his relationship with Veronica, his depressive, suicidal wife. "With you," Caroline says in one of her apostrophes to her dead father, ". . . everything had its aesthetic raison d'être, even Mother—her illness, her beauty. She fit somehow perfectly into your world view, your particular brand of romanticism, your nihilism, your cynicism" (126). Indeed, Maso's description of Veronica's deterioration suggests the chaotic experience from which modernist artists retreated into the containment of their impersonal art: "She was losing detail. . . . [D]isappearing into chaos, dissolving, losing all life" (87). In ironic counterpoint to Max's penchant for art's "transcendent nature" (185), Veronica's fatal depression weighs her body downward, in one metaphorically rich scene seeming actually to transubstantiate into stone too heavy for Max to lift. Finding it "too frightening to go to the place she was" (45), Max recoils into the only order he knows, the palliative coherence of art, keeping "at a distance" the disordered world personified in his ill wife by attempting to "paint her back into a body, lengthen her thick dark hair and climb it, *use it as a rope ladder out of here*" (185, italics mine). In modernist fashion Max aspires to "an iconic poetic of transcendence," which, William V. Spanos argues, requires a withdrawal from "existential time" in pursuit of an "aesthetics of *stasis,*" an art "the iconic—and autotelic—nature of which *arrests* the mind—neutralizes the anguish, the schism in the spirit—and raises it above . . . the realm of radical motion, of contingency, of historicity" (158, 160, italics Spanos's). Veronica, who "holds still" for thirty years and then commits suicide (190), ironically embodies the stasis to which Max and modernism aspire, suggesting the covert truth of impersonal, iconic art: its "impulse to transcend the historicity of the human condition" (Spanos 111) is, finally, life-denying.

Of course, Max is already dead when the novel begins, and though Caroline's memories of and imaginary conversations with Max comprise a major portion of Maso's narrative, the real purpose of Caroline's ruminations is not to achieve a better understanding of her dead father so much as of herself. "[F]or better or for worse,"

Caroline realizes, "I am my father's daughter" (113). Like Max, Caroline fears life's contingencies. A decade after her brilliantly successful first novel, she still has not written a second work because "Novels seemed just a little too dangerous" (27). Also like Max, Caroline attempts to evade life's hazards by retreating into a modernist conception of art, symbolized in the novel by the Cummington Community of the Arts, where, Caroline says matter of factly, "we turn everything into art" (70). Evoking the modernist aesthetics of stasis, Cummington provides the required distance from reality modernist criticism demands: "Plastic covers the windows. . . . It's supposed to keep us safe and warm. The outside, seen through plastic, seems a long way off, unreal" (170). Although Caroline is able to keep death "At arm's length" for "an entire year" (41), Max's demise obliges her to leave Cummington and return to Manhattan, which, Caroline discovers, has deteriorated into an Eliotic "unreal city" of homelessness and dying, the twin scourges of the Reagan eighties.[3] The shock of "So much death" (89) convinces Caroline to begin writing again as a way of "nearing the truth" (15). Until the last section of *The Art Lover*, however—when, as shall be seen, Caroline, like Maso herself, discards the modernist aesthetic—Caroline's novel-in-progress, segments of which are interspersed throughout Maso's narrative, evinces the same evasive desire to master aesthetically the radical contingencies of modern experience that characterizes the view of art she learned from her father.

Maso has said that "the fictive family Caroline writes about" was actually the novel Maso herself had intended to write before Gary Falk contracted AIDS (Cooley 35). At that point, Maso began to write Caroline's story, assigning her original novel to Caroline as a novel-within-a-novel-*within*-a-novel, the outermost frame, of course, being Maso's starkly nonfictional account of her relationship with Gary Falk during his last days, which became the penultimate section of *The Art Lover*. What we have, then, is Carole Maso trying to come to terms with the fatal illness of her best friend by writing a novel about a writer trying to come to terms with the death of her father and, eventually, the fatal illness of *her* best friend by writing a novel about a mother and two daughters trying to adjust to the absence of the husband/father who has deserted them. Until the subversive fifth section of Maso's novel, both Maso's story of Caroline and Caroline's novel-within-the-novel observe the conventions of what Wellek and Warren term subjective literature. In *Theory of Literature*, for over thirty years the Bible of modernist approaches to literature, Wellek and Warren argue that the difference between the "objective poet," who stresses "the obliteration of his [*sic*] concrete personality" (77), and the "subjective poet," who writes autobiographically, is not great.

> Even when a work of art contains elements which can be surely identified as biographical, these elements will be so rearranged and transformed in a work that they lose all their specifically personal meaning and become simply concrete human material, integral elements of a work. . . . The whole view that art is self-expression pure and simple, the transcript of personal feelings and experiences, is demonstrably false. . . . A work of art may rather embody the "dream" of an author than his actual life, or it may be the "mask," the "anti-self," behind which his real person is hiding, or it may be a picture of the life from which the author wants to escape. (78)

That Caroline begins her novel as a defensive maneuver, a modernist deflection of "the life from which the author wants to escape," is suggested in the first few pages of *The Art Lover* (which opens, interestingly enough, not with Maso's story of Caroline but with the first two numbered chapters of Caroline's novel-in-progress). In a series of statements implicitly comparing her initial motives for writing the novel to Max's reasons for painting portraits of Veronica, Caroline evokes the modernist characteristics of distance, impersonality, and order: "Writing too can keep the world at a distance. One uses 'one' instead of 'I.' . . . One turns flesh . . . into words on a page. . . . The temptation is to make it beautiful or perfect or have it make sense. The temptation is to control things, to make something to help ease the difficulty" (16). This longing to stabilize the flux of experience threatening her equanimity informs one of Caroline's earliest descriptions of her fictional family, who, picnicking in a meadow, are portrayed from "some distance" (7). At this point, Caroline writes, the family is "still just a lovely picture, a word picture" (8), suggesting her desire to achieve the static transcendence of the verbal icon. The "figures appear static," Caroline explains, because that is her "wish for them: that they stay together, that the light remain" (8).

Of course the central conflict of Caroline's novel arises from the fact that the family doesn't stay together. To gain distance from a seemingly disintegrating world, Caroline transfers the threatening emotions associated with that world to her characters. Thus Henry, the untouchable father, is clearly a "mask" for Max, although instead of dying he deserts his family for another woman. His motive for withdrawal, like modernist Max's, seems to be a fear of existential time. "He's become a cliché," scoffs Candance. "Another middle-aged man who is afraid to die" (56). Also like Max, Henry, a composer of music, aestheticizes experience, containing his most deeply felt emotions in formal strategies. Rather than telling Maggie that his mother is dying, for example, Henry writes the news in a note which he places on Maggie's pillow, even though he's standing in the room while she reads the note. Writing, Maggie understands, is Henry's "way of coping with the most intense of experiences. Ordering them," making "them seem more real" (226). For Henry, then, as with Eliot, the unobjectified emotion seems terrifying in its insubstantiality. As a "mask" for Caroline, Maggie has also learned well the lessons of modernist criticism. In a telling recapitulation of Caroline's iconic description of the picnicking family, Maggie, viewing her family from a distance, quickly arranges them into a tableau, using her youngest daughter Alison, as Stevens used the jar in Tennessee and Williams the red wheelbarrow, as the "unifying element" in her visual frame. "To watch these shifting forms fall into order and balance—there is no greater joy than this," she thinks, relying on her aesthetic "vision" to "steady the chaos . . . stabilize the scene" (18). Preferring ordered art to vicissitudinous life, Maggie tries to adjust to her husband's desertion by wandering "from one painter to the next searching for solace" (61).

By my count, Maso distributes a total of thirty-five separate "excerpts" from Caroline's novel throughout *The Art Lover*, the majority of these segments falling into the first three titled sections of Maso's novel. Until the final section—"Spring 1986"—Caroline's characters, especially Maggie, continue to seek aesthetic control of a world grown frightening in its disconnectedness and fragmentation. Their behavior, once again, reflects Caroline's own desperate need to aestheticize experience. Her compulsion to impose form on chaos by arranging things in lists and categories, for example, is bestowed as a character trait on both Maggie and Alison, who label trees, make lists of poisonous plants, and invent "an elaborate coding system with colors" (95) to file the labels. Only Candace, the elder daughter, seems immediately able to throw off the conceptual blinders of modernist aesthetic postulates. For this reason, she becomes a key character, representing not only the subject position Caroline eventually comes to occupy (the first letter of Candace's name associates her metonymically with her creator, Caroline, and with Caroline's creator, Carole Maso) but the link between the emotionally and literally absent fathers of Maso's novel and the androcentric nature of the impersonal view of art.

From the moment her father abandons the family, Candace's dominant emotion is rage. Indeed, one of her functions is to allow Caroline to manipulate the conventions of "subjective" narrative in order to displace her deep-seated and unarticulated anger at Max's emotional aridity.[4] In one of the novel's few humorous scenes, for example, Candace provides an extensive and unflattering description of her father's mistress in a telephone conversation with Alison. Not only the name of Henry's mistress but her unattractive personal attributes correspond to Max's last mistress (throughout the description, Caroline imagines Max interrupting to protest her characterization of Biddy). But if the immediate target of Candace's anger is her absent father, that rage eventually extends to a patriarchal culture whose objectifying representations, Candace comes to realize, have disempowered women. In a memorable scene Candace first writes, "I do not believe we are powerless" in her notebook, then scrawls "I do not believe in the limitations of art" on the wall in bright red lipstick. Opening the window overlooking Eleventh Street, the address of both Max's and Henry's New York apartments, Candace screams imprecations at the patriarchy.

> "I do not believe in Ronald Reagan," she shouts. " I do not believe in Ed Koch!"
>
> "Neither do I!" someone shouts back.
>
> "I do not believe in Sigmund Freud. I am not smiling when I say this.
>
> "*I do not believe in any of the fathers*. I do not believe in Science or Medicine. I do not believe in NASA. I do not believe in God. I do not accept that it is a man's world." (160, italics mine)

That Maso intends to link Candace's protest to an aesthetic—or, more appropriately, a counteraesthetic—that opposes the modernist view of art espoused by Candace's parents is suggested not only by Candace's explicit rejection of art's limitations at the onset of her outburst but by the juxtaposition of two visual images associated with feminist art that immediately follow this scene. The facing page (161) displays photographs of a pair of Guerrilla Girls posters denouncing sexism and racism in the contemporary art world. The Guerrilla Girls, as Ali informs Maggie, are a "group of women artists" who present themselves as " 'the conscience of the art world' " (221). Working collectively and anonymously (they wear gorilla masks), the Guerrilla Girls use posters, billboards, and other protest actions to call attention to the andro/eurocentric nature of the art establishment and to the women and artists of color whose work is underrepresented in New York City galleries and museums. The second visual image, displayed on the page immediately following the Guerilla Girls posters, is a print by Barbara Kruger. Employing postmodernist tactics in the interest of feminist politics, Kruger's print reveals the hunched silhouette of a woman, who is quite literally pinned down, over which a superimposed caption reads, "We have received orders not to move" (162). The print sets off a concatenation of associations, linking the caption with Veronica, who held still for thirty years and then died; the pins fastening the woman in

Kruger's picture to the mat, as it were, with Veronica's immobilizing depression; and the objectifying male gaze and the concomitant representations of women's bodies that, Kruger implies, keep the impaled woman in her picture securely in place, with Max, who adjudges his wife a "wonderful model" because she "never moved" (14).

That Candace eventually comes to embrace the counteraesthetic implied by the posters and Kruger's print becomes explicit near the novel's conclusion when we learn that she has decided to become a painter and to join the Guerrilla Girls. Something of the nature of this counteraesthetic had been predicted in Candace's earlier denunciation of her mother's love of Poussin, in whose "balance and grace . . . proportion, harmony" (61) Maggie sought solace: "Fuck Poussin, Mother. Your husband left you for a twenty-nine-year-old. Let's show a little emotion. Stop looking for the perfect order, reason, symmetry. There's no such thing" (96). Candace's tirade contains an implicit critique of the modernist/androcentric view of art, whose valorization of the depersonalized art object, Candace strongly suggests, is based in an objectivist illusion. Just as Candace's desire to join the Guerrilla Girls implies a feminist aesthetics of engagement that merges the political and the personal, her insistence that Maggie "show a little emotion" implies a preference for experience unmediated by modernist aesthetic conventions.

Because she is a mask for Caroline, Candace's aesthetic conversion reflects Caroline's own changing views regarding modernist definitions of art. This change emerges slowly. Although she is able "to find a manageable shape" for Max's death (117), the emotions evoked by Steven's catastrophic illness exceed Caroline's ability to order them artistically. Her first reaction to this impasse—poignantly expressed in the brief stanzaic segment entitled "Chaos," which refers, respectively, to Max's death, Steven's illness, and Veronica's suicide—is to blame art itself:

Despite my penchant for order. This is the world. We name it.
And what good does it do? We arrange it on a page.
    You were here and now you're gone.
    You were well and now you're sick.
    You were a painting by Matisse, but you took sleeping pills. (138)

"[F]rightened of the things there were still no names for" (174-75)—"the inexpressibly horrible," to recall Eliot's diagnosis of *Hamlet*'s purported fatal flaw—Caroline virtually stops writing. "Now and then," she tells herself after a visit to her dying friend in the hospital, "you still think of Maggie and Alison, of Candace and Henry" (150). But "Winter," the long fourth section in which Steven's steady decline is detailed, contains only four brief fragments from Caroline's novel-in-progress, by far the fewest number to appear in any of the novel's major sections, with the obvious exception of the nonfictional fifth section.

Caroline, of course, is a mask for Maso, whose faith in the power of literature was also challenged by Gary Falk's illness. "All the way through writing this book," she told an interviewer, "I thought that, quite possibly, I'm not going to be able to believe in writing enough anymore to be able to do it" (Hackett 66). Working on *The Art Lover* in the mornings and visiting Falk in the hospital in the afternoons, Maso was suddenly seized by an overwhelming sense of futility. "I thought, this is so absurd, you are such a fool if you think you can create and control all these things. . . . I just . . . felt like I don't have any language for this so I'm not going to write" (Cooley 36). Maso stopped writing for an entire year.

Caroline—like Maso, one presumes—returns to her novel when she realizes that what has failed is not art itself but the unrealistic expectations imposed on art by modernist definitions. Unable to find an external equivalent for her emotions that will allow her to express them objectively, Caroline eventually questions the efficacy of impersonal art and its requisite transmutation of emotion. Indeed, like her character Candace, Caroline comes to associate the modernist aesthetic with deception. "I am tired of things that . . . become anything other than themselves. . . . I am tired of any deception. The cells of my brain that bring you back, Max. I am sick of myself trying to give shape to all this sorrow, all this rage, all this loss—and failing" (148). Caroline's breakthrough moment occurs when, rejecting the modernist principle of distance, she refuses to transmute her dying friend into an art object: "I flesh him out. *I will not turn him into paint and canvas, where he'll be manageable*. He won't allow it" (142, italics added). Unlike the modernist epiphany, however, with its religious overtones of clarity and transcendence, Caroline's realization returns her to the contingency and messiness of the existential world, whose "unbreakable code" refuses "to give up its logic" (216).[5]

Caroline's aesthetic conversion, like her character Candace's and her creator Maso's, implies two major separate but overlapping critiques of modernism that figure prominently in the construction of *The Art Lover*: postmodernism and feminism. Whereas modernism, as discussed, recoils from the messiness of experience into the putatively transcendent harmonies of formal art, *postmodernism*, as Wilde points out, accepts "the impossibility of making any sense whatever of the world as a whole" (44), not only tolerating but in some cases celebrating incoherence, randomness, uncertainty—in a word, the irreducible disorderliness and messiness of human experience. Building into its formal structures the ontological certainty of uncertainty, postmodernist art problematizes and deconstructs universalizing ideologies rather than endorsing any single political position. Feminism, on the other hand, associates the universalizing tendencies of humanist ideologies with androcentricism, thereby wearing its politics on its sleeve. Its goal, according to Linda Hutcheon, is "to effect a real transformation of art that can only come with a transformation of patriarchal social practices" (168). An important element of this transformation involves the privileging and the politicizing of the personal. If postmodernist critics and artists attempt to dispel objectivist definitions of art out of a general suspicion of forms that present themselves as coherent, organic, and complete, feminist critics and artists reject such definitions because women have themselves suffered a history of objectification.

Caroline's refusal to turn Steven into an art object must be seen, then, not only as a rejection of the impersonal theory of art but as an implied critique of the patriarchal underpinnings of that theory. This refusal enables her to begin writing again, excerpts from Caroline's novel comprising over a third of the titled segments in the sixth and final section of *The Art Lover*. In this section, moreover, the effects of Caroline's transformation are passed on to her characters. Candace, as has been seen, embraces feminist art and resolves to join the Guerrilla Girls. But Maggie also rejects the androcentricity that has generally passed as the universal, plunging back into the messy materialism of a postmodernist world. "It's all so wonderful," she exclaims, in an exaltation heretofore reserved only for art. "The world. All this dirt everywhere. And cow shit. My God" (220). Significantly, Maggie's effusive embrace of the untidy world is followed almost immediately by her recollection of the names of women artists:

> And the painting she could now see in her mind's eye. Mary Cassatt, she said. Why had she never thought of Mary Cassatt before? Or any of the others? Vanessa Bell, she said to herself. Frida Kahlo. Sonia Delaunay. Georgia O'Keefe. . . .
>
> Rosa Bonheur, Paula Modersohn-Becker. Florine Stettheimer and Käthe Kollwitz. She thought she had barely known their names, but now they all came back, in an instant. (220)

The juxtaposition of these two scenes—Maggie's realization of "the beauty of her surroundings" as if "for the first time" (222) and her catalog of feminist artists—suggests that Maggie has liberated herself from the "immasculation" of the modernist critical tradition and the objectivism that buttresses it.[6] It should be emphasized, however, that Maggie—and, ultimately, *The Art Lover*—rejects male-centered *definitions* of art, not necessarily art by men. Indeed, a painting by a man, Van Gogh's *Crows over the Wheatfield*, helps lead Maggie back "into the pain of the world" (235). But whereas she had earlier sought solace in art's distancing and stabilizing qualities, it is the postmodernist quality of Van Gogh's painting, its passionate desire to relate to rather than disengage from the churning world, that now magnetizes Maggie. "Everything moving toward us. The whole world moving toward us. *She feels the longing for everything in this world.* She shrieks and shrieks: 'Why these roads? Why these crows?' " (234, italics added). Earlier in the novel, Maso interposes within the text a reading of Vermeer's *Head of a Young Girl* that similarly invokes "all that art is supposed to keep at bay" (58). To look at the woman in Vermeer's picture, writes art historian Edward Snow in the interposed fragment, "is to be implicated in a relationship so urgent that to take an instinctive step backward into aesthetic appreciation would seem in this case a defensive measure, an act of betrayal and bad faith. . . . Indeed, it seems the essence of the image to subvert the distance between seeing and feeling, to deny the whole vocabulary of 'objective' and 'subjective' " (58).

Their insistence on compressing the distance between artist, text, viewer/reader, and, ultimately, world sharply differentiates the paintings by Van Gogh and Vermeer, or at least the readings of those paintings incorporated into Maso's novel, from the Giotto fresco and Stubblebine's interpretation of it. Fettered by modernist ways of seeing, Caroline could never "quite see in," could never "seem to get dirty enough" (212); only her willingness to relate to a world divested of her ordering imagination, "to love not only the names of the trees but gradually the trees themselves" (227), to relinquish the need "to name or arrange anything" (222), returns Caroline and her characters to the teeming, incoherent world and that world to them. The pristine promise of Giotto's fresco—transfiguration, transcendence, the ultimate mending of death's final fracture—implies a world of mastery and submission, distance and control, a world, as the fourth detail from *Noli me tangere* makes clear, which is fundamentally androcentric. While the longing to rise remains strong—after all, Caroline does include the fourth detail from Giotto's fresco among her "hieroglyphs of hope"—Maso's narrator eventually concludes that the desire for transcendence is a "final fiction" (229).

The Art Lover could easily have concluded with Caroline's recognition of the deceptions of the modernist critical tradition and her ensuing integration of that understanding into the theme of her own "subjective" novel. That is, Maso could have decided to delete "More Winter," the transgressive fifth section of *The Art Lover*, which is precisely what her editor at North Point tried to persuade her to do (Cooley 33). Maso must have realized, however, that to make that choice would have constituted a kind of betrayal, not only of her artistic integrity but of Gary Falk as well. For without the fifth section, *The Art Lover* becomes an affecting, well-crafted, but—despite the distinctive use of graphics (which Maso's editor also wanted her to excise)—generally *conventional* example of "subjective" literature, in Welleck and Warren's sense of the term. That is, without the convention-defying fifth section, *The Art Lover* would have imposed an unproblematized frame, a mediating order, on an event that Maso had experienced as shattering, chaotic, and deeply personal, in the process transmuting that experience, and her friend Gary Falk, into impersonal art.

Now I want to state carefully the claims I am making for section 5 of *The Art Lover*. By writing a straightforward and unabashedly personal account of her dying friend's last days, Maso reverses the distancing impulse of modernism, violating the traditional boundary between art and the chaotic real. More specifically, by temporarily discarding the twin frames formed by Caroline's story and Caroline's novel and by referring to herself throughout the section as Carole and to Falk as Gary, Maso narrows the aesthetic distance separating both the author and the readers of *The Art Lover* from the real-life prototypes for the characters in her novel. And yet, despite Maso's innovative efforts to personalize *The Art Lover*, in reading the novel we encounter not a subjectivity but, inevitably, a printed text, the trace of a subjectivity that is no longer there. Furthermore, no matter how disruptive section five is, it takes its place nonetheless as a constituent element in the overall structure of the novel, asking to be read as part of—indeed, performing its disruptive function *only if* read as part of—the entire novel.

Section 5, then, is best read as an *intervention*, a problematization of the novelistic tradition that ineluctably subtends even such disruptive texts as *The Art Lover*. Maso, that is, does not attempt to dispel the inherited novelistic discourse inscribed with the conventions and values of patriarchy; to do so would have risked moving outside of the boundaries of discursive coherence. Rather, Maso develops a subversive rewriting of that discourse, first by constructing the first four sections of her novel in general accordance with the traditional conventions of "subjective" literature, then by unsettling those conventions and the patriarchal assumptions underlying them in the transgressive fifth section. Working within the received framework of patriarchal discourse, Maso clears a space for her own personal voice. It is a self-consciously feminine voice we hear, spoken without the masks of protective, distancing personae, gently yet insistently challenging the canons of impersonal, objectivist art and, with them, modernist pretensions to universal, univocal truth.

Then, suddenly, with the beginning of section 6, "Spring 1986," we are back inside Caroline's story, the twin frames of Maso's novel closing over the "rupture" (Hackett 65) in the text like skin over a wound. Yet, to change the metaphor once more, the intervening fifth section continues to work like a virus, "infecting" in significant ways the conventions of subjective literature to which the novel's final section returns. Thematically, as we have seen, the sixth section moves the novel toward resolution: Candace becomes a feminist artist, Maggie returns to the world, Caroline frees herself from the mandates of modernist art. Structurally, too, the novel's final section demonstrates the destabilizing impact of section 5. Whereas the three frames of the novel had maintained a strict demarcation through the first five sections of *The Art Lover*, with Caroline's novel always clearly delimited within Caroline's story and the nonfictional fifth section formally segregated from the rest of the novel, in the final section these structural boundaries begin to buckle and perforate, as though from the weight of Maso's critique. The segment entitled "The Sky at Night," for example, while ostensibly an excerpt from Caroline's novel, oscillates wildly from frame to frame, as Max's commentary on Van Gogh's *Wheatfield* interpenetrates Maggie's reaction to the painting, and a scene on a boat in which Maggie holds Alison's hand is interrupted by an imagined conversation between Veronica and Caroline about Caroline's infancy. So complete is this intermingling that the section's—and the novel's—final segment, entitled "Author's Note," in which Maso again speaks in the first person about Gary Falk's final days, seems less an addendum than an integral component of the section and work, just as the concluding photograph of Maso and Falk seems to fall naturally among the graphics so effectively interwoven into the novel's total fabric. By the novel's end, that is, the narrative barriers enforcing the requisite distance between the author and the experiences refracted through her text have all but collapsed.

Finally, the pattern of imagery developed by Maso over the course of the novel culminates in the sixth section. This pattern is particularly complex because Maso assigns what seem to be contradictory values to single images. Stars, for example, ranging from the omnipresent Halley's Comet to the Big Dipper to the spiral galaxy Andromeda to the star of Bethlehem, seem, on the one hand, to represent transcendence, rising. Yet stars in other contexts—Max's aneurysm (described as a starburst in his head), the medicinal spiral taped to Steven's chest, the fatal star on Christ's forehead—are associated with death and disintegration. Light and dark images similarly commingle: Halley's Comet's "absolutely black" (241) nucleus, the black hole at the center of our galaxy, a black tulip. Fathers simultaneously protect and desert; bears both threaten and transmogrify into stars; Christ is concurrently the hope for salvation and a befuddled buffoon who "can't save anyone" (176).

Of course, modernist criticism has taught us to prize complicated imagery, since complexity in literature corresponds to our complex experiences of the world. Yet towering above the modernist valorization of multivalence, tension, ambiguity, and paradox is the principle of coherence, the poet's role being to "fuse the irrelevant and discordant" into ordered, significant form (Brooks 77). But Maso leaves ambiguity determinedly unresolved, refusing to diminish chaos by containing the antipathies her images generate. This is particularly apparent in Alison's dream, in which Candace encourages her younger sister to look upward at the stars:

> "That's right," Candace said, helping Alison slowly navigate her way. They found the Big Dipper, tipped, and with their infinitesimal fingers they connected the stars. In the handle now she saw the tail and in the bowl, the back. She heard her father's voice louder, clearer. "I will protect you forever. I will keep you safe from all bears." And baffled and angered and aching, Alison continued. "I will never leave you." There was the giant head, the body, the paws. And finally, with great effort, she cast it into the sky, Ursa Major, the family bear, and cried. (224)

Bears and stars, terror and solace, fidelity and betrayal, faith and loss clash and intermingle in the cacophonous imagery of Alison's dream, which is not unlike Maggie's description of Van Gogh's painting a few pages later. The chiaroscuro effect of that painting, we recall, led Maggie "into the world," a world in which "light and dark [are] intermingled. Together. One world" (235). Similarly, the suspended uncertainties of Alison's dream suggest a world impervious to the formalist's totalizing rage for order.

Modernist Max, aestheticizing experience, cared only for "what the light looks like" (242), for a life shaped by art. Caroline, his postmodernist daughter, learns also to allow the darkness in, to accept the messiness of unaestheticized experience. At some point during the long dying of her friend Gary Falk, Carole Maso came to understand that writing *The Art Lover* could not save him, an understanding she includes explicitly in the fifth section of *The Art Lover* (206). It was at that point, perhaps, that she became a postmodernist and a feminist writer. "In an attempt to ward off death with its chaos and mess," Maso says, "traditional fiction had flourished. Its attempts to organize, make manageable and comprehensible with its reassuring logic, in effect, reassure no one. I do not think I am overstating it when I say that mainstream fiction has *become* death with its complacent, unequivocal truths, its reductive assignment of meaning, its manipulations, its predictability and stasis" ("One Moment" 4). As an alternative to and a critique of traditional fiction, *The Art Lover* plunges art into the maelstrom of unaestheticized life, refusing to reconcile the oppositions and contraries of everyday experience, to tidy up the mess, as it were, with a formalistic broom. Instead, Maso's novel maintains and expresses a contact with the world as perceived apart from the aestheticizing consciousness, in which "nothing is finished or put away" (213). Carole Maso does not reject art, but a particular view of art, helping to lay to rest the Dead Fathers of modernism by evoking in order to subvert their aesthetic imperatives.

NOTES

[1]One of the novel's controlling conceits is that this page as well as the details from paintings reproduced in the novel have been torn by Caroline from a book in Max's "art history library" (16) after Max's death. In addition to pages "torn" from art books, Maso includes a wide range of other visual images—clippings from the *New York Times*, sign language cards, lost pet notices, photographs of fanlights in the form of starbursts, excerpts from poems, among others—that, as Linda Bellamy observes, "are not illustrations, but are an integral part of the biological impact of the text" (112). A total of sixty-seven images, some of which appear more than once, punctuate the novel.

[2]The formulation, of course, is Eliot's famous definition of the *objective correlative* in "Hamlet and His Problems." As shall be suggested, Eliot may be the Dead Father whose shade most prominently haunts Maso's novel.

[3]In a funny scene Maso seems to associate Reagan's geopolitics with the modernist aesthetics of distance, although instead of verbal icons, Reagan's sanctuary is an invisible shield. "Max, last night I dreamt that a B movie actor decided as a joke to run for president and got elected and then started a zany military program called Star Wars, like the movie, while everyone on the earth was dying or starving to death. A big dome in the sky that would keep out all the bad guys" (183).

[4] "Do I put my rage for you into art, where it is acceptable?" (117), Caroline asks Max in one of her imaginary colloquies.

[5]Of the epiphanic moment, Maso has said, "That's not true to my experience of the world. Things aren't resolved in that way. . . . It's this whole way of perceiving the universe which is . . . quite male, I think. It's not ours. It didn't come from us at all" (Cooley 34).

[6]*Immasculation* is Judith Fetterley's term for the cultural process by which women are inscribed into a male system of values.

WORKS CITED

Bellamy, Linda. [Review of *The Art Lover*]. *Calyx* 13.3 (1992): 111-12.

Brooks, Cleanth. "Irony as a Principle of Structure." *Literary Opinion in America*. Ed. Morton D. Zabel. New York: Viking, 1949: 729-41. Rpt. in *Contexts for Criticism*. Ed. Donald Keesey. 2nd ed. Mountain View, CA: Mayfield, 1987: 74-81.

Confessions of the Guerrilla Girls. New York: Harper, 1995.

Cooley, Nicole. "Carole Maso: An Interview." *American Poetry Review* March-April 1995: 32-36.

Eliot, T. S. *The Sacred Wood: Essays on Poetry and Criticism*. New York: Barnes and Noble, 1960.

Fetterley, Judith. *The Resisting Reader: A Feminist Approach to American Fiction*. Bloomington: Indiana UP, 1978.

Hackett, Joyce. "An Interview with Carole Maso." *Poets and Writers* May/June 1996: 64-73.

Hutcheon, Linda. *The Politics of Postmodernism*. New York: Routledge, 1989.

Maso, Carole. *The Art Lover*. San Francisco: North Point Press, 1990.

———. "One Moment of True Freedom." *Belles Lettres* 8.4 (1993): 3-5.

Spanos, William V. "The Detective and the Boundary: Some Notes on the Postmodern Literary Imagination." *boundary 2* 1.1 (Fall 1972): 147-68.

Wellek, René, and Austin Warren. *Theory of Literature*. 1949. 3rd ed. New York: Harcourt, 1962.

Wilde, Alan. *Horizons of Assent: Modernism, Postmodernism, and the Ironic Imagination*. Baltimore: Johns Hopkins UP, 1981.

Emancipating the Proclamation: Gender and Genre in AVA

Victoria Frenkel Harris

> Always she seemed to be listening to the echo of some foray in the blood that had no known setting.
>
> —Djuna Barnes, *Nightwood*

In *An Atlas of the Difficult World*, Adrienne Rich writes:

> I promised to show you a map you say but this is a mural
> then yes let it be these are small distinctions
> where do we see it from is the question.

If we concur with Richard Rorty that as social beings we construct our realities, then "where . . . we see it from" relates inextricably to the question of who we are. When the foundations of legitimizing accounts began to crumble, when, as Susan Bordo suggests, "accounts could no longer claim to descend from the heavens of pure rationality or to reflect the inevitable and progressive logic of intellectual or scientific discovery," then "the imperial categories that had provided justification for those accounts—Reason, Truth, Human Nature, History, Tradition—become displaced by the (historical/social) questions: *Whose* truth? *Whose* nature? *Whose* version of reason? *Whose* history? *Whose* tradition?" (137). Denial of either the anteriority of truth or of the Cartesian postulating subject requires a dialogic stance from which one enters the dialogue committed to acts of agency, points of affiliation, and the stakes of the commitment. Those places of entrance and involvement continually construct an ongoing and shifting subject position in service neither to closed information systems—those political and aesthetic as well as topographical maps—nor to a self-enclosed identity.

Throughout *AVA,* Carole Maso's third novel, Ava's ruminations on literature suggest that dialogism applies even to how we receive a literary text: "The poem demands the demise of the poet who writes it and the birth of the poet who reads it" (65). Textual parameters, in turn, extend to broader ideological concerns: "Each page is completely entitled to be the first page" (58) in "literary texts that tolerate all kinds of freedom . . . which are not . . . texts of territory with neat borders" (113). *AVA* is thus both text and metatext, a narrator's story and the story of a narration committed to interactive multiplicity. The protagonist, like the text of *AVA*, opts for resisting closure; indeed, *AVA* is a moving symphonic rendering of how one life accumulates memory and desire and that life's narrative equivalent, a narrative that, among other literary transgressions, undercuts chronological sequence ("My students and I celebrating the death of plot" [161], Ava says at one point). Maso's textual view of reality—as inevitably shaped by the stories we choose to tell and the stories that we are told—is structured by her determination "to reshape the world according to the dictates of desire" (6) in an emplotment of the sexuated female body that is erotically attentive to the material world; matter matters to Maso. On a broader level, her call for an open-endedness to the nature of inquiry and for an ongoing inquiry into and denaturalization of the subject interrogates strategies of closure and their usual concomitant gestures of isolationism and desires for power.

Self-enclosed identity is incommensurate to the text of *AVA*/Ava; thereby Maso imagistically and metaphorically inscribes an alternative to political and aesthetic closed information systems—her ongoing inquiring and denaturalized subject crucially redressing the inevitable and necessary omissions of such systems. On a literal and symbolic level *AVA* is very much a novel about the body of its eponymous central character. During the breakdown of her physical body, Ava's celebrated "interior multiplicity" (176)—Maso's metonym for a perspectival aesthetic—is traversed by a medical profession that perceives the human body as self-contained and whose articulations of and practices upon the body are synecdoches of the discourses and power operations in the larger cultural context. Maso, on the other hand, is interested in theories of identity based upon sexual object choice, upon the gendered body and its lability. Such investment resists reactionary sexual prohibitions fostered by anxiety over contamination by a sexual "other," as seen, for instance, in the AIDS hysteria.

Such anxieties extend to the body politic, as well, which forms a backdrop to the novel and which is treated throughout with images of containment, power, and invasion: "Iraq invades Kuwait," Maso writes at one point in the narrative, "The president draws a line in the sand" (88). Similarly, Ava's family are victims and survivors of the holocaust, a genocide enabled by the literal and paradigmatic enclosure of an entire human population. Even the name of Ava's doctor, Dr. Oppenheim, who is treating, irradiating, the cancerous Ava, in evoking the name of J. Robert Oppenheimer, who helped develop the A-bomb, then later spoke out against America's Cold War McCarthyite intolerance, suggests totalizing boundaries, the way that activities of science implode upon political activities, and the "liars who are holding power over others" (17).

For Maso, this all ties into "the seduction that is, that has always been language" (226)—language that is both adored and responsible. Throughout *AVA*, Maso insists that since inscriptions forge our realities, language use must be ethical, to this end citing Paz: "The writer's morality . . . [lies] in his behavior toward language" (63); Neruda: "Form and content constantly shape each other like elements of the ecosystem and this allows truth, infinite possibilities for expression" (90); and Wittig: action "is the overflow not only of words, but of the reality and the traditions these words have fashioned and perpetuated" (29). While enthralled by the hold language has, Maso equates overtelling with totalizing: "Words are less integers than points in a continuum. Indeed one might well describe the structure of the lyric as the expression of the interval" (40). And interval and narrative fragment play interventive roles, replacing the appearance of totalization with a mood of narrative flow—Ava's stream-of-consciousness collage of memory and desire. Thus the work, though always about language, is also about reading. Ava's life of passionate and promiscuous reading portrays the way a life accumulates resonance and how a writer might evoke a resonant narrative equivalent, flooding the protagonist's and reader's minds with multiple voices. Yet, on her deathbed, Ava is also not afraid to "listen to the music that is silence" (123). Indeed, silence, bound to the love and inner necessities of language, its shaping forms, performs a semiotic function in Maso's novel: "let silence have its share and allow for a fuller meditative field than is possible in linear narrative or analysis" (184).

AVA situates a composing mind under the pressures of context—historical, cultural, and biological. But the widening notions of just what constitutes a text include what constitutes a subject; and the interruptions of linearity by silences, syncopation, indeterminacy, disarticulation, and recursion are the undulations of a different kind of semantic field. A text such as *AVA*, which replicates a mind's recursions, repetitions, drifts, and motives, renders notions such as non sequitur or self-sustaining unity inapplicable. Silences, furthermore, constitute omissions only in texts that promise the aesthetic mastery of experience, that present themselves as a totalized *work* in the Barthesian sense of the term. Yet, Ava concludes, "As seemingly random as it all appears—there are accumulated meanings. I believe that" (129). The synecdochal aspect of the novel-to-world relationship in *AVA* insinuates process, the dilatory, and the incomplete as hedges against totalization when notions of completion spawn cidal exclusionary economies.

Thus *AVA*, like each of Maso's five novels, performs valuable cultural work. Nonetheless, in an era in which, as Michael Riffaterre observes, academic critics and theorists (in particular) tend to dismiss "aesthetic features" as "historical variables or as suspect vestiges of the styles and reading practices of the embattled canon" (15), *AVA* remains determinedly literary, with both artifice and textuality foregrounded. Yet, even from its self-consciousness as *aesthetic* artifact, Maso interrogates the traditional valorization of objectivity, ideological neutrality, and disinterested art, which is under scrutiny by much contemporary theory. Language operates, in Riffaterre's formulation, less as "sociolect," which is largely mimetic, than as "ideolect," the "self-sufficient" imagistic codes which disclaim referentiality. Moving "from a denotative to a connotative status" (14), such codes gain salience formally, not mimetically; contextually, not referentially. "We are . . . dealing," Riffaterre concludes, "with a mode of expression whose basic unit is likely to be a text, rather than a word, a sentence, or a trope" (15). Such texts impel a "move from passive to participatory reading" (4), an attendance to significance rather than uncontextualized meanings, relying on the cumulative power of images that subvert "the principle of substitutability" (15). Formally and aesthetically, in other words, *AVA* is not a text at all analogous to realism, unless its referentiality is to the mind that negates linear or rationalistic orchestration.

Despite its literariness, however, Maso abjures high modernist hermeticism, that Eliotic valorization of the autonomous text, which claims to escape from the personality of both the writer and reader. The personal pervades, and Maso discusses *AVA* in the most personal of terms: "No other book eludes me like *AVA*. It reaches for things just outside the grasp of my mind, my body, the grasp of my imagination. It brings me up close to the limits of my own comprehension, pointing out, as Kafka says, the incompleteness of any life—not because it is too short, but because it is a human life"("One Moment" 3). Moreover, Maso evokes the *reader's* personal as well as rhetorical engagement, not merely because formal difficulty demands "a more conscious, more thorough reader-response" (Riffaterre 14) but because the reader's participation is built into the aesthetic strategies of the text. Maso, for example, complaining of the usurpation of "the reader's freedoms" by traditional narratives, which "left no place in the text for the reader," attempts in *AVA* "to write lines the reader (and the writer) might meditate to, recombine, rewrite as he or she pleases" ("One Moment" 4). Furthermore, Maso undermines privatized "originality" by presenting herself as participant in the current cultural/epistemological sea change that resists notions of ideational enclosure (whether the entity enclosed be a construction of self, body, or literary genre), that views knowledges as situated and implicated, that displaces dichotomy, autonomy, and determinateness with relationship, mutuality, and openness—in short, to return to the quotation from Rich with which I began, that prefers murals to maps.

There is no pattern in *AVA* for that which is complete and self-contained or without apparent authorship. There are no authoritative and neutral representations—for a world that is always already given, objectively "out there," rather than constantly undergoing construction. The literary conscription here is into *AVA*'s mode and content of affiliation, not into the service of impartial perspectives implementing a rhetoric of objectivity. *AVA*'s world is constitutionally perspectival, thereby destabilizing objectivism. Multivocality, uncertainty, complications, and paradox resist monologism and a worldview that normalizes its own biases through historical, rationalistic, and scientific fictions of unity. What distinguishes Maso's use of polyvocality, uncertainty, paradox, etc., from similar techniques in modernist texts is the foregrounded *implicatedness* of the author in her text and the reader in its reading as well as the avoidance of stability-intending resolution. If anything is consistent, it is the modulations of change and shift and the necessity of acknowledging implicatedness in Maso's politics of location. "Where do we see it from is [indeed] the question" to be asked. Situatedness is all.

Maso writes herself into her historical situation by actively infusing her work with other texts whose status as cultural products is acknowledged by footnotes, which in turn self-consciously mark the texts' relationships to, complicities with, and dismantlings of contemporaneous and historical texts. This move serves to elasticize textual boundaries—enlarging *work* into Barthesian *text*, extending beyond the enclosures of the book's covers. Generous allusion acknowledges acculturation and avoids in the process the sense of either cutting off through enclosure or progressing through linearity. While Maso's footnotes refer largely to the Western canon, the multivocality within her text challenges sedimented notions of master narratives emanating from sequestered originating poets. Her situatedness admits to different knowledges, and this notational gesture allows her to display intelligence, precision, and erudition, instantiating multiplicity, while disclaiming a unitary source of originality. The inspirational and generative heteroglossia differs from the more conservative influence model of the modernists, which alludes not only to the author's erudition but also to a parochial envisionment of canonic homogeneity, Eliot's "monuments." Unlike "influences," which would still embody the notion of containment, this textual weaving asserts our own social construction. Voice, therefore, eddies into multiple voices in *AVA*, countering centrist humanist notions of being as well as any appearance of omniscience or neutrality.

Not surprisingly, Maso writes her readers into the text, making available "in the text a 'reading function' that allows for a shift in enunciative and denotative positionality—in other words for movement beyond what the text says" (Rajan 67). In her conscious deployment of intertextuality, Maso insists upon her own intentionalities and positionalities while honoring competing discourses, even providing gaps and silences in her work's formal dimension that invite dialogic interchange with the reader, whose intentionalities and positionalities are also acknowledged. *AVA* presents itself, then, as a consciously crafted aesthetic construct while simultaneously opening itself to palimpsestic interaction with past and current cultural texts and dialogic interchanges between author and reader.

I would like to consider what I think is a major symbolic dimension of Maso's use of textual multiplicity in *AVA* to undercut detachment, neutrality, and universality as value judgments disguised as both positionless and aesthetically august. The prestige of allopathy in this country seems to have secured the notion of the body as an enclosed space, "normal" if healthy in its pristine, atomistic terms, but susceptible to invasion by voracious, self-multiplying cells. Such multiplication within an enclosed system leads to sure collapse of that enclosed space. Without trivializing in any way the ravages of cancer and other diseases, I mean to suggest that this invasion metaphor, issuing from our culture's preeminently esteemed scientistic discourse of the body, extends to our terms of securing normal status by protecting the empowered from rampant invasions by the unempowered. The altern/subaltern terms of colonization exist in the invasion metaphors informing homophobia, racism, sexism—in general, any discourse of the other that projects evil invasions wreaking havoc upon the harmonious and the "normal" (the normal body-state, for example, or the nuclear family). Not only through its transgressive form but through its central image of a woman dying of an *incurable* disease, *AVA* symbolically critiques the universalist and humanistic perspective that imposes value-laden sound bites on a population extremely distressed by the failure of all that such truisms were meant to secure. To allow Ava's body to be cured through such logic would be tantamount to assuring the success of blindered telescopic scrutiny—even of the body. Under such a predilection, the splendid physical and metaphorical sexuality celebrated in the novel collapses. In resisting "cure" by the rigid domain of allopathic procedures, Ava's body also resists the body of science that seeks to enclose its specimen while ridding it of contaminants. If Ava were cured, if Maso narrated success from such centrist practices, she would, in some ways, collude with those practices, in the process succumbing to a metaphysics of closure her narrative resists at every turn.

Although *AVA*/Ava concludes/dies, Maso never relinquishes her investment in opposing the logic of exclusion—such as that definitional appropriation of the other/the self. Ava's story as an embodiment of openness precludes any preconfirmed sense of an otherness that ought to be avoided, like a citizenship that bans foreigners. The novel's lack of closure, at all levels, parallels its investment in multiple textuality, in the palimpsest, the trace. Ava's wish for daughters, maybe hundreds of them, is potentiated, not through the essential body, but through the text. Her issue results from the same formal greening up of the status of the book—an inability to seal off the text as novel, as narrative, bound to genre assumptions about closure, character, plot, and, implicitly, subjectivity. Perhaps if Maso's gesture of opening that which formerly was conceived of as enclosed were extended to the vocabulary of science, prevalent diagnostic vocabularies of normalcy and disease would throw off metaphors of insulation, isolation, and invasion, leading to more effective treatment of cancer and AIDS.

As we become more liberated from discourses of separation and autonomy, from any ecological effacement in service to personal gain, we concomitantly must find rapprochement for the denounced other, seeking, for example, not only refuge for the homeless but a reassessment of just what we mean by *home*. Maso characterizes homelessness partially in terms of locating a language to make space for the feminine, which is described explicitly as linguistically nonexistent, having thus no "at home." As Maso states her notion: "So primary is homesickness as a motive for writing fiction, so powerful the yearning to memorialize what we've lived, inhabited, been hurt by and loved—"(176). Homelessness may be seen as an imagistic portrayal suggesting life outside a transgression/rule dilemma. Suggesting, however, that Ava's actions be identified as transgressions would solidify the concept of the rule. Homelessness may imply not a situation of being away from home, but an adriftness, an alterity—indecipherable within the purview of transgression/norm. Maso moves into the postmodern by deconstructing that binary, refusing to signify against a norm and furthermore not instantiating a humanistic mode of toleration for the anomalous.

Maso swerves away from both fixed identity and repudiation of a fixed subject position with the figure of the nomad, for one example.

Marked by unlocatability, the nomad's lack of fixity carries both the potential burden and freedom implicit in dialogue, interaction, incompletion, and accountability without the bourgeois or cold war (I-you, us-them) bifurcations. *AVA* presents the shifting nature of involvements that continually construct a fluctuating subject position, one not inherited and complete but continually responsible and responsive in its ongoing constitution. Being a nomad in the collapsing eco- and immune system, Ava repeatedly recalls Schubert's *Wanderer* Symphony. "It is difficult," Maso writes, "to convey in English the exact meaning of the word *Wandern*. Perhaps 'to roam' comes nearest to a definition of that half-joyous, half-melancholy notion. Wandern serves both as a symbol of freedom, of not being weighted down by responsibilities, and as a symbol of not belonging, of homelessness" (98). By calling attention to the untranslatability of *wandern*, Maso suggests the need to elasticize boundaries—of language norms and of dichotomous assertions of home/homeless. No rule exists from which to grant exceptions—perhaps, then, this portrayal indicates Maso's ability to metonymize ec-centrism.

Citing Hélène Cixous, Maso associates this liberating ec-centricity with women's bodies. "Language for women is closely linked with sexuality for Cixous. She believes that because women are endowed with a more passive and consequently more receptive sexualilty, not centered on the penis, they are more open than men to create liberated forms of discourse" (51). Arguments about passivity aside, Maso concurs with Cixous's contention that "We've been turned away from our bodies, shamefully taught to ignore them, to strike them with that stupid sexual modesty" (56). Rejecting all objectifying representations of the feminine, Maso asserts that "Feminine can be read as the living, as something that continues to escape all boundaries, that cannot be pinned down, controlled or even conceptualized" (160). Affiliation and networking in *AVA* suggest not lassitude but involvement. A totalized tale is withheld because the desire for totalization is itself being mocked. The reader must enter at a place, insert particularity and identifiability, locate her space and haul along a packet of affiliations which must provide perspective and require scrutiny. Both moves—by author and reader—share the activity of silence and voice, suggest not fullness but invite enunciations that are uncorseted by mandates for universal, abstract discourse that marginalizes a sexual subject.

Maso expresses the body—book, protagonist, world—in a narrative form that parallels Ava's life: that which expands and contracts as respiration pulsates within the body. Maso cites Sarraute's notion that "the genuine response to art is on an immediate and personal level. It is essentially a wordless conversation between the author and the reader and his or her willingness to assume the same responsibilities and prerogatives as the author" (61). Ava's repeated recourse to music—she in fact aspires to the state of music—metaphorically suggests alertness to resonance and nuance, in a throbbing network of recollection in repetition like musical variations. Unlike musicality, however, *AVA* possesses semiotic materiality, and Maso, as suggested, is invested in a world without revulsion toward matter. "In between waves and heat, a conversation, bits of conversation carried to me on the air. . . . If I did not care about making this a better world" (66). A world inhabited by agents bound to render matter precisely, to attend to it and care for it, would be a world—in other words—not headed toward heedless destruction. As readers, we, too, are compelled to make contact actively with the materiality of this novel while asking, in fact inventing, the means to adapt to its shifting ground of shapes, allegiances, and form, constructing ourselves along the way—implicatively and metaphorically—with a dying body in microcosm, a dying population or form in the macrocosm. Unlike a bourgeois tourist who aloofly observes the devastation of an *other,* we become accomplices in alternative social constructions.

Throughout *AVA*, cultural vocabularies fall short of "The ideal, or the dream, . . . to arrive at a language that heals as much as it separates" (250). In a quintessential scene Ava reacts to an advertising executive's smirking remark, "So I see you are into kinky sex." Ava is not personally offended; rather, she is put off by the executive's censorial and exclusionary construction of her sexuality. "[S]omething about 'into kinky sex' bothered me," she reflects. "He had committed a sin of language and I never saw him again" (58). The erotic body in Maso's work is not susceptible to normative summary; the oppressive constructions of altern/subaltern are unacceptable as well. Maso implicitly finesses even the current theoretical either-or critical bifurcation in feminism pertaining to essentialism and social constructionism, retaining instead an investment in the bodily while avoiding charges of being a precritical essentialist.

Readers are left being told to "pray for peace" and to imagine a healing language in a world ravaged by discursive patterns of separation and ghettoization. Yet, to conclude where I began, to the extent that we are socially and linguistically constructed, inscription of failures of articulated structures inaugurates possibilities for alternative inscriptions. The semiotics of space and recursion in *AVA* amend the slices of the sharp scalpel of linear language, leaving room also for that which we are repeatedly told to love: questions (171). We are seduced by Maso's portrayal of Ava's urgent promiscuity as suiting "some interior multiplicity" (176). We love Ava's will to love. Furthermore, *AVA* metaphorically engenders a global economy that will not tolerate economies of isolationism which foster exclusionism and elitism, homicides and genocides, at the expense of some constructed subaltern other.

The tragic element here comes from witnessing the extinction of "a rare bird," as Ava—*rara avis*—is repeatedly called. All this sensuous bodily care and delight remain housed in a suffocating ecosphere—a metonym for the annihilation of several kinds of life, spoken by one author or one character, who loves the imbricating textures of life's events. Yet this shape-shifting psyche weaves into extinction—like a note into air—sensuously and particularly. The protagonist, like the novel, loses shape and closure while making the reader dance to Ava's music, follow her suit and love it, respond to her demands for an attentive and sensuous mind in harmony with that of both author and character. A novel that revels against plot, *AVA* transgresses some of its own inherited premises, inaugurating replenishment, metaphorically what the body of this protagonist cannot achieve. The thrumming energy of the text contains and continues beyond the endurance of this figure in its rushes and halts, spillovers of Ava's psyche—the only imposition of linearity of narrative progression signified by the "Morning," "Afternoon," and "Night" markers.

The conclusion of *AVA*/Ava avoids conventional closure. The tragedy is not that the drift cannot take shape but that this source cannot remain alive. This body cannot be sustained by the trust in what's so sensual. That which has been trusted may not be retained. The tragedy, then, is not a deathbed scene, not a grieving for this one body's submission to cancer—our bogus category for any number of various illnesses plaguing a population with damaged immune systems. The pathos, rather, results from our inability to have this music, its sensuous indeterminacies, exist as recognizable form. Unfamiliarity with such attentiveness makes us accomplices to the destruction of that which is indeterminable in our regnant grammar. And yet do not the principles guiding a reading of *AVA* generate filiation?

"No more second opinions. It's OK," Ava says, dismissing the deficient treatment.

No more binary logic applied to the body.

Or to the life, the book, the loves, the culture.

"I'm feeling the form—finally."

And then:

"A more spacious form. After all this time" (212).

WORKS CITED

Barthes, Roland. "From Work to Text [1971]." *Image, Music, Text*. Trans. Stephen Heath. New York: Hill and Wang, 1988. 155-164.

Bordo, Susan. "Feminism, Postmodernism, and Gender-Scepticism." *Feminism / Postmodernism*. Ed. Linda J. Nicholson. New York: Routledge, 1990. 133-56.

Maso, Carole. *AVA*. Normal, IL: Dalkey Archive Press, 1993.

———. "One Moment of True Freedom." *Belles Lettres* 8.4 (1993): 3-5.

Rich, Adrienne. *An Atlas of the Difficult World: Poems 1988-1991*. New York: Norton, 1991.

Rajan, Tilotama. "Intertextuality and the Subject of Reading/Writing." *Influence and Intertextuality in Literary History*. Ed. Jay Clayton and Eric Rothstein. Madison: U of Wisconsin P, 1991. 61-74.

Riffaterre, Michael. "How Do Images Signify?" *Diacritics* 24.1 (1994): 3-15.

"There's Not One Story That Will Change This": The American Woman in the Chinese Hat

Nicole Cooley

In *The American Woman in the Chinese Hat* Carole Maso states that she "was interested in investigating the collapse of a belief system and what effect it would have both on subject and language" (Moore 189). *The American Woman in the Chinese Hat* is a novel which is literally about the act of narration. We are told in the first sentence of the novel that Catherine, the narrator, has come to the Côte d'Azur "to write" (5). The text opens with the modernist trope of the expatriate writer familiar to early twentieth-century literature.

Like *The Art Lover, The American Woman in the Chinese Hat* not only depicts the writing of a novel but also allows us to enter the novel that is being written. But whereas in *The Art Lover* Caroline's own story and the story of the family she invents are separated by both typography and the use of titled sections, in *The American Woman in the Chinese Hat* the narratives blur, and, finally, the narratives break down. The novel thematizes both the breakdown of narration and the breakdown of the narrating subject. In this essay I will first examine Maso's construction of Catherine as a woman writer in terms of a breakdown of identity and then discuss the challenge to literary forms articulated in this novel as a disruption of modernist modes of writing.

The American Woman in the Chinese Hat offers a critique of the modernist notion of "genius," the myth of the great, transcendent artist. Specifically, Maso invokes the writing of genius found in Gertrude Stein's work. Stein's *The Autobiography of Alice B. Toklas* addresses the notion of genius in terms of the woman subject and the lesbian subject.[1] Maso adopts the modernist notion of genius found in Stein only to disrupt it through postmodern writing strategies. While genius depends on a unitary construction of self, Maso's text decenters unitary subjectivity by alternating "she" and "I" as its point of view: we are simultaneously within Maso's novel and the novel Catherine is writing in her notebook. We see the identity of the woman writer thematized as a very literal emotional breakdown. Maso acknowledges that "I've been looking at mental illness from afar and that has informed all the books."[2] She goes on to link *Ghost Dance* and *The American Woman in the Chinese Hat* in this respect: "I think that Christine Wing from *Ghost Dance* becomes Catherine, or is a version. But I was too afraid when I was twenty-one to write Catherine, and so I gave the suffering, the illness, to the mother back then" (Cooley 1995: 34).[3]

Catherine continually insists that "Except for the cahier I carry, I am just like everyone else" (39) and "Except for the cahier, and the French workbook, and the Chinese hat, and all the crying, I am just like a resident of Vence these days" (40). Such claims would seem to disprove her own desire for genius. Here, Catherine, who exists on the margins of the town, tries to identify with the center.

Linda Hutcheon identifies a central paradox of postmodernist writing when she contends, "The ex-centric, the off-center, is ineluctably identified with the center it desires but is denied" (Hutcheon 60). Not only is Catherine, who exists on the margins of the town, trying to identify with the center but she defines the difference between herself and the town in terms of the documents she carries with her. It is, significantly, always her notebook that creates her status as *other*. At the end of the novel, as part of Catherine's breakdown, the notebook disappears from the text and she burns her passport, the document that has allowed her legally to remain on the margins of a foreign country. With these actions, she says "she slips out of this last credential of self" (190). Thus Maso establishes the self, even the self of the writer, as discursively constructed. Catherine often asserts her own identity in the novel, but this assertion becomes increasingly troubling as the narrative progresses. Repeated often in the text is the sentence: "I am known as the American woman in the Chinese hat who writes" (7). Rather than conferring an identity upon her, this statement becomes a symptom of Catherine's own troubled narration. Language enacts her breakdown through repetition.

As Catherine reports it, Lola tells her that she is leaving her because "She can no longer be a slave to my genius" (14). After Lola has left Catherine, she is haunted by the notion of "genius" and its relation to her life, as in the following passage:

> What is this pervasive feeling of danger? Of doom? A woman, a bed, a half-eaten loaf of brioche, many empty wine bottles, a swirl of vomit, the radio playing its handful of sad songs, a notebook.
>
> The word *genius* catches fire in her head. What *genius?* (16)

In this passage Maso shows the inability of genius to act as a saving power. In accordance with her desire to believe in genius, Catherine views her writing as a way to ward off "danger" and "doom." But Catherine eventually admits that genius fails; she states, "I thought the work I was doing was more important than it actually was" (119).

The construction of "genius" in this novel is also linked to alcoholism. It is significant in this respect that Catherine makes several references to the American fiction writer Raymond Carver. She buys a copy of the *Herald-Tribune* and finds the news of his death. Carver died of lung cancer, but the fact that he was a recovering alcoholic is well-known. Part of Catherine's personal deterioration in this novel has to do with the fact that she sits in the café all day, drinking. In fact, at one point her lover Lucien tells her she drinks too much: "In France women don't sit at a table in the center of town in the middle of the day and drink three, four pastis" (85). Catherine's actions are transgressive because she is a woman, and the alcoholic genius may be male but not female.

Catherine's identity is constantly being disrupted by Maso's narrative practices. The point of view in this novel alternates within sentences and paragraphs. At first, the divisions are clear, the reasons explained: "Often these days she finds she refers to herself in the third person as if she were someone else. Watching from afar" (21). As the narration progresses, the alternation becomes more frequent and often occurs in midparagraph: "Elle est complétement folle. Elle est seule. Elle est belle. I am still trying to give her a firm identity. The American woman in the Chinese hat who cries and writes" (57).

At the end of the novel the split between "I" and "she," as opposed to being neatly resolved, is further intensified:

> I touch the American woman gently on the shoulder. She smiles at me. "You think we wouldn't have needed much."
>
> She whispers to me, "It's OK." She whispers. "Thank you for everything. For the fruit, and the light, and the hat." (192)

The division between "I" and "she" disrupts the notion of a single, individual speaking subject. Again, Maso offers a postmodern critique, as "the modernist concept of single and alienated otherness is challenged by the postmodern questioning of binaries that conceal hierarchies" (Hutcheon 61). The movement within the point of view in this novel also suggests that identity is mobile, shifting, and irreducible to a single term:

> I am losing the ability to dream her, to make her up—this lovely construction of self. The stories had said: I exist. Even when they were sad. It was something. The stories were shelter for a while. Company.
>
> I was hoping to tame my terror with sex or language, to bear the solitude with stories or—(185)

The postmodern self, the identity of the woman writer described here, is explicitly a "construction." While identity might have been conferred by the "stories," in the process of the novel we see that the stories can no longer offer Catherine any "shelter." When the relief of "terror" is hoped for with "sex or language," Maso links sexuality and language, a connection she will exploit further in the novel. Writing, as it is represented by Catherine's expatriate café life and her desire to be a genius, necessarily fails: "There's not one story that will change this. That makes any sense. No beginning, no middle, no end. Most of all not a story like that" (189), and "It's not possible to come up with one true sentence, one arrangement of words that would mean anything" (189).[4] Instead of writing offering truth, writing enacts difference.

Language as difference is enacted in *The American Woman in the Chinese Hat* in terms of the trope of *translation*. The critique of writing as a mode of representation is apparent in the use of translation as a figure in the novel. Hutcheon argues, "It is through language that the status of difference as ex-centricity is thematized" (Hutcheon 73). Translation functions as a challenge to the signifier by defining language as perpetually double throughout the novel. French and English are both employed in Maso's text. The beauty of language, its status as an object, is frequently remarked upon by Catherine. The materiality of language is foregrounded: "Ciel is both the word for heaven and for sky. I think. I pick words out: Toujours. Sans doute. Sans exception. L'éternité. Such beautiful words" (12). Catherine often gives the reader definitions of French words, as in the following passage:

> Vouloir is to want.
> Attendre is to wait.
> Manquer is to miss. (10)

In this passage Maso proposes three definitions, all relating to desire, absence, and loss. But these lines sound like exercises from a grammar book, and they are premised on one language being equivalent to another. Translation functions as a rhetorical strategy within the text, as a form of repetition: "The next day in Vence I go to the municipal pool. La piscine municipale" (21).

Catherine cannot speak to her male lover Lucien without translation. She states, "It is foolish to believe that because we do not have much language that we cannot hurt each other" (82). Significantly, he is the first person with whom she discusses her writing: she tells him she has written "Deux livres," and he asks if her cahier's purpose is "To write down the book" (73). When he asks her "What kind of book are you writing?" she tells him, "Un roman d'amour" (73). This description of Catherine's writing is performed in both French and English, in a double dialogue. But a reversal is operating: Catherine is speaking in French while Lucien speaks in English.

In this novel translation is not purely linguistic; it thematizes sexuality. Heterosexuality is figured as a translation. The connection between writing and sexual acts is enforced when Catherine tells Lucien, "I would like to write you a book in which one side of the page is in English, and the other side of the page is the French translation, and every time the book is closed the two sides would kiss" (129). The interactions between Lucien and Catherine are performed as translations. When he first sees her and asks, "Vous parlez français?" ("Do you speak French?"), she responds, "Non. Oui. Non. Un peu" (71). At their first arranged meeting at a bar, translation is their conversational mode:

> He speaks quickly and she has a difficult time understanding what he says. And when she speaks in her simple English he whispers slower, more slowly. They smile at not being able to understand each other. They are guests of this earth—not really at home here. It is easy to see. The waitress offers her a French/English dictionary. But what good would a dictionary do? Even now it is already too late. "Non," he says quickly. It would violate some unspoken agreement they have already entered. "Non." (72)

They cannot understand each other, and the misunderstanding, the linguistic difference, is evoked as pleasurable. While Catherine and Lucien seem to be allied in their ex-centric status, since "they are guests of this earth—not really at home here," in reality Catherine is alone on the margins.

The translation of language becomes a translation of bodies. Lucien is a man whom Catherine desires as a woman, specifically, as Lola who is now lost to her. The "dictionary" is "useless" because Lucien cannot become a woman, he cannot become Lola. Catherine tries to "translate" Lucien into Lola; she observes, "It is a beautiful back. It is a back like hers" (86). She is first attracted to him because of his long hair: "His hair is longer than hers was when I left" (85). She thinks of him: "you are so beautiful, like a woman" (120). He is attracted to her because she resembles a famous German actress. "It's what immediately attracted him, he says, of course" (89). They are both drawn to one another because of the "other" whom each resembles, a false identity only inscribed on the surface of the body. She says, "It occurs to her that it's possible that the idea of the beautiful stranger is more interesting than the stranger himself" (103). Lucien's "surface" does not translate.

While Maso represents sexuality in this novel as largely unfixed and mobile, Catherine's own self-identification as a lesbian is made explicit in the text. When she tells him about Lola, Lucien asks, "You are a lesbian then?" "Oui," she responds. It is significant that Catherine answers the Frenchman's English question in French. For the lesbian subject, this translation will always be necessarily incomplete. One term, one body, cannot be substituted for another, as Catherine learns. While her sexual life with Lola (which we only see in flashback) is not described as a translation, her sexual acts with Lucien, the novel's invocation of heterosexuality, are figured as translation. The original is not equivalent to the translation. Translation is therefore another binary in the novel which is decentered, refigured as a structure of *difference*.

Thus lesbian becomes the original, heterosexuality the copy. In light of this reversal, it is crucial that one of Catherine's only attachments in Vence is Sylvia, a woman who is "at least seventy" (33) and who likes to tell Catherine stories of salon life and her dead lover Monique. Sylvia and Monique provide another echo of Gertrude Stein and her lover Alice B. Toklas. Sylvia is the person whom she tells about her affair with Lucien and who responds, "I thought you were one of the girls" (124). Sylvia then relates what she heard on a London radio program: "A woman got on and said, 'Because we can no longer say "lesbian" on the air, from now on we will refer to lesbians as "the women in comfortable shoes" ' " (162). Within the terms of this joke, lesbians are renamed. To understand who is a lesbian, we have to translate the phrase.

Finally, all language becomes translation, and translation is a figure for inadequacy. When Catherine's American friends visit her, she notes that everything they say "sounds like a translation" (43). The world can only be translated in terms of its bright surfaces. Catherine writes, "What is it that is so dangerous under this bright surface of saluts and kisses and ice cream and many-colored drinks in the dazzling afternoon?" (9). The novel's distrust of literary representation is evident because this surface of "saluts and kisses," of words and gestures, like the materiality of the signifier on which modernism is predicated, does not translate to reveal anything.

The distrust of representation is exemplified by the fact that the text will not allow us to name it as a novel or as autobiography. The cover of the book is a drawing of Carole Maso wearing a Chinese hat. On the copyright page of the book, Maso acknowledges a foundation in Vence, France, where she says she wrote the book; Vence is the city where the action of the book takes place. In addition, we find the statement: "This book is an invention, an act of the imagination, and in no way should be mistaken for reality, the place where much good invention originates." Furthermore, on the last page of the novel Maso lists "Acknowledgments" and makes two lists of people titled "Je t'embrasse" and "Merci mille fois." We can never be sure if we are to read Catherine as Carole Maso or Carole Maso as Catherine. The book continually invokes and then challenges autobiographical representation, leaving the reader on shifting narrative ground.

Early in *The American Woman in the Chinese Hat,* Catherine writes in her notebook, "One feels safe from grief here" (6), referring, I believe, to both the town of Vence and to the notebook or cahier in which she will live her invented life. Yet, finally, this statement functions in a sadly ironic fashion. *The American Woman in the Chinese Hat* is a novel that forces us to consider a world, a fiction, a text without safety and without transcendence.

NOTES

[1]In *The Autobiography of Alice B. Toklas* Stein, writing as Alice, states, "I may say that only three times in my life have I met a genius and each time a bell within me rang and I was not mistaken, and I may say in each case it was before there was any general recognition of the quality of genius in them. The three geniuses of whom I wish to speak are Gertrude Stein, Pablo Picasso and Alfred Whitehead. I have met many important people, I have met several great people but I have only known three first class geniuses and in each case on sight something within me rang" (8). Many Stein critics, past and present, voice their anger at Stein's assumption of her own genius because, I believe, she is woman writer and she is a lesbian writer, and definitions of genius do not include these categories.

[2]*Ghost Dance* is the site of Maso's early explorations of female identity and mental illness in terms of the woman writer. Christine Wing is a poet who suffers from periodic bouts of depression and erratic behavior, an illness that is represented by the figure of the "Topaz Bird." While this early novel is narrated by Vanessa, Christine's daughter, the books that follow *Ghost Dance* approach the woman writer from her own point of view, focusing on the grief of the writer herself and the relationship between writing and loss.

[3]In *The American Woman* Catherine asks Lucien, "Tu connais *Nadja* de Breton?" ("Do you know *Nadja* by Breton?"), but he does not (108). It is significant that Maso references André Breton's novel *Nadja* (1928) because *Nadja* is a modernist novel heavily dependent on the myth of "genius." It also installs the subject and object positions of art-making along gendered lines: man as subject, woman as object. *Nadja* portrays the woman who is the male artist's muse and art object as mentally ill.

[4]The notion of writing "one true sentence" which Maso is referencing derives from Hemingway's essay "Miss Stein Instructs." Early in the essay, Hemingway writes, "I would stand and look out over the roofs of Paris and

think, 'Do not worry, you have always written before and you will write now. All you have to do is write one true sentence. Write the truest sentence that you know" (12). I find it interesting in terms of Maso's text that later in this essay Hemingway reveals his own anxiety over Stein's lesbianism.

WORKS CITED

Cooley, Nicole. "Carole Maso: An Interview by Nicole Cooley." *American Poetry Review* March-April 1995: 32-35.

Hemingway, Ernest. *A Moveable Feast*. New York: Scribner's, 1964.

Hutcheon, Linda. *A Poetics of Postmodernism: History, Theory, Fiction*. New York: Routledge, 1989.

Maso, Carole. *The American Woman in the Chinese Hat*. Normal, IL: Dalkey Archive Press, 1994.

Maso, Carole. *Ghost Dance*. San Francisco: North Point Press, 1986.

Moore, Steven. "An Interview with Carole Maso." *Review of Contemporary Fiction* 14.2 (1994): 186-91.

Stein, Gertrude. *The Autobiography of Alice B. Toklas*. New York: Vintage, 1933.

Between the Winding Sheets: The American Woman in the Chinese Hat

Jeffrey DeShell

The approximate distance between:
Vence, France, and New York City, USA—4080 miles;
Vence, France, and Bloomington, IL, USA—4720 miles

This is a story of distances; this is a story where distance is *critical.*

The *between* effect: a word that both separates and joins. Distance always requires some relationship between the two poles, whether they be cities, people, languages, words. One example among many: the distance between a novel and a critique of that novel.

I am (written) *in* this novel, *between* the covers of the book, page 201, my name among others both living and dead, a postscript, after the *fin* but before the flyleaf. And now I am writing *on* this story, about this story: I am writing on from between and within. A provisional schizophrenia: I will have to separate my writing self from my written self. I will have to create a distance between my writing and written selves, between the "I" who writes these sentences and the "Jeffrey DeShell" who is written in the acknowledgments of *The American Woman in the Chinese Hat.*

This is not about me.

I recognize a few names.

I know a few of their stories.

Distance is necessary to experience both art and desire. We need aesthetic distance in order to appreciate beauty, just as we need obstacles and separation in order to want something or someone. The distance in any case needs to be exact, precisely measured. If the distance disappears, if the desiring, looking subject collapses into the object of desire, of the gaze, then the whole house

Benjamin

falls down; "'Protect me from what I want,' it says" (32). If this distance grows too great, if the subject loses track of or forgets the object, then the subject simply sublimates the desire onto something or someone else; "Back in the dark city I take another lover. And then another. I don't know what I could have been thinking. What I wanted" (117).

"Usher"

Proust

The story begins with separations, with creations or articulations of distance: at least four of them in the first fifteen pages. The narrator, Catherine, has come to France leaving a lover, Lola, behind; "But I'm not kissing anyone; I'm waiting for her" (5).

As Maria begins to light her cigarette from the gas stove we hear the sound of a soccer match on the radio. Germany will beat Hungary 1-0.

This temporary separation turns more permanent a few pages later:

> "I'm seeing someone else," she whispers.
> "No, I don't believe you."
> "It's true."
> And then she begins. She says she can't stand the separations anymore. She says she can't believe she's put up with so much. She says something about all my affairs. She can't go on. She says she loves me but she is worn out. She can no longer be a slave to my genius. (14)

Catherine is in fact finishing another relationship: her second novel is complete and about to be published.

> "Your first book was so sad."
> "The second too," I say. "It will be out soon." (19)

A most interesting split happens after Lola has informed Catherine about her decision to break up. The narrative changes from first person to third, from "I close my eyes and see colors" (14) to "She is writing everywhere on scraps of paper" (15). This change is not permanent, but a separation has occurred, a distance has been established, the distance between "I" and "she," a distance between one who writes and one who is written, between one who describes and one who is described. This split, this schism, this distance, is what figures both *The American Woman in the*

Blanchot

Chinese Hat and the American woman in the Chinese hat, both the novel and the heroine.

What is the distance between I and "I"? Between she and *she?* Between she and I?

"Ecstacy. From Gr. *ekstasis, ek* out + *histanai* to set or stand. State of being beside oneself . . ."

"For once she'd like to understand the terrible distance in herself" (43).

More distances: between Catherine and Carole, between Catherine and her notebook, between Catherine and *The American Woman in the Chinese Hat,* between Carole and *The American Woman in the Chinese Hat,* between Catherine and Lucien, between September and *septembre.* This is a novel of distances; a novel where the story takes place in between.

Distance between Gazimagusa, Turkish Republic of Northern Cyprus and Providence, RI, USA—5310 miles.

In a novel of distances, movement is vital. There is constant going *(aller)* and coming *(venir),* constant adjustment and readjustment of the distance. *Sans ârreter.* At least at the beginning. At least until *le fin.*

"For a moment I am afraid, not of him, but of myself. I am frightened in the moment I realize that I don't care what happens to me anymore. It's what makes me move" (31). Which "me" are we talking about here? Who is afraid? Who is moving? The next page: "How she suffers. And she is a little in love with it. This romance of sex and sorrow" (32). Which "she"? Who is suffering? And who is in love with her suffering? Is it even the same she who suffers and who is in love with suffering? It is as if one self is experimenting with the other, putting the other into play. But which one?

Always the question.

Part 1—after the arrival in France and the breakup with Lola, a stream of lovers: a "young poet," "The Young Arlesian," the "fascist," "a pompier in a yellow coat," "Pascal," "the noir" and "la femme" (all of the quotation marks are Maso's [or Catherine's]). The encounters with the first two women (the "young poet," "The Young Arlesian") are somewhat erotic and seductive, especially when compared to those with the men, but the repetition makes them seem almost

Hello "young poet."

Aren't all lovers in quotation marks?

frightening in their meaninglessness, their randomness, in their self-destructiveness:

"F.N. What is it? What does it stand for? F.N. on your keys?"
"Front National," he says.
"What is that?"
He whispers as if someone may be listening. "A political party."
Suddenly it all makes sense. Le Pen's party. France for the French. . . .
She tells him she hates Le Pen.
He smiles. The very name seems to arouse him. I know what this passion in him is now. This intensity. He is so ugly suddenly. So large with hate. . . .
He kisses me hard. I know what he is and allow him to do this. To fuck me over and over and it is not even to save my life or bring meat to hungry children or get a secret. (30-31)

Why does sex always have to have meaning? Especially for women?

Fucking for nothing, "not even to save my life . . . or get a secret." Inflamed by a word, a name, a cognate, a pun, the Pen, le Pen(is), The Pen(al) Colony, he fucks her hard, over and over, leaving his sentence on her neck, literally splitting her in two:

The next day what is left is the imprint of his lips, a bloody red rose, a swastika on *her* neck. And it makes *her* feel sick. (31, italics mine)

" 'BE JUST!' is what is written there . . . surely you can read it now."

To repeat, the destruction of self through sex. But which self?

The lesson of *The Art Lover*. Anything can be used.

In Part 2 we read of a possible salvation through physical beauty. In the square, by the fountain, Catherine sees a man:

His is a beauty so perfect, so complete, that it makes all else seem inconsequential. Nothing else means anything. Nothing else matters. With a savage turn of his dazzling head the rest of the world turns black. (68)

Another chance meeting. With ultimately the same result: "three young girls . . . and a long-haired boy of about fourteen. Aschenbach noticed with astonishment the lad's

This is the man with the "cheveux longs." He is what she thought she needed:

perfect beauty. His face recalled the noblest moment of Greek sculpture."

> I needed the kind of beauty that renders all other things meaningless. That was the kind of beauty I longed for and sought. I was looking for a loveliness I had known in women and was beginning to recognize in some French men. But this—I wasn't expecting this. (70)

The trauma of his beauty, the shock of his perfection, immediately causes her to split: the point of view oscillates between first and third person:

> When he turns away she realizes she would enter this without thought of the consequences. As he turned away I knew I wanted him, whatever that would mean. (70)

" 'Protect me from what I want,' it says" (32).

Pygmalion and Galatea revisited, with genders reversed:

The difference between "Vence" and "Venice" is an "i."

> He is a world-weary statue, tired of everything. Tired of gazing out into perfect light, the fountain, the tourists. Bored by his own face. His eyes show it. They have the glaze of marble, there is something dead in them—it is his only flaw. (71)

The moving woman meets the dead statue, and is, for a while, stopped, "Arrested" (71). But only for a while. Soon, we suspect, something or someone will have to give. Or be given. Sacrificed.

Bataille

Ghost Dance—Christine Wing
The Art Lover—Gary Falk
AVA—Ava Klein
The American Woman in the Chinese Hat—?

Beyond the Pleasure Principle. The Death Instinct.

The story continues: the gradual disintegration of Catherine as the distance between her and what she desires, the man with the "cheveux

"Literature can be shown to accomplish in its terms a deconstruction that parallels the psychological

longs," begins to shrink. In the second part we have a foreshadowing of this: " 'C'est ne pas bon,' he says as he moves into me, *disappears into me"* (97, my emphasis). He disappears into her, he disappears, ceases to exist, is absorbed by her. He cannot save her if he does not exist. The quote continues, " 'What will it say in the book?' That he tried to save her, I think to myself, but could not" (97). And so she is left alone. Not alone, exactly, but by or with her self. Left by her self with her writing, her eye for (his) beauty, and her images, "They don't understand that this image of him in the water is all I really want. The ability to conjure him" (128). Alone, by her self, in a foreign country, a place between languages, a place where all language is foreign, "She knows she's speaking English like a foreign language. She's forgetting the meanings" (102). By her self with her cahier (which means she is or can never be alone, there is or will always be the written self to keep the writing self company), she writes, turning her life into fiction, her friends and lovers into characters:

deconstruction of selfhood in Freud."

Benjamin

The perfect situation for a writer: "A writer is someone for whom language constitutes a problem."

> "You use me," he says. "I see how you stare. You use my profile, my walk. I read while you slept about 'the particular beauty of the French.' I read about the nose, the long hair, everything. I recognized myself there."
> "So?" (125)

Everything and everyone can be used. Everyone becomes a character, everyone becomes internalized and fictionalized, everyone is written between quotation marks: the man with the cheveux longs, Catherine's friend, Sylvie, and the American woman in the Chinese hat. If you are a writer, when do you stop writing? "A writer's real life is when and where she is writing, she thinks. She is not running away in these pages, she is running forward, embracing her real life" (89).

What does it mean to stop writing?

The question of autobiography is unavoidable here. On the copyright page, a page meant to establish stable, legal identity and ownership, on a

"On the usual view, the work arises out of and by means of the activity of the artist. But by what and hence is the artist what he is? By the work; for to say that the work does credit to the master

page which by definition is outside of the fiction, we read:

means that it is the work that first lets the artist emerge as master of his art. The artist is the origin of the work. The work is the origin of the artist. Neither is without the other."

> © Carole Maso
>
> First Edition, May 1994
>
> This book was written at the Michael Karolyi Foundation in Vence, France, with the added support of a literature grant from the National Endowment for the Arts.
>
> This book is an invention, an act of the imagination, and in no way should be mistaken for reality, the place where much good invention originates. (iv)

Carole Maso, the legal owner of the copyright, the living, breathing person who in reality wrote this book actually went to Vence to write this book, a book about a writer going to Vence to write a book. This novel, we are told next, "in no way should be mistaken for reality." In other words, there is a distance or difference *between* this book and reality, just as there is a distance or difference *between* the character Catherine and the person Carole, although both are writers, and both, in a sense, are written. We are then told that reality is "the place where much good invention originates," the implication being that this novel, or invention, somehow originated in a reality: so perhaps this novel is a record of events that happened to Carole, in some form or another, when she went to Vence to write a book, a book that ended up being about a writer going to France to write a book.

Scheherazade

As the distance between them begins to shrink, the stories they tell each other, the stories she tells and hears, multiply. We read, "He's becoming addicted to her body. She can tell by the way he touches her now. And the stories. So many stories" (150). The stories she tells, stories of women, simultaneously attract and repel, fascinate and wound Lucien:

The idea of "a language that heals as much as it separates" frightens me.

> He laughs. "Tell me another one."I tell him I have been with women who love men.
>
> "You mean women who are not lesbians?"

"Oui."

"How many?"

Sade

"Beaucoup. I meet them. They are everywhere. I tell them how I will make them feel. And exactly how I will do it". . . .

He laughs again. It's nervous laughter.

"Women are so beautiful in their curiosity," I say, "their openness to everything. They are not like men."

He turns away.

It is a mistake to think that because our vocabularies are not large we cannot hurt each other. (151)

On the next page, Catherine begins to work her way through the alphabet:

"Go through the alphabet," he says.

Abish

"Oui?"

"Commence avec A."

"OK," I say. "A is for Annalise."

Sade

"Annalise," he repeats.

"B—Brett."

"Brett."

"C would have to be Cynthia. She was my first girlfriend. We were in high school."

He smiles. A universe of women. . . .

I never get to L. (152)

This is the place where language is successful, where it works to maintain the distance, the distance of separation and connection. But only for a while.

" 'You are already far away,' he says. 'How far do you want to go?' " (105-6).

In Part 3—the distance between Catherine and Lucien begins to disappear completely, along with the desire. Lola decides to come to Vence, to close the distance between them, to try to rescue Catherine and/or the relationship. But distance is what she needs. Near *le fin:*

She looks at the young French man she imagined she could die for. She tries to recall the enormity of her

Lola is also a writer: "She picks up a pen and writes 'important' in the margins. She puts a question mark next to

> desire. What does she desire now? She can think of nothing in this world. (188)

the part about Aschenbach's fear of being ridiculous; for what could be ridiculous in his pure search for beauty?"

To desire nothing in this world, to desire nothing in *this* world, to desire *nothing*. Nothing left.

The first death, offstage, "'Where is your cahier?' She scares him, this American. 'Gone,' she says. 'All gone' " (190).

What does it mean to stop writing?

Without writing she is no longer a writer. She is already, in a sense, dead. The self-slice at the fountain prefigured, predetermined, redundant:

> She reaches. Reaches for the knife. She thinks she should be afraid at this moment, but she is not. One should feel something more.
>
> How small she is suddenly. And her small offrandes. Love. All those lights were people's lives.
>
> She watches her veins open—a cathedral of light. Her blood rings like bells. Confetti. Angel. Stranger. (198)

Isn't death always a little ridiculous?

She is dead. But who is this she?

Autobiography—"A biography written by the subject of it; memoirs of one's own life written by oneself." Auto—self; bio—life; graph—to write. In the world, the world of life and breath, of copyright and disclaimer, of Carole Maso of Brown University, writing an autobiographical novel is a way to recount and remember, to reconstruct and re-create: to record events and feelings that either have, should or might have happened. The positive, safe aspect of biography—to put into writing in order to remember the events of one's life, "Écrire is to write. Souvenir is to remember" (174).

Duras

Writing, remembering, re-creating a past. Memory and distance. Writing in order to remember, and maintain a distance. A distance between two selves: a self that was, and a self that is. Trying to make sense out of what she (I) was. By negating (killing) that self that was her (me).

Proust again

"I know I am sounding less and less like myself. More like—quoi? a nouveau roman perhaps—a borrowed voice" (139).

How do you recount your own death, the death of your self? How do you find the right distance to watch your self die? "Often these days she finds she refers to herself in the third person as if she were someone else. Watching from afar" (21).

Language, writing, the means the writer uses to remember one's life, is precisely that which puts "life" into quotation marks, is precisely that which makes the writer forget life, that which makes the writer forget the life which is not writing, "A writer's real life is when and where she is writing" (89). We read in Blanchot:

A French writer, Maurice Blanchot!

> The journal is not essentially confessional; it is not one's own story. It is a memorial. What must the writer remember? Himself: who he is when he isn't writing, when he lives daily life, when he is alive and true, not dying or bereft of truth. But the tool he uses in order to recollect himself is, strangely, the very element of forgetfulness: writing.

The writer writes in order to remember, to remember who she is when she is not writing; but writing simultaneously erases the person who is not writing; writing forgets and causes the writer to forget the part of the writer who is not writing.

" 'Plus loin,' she says. 'More far. Farther' " (106).

By writing, you are already erasing. Or, to go further, you are killing:

> For me to say, "This woman," I must somehow take her flesh and blood reality away from her, cause her to be absent, annihi-late her. . . . The word is the absence of that being, its nothingness, what is left of it after it has lost being—the very fact that it does not exist. . . . Of course my language does not kill anyone. And yet, when I say, "This woman," real death has been announced and is already present in my language; my language means that this person, who is here right now, can be detached from herself, removed from her

A woman's corpse.

existence and her presence, and suddenly plunged into a nothingness in which there is no existence or presence.

Why is it always a woman's corpse?

To write in the third person: murder. To cause the death of one who is not you, of one who is distanced from you. The death of the other: an experience of death that distances you from death. A distancing from death that perhaps kills.

"William Wilson"

To write in first person: a simultaneous doubling and murder. To create an other (self) only to kill that other (self). But which one dies?

Despair

Catherine sacrifices the "she," the she who writes (and is written), by making her (self) burn her cahier.

A sacrifice which is also a suicide.

And she in turn is sacrificed by Carole, the blood flowing from her wrists.

Like ink.

The destruction of language that takes place in language, between languages, between the I and the she. The writing of the destruction of writing.

Writing between cruelty and ecstasy. An ecstasy which can never be contained.

An ecstasy that prefigures the self: that is the condition of the self's existence (L. from *eks* out + *sistere* to cause to stand). To write is to exist, to stand out, distanced from the self, the I watching the she, the first person the third. And vice versa. In the ecstasy of language.

"The cruelty of language comes from the fact that it endlessly evokes its death without being able to die."

Writing also negates: to write a life is to negate a life, to record and repeat what that life is *not.* To write a life is to drain the life from that life: it is to kill. Autobiography is always suicide.

By the same token, to write one's death is to negate that death: to write a death is to imagine what it can*not* and will *not* be, for who can imagine death, which is by definition beyond images and beyond words. *The American Woman in the Chinese Hat* can be read as a sort of talisman, a ghost dance, an attempt at immunization. A writing and imagining of a death (and a series of "little deaths") in order to forestall that very death, in order to keep that very death *at a distance.*

"I had done Sylvia—this woman whom I had so admired, even loved—a disservice. I had turned her into a character. I saw that now. A literary invention. I had imposed a false shape on her. I had diminished her in an attempt to understand something about

"We can never drive far enough" (117).

A distance which connects.

What does it mean to stop writing?

Most quotations in this column are taken from Carole Maso's novel, *The American Woman in the Chinese Hat* (Normal, IL: Dalkey Archive Press, 1994). The first Blanchot quote is from *The Space of Literature,* trans. Ann Smock (Lincoln: Univ. of Nebraska Press, 1982), 19. The second quote is from "Literature and the Right to Death," trans. by Lydia Davis, in *The Work of Fire,* trans. by Charlotte Mandel (Stanford: Stanford Univ. Press), 1995, 322-23.

my life. I had been in need of comfort, in need of consolation. I had invented her to give me courage, to ease my pain. For who was the real Sylvia, after all?" The paraphrase near the beginning is from *The Marriage of Maria Braun,* directed by R.W. Fassbinder, with Hanna Schygulla and Klaus Lowitsch, 1979. The first quote is from Franz Kafka's "In the Penal Colony," trans. Willa and Edwin Muir, in *The Complete Stories* (New York: Schocken, 1971), 161. The second quote is from Thomas Mann, *Death in Venice,* trans. H. T. Lowe-Porter (London: Penguin, 1971), 30. The third quote is from Paul de Man, "Self (Pygmalion)," in *Allegories of Reading* (New Haven: Yale Univ. Press, 1979), 174. The fourth quote is from Roland Barthes, *Criticism and Truth,* trans. Katrine Pilcher Keunemen (Minneapolis: Univ. of Minnesota Press, 1987), 64. The quotation following is from Martin Heidegger, "The Origin of the Work of Art," in *Poetry, Language, Thought,* trans. Albert Hofstadter (New York: Harper & Row, 1971), 17. Following is a quote from Carole Maso, *The American Woman in the Chinese Hat,* 165. The next quote is from Maurice Blanchot, "Kafka and Literature," in *The Work of Fire,* trans. Charlotte Mandel (Stanford: Stanford Univ. Press, 1995), 23. The final quotation is from *The American Woman in the Chinese Hat,* 176.

A New Language for Desire: Aureole

Steven Moore

> Sleepers awaking, our grey flesh tingling beneath the warm tongues of sister suns, the old dreams stirred; our blood flowed fast now, darkening, already inventing a new language for Desire.
>
> —Rikki Ducornet, *The Complete Butcher's Tales*

"We were working on an erotic song cycle" the dying Ava Klein remembers in Carole Maso's *AVA,* recalling its tentative titles throughout the novel (*A Place We Can Still Go; Toward a Female Subject; In the Joie de Vivre Room*—which was the original title for *AVA*). In a sense, *Aureole* is the song cycle Ava Klein didn't live to complete, musical in its lyrical style and decidedly erotic. Like Schubert's song cycle *Die Winterreise,* mentioned near the end of *Aureole,* Maso's individual "songs" are united by a common theme: desire. But rarely in literature has desire been explored with the intensity Maso brings to *Aureole:* a pyrotechnic display almost reckless in its abandon, daring in its subversion of literary propriety, and voracious in its erotic hunger.

In *Aureole* (Ecco, 1996) Maso exhibits the kind of bravado and self-exposure that I associate more with rock music divas than with her literary sisters. She has something of Courtney Love's swagger, P. J. Harvey's erotomania (both are mentioned on p. 81 of her book), Liz Phair's bluntness, Kate Bush's bookish romanticism, Siouxsie Sioux's dramatic flair, Jane Siberry's wit, Liz Fraser's mellifluousness, Shirley Manson's aggressive sexuality, Tori Amos's introspection, and Lisa Germano's heartbreaking insecurity. Maso even seems to borrow techniques from the more experimental female musicians working today, "sampling" older books and films (like the women in Single Gun Theory), using words occasionally as "noise and effects" (as Lisa Germano uses her violin), creating loops of recurring phrases (like Sarah Peacock of Seefeel), and so on. The individual pieces in *Aureole* cry out for performance, preferably with a backing track mixed by Betty and released on the innovative 4AD label.

But the overt musicality of *Aureole* owes just as much to the literary tradition of lyric women writers Maso aligns herself with by way of citation. In this book she names and quotes Sappho, Mirabai, Emily Dickinson, Gertrude Stein, Anna Kavan, and Marguerite

Duras. A woman writer she doesn't name is Elizabeth Smart, whose novel *By Grand Central Station I Sat Down and Wept* provides an instructive parallel to *Aureole.* Smart's 1945 novel, which remains criminally neglected, is a torch song of a book, an operatic lament written in an intense, overwrought style that is by turns biblical, poetic, and impertinent. The story is simple: a young woman falls obsessively in love with a married man, enjoys some blissful moments of illicit sex with him, and is left to bear their children. But the plot is hard to follow, for the text is hardly what you'd call "composed"; instead, its lipstick is smeared, its hair a mess, its mascara running as the nameless narrator rhapsodizes over love's joys and desolations. The novel lacks decorum, is shameless in its excesses, and resembles those madwomen scenes in Elizabethan drama where disorderly prose breaks through the orderly boundaries of verse. The story doesn't flow, it hemorrhages. (All this is praise, not censure.) The effect is overwhelming, emotionally draining, the greatest love story ever written if you define *love* as naked yearning so powerful and lawless that it resembles demonic possession.

Aureole is the only book I know to match the intensity and stylistic daring of Smart's. The narrative of *Aureole* is even more deeply buried than that in *By Grand Central,* but it can be unearthed if one wishes to consider the book a novel (which is useful if not strictly necessary). The nameless protagonist is an autobiographical figure whose erotic life traces a trajectory of desire from youth and the giddiness of her first lesbian experience, through the agony and ecstasy of various adult relationships, concluding in what might be the afterlife in a lesbian paradise. Like Smart, Maso isn't interested in standard exposition or in providing her figures with detailed backgrounds. (It's more useful to speak of figures than characters in *Aureole;* they're more like figures in a painting, or fantasy figures, than characters in a conventional novel.) But the overarching narrative concerns the writer/protagonist's search for a new language for desire. Maso goes further than Smart, further than anyone, in exploring "the hanging, gorgeous strange place between poetry and prose" (6), dispensing with the clichés of most erotic writing to develop a more physical kind of writing to simulate the various physical states of desire. Braving the imitative fallacy, Maso's sentences moan, babble, stutter, shout. The novel is a record of finding this language. Glance at the opening and closing pages of *Aureole* for a preview of the process: from normal-looking paragraphs and complete sentences, to isolated phrases, then blissed-out words, winding down to suspension points and finally an open-ended dash, yearning for "more—" (211). If language is seen as the protagonist, then its development can be tracked as easily as Jane Eyre's.

After a brief preface (in which Maso explains what she's up to better than I ever could), the novel opens with "The Women Wash Lentils." Stylistically, it encapsulates the stylistic development of the entire work, much as an opera's overture does: it begins with orderly sentences, standard paragraphing, and so on, but soon starts breaking up into fragments, lists, two-word paragraphs, where incantation replaces narrative. Ostensibly, the chapter concerns two young women in Paris, discussing French slang, though it is more likely an erotic fantasy invented by two older women, pretending to be in Paris and taking on the roles of two straight girls having their first lesbian experience. (In fact, in much of the novel it is impossible to say what is "really" going on and what is fantasy; it is set in the place in between the two.) One of the women is American, the other French (or pretends to be), and exploring a foreign language becomes synonymous with exploring a foreign body: "When they are in love with language, as they always are when they are French they explore each word, as they explore each other" (9). Throughout the novel Maso explores English with the care and curiosity with which one studies a foreign tongue: intrigued by its idioms, amused by its slang, puzzled by its grammar, going so far as to use English in the nonidiomatic way a foreigner would ("You Were Dazzle" is the title of a later chapter). She is defamiliarizing the language, both for herself and her readers, in order to rediscover its metaphoric capacity and to tease out its erotic potential (as in "a foreign tongue"). In this first chapter Maso establishes the equivalency of "lovemaking, language making" (15), where reading and writing are aphrodisiacal acts, and where sexual energy becomes a goal to achieve in writing: "And I'd like to do with any sentence what I'm about to do to you . . ." (10).

Maso's achievement of this goal is what distinguishes *Aureole* from standard erotica. Most erotic writing is erotic in content only, not in style or form. The average erotic novel uses the same syntax and paragraph organization as the average murder mystery or sci-fi adventure and is heavily reliant on clichés. Maso wants to capture states of desire "Between the event and its many formulations in the mind" (15), before it gets translated into those standard sentences and paragraphs. This means risking unintelligibility, slurring the language rather than seeking clarity, inducing a trance rather than providing a straightforward narrative, but Maso is willing to take these risks. Reversing the procedure of the Elizabethans I mentioned earlier, she disrupts orderly prose for a disorderly poetry of desire.

The young writer of the first chapter is next seen in a café in "Her Ink-Stained Hands," talking with her male lover, a butcher who is practicing abstinence. Their previous sexual bouts were physically brutal, and she still has the bruises and scars to show for it. She wants him still, but since he has withdrawn himself from her, she writes about him instead, another instance where writing becomes an extension of sex. The two have grown apart, mimetically signaled by the layout of the text: there are blank spaces between their utterances, with many of their sentences likewise interrupted by space. The blood, scars, and ink-stained hands metamorphose into religious images of crucifixion and stigmata, continuing the blending of religious and sexual images from the first chapter (where it is noted that *voir les anges*—to see the angels—is French slang for orgasm [22]). The chapter is a quiet piece, a meditation on the sublimation of sexual energy. It ends with the woman imagining kissing a bisexual triathlete, who takes the stage in the next chapter, "Make Me Dazzle," which is as explosive as the previous chapter is muted.

Dazzle is a key word in *Aureole,* used in two of its chapter titles and recurring throughout the novel. Maso has rescued the word from overuse in advertisements in women's magazines and recovered its more powerful original meaning of becoming overwhelmed by something, blinded, stupefied. In *Aureole* the word carries the full force of the impassioned boast of Shakespeare's Henry the Fifth: "I will rise there with so full a glory / That I will dazzle all the eyes of France, / Yea, strike the Dauphin blind to look on us" (*Henry V* part l, 1.2.279-81). Or for a more modern instance, listen to Siouxsie and the Banshees' magnificent song "Dazzle" (from *Hyaena,* 1984), where the word conveys an exultant derangement of the senses. In "Make Me Dazzle" the woman writer of the first two chapters is now a professor, vacationing in what sounds like Provincetown off-season. Walking along the beach, she encounters a woman named Aurelie, a bisexual triathlete, and they begin a torrid affair. Dazzled by the woman, the professor's language falls apart. "A deep deranging of the sentence—disorder" (49) sets in, and she has trouble forming coherent sentences. Mixed metaphors, synaesthesia, disrupted syntax, and almost preverbal babbling effectively convey her dazzled state of mind, the seashore setting providing some intoxicating Dylan Thomasesque sea imagery as she goes down (in all senses): "Sea drunk and snow they can barely hear each other / over the moan of the lighthouse and the ocean and roses" (43) could almost be a couplet out of his *Under Milk Wood.* "Rising from their sexual wreckage" (71) near the end of the chapter, the professor enters a stupefied dream-state, "singing demented songs dazzling songs," and indeed in the next chapter she becomes Ophelia and sings the most demented, dazzling song in the novel.

"Dreaming Steven Lighthouse Keeper" is a reverie conveyed in nursery rhymes and poetic prose in a state of post-orgasmic bliss. The narrator imagines that the lighthouse nearby is inhabited by a man who overhears the love-talk of the professor and the triathlete, then invents a background for him: a married man who left his wife, children, and the big city for a lonely existence as a lighthouse keeper. The narrator imagines Steven in love with an array of women, most identified winsomely by their relationships (the schoolmaster's daughter, the butcher's bride, the piano-tuner's assistant), others romantically mad (an opium addict, a crazy white-haired girl who scribbles poetry and who, in one sense, is the author of this chapter). His is an isolated, masturbatory existence, but Maso wraps it in a cocoon of enchanting fantasies and sing-song poetry, like a mother cooing nonsense over her sleeping baby.

Turning from this chapter to the next, "The Changing Room," is like getting a bucket of water in the face. It recounts a brief, urgent coupling between a man and a woman in breathless prose that is almost over before it begins. (It is the shortest chapter in the book.) The encounter takes place on a foggy night in March in a beach cabana, illuminated by a car's headlights. The woman repeats a line ("must have been an angel") from "Her Ink-Stained Hands" and is presumably the same; another line ("you are gentle") links this chapter to the next, the longest chapter in the book.

"Anju Flying Streamers After" begins with what sounds like a line from Wallace Stevens—"On the nighttable: a pomegranate" (89)—an obvious and important influence on Maso. But "Anju" is more influenced by film: directly by Marguerite Duras's *India Song,* which is quoted throughout the rest of the novel, and indirectly by the films of Satyajit Ray and Maya Deren. The professor of "Make Me Dazzle" is still in off-season Provincetown when she conjures up Anju, an Indian woman who inspires Maso's most trancelike writing. One can almost hear the drone of sitars and tambouras as the narrator rhapsodizes over Anju, abandoning linear narrative for a series of intoxicating visual images. The narrative method here is "chanting chanting / weaving slurring bobbing" (109), single words and phrases, as though the narrator is so "deranged by desire" (121) that she cannot form a coherent sentence: "sexual energy propels the sentence . . . her body disorders how you—" she trails off, allowing Anju's body to disorder the very sentences we are reading. The water imagery of "Make Me Dazzle" and "Dreaming Steven" is replaced here by fire imagery, as the narrator almost literally burns with desire for her luscious Indian beauty. Likewise, there are images of food and eating that are almost literalized as the narrator feasts on her beloved's body, eats from her fingers, eats a mango from between her legs, smothers her with spices. Possessed by erotomania, the narrator reverts to pure orality, the earliest stage of psychosexual development in psychoanalytic theory. The willing reader is sucked into this whirlpool, and only with difficulty realizes that Anju is a former student or disciple of the professor's, and who intriguingly enough believes she saw her teacher in India many years ago, the mysterious "woman on the bridge" who drifts through *Aureole* in various disguises (a persona for the narrator). Like the Song of Solomon, "Anju Flying Streamers After" is ravishing.

"The Devotions," the next chapter, continues with quotations from *India Song,* but the fires of desire have been extinguished for a meditation on the ephemerality of things, including art. This is followed by another brief chapter, "As We Form Our First Words." By this point in the novel, narrative has all but disappeared. This chapter contains fragments from most of the preceding chapters and represents a kind of breathing place as the narrator conjures up the persona for the next chapter.

"Sappho Sings the World Ecstatic" echoes the title of Whitman's "I Sing the Body Electric" and delivers another burst of sexual energy to the novel. (It will be noticed that there is a sexual rhythm to the novel, as chapters representing sexual insatiability alternate with ones in which, temporarily satiated, the narrator can fantasize about other figures or recall sexual episodes from her past.) With Whitmanesque exuberance Maso sings of the joys of lesbian sex, channeling Sappho as her narrative persona. Sappho, of course, has been present throughout the novel, quoted in several of the chapters and obviously a presiding muse over the novel. (The fragmented form in which her work survives can even be seen as a formal model for Maso's deliberately fragmented style.) Maso evokes the Greek poet in her most lilting, lyrical language yet, setting her in an erotic landscape (where a reclining nymph's hip can turn into a cliff's edge) and allowing her in a "fever dream" to see Maya Deren's dreamy film *At Land,* whose filmscript is excerpted throughout the chapter. The chapter itself is a kind of fever dream, where different levels of narrative surrealistically waltz together "In a medium unknown at the lip of the hypnotic word and Maya, key, asleep" (160). This sentence introduces Maya Deren, but also evokes the Vedantic concept of *maya,* the illusory world of the senses, which Maso represents so seductively here. A sensuous languour infuses the chapter to the point where the narrator becomes giddy and silly: "Sappho sings and sells sea shells. Sappho sings by the seashore" (166). Such playfulness explains Gertrude Stein's presence in the chapter, another woman conjured up by

Sappho from the strings of her lyre (164). In one sense Sappho is creating the lesbian paradise of the novel's final chapter; in another, all this is another reverie of the narrator, and ultimately of Carole Maso herself, our postmodern Sappho.

The narrator is jerked back to reality in "You Were Dazzle" (that word again), remembering a messy affair with a rich, cultured woman. The soft seas of Sappho's Greece give way to "the slam of the ocean" (170) back in the States, the "girly girls" (167) of Sappho's dream pushed aside by two strong-willed women filled with "rage and sorrow and hurt" (171). The prose is as wild and reckless as the women, with striking images flung in the reader's face, rage and lust preventing the impatient narrator from forming complete sentences. Lust here isn't the devouring hunger of "Anju" or the sexy games of "Make Me Dazzle" but "sex addiction" (172), that dreary concept from 1980s pop psychology that seems to have some validity here. The narrator resents her lover, even going so far as to turn her faults into a kind of poem (174), but admits "We were tangle and pull and gag but we were dazzle" (173). That sentence makes sense even though ungrammatical, and their affair made sense the same way.

"We were strung out," the narrator of "You Were Dazzle" says several times. In the next chapter, "Exquisite Hour," the narrator draws a parallel between sex addiction and drug addiction. The "you" addressed throughout this chapter is a composite figure, partly the opium addict with her snowy globe from "Dreaming Steven Lighthouse Keeper" and partly Anna Kavan (1904-68), a British novelist and short-story writer who was a heroin addict most of her adult life. The language itself is drugged, drifting in a haze, nonlinear, indolent, obsessive, beautiful in an icy kind of way. It is difficult, consequently, to determine what exactly happens. Is the "he" who addresses the opium addict Steven? Is the narrator herself the one strung out on drugs? On page 188 there is a quotation from David Callard's biography of Kavan (acknowledged in the notes at the back of *Aureole*): "The heroin makes one's eyes beautiful. There is no doubt I am attractive. I watched myself in the glass for a long time, which gave me pleasure." This suggests the narrator is addressing herself throughout, staring into a snow globe (179) in a drugged state. Snow and ice are the dominant images; one of Kavan's best novels is entitled *Ice,* and in her story "High in the Mountains" she praises heroin: "a clean white powder is not repulsive; it looks pure, it glitters, the pure white crystals sparkle like snow" (quoted in Callard, 47). And of course *snow* is slang for heroin as well as cocaine.

The aggressive sexuality of the previous chapter relaxes here into passive submission: to drugs, obviously, but also to a "*maitre*" who is partly a fencing instructor (Maso studied fencing as a teenager). But the narrator is also learning to submit to a new kind of writing, to "the sensuous lexicon of falling, where I write, where I like to write, more and more often now. Charting a motion and its many permutations, its many fallings into desire, language—waywardness, hope . . ." She goes on to justify drug use because "you just wanted to be taken away. Taken out—to become silent because there wasn't any language for this" (193). But at this point in the chapter the male voices (the "he" of the opening pages, the fencing master, even the "yowling mouth of Dietrich Fischer-Dieskau" singing *Die Winterreise*) are drowned out by the voice of "a woman singing only slightly out of phase . . . the woman with the velvet voice. Exquisite. Salvation. Lady Day" (194). Listening to Billie Holiday, the narrator sees a "Halo. Aureole. I lift my arms to the glare" (194). "A strange paradise enters" (194), glare and fire melt the snow and ice, couples dance, and the narrator walks "out of all enclosures, all that has confined you . . . away from all that has kept me in place. Afraid" (196). Thus "Exquisite Hour" can be read as an account of an aesthetic crisis, where the narrator turns to drugs in despair of finding an appropriate language for herself, is confined in an enclosure of patriarchal expectations—the fencing master's (read agent's, publisher's) repeated demand for a masterpiece—then finds in Lady Day's voice the courage to forge a new language like that so triumphantly on display here and throughout *Aureole*. "At last you see—at last—someone in the mirror you think you recognize. And I am happier than I have ever felt, she thinks" (200).

This feeling of triumph at the end of "Exquisite Hour"—the most daring and complex chapter in the book—is carried over to *Aureole*'s concluding chapter, a kind of coda entitled "In the Last Village." A few pages back the narrator had said "A strange paradise enters," and this brief prose poem describes her personal paradise, a lesbian utopia populated by her friends and mentors. Various phrases from earlier chapters are chanted in a final state of post-orgasmic bliss, where all aesthetic and erotic difficulties have been resolved.

It's a lovely conclusion to Maso's most innovative book to date. Each of her preceding novels pushed the envelope of what prose fiction could do, especially the groundbreaking *AVA*, but *Aureole* takes greater risks, dares more, shows greater variety than anything she's done before. Though it will probably be categorized as lesbian erotica—and deserves to become a classic of the genre—it's more an aesthetic adventure of self-discovery, of seeing how far a gifted writer can go to forge a new language for desire. Borrowing techniques from film and poetry, nursery rhymes and pornography, rock music and painting, Maso goes further than any writer working today to create a style that does justice to the polymorphously perverse energy of eros. Carole Maso will make you see the angels.

A Carole Maso Checklist

Ghost Dance. San Francisco: North Point Press, 1986; Hopewell, NJ: Ecco, 1995.

The Art Lover. San Francisco: North Point Press, 1990; Hopewell, NJ: Ecco, 1995.

AVA. Normal, IL: Dalkey Archive Press, 1993.

The American Woman in the Chinese Hat. Normal, IL: Dalkey Archive Press, 1994; New York: Plume, 1995.

Aureole. Hopewell, NJ: Ecco, 1996.

Book Reviews

Thomas Pynchon. *Mason & Dixon*. Henry Holt, 1997. 773 pp. $27.50.

In 1990, when, after seventeen novel-less years, Thomas Pynchon published *Vineland,* old Pynchon hands everywhere moaned: we waited so long for *this? This* is the successor to *Gravity's Rainbow?* Well, after teaching it several times, I've developed a lot of respect and affection for *Vineland*. Still, *this* time there's to be no moaning: *Mason & Dixon* is the real thing, the novel we've been waiting for, and, yes, it turns out to have been worth the wait. Like *Gravity's Rainbow*, it is an encyclopedia of esoteric knowledge, it brings together everyday, historical, and fantastic characters, it passionately opposes the forces of objectification and control, but not without making problematic those who represent life and freedom, it contains both outrageous jokes and passages so beautiful you want to cry.

The novel focuses on astronomer Charles Mason, surveyor Jeremiah Dixon, and their lines, most famously the Line they measured separating Pennsylvania and Maryland and thus the North from the South in just-pre-Revolutionary America, but also the line made by Venus as it crosses the face of the sun, the lines representing Mason's and Dixon's life stories and the narrative we're reading, the "lines" Mason, Dixon, and the other characters speak, fishing lines, and, perhaps most important, the lines connecting one person to another. The central image of the novel, the Mason-Dixon Line seems to represent, in the words of Tyrone Slothrop of *Gravity's Rainbow*, "the fork in the road America never took, the singular point she jumped the wrong way from." Of course, the America Mason and Dixon find is hardly Edenic; the coffeehouses of Philadelphia, Annapolis, and New York seethe with the machinations of various nations, religions, political factions, and mysterious controlling forces—including the Royal Society and the Jesuits. Still, the Line represents the processes of division, rationalization, and control that have resulted in the America we have inherited. On the one hand, the Line manifests America's Original Sins, both westward expansion, as Mason and Dixon cut their line through the forests and encroach on Indian lands, and the separation of America into "free" and slave-holding territories. But on the other hand, the Line, as it is being measured, draws to itself an increasingly strange collection of oddballs and outcasts—a great French chef and the mechanical duck impossibly in love with him, a Chinese geomancer on the run from the Jesuits, a woman who is compelled to perform as a street show a miniature re-creation of the Battle of Leuthen, a secret agent from an unknown northern land posing as a Swedish axman—people who in all likelihood won't fit in to the America Mason and Dixon are helping to define. Moreover, as they move west, farther from the more settled, civilized, and rationalized east, they come into contact more frequently with the marvelous and the fantastic—my favorite: a were-beaver who loses a tree-cutting contest when a lunar eclipse, unpredicted by the astronomers, inconveniently turns him back into a human.

If this potential for ad hoc community and the magical is part of what is lost to America as a result of the Line, the novel also recognizes the potential for love among people. Mason and Dixon spend years together, coming into conflict personally and professionally, bickering endlessly, and it is only in their last meetings, annual fishing expeditions in the north of England, that they come tentatively and inarticulately to recognize their affection for each other and to use this affection as a way of connecting with others in their lives—parents, spouses, children. If *Gravity's Rainbow* ends with disturbing, apocalyptic power, *Mason & Dixon* ends touchingly, with nostalgia for what's been lost and hope for what might, even now, be found.

There are reminders of other authors here—the Barth of *The Sot-Weed Factor,* the Vollmann of the *Seven Dreams* series—but I am most reminded of Pynchon at his best, especially *Gravity's Rainbow*. My guess is that *Mason & Dixon* is an easier first read than *Gravity's Rainbow* but that a first reading gives only a hint of what the novel offers: Pynchon scholars—as if they weren't busy enough—will find plenty here to occupy their time into the next century. *Mason & Dixon* is an amazing achievement, certainly the novel of the year, possibly the novel of our time. [Robert L. McLaughlin]

Don DeLillo. *Underworld*. Scribner, 1997. 827 pp. $27.50.

The word *underworld* suggests many associations: (1) The criminal element of American society (the mobs in the Bronx, including Nick, his bookie father, and their desire to fashion a private world); (2) the regions of hell; (3) the repressed memories of the past (an underworld of murder, victimization, shame); (4) the "waste" of language itself (including the change of the Latin of the Church and the street dialect of Italian). And to complicate matters there is the exploration of "under" as failure (as represented let's say by the losing Dodger, Ralph Branca) and success. It is possible to read any page to see references to *un*knowing, *un*doing and other words using this prefix.

DeLillo is, in effect, posing philosophical questions about the nature of knowledge and ontology. Underworld suggests the notion of mystery, occult, and secret forces. But is there an underworld opposed to *the* "world"? What are the limits or boundaries of "under"? Is there any routine, known "world" which the "under" subverts? Perhaps the linkage of Branca and Thompson—the loser and the winner—recur throughout the novel to remind us that opposites are somehow always linked. High and low are relative—are, indeed, married.

I want to quote two passages that demonstrate the careful and subtle "logic and metaphor." The first is from the prologue in the Polo Grounds in the 1951 baseball game. J. Edgar Hoover, Jackie Gleason, Frank Sinatra—all successful "heroes"—sit close to the action of the game. When Thompson hits his home run the fans in the cheap seats (the failures in our capitalist society?) throw down papers of various kinds onto Hoover: "In the box seats J. Edgar Hoover plucks a magazine page off his shoulder, where the thing has lighted and stuck. At first he's annoyed that the object has come in contact with his body. Then his eyes fall upon the page. It is a color reproduction of a painting crowded with medieval figures who are dying or dead—a landscape of visionary havoc and ruin."

Almost every word explodes with associations, and these associations recur throughout the entire novel. Hoover regards people, texts, files, and bodies as things. He opposes thing and being. He hates "contact." He wants pure distinction. His eyes—his perceptions—are distorted. They don't see the full picture. The reproduction is of *The Triumph of Death*, Breugel's painting. It is a visionary (remember Hoover's vision) work of havoc and ruin. The novel is also a work of havoc and ruin. There is a connection between text and painting. Significantly, the prologue is called "The Triumph of Death."

Much later in the novel, Klara, an artist and the mistress of the adolescent Nick, attends a secret showing of a lost Eisenstein film called *Unterwelt* (consider the relation of film to painting to text). The German title, of course, brings to mind DeLillo's obsession with Nazi havoc in *White Noise* and *Running Dog*. Klara is told by her friend: "I think you ought to see the film and figure it out for yourself. I'll only tell that word got around, early on, that Eisenstein made a film with a powerful theme and the footage has been hidden away all these decades because the theme deals on some level with people living in the shadows, and the government, or the governments, the GDR and the Soviets, have suppressed the film until now."

The words reverberate with meaning. Eisenstein is known for his use of montage and the DeLillo text is a montage, a layering of levels. Eisenstein was homosexual. Nick, the protagonist, by using Klara as his woman years ago was, in effect, seducing the woman married to his teacher, his substitute father. The homosexual's "world" is coded, secretive, and subversive. Notice that the film is full of shadows; it deals with the shadows of the repressed masses. The entire passage forces us to recognize that power is perhaps the "real" theme of the novel. [Irving Malin]

Christine Schutt. *Nightwork.* Knopf, 1996. 129 pp. $20.00.

Buzzing with the hothouse sexual latency of a Sally Mann or Jock Sturgess nude, the stories in Christine Schutt's debut collection inhabit a dangerous space between incest, fear, and desire. Many of Schutt's seventeen stories revolve around couples coupling—and the anticipation or threat of coupling between figures in a family. Everyone wants something here: daughter covets father, and mother her son. In "You Drive" the collection leads off with such a transgressive enticement: "She brought him what she had promised, and they did it in his car, on the top floor of the car park . . . and she said, or thought she said, 'I like your skin,' when what she really liked was the color of her father's skin. . . . "

Though incest verges on becoming a stock situation in recent fiction, these are not conventional tales of familial lust and abuse. The dreamlike and poetically rendered stories in *Nightwork* resist a casual reader's attempt to shape out intentional plot or design. Throughout the collection, meaning is pleasurably associative and indirect. These stories rely upon memory and meandering thought, and nothing much usually happens. "Good Night, Sweetheart" deliciously recalls a woman's sexual dread while on a date with an elderly man. In "Daywork" two sisters simply banter while emptying the attic of their infirm mother's belongings. "What Have You Been Doing" follows how a kiss between a mother and son evolves like expanding pearls in a necklace into an overtly Oedipal liaison—a burning central gem at the story's end. Schutt discards plot mechanics; almost every story explores some overintimacy of characters, relatives locked in the old transactional systems of family, though without the normal moral order of values, familial or otherwise.

The reward for reading *Nightwork* lies in the wonderful line-by-line sensuality of Schutt's language and in the intensity of each worked line. Often her stories contain leaps of prose which thrill like virtuoso moments in dance. Onomatopoeic words and neologisms ornament this work. A shoe doesn't slip on and off but *shucks* against a heel. Debris beneath a table becomes "bread crusts and withered peas always more, and furred with such a dust that I think they come alive at night and breed." Though the stories in *Nightwork* are brief, you may want to take your time with them and read each piece with deliberation and slowness. [William Tester]

Seamus Deane. *Reading in the Dark.* Knopf, 1997. 246 pp. $23.00

Deane's first novel arrives in the wake of the numerous volumes of poetry and criticism which have gained him an international reputation as an original, complex, and sometimes controversial writer and thinker. Although his work as both poet and scholar has distinguished him, this previous work is dwarfed by the magnificence of *Reading in the Dark,* a novel which seems destined to be regarded as one of the great Irish novels published this century. The novel is set in Derry, Northern Ireland, between the 1940s and 1960s. On one level it is a coming-of-age novel which traces the growth into manhood, knowledge, and experience of a male hero. However, in addition to coming to terms with body and soul, this young man is forced to discover and accept the hard secrets which have burdened his family and to come to grips with the history of Derry and Ireland. Out of a natural curiosity, the boy discovers the roles played by members of both his maternal and paternal families in the I.R.A. and how both families and their interrelationships have been undermined by desertion, treachery, and wrongful execution: "You poor Child—My poor family," his mother tells him. The boy learns all of these family secrets, becomes their repository, but must become a man before he can learn to live with them.

What makes this novel succeed so magnificently is the quality of the writing. Each chapter is brief, generally no more than 1500 words in length, with the narrative growing more complex as the boy grows older. Deane seems to distill from Derry all that is important in both public and family life and to relate one to the other. He provides a deep sense of how claustrophobic and difficult it can be to grow up in the turmoil of Northern Ireland and how past events can draw in and destroy the lives of the living. By his adroit use of a first-person narrative, Deane underlines the truth that in the less-well-off neighborhoods of Northern Ireland there can be no separation of the personal and the political. Each short chapter is carefully and elegantly written and complete. However, the novel also accrues in power from chapter to chapter with a kind of deep, tragic sense of doom. In some respects one is reminded of Joyce's *Portrait,* of Koestler's *Darkness at Noon,* of the works of Faulkner: *Reading in the Dark* is that good. This is a novel which comes to America with a big reputation and one that is completely deserved. [Eamonn Wall]

Steve Erickson. *American Nomad.* Henry Holt, 1997. 256 pp. $25.00.

Steve Erickson's imaginative documentary of the 1996 Presidential election began when *Rolling Stone* hired him to report on the campaign as if it were a novel. The magazine's editors quickly tired of the novelist's narrative style and fired him after the New Hampshire primary, so he lit out on his own nomadic journey, "one last rampage through the national asylum," into the heart, mind, and soul of America. In Erickson's view the election was "a war for the soul of America." More than a mere chronicler, Erickson serves as our war correspondent in the apocalyptic trenches of millennial America. Although *Leap Year*, Erickson's account of the 1988 election, pictures an America caught in the grip of inertia, America 1996 faces a more insidious, less benign threat from within—us. He contrasts the "moral generosity" of Lincoln's second inaugural speech with the exclusionary rhetoric of today's politicians and concludes that "America wearies of democracy." Beset by rage, hypocrisy, and selfish interests, millennial America is in an entropic slide. As Americans feel increasingly oppressed by individual freedom, political options move further out toward extremes of conformity hostile to any "moral nuance." Erickson's narrative historicizes America's contradictory desires and works to restore this moral middle ground. *American Nomad* deserves to be compared with the best political and cultural journalism of Norman Mailer and Hunter S. Thompson (Erickson even accosts Bob Dole in a men's room, recalling the legendary Thompson-McGovern meeting in *Fear and Loathing on the Campaign Trail, '72*), yet Erickson's style is less self-indulgent, less overwhelmed by the observing author's persona. Remarkably insightful, sharply funny, complex, and provocative, *American Nomad* rates a space on the short shelf of books about politics and life at the end of the twentieth century. [Trey Strecker]

John Banville. *The Untouchable*. Knopf, 1997. 367 pp. $25.00.

Banville writes novels which question the truths of biography; his historical novels about Copernicus, Newton, and Kepler subvert usual conceptions. *The Untouchable,* his most recent novel, is another "antibiography." He uses the story of Blunt, the British art historian and Russian mole, to develop his own obsessive search for truth. Blunt is, in many ways, his secret sharer.

The novel is a mixture of reportage, biography, and meditation. It is, in a perverse way, an occult, secretive work about the hidden world of homosexuality and spying. Form and content are reflective. Banville understands the marriage of homosexuality and spying. Both realms dwell upon coded messages, gestures, and obscure pleasures. He makes us wonder whether family nurtures or creates untouchables (or vice versa). The novel's opening lines are clues: "First day of the new life. Very strange. Feeling almost skittish all day. Exhausted now yet feverish also, like a child at the end of a party. Like a child, yes; as if I had suffered a grotesque rebirth. Yet this morning I realized for the first time that I am an old man." The sentences seem to be unbalanced; the oppositions of new/child and end/old are deliberately presented in a jittery way. They make me wonder whether I can trust Victor's confession-text.

This novel reinforces my contention that Banville is one of our most daring, erudite novelists. He deserves close reading. [Irving Malin]

Hervé Guibert. *Blindsight*. Trans. James Kirkup. George Braziller, 1996. 119 pp. $20.00.

Hervé Guibert is best known for his works dealing with AIDS (*To the Friend Who Did Not Save My Life* and *The Compassion Protocol*)—dead-pan accounts of his grappling with, and sometimes perverse embracement of, the disease. His current stature is evident in the fact that this English translation of his rather patchworked novel *Des aveugles* has appeared only a year after its posthumous publication in France. Arising from an experiment that he carried out among the blind and his experience as a reading volunteer,

Blindsight describes a borderland world filled with fierce, proud, and ultimately ruthless characters, whose blindness acts not only as a defiant rejection of the outer world but as an embracement of an inner, almost childish one of freeplaying impulse and cruelty. As the narrator states midway through the novel, Guibert is less concerned with a sympathetic portrayal of the blind than with flying "in the face of conscience or charity."

After a bit of uncertain groping about, the novel finally focuses on three characters: Robert and Josette, a young married couple at an institute for the blind, and Taillegueur, a brutal con man and clammy-handed masseur whose odor seduces Josette, setting off a sordid series of erotic and sadistic games. The plot, if at first spotty, finally plays itself out like a horror comic book, particularly in an odd episode involving the narrator as a volunteer-reader turned sacrificial victim. What makes the book of interest, however, is not its story as much as the world it attempts to describe. At the institute, run and inhabited by the blind, surface is sight. *Everything* is surface, and if depth (psychological or otherwise) manifests itself, it is as the depth of a needle into an eye or the void through which a misguided body might fall. Across this synesthetic horizon, touch becomes noisy, smells become sights, and faces become as undefined as desires.

This ambiguity of definition is what ultimately creates the novel's suspense.The characters remain hovering between childhood and adulthood, like the proudly cruel adolescents of Jean Cocteau's work; victims and victimizers blur into each other, both in relation to their private games and in relation to the world of the sighted. The institute is located at the border between the city and the countryside, and the text itself carries an open visa between the actual experience to which Guibert alludes at the novel's opening and the slight feverishness of his own imagination.

Blindsight is of decided interest to anyone wanting a fuller range of Guibert's work. [Marc Lowenthal]

Samuel R. Delany. *Longer Views.* Wesleyan Univ. Press, 1996. 342 pp. $50.00; Paper: $22.00. *Atlantis: Three Tales.* Wesleyan Univ. Press, 1997. 212 pp. $24.95.

We witness a strange period in which it seems that, at the same time the canon of approved, proper literature narrows, we have ever greater access (through translations, small-press publications, courageous university presses) to the fullest range of literary possibility: Delany, for instance.

Author of thirty or so books, a cornerstone of contemporary science fiction with novels such as *Dhalgren* and *Triton*, praised by the likes of Umberto Eco for the innovation and imaginative force of his fantasy quartet *Return to Nevèrÿon,* Delany is a national treasure unknown to the majority of readers. He is also, as earlier books such as *Silent Interviews* and *The Straits of Messina* suggest and as *Longer Views* affirms once and for all, a formidable, engaging critic.

Opening with a graceful introduction from Ken James, *Longer Views* goes on to reprise Delany's brilliant, evocative investigation of modernity, "Wagner/Artaud"; a reading of Donna Haraway's feminist "Manifesto for Cyborgs"; a self-interrogation into the nature of personal and social sexual experience ("Aversion/Perversion/Diversion"); the collagelike, darting, glancing "Shadow and Ash"; and a marvelous essay on Hart Crane written simultaneously with composition of Delany's short novel "Atlantis: Model 1924." An earlier essay, "Shadow," is included as appendix.

Ken James points out that in previous critical work Delany largely restricted himself to standard essay forms, while here, importing techniques from his later fiction—framing structures, multiple-intersection stories, conflation of personal, social, and historical voices—he comes onto something new in the world, "an experience which simply cannot be found anywhere else in the current American literary landscape."

Atlantis: Three Tales brings into paperback Delany's most recent medium-length writing. "Atlantis: Model 1924" supposes a meeting of Delany's father, newly arrived in New York, with Hart Crane; it's as densely allusive, as written-over and frought with cultural cargo as anything of Joyce's, truly a major work. In a sort of inversion of intent, "Citre et Trans" fictionalizes, or reimagines, actual episodes of Delany's travels in Greece. The model here is Paul Blackburn, stories that seem all fictive *stuff,* not at all arranged. "Eric, Gwen, and D. H. Lawerence's Esthetic of Unrectified Feeling" seems at first a memoir on the model of Delany's earlier *Heavenly Breakfast* or *The Motion of Light in Water.* Probing at his early fascination with science fiction, his simultaneous awakening to art and to his own homosexuality, quickly the "essay" takes on the texture and heft of fiction, those "neat and headlong narratives."

Wesleyan University Press, meanwhile, is to be roundly commended both for its publication of new Delany, such as *Longer Views* and *Atlantis*, and for its reissues of classic Delany fiction: *Dhalgren*, *Triton*, the *Return to Nevèrÿon* quartet. [James Sallis]

Eric Chevillard. *The Crab Nebula*. Trans. Jordan Stump and Eleanor Hardin. Univ. of Nebraska Press, 1997. 126 pp. $35.00; Paper: $12.00.

The celestial Crab nebula, in the constellation Taurus, is the debris of a supernova observed in 1054 and the source of strong radio waves. These astral facts serve as metaphor for Eric Chevillard's *The Crab Nebula*, about a man named Crab: the volume is full of verbal debris contained between its covers, but beyond that, having little coherence. Its language signals are strong, mainly composed of exuberant and authoritative-seeming declarative sentences, making absolute statements that are subsequently contradicted and reversed. As we are told, "Crab is ungraspable, not evasive or deceptive but blurry, as if his congenital myopia had little by little clouded his contours."

The Crab Nebula has fifty-two small chapters and if readers were so inclined, they could invent some thematic consistency within each one that would justify the isolation of those sentences into a chapter. Chapter 4, for instance, seems to be concerned with Crab's body parts: a wax tongue, mercury eyelids, gold teeth, nails made of frost, scales, feathers, a saltpeter belly, feet of different lengths a scrotum under his chin. But, then, most of the chapters have something in them about Crab's body parts.

Philosophically French, the book is existential and postmodern, since its outlook on life is both bleak and filled with non sequiturs: "Crab believes that he deserves a full day of rest tomorrow. . . . It will have to wait. It's simply been too long since Crab was last tormented by his rheumatism. And there are other experiences he has yet to go through, experiences that count for something in the destiny of a man, and of which he has so far inexplicably been deprived. There are plans for a house fire. . . ." Yet *The Crab Nebula* is, despite its melancholy, light and humorous, a crazy dream full of terrors dressed like a sad, accepting clown who knows his part is to amuse. [Ellen G. Friedman]

Jeanette Winterson. *Gut Symmetries*. Knopf, 1997. 223 pp. $22.00.

Winterson's latest novel compares favorably with her previous work, particularly her brilliant *Sexing the Cherry*. *Gut Symmetries* is an alchemical blend of multiple narrators, fairy-tale allusions, and quantum physics theory. Winterson displays the same well-crafted, seraphic prose that has established her as one of Britain's most intriguing and prodigious younger authors.

Gut Symmetries revolves around Alice, a young British physicist who has become the defining corner of a bizarre love triangle. She finds herself involved with a distinguished peer, Jove, whose pragmatic theories are the "future" of physics. His assured demeanor provides a point of reference for the uncertain Alice: "I could not define myself in relation to the shifting poles of certainty that seemed so reliable. What was the true nature of the world? What was the true nature of myself in it?" Jove's wife Stella has grown intolerant of his affairs and arranges to confront Alice. Their meeting turns erotic and they become involved in a meaningful relationship of their own. Caught in the middle and yet on both sides of a marital feud, Alice struggles to find solid ground in a newly decentered reality.

Winterson's use of structure and language is self-reflexive. Each chapter provides a shift between the perspective of characters, and perspectives shift with the dynamic nature of their three-way relationship. Seemingly uncontextualized sentences early in the novel reflect the physical and spirtual theories of an uncertain Alice. As the novel progresses, these sentences reappear and eventually become contextualized in symmetrical GUTs: the Grand Unified Theories needed to cope with a transmogrifying existence.

Gut Symmetries proves Winterson's dynamic sense of language. It is a solid addition to an already stellar body of work. [Christopher Paddock]

Patrick Chamoiseau. *School Days.* Trans. Linda Coverdale. Univ. of Nebraska Press, 1997. 146 pp. Paper: $13.00.

In *School Days* Patrick Chamoiseau (winner of the 1992 Prix Goncourt) recounts with bitter charm his introduction to the colonial education in the Martinique of the 1950s—the days when "the blue-eyed Gaul with hair as yellow as wheat was everybody's ancestor." The child Chamoiseau, "the little boy," desperately hungry for exploration of the outside world, latches onto school as the pathway to it, only to discover that this path demands the eradication of the "barbarous," "ol'-nigger ways" of Creole. This is undertaken by the "Teacher," a humorous exemplar of official culture with unhumorous methods of beating barbarity out of his students.

The little boy's induction into the confining, yet ultimately salvatory, horizon of language takes place under the shadows of two mentors: the Teacher, the enforcer of the written word, and Big

Bellybutton, the class outcast, the unknowing preserver of the underground spoken word, and keeper of the Creole legend. It is this tension between improper Creole tongue and proper French text that defines much of Chamoiseau's work and provides much of this novel's humor and delightfully ribald episodes. Chamoiseau's writing, via Coverdale's charged and inventive translation, bristles with energy, opening up portals into the Creole dialect with Rabelaisian gusto.

The humor carries a weight, though. Chamoiseau's classmates are for the most part ostracized from any hope of a future in the colonies, and Big Bellybutton's inability to culturally assimilate ultimately crushes his spirit. It is left to the author to try to salvage whatever troubled identity is left to the Caribbean individual, an effort that takes up where Aimé Cesaire's "négritude" left off. The novel locates a meeting point for speech and writing that should carry resonance for anyone concerned with the politics of identity and language.

Chamoiseau's novel *Texaco* won him the Prix Goncourt in 1992, and his *Creole Folktales* is already available in English. This novel should do well in bringing him further to an English-speaking audience. [Marc Lowenthal]

Rick Moody. *Purple America*. Little, Brown, 1997. 298 pp. $23.95

In a traditional allegory characters stand in for their qualities. Goodness, Courage, and Charity stride about, going head-to-head and hand-to-hand with their well-known evil twins. In both *The Ice Storm*, his last novel, and *Purple America*, Rick Moody writes a kind of demographic allegory. Characters in the novel are at once people in an unfolding drama as well as a segment of the American population, recognizable pieces of the most recent census, say, people of a certain educational background, a certain size house, a certain quality of clothing, a certain grade of household appliances.

The Raitliffes, a nuclear family in the early stages of meltdown, are the primary characters in this novel, and Billie, her son Hex, and Lou Sloane, Billie's second husband, are real to more than their own emotions. Reality here is not just the frayed inner reality of characters in trouble; there are national troubles afoot as well, and the characters are never separate from them. These crises and conflicts that summon Hex from New York City, cause Lou to leave Billie, and bring Billie to the point where she wishes to die would never survive a summary. Suffice it to say that the novel never feels overburdened with too much conflict or, more miraculously, ruined by a resolution that's too tidy.

What distinguishes *Purple America* is not its family plot, but what Moody does in addition to it. His novel is as rich in specifics as it is in generalities, patterns, economic forces, social history, and cultural observations, all the huge, gravitational movements of people toward some state of mind nobody has a name for yet. Some passages begin in generality: "Misfits and idiot savants, coveters of weapons-related data, fundamentalists, borderline personalities, pot smokers, people who fell through the cracks of a franchise-fueled economy; these were the guardians of the atomic age." This roll call of types is followed by Lou Sloane's closer observation of one such guardian—"Dave McCluskey, his name was"—who is just one individual at a nuclear power plant where both are employed.

Surprisingly, generalities and specifics work well together. The writing on large patterns that overcome characters lends credence to the specific predicaments of those characters. Similarly, specifics insure that the generalities never lapse into the universal. Micro and macro, specific and general, *Purple America* is at once set specifically in Connecticut and, generally, in a wider world. This is a family story that is unafraid to be larger than the dinner table, weightier than the average couch, and not so still as the view from many fictional windows. Moody has found a way to take the family narrative and open it up to what's forever outside and often unacknowledged. *Purple America* is an inviting and generous novel. [Paul Maliszewski]

Maurice Blanchot. *Awaiting Oblivion.* Trans. John Gregg. Univ. of Nebraska Press, 1997. 86 pp. $26.00.

Blanchot is a terrifying writer. The action takes place in a hotel room; a man and woman make cryptic remarks about such subjects as waiting, writing, time, and death. But the man and woman seem to melt into other ghosts—these may or may not be another man and woman or their secretive doubles. "He" and "she"—and "I," the author—become ambiguous pronouns so that identities remain obscure. And, to complicate matters, the author seems to intrude into the text—but isn't the text *his* own creation?—and to offer circular aphorisms. Thus the text is, in effect, a philosophical inquiry "posing" as a fiction (or vice versa), a work which is more complex than *Waiting for Godot* or *The Beast in the Jungle,* James's text about waiting for a finality, a *revelation.*

I want to quote one passage to indicate the terrible beauty of this shocking text: "No one likes to remain face to face with that which is hidden. 'Face to face would be easy, but not in an oblique relation.' " Notice that the first statement is written by the author. "Face to face" seems to contradict *hidden*. How can I confront something (a state of mind) which is *hidden?* But how do I know what is hidden if I can see or think or write it? The second sentence is presumably spoken by the "he" of the story. It is comic and bleak because it counterpoints rational inquiry into the nature of things with "oblique relation." The statement itself is an "oblique relation." Blanchot's text is full of turns and counterturns. And this strange linguistic strategy is perhaps at the heart of the text. [Irving Malin]

Linda Lê. *Slander.* Trans. Esther Allen. Univ. of Nebraska Press, 1996. 156 pp. Paper: $14.00.

In *Slander*, Linda Lê's fifth novel, a young writer, with obvious resemblances to the author, seeks information from her mad uncle concerning her unknown father; the uncle in turn begrudgingly provides a report on her family's history, and the novel unfolds in alternating chapters from their two perspectives.

Slander concerns itself with a quintessential *foreigness*, an almost ferocious pride in not belonging. The writer's mad uncle describes her as a "*météque*, a dirty foreigner who writes in French. For her, the French language is what madness had been for me: a way of escaping the family, of safeguarding her solitude, her mental integrity." But Lê's conflicted background (she came to France from Vietnam at the age of fourteen) scarecly accounts for the desperate freakshow nature of her estranged characters: screaming and homicidal madmen, suicides, a shoe repairman with a legless mother (a half-woman who starts eating enough for two), and idealists who sink into pathetic crimes of failed passion and bitter misogeny. Lê plays a bleak tune on the registers of love, with a fierce antipathy for blood ties, a dispirited outlook on romantic ones, with the closest ideal being that of the impassioned incest at the root of her uncle's madness. But while her uncle's shared loathing for their family brings the two narrators together, it also divides them. As the uncle states at one point: "She is my enemy because there can't be two escapes in this family." This inability to coexist creates the novel's structure.

The writing is good, but tends to announce itself as such. *Slander* offers a relentless and voyeurisitc gaze on uncongeniality. Lê is an author to keep an eye on. [Marc Lowenthal]

Guillermo Cabrera Infante. *Holy Smoke*. Overlook, 1997. 329 pp. $24.95.

A self-professed cigar aficionado, Infante chronicles the history of his first love, tobacco, from its discovery by a skeptical Colombus to its eventual acceptance as a worldwide vice. For the Cuban born author, this book—previously published by Harper and Row—is "an autobiography written with smoke, cigar smoke but also cigarettes and pipes and even snuff." The term *autobiography* describes in part Infante's historical essay as it contains many personal anecdotes relating his lifelong love affair with the cigar. Along with his memoirs, Infante uses the myriad voices of history, literature, music, and especially film to tell the cigar's tale.

A true cinephile, Infante utilizes even the most obscure moments in cinematic history to explain the manners and customs of smoking. His attention to detail will make you want to view your favorite movies in a different light. Clint Eastwood, for instance, is revealed not only to have extremely poor taste in cigars but also to have exhibited bad smoking technique (his spaghetti westerns are a prime example). Marlene Dietrich maintained a permanent smoky aura about her with an ever-present lit cigarette; cigarettes were an extension of her persona, and as Infante quips, probably contributed to her emphysmatic screen presence in *Shanghai Express.*

Infante also reserves his humor for his political views. As an exile, he often channels his acerbity toward Castro, portraying him as an imposing cigar hog who leaves behind him a trail of barely smoked stogies. Rationalizing his disdain for Cuban cigars, Infante explains, "It would be as if a German Jew, in 1933, bought sauerkraut from Hitler."

Humorous and opinionated, Infante is one of the most inventive Spanish-language authors currently writing (incidentally, he wrote this in English, demonstrating a stunning eloquence and a wily Wildean wit that would put virtually any native English speaker to shame). Engaged in constant wordplay, his prose has a certain vaudevillian quality—sometimes bordering on cliché—reminiscent of Groucho Marx, who, by the way, makes an appearance here. [Kent D. Wolf]

Sherril Jaffe. *Interior Designs*. Black Sparrow Press, 1996. 240 pp. $25.00; paper: $14.00.

Literally and symbolically, *Interior Designs* is about interior and exterior designs. Its form parallels its content: it is divided into four major sections, each with approximately twenty chapters of between one and four pages. Instead of relying on plot, Jaffe writes short passages to illustrate various aspects of design, primarily the architecture of houses. In these passages the narrator describes all the houses she has lived in, none of which she has occupied for more than three years. In the section entitled "The First House," the narrator and her husband, a rabbi, look for a new house. Instead of finding the right house, the right house seems to find them (throughout the novel structural components such as doors and windows are personified). The new house also has light shining from more than one direction, an entry for proper greetings and farewells, and a sense of solidity, all of which make the narrator feel infinite. Upon moving to the house, the narrator considers philosophical questions concerning fate, luck, guilt, and desire. These questions are exemplary of the novel's themes—in every chapter of the novel, some aspect of exterior design is portrayed literally to illustrate metaphorically human emotions or philosophical issues. Sometimes the metaphors are a bit too obvious, and occasionally the narrator intrudes to explain them lest they slip past readers. For example, when looking at a house she decides against, she says all except one structural flaw is amendable. The minor flaws in the house are like "little and medium-sized mistakes we all make in life—they were not irrevocable." For the most part, however, Jaffe has a wonderfully poetic style; remarkably enough, despite the lack of plot, the novel moves forward at a quick pace. The idea that you can't go home again recurs throughout the novel, but the implication is interestingly reversed, suggesting that to return to an earlier phase in one's life would be to backslide. Textual and symbolic circular patterns develop in the novel that integrate the chapters with the text as a whole and that unite individuals with others and in a spiritual sense with the universe. Entertaining, witty, and full of philosophical insights, *Interior Designs* explores ways to find and maintain personal and spiritual peace. [Laurie Champion]

Francine Prose. *Guided Tours of Hell*. Metropolitan Books/Henry Holt, 1997. 241 pp. $23.00.

To the list of recent—and classic—books tracing the moral adventures of Americans in Europe we must add the two novellas collected together under the title *Guided Tours of Hell*. Landau, the protagonist of Francine Prose's sixty-eight-page title work, is a third-rate American playwright visiting Prague for the First International Kafka Congress (his play for one actress—*Letters from Felice*—imagines the lost half of Kafka's famous love correspondence). We follow a claque of frumpy, ego-jostling, middle-aged academics on a tour of the Terrezenstadt Nazi concentration camp where Landau wrestles mightily—against his own jealousies and under a cruelly blazing sun—to construe justly and objectively his flamboyant yet vexing rival, Jiri Krakauer, star writer and academic, who, although deserving of sympathy as a one-time inmate of the very camp, is arguably a fraud.

The second, longer work, "Three Pigs in Five Days," follows Nina, a thirty-something American travel writer, to Paris and to the Hotel Danton, where her lover, also her boss at *Allo!* magazine, has apparently banished her. At the hotel, itself little more than a brothel, she lies in bed emotionally paralyzed, watching a television that carries only broadcasts of peasant farm couples slaughtering pigs to make sausages. The story plays itself out amid the Paris monuments to the dead including gloomy catacombs, Marie Antoinette's execution spot, and Simone de Beauvoir's grave site.

Putting aside Prose's Paris and Prague, both brilliantly realized, the author's true dark landscape here is mentation itself. It's not just that she identifies uncertainty and ambivalence as one's lot but that she's so knowledgeable a tour guide of those terrains. Here is a writer whose eye is sharp, whose prose is smart, whose allusions are both erudite and funky, whose humor is wry. [Rod Kessler]

Bharati Mukherjee. *Leave It to Me*. 288 pp. Knopf, 1997. $23.00.

Bharati Mukherjee's ninth novel, *Leave it to Me*, resembles a Hollywood thriller fantasy: an orphan, adopted by a hardworking, religious couple in upstate New York is transformed from Debby DiMartino who telemarkets Elastonomics in Schenectady, to Devi Dee, named after the many-armed Hindu goddess, who uses fire, an ax, and a well-timed earthquake to wreck vengeance on the fabulously rich and interesting evil people, some of them Asian, who betray her. This cartoon plot is quick and complicated, and the pages turn almost faster than one can read.

The orphan plot is quintessentially American. Many postmodern American protagonists and poetic personae, as they used to call them when I was a student, are literal, virtual, or metaphorical orphans, on a futile search for home, father, and origins. Mukherjee's *Leave it to Me* varies this paradigm in ways worth paying attention to. Devi Dee, unlike her modernist oedipal counterparts, is a female looking for her mother. In San Francisco she finds the ex-hippie flower child whom she presumes is her "Bio-Mom" and, Electra-like, abets her murder, as well as has sex with the man she believes is her "Bio-Dad." When he is ax-murdered by the mother's former lover who has also killed her mother, she returns the favor. As the police make their way to the crime scene, an earthquake diverts their attention and she escapes them. She rides out the earthquake bobbing up and down in the crime scene, a boat in the waters off Sausalito, the location from which she begins to tell us her story.

A female, post-Freudian, new-millennium Huckleberry Finn, Devi Dee is one of a small but growing list of female protagonists who navigate through their plots mostly alone and under their own steam and emerge at the end triumphant to some degree, without parents or men deciding their fates. Add to that the multiraced cast of characters and you have a novel of new realism, postfeminist and postcanonical American narratology. [Ellen G. Friedman]

Christoph Ransmayr. *The Dog King*. Trans. John E. Woods. Knopf, 1997. 355 pp. $24.00.

Christoph Ransmayr's *The Dog King* portrays the mythic, vulnerable, and often violent town of Moor, a microcosm of post-W.W. II Germany. Essentially, he presents a defeated Germany, depicting a mostly unspoken yet deeply felt humiliation and rage, perhaps echoing Treaty-of-Versailles sentiments. It's clear Ransmayr empathizes with the people of Moor as victims. In accordance with the Peace of Oranienburg, Moor is forced "Back! . . . Back to the Stone Age!" And Moor does indeed decay into a machineless, farming, violent culture while literally working with stones, mining the quarry, which was the site of a small concentration camp. The novel begins with macabre descriptions of three dead people on an "uninhabited" Brazilian island, then unravels who and how. The main portion of the novel exhibits Moor's decay through three main characters: Ambras, the Dog King; Bering, his blacksmith/bodyguard; and Lilly the mysterious, Brazilian black-market dealer. As in Ransmayr's *The Terrors of Ice and Darkness*, landscape figures prominently. Similar to German myth, land is strong and virile though it's plundered of prewar glory. The quarry is stripped; buildings and roads are neglected. Eventually, Moor is to be used as a military practice zone and has to be evacuated. Ambras the Dog King relays these orders, yet Moor seems to blame him in part. As a Moor camp survivor, he's the Allies' surrogate overseer of Moor. He is haunted by his past—a past that has little meaning for decaying Moor. He is left isolated, heartless, and almost maniacal, killing some wild dogs with his bare hands and training the rest to guard his crumbling villa. I recommend reading this imaginative work. [Robert Manaster]

Frederic Tuten. *Van Gogh's Bad Café: A Love Story*. William Morrow, 1997. 163 pp. $20.00.

"Art finally undecorated by sentiment, free from human rhetoric—art pure"—such is the ideal espoused by Ursula, photographer, morphine addict, and lover of the Dutch painter in Frederic Tuten's fourth novel. The hallucinatory, anachronistic form of the narrative allows Ursula to be displaced from the French fin de siècle to late-twentieth-century New York, where she experiments with modern cameras (and crack) and trades in her 1890s utopia for a postmodern one: "the final democratic ideal, everyone his/her own work of art, the body as canvas, the body as sculpture, the body as an arena in process, a show, a spectacle, one among the millions of spectacles." The novel intelligently contemplates the validity of the aesthetic in an age that has threatened to strike art silent: "Ursula had no words for it, the twentieth century; it was beyond horror, and comprehension." Like Tuten's recent *Tintin in the New World* (1993), where Hergé's pastoral was engulfed by historical reality, *Van Gogh's Bad Café* explores the seductions of escapist and utopian art, but without passing judgment, recognizing instead the humanity of the impulse to seek a refuge, whether in "sentiment" or intoxicants (or, in the case of Van Gogh, both).

The impressionist movement is denigrated these days for its complicity with bourgeois leisure: Pissarro, Gauguin, and Manet stand accused of absconding from class politics to the false idyll of the countryside, the primitive, and the picnic. The postimpressionist Van Gogh, with his fields and sunflowers, could be similarly categorized. Tuten's novel holds in balance cynical and romanticized versions of the Dutch icon. "Vincent did not paint light, he painted his hysteria, which just happened to be interesting as painting"; " 'He flaunted goodness as a principle in art' "; " 'He was the best, but he thrived on rejections,' " Ursula says, and the contradictions ring true.

Tuten's style is a masterly blend of gritty speech rhythms and the prose equivalent of cherry blossoms. He treats Van Gogh's devotion to beauty with honesty and tact, revealing horror, like a geological seam, beneath the radiant haze of the canvases. If art is an escape from such, so much the better: there are worse things than sentiment. Ambitious, original, benign, Tuten stakes out a place for human rhetoric in art pure. [Philip Landon]

Stephen Dixon. *Gould: A Novel in Two Novels.* Henry Holt, 1997. 277 pp. $24.00.

The strength of these two connected novellas, "Abortions" and "Evangeline," lies in their stimulating treatment of two familiar themes: the mutual deceptions of lovers and the anxieties of becoming, or of trying to avoid becoming, a parent. Written in Dixon's trademark style (long paragraphs with rapid-fire dialogue and abrupt temporal leaps and compressions), *Gould* portrays a dizzying variety of oral and written mendacities between lovers and documents one man's gradual transformation from selfish lout to caring husband and father. In "Abortions" Dixon takes us from Gould Bookbinder's first long-term relationship at age seventeen through five more relationships. Each is recounted with exceptional economy and virtuosity, and each ends with some form of abortion. Some of these abortions occur in dangerous and illegal conditions; some possibly never take place; some Gould wishes he could have prevented; one is accidental. Initially, Gould cannot tolerate his lovers' social, intellectual, and physical shortcomings, and he betrays them in various ways in order to avoid taking on the responsibilities of marriage and parenthood. Eventually, he settles down, has two daughters, remains devoted to his ailing wife, yet is haunted by a desire to have a third child. The mother of the boy who may have catalyzed his transformation is the subject of the second novella, "Evangeline." Although Dixon devotes many more pages to this relationship than to any of the six covered in "Abortions," we realize that this was neither the longest nor the most significant one in Gould's life. But Dixon lends an elegiac tone to Gould's memories of it, perhaps because these memories ultimately provide him with the third child he has been longing for. With admirable detachment and without lapsing into heavy-handedness, Dixon has written a profound meditation on what makes both romantic and parental love maddening yet irresistible, on what it takes to become and remain a parent, and on how twentieth-century American social conflicts and mores complicate both of these endeavors. Like good poetry, *Gould* implies and evokes more than it specifies and resolves, and it is well worth reading more than once for the insights it affords. [Thomas Hove]

Lance Olsen. *Time Famine.* Permeable Press, 1996. 324 pp. $12.95.

The time is the twenty-first century. Lance Olsen's America is a corporate-owned wasteland where poverty and social marginalization have provoked riots that are quickly and efficiently suppressed by private security companies. But the terrain stays dangerous. Even the White House is subject to mortar attacks. Klub Med, a huge theme park complex in southern California, suffers a massive reactor meltdown in an earthquake that releases a radioactive cloud into the atmosphere, an event the company immediately stifles by expert media management. For Olsen's world, like that of Pynchon to which it owes an obvious debt, is a totally constructed environment traversed by different control systems. On the whole he focuses his narrative through different victims of these systems. The nuclear incident induces Chrono-Unific Deficiency Syndrome—CHRUDS for short—where subjects fall into catalepsy while they are pulled into other time periods. So a wanderer named Uly (for Ulysses) finds himself displaced into the incredible hardships of the Donner exploration party trekking through the wilds of nineteenth-century Nevada. In a world where the power of commercial technology is paramount there is no dimension to experience, not even time itself, which stays exempt from manipulation and commodification. Olsen places his novel within the dystopian tradition by depicting a space station named Erewhon One which offers to those who can afford it a cultural nostalgia for a period rather like the 1960s viewed in retrospect that never existed. It would do an injustice to this novel's complexity to argue that Olsen lines up corporations against individuals; instead one of his minor characters insists that everything interconnects and some of the most powerful moments in the narrative occur when characters discover this connectedness. There is literally no sustainable distinction between inside and outside, as a figure called Krystal realizes when she learns that she has an electronic implant in her brain. It is no coincidence that Olsen has written a study of William Gibson because his own novel clearly connects at many points with cyberpunk fiction. His characters here and in his earlier novel *Tonguing the Zeitgeist* (1994) at their most minimal are not much more than animated intersections within media systems. There is a suspicion running throughout *Time Famine* that anonymous forces are at work in America. The Cold War may be over but information on covert government and military industrial operations runs with smooth continuity into the next century. The novel's off-beat humor, surrealism, and strategic repetitions (with some debt here to Burroughs) all paint a bleakly powerful picture of the "Nort Amerika" (Nor-Am) to come. [David Seed]

Percival Everett. *Frenzy*. Graywolf, 1997. 165 pp. $12.95.

This novel is a brave attempt to define and to employ frenzy. Frenzy is a synonym for ecstasy, rapture, epiphany—that "still point" in which the human suddenly sees the superhuman and also recognizes the gap between daily life and eternity. Everett, in effect, tries to confront holiness. And although he is not completely successful, he deserves our close attention.

Dionysus is one of the strangest pagan gods. He is half man, half god—according to mythology—and he is aware that he can never be complete, despite his excessive, eccentric rituals of transfiguration. His "mortal bookmark" is Vleppo, who tries to explore the meanings of time and love. The novel collapses past and present, fuses wit and horror; it is meant to confuse us, to destroy the safe logic we embrace. Everett's novel works because of the odd conversations of Vleppo and Dionysus. We don't know what to make of their exchanges. They, at times, remind me of the confrontations in Merrill's *Sandover*. Somehow words take on a strange, new meaning; they are twisted, frenzied, impure. And the single meanings no longer exist—especially when Vleppo tries to explore his consciousness: "And then I was atop my own head, peering through a rather clear window into myself, knowing full well it to be myself, and there in the deepness of me I saw nothing, felt nothing."

This novel is surely mad. But it knows that it is. It lives. And it makes other novels seem lifeless. [Irving Malin]

Ralph Ellison. *Flying Home and Other Stories,* Ed. John F. Callahan. Random House, 1996. 179 pp. $23.00.

This collection of stories shows Ellison becoming the masterful writer of *Invisible Man;* its stories reveal Ellison's great gift for communicating not only the African-American experience but also the twentieth-century experience. (Many later published works of short fiction—those appearing after *Invisible Man*—were actually parts of the novel-in-progress that readers have been awaiting for forty-five years, and so editor John F. Callahan—in hopes of that novel's eventual publication—has chosen not to include them here.) It's true that some of these pieces of early fiction feel more like scenes (and perhaps *are* simply scenes) than full-blown stories; two were untitled until Callahan attached titles to them. But even in short works like "Hymie's Bull" and "I Did Not Learn Their Names" which have little narrative arc, we see Ellison's growing mastery of the simplicity and directness of the American language as well as the more lyrical—perhaps musical—language that characterized his best work.

But among the other stories, we find such gems as "A Party Down at the Square," an account of a Southern lynching from the perspective of a white boy from Cincinnati that feels its way obliquely toward its powerful conclusion; "A Coupla Scalped Indians," the best of four stories featuring the boys Buster and Riley, and an initiation story worthy of inclusion alongside Hemingway's "Indian Camp" or "The Doctor and the Doctor's Wife"; and, of course, the justly celebrated "King of the Bingo Game," one of the most powerful and moving short stories written by any American author. The music is still there. Although writing about music as to render the feeling of it is supremely difficult, Ellison makes it look easy. The collection boasts a masterful use of call and response in "Mister Toussan" and of jazz in "A Coupla Scalped Indians." And the music is there, soaring and tender and tough in lyrical descriptions interspersed throughout the stories. [Greg Garrett]

Lidia Yuknavitch. *Her Other Mouths*. House of Bones, 1997. 120 pp. Paper: $8.95.

Lidia Yuknavitch's first collection of stories is a collision between language and the body. Slowing down to gaze unflinchingly at the wreckage, her stories examine the wounds inflicted by need, desire, rage, and stifled communication. The mouths of her title are savagely mute; the psychic wounds of her protagonists find expression only in the physical wounding of themselves and others. Self-mutilation, scarification, and drug injection carve new mouths in the flesh of her characters, who, often, turn their rage outward and torture others. These mouths gnash, curse, and bite, but rarely do they speak: the private language of these women's other mouths goes unheard by others. As Dora, a reappropriated version of Freud's famous case study, observes in a letter to the painter Francis Bacon: "I don't want to talk anymore since that's not what mouths are for." Throughout the collection, Yuknavitch knowingly pirates Freud's vocabulary of orifices and repression and plays it off against Bacon's gallery of mutilated figures with voracious mouths. Even in stories which do not turn on a violent image—such as "Chronology of Water" or "Strata"—painful memories of the body's experience are never far from the surface. Biography, Yuknavitch suggests, is nothing but the story of a body, and can only be told through corporeal means. Yuknavitch herself writes in an unsparing prose, a difficult mixture of painful lyricism and staccato abstraction which voices her characters' desperate inarticulacy. Substituting violence and pain for expression and understanding, Yuknavitch attempts to clear space for a new sort of understanding and beauty. There is little room for irony in her prose, and virtually no humor, but her female protagonists emerge with a sympathy which defies the brutal silence in which they live. When we are privy to the secret writings of a heroin addict who has been taken as a subject for a sociological study, or find that a sixteen-year old self-mutilator understands her motivations much more clearly than her psychiatrist ever could, we see that Yuknavitch's characters are looking beyond language to a place where there are no thoughts without a body and where the only words are wounds. [Graham Fraser]

William Trevor. *After Rain*. Viking, 1996. 213 pp. $22.95.

Because he has published twenty-two books—short-story collections, novellas and novels, certainly, but also plays, nonfiction, and a children's book—because he has won such prestigious prizes as the Heinemann Award and the Whitbread (twice, so far), because his stories appear not only in *Antaeus* but, frequently, in the *New Yorker* and *Harpers,* and because he's considered by some critics as "the greatest living writer of short stories," it's likely that readers will know the work of William Trevor, whose new collection of short stories, *After Rain,* has just appeared. For such readers, suffice it to say that in these twelve stories—about wives, husbands, lovers, and heartbreak; about children and parents and heartbreak; about friends and thieves—Trevor displays both his usual craftsmanship and his uncanny insight into the human heart.

But what of William Trevor for the as-yet-uninitiated? Except for the Italy of its title story, the stories are set in his native Ireland and in England and Northern Ireland, where Trevor has spent his life. Trevor has observed of his own earlier writing, "I think I am interested in people who are not necessarily the victims of other people, but simply the victims of circumstances. . . . I'm very interested in the sadness of fate, the things that just happen to people." One thinks of his "Child's Play," about the two unrelated children thrown intimately together after their adulterous parents swap marital partners for a brave new family.

If critics have a complaint against Trevor, it is that some find his prose "dispassionate"—dry and emotionally flat. In fact, he is scrupulous in leaving it to readers to probe the depths of his observations in the echo chambers of their own hearts. This is perfect subtlety, and *After Rain* is a literary achievement best left to those who don't need a laugh track to get it. [Rod Kessler]

Rick Harsch.*The Driftless Zone: Or A Novel Concerning the Selective Outmigration from Small Cities*. Steerforth, 1997. 201 pp. $21.00.

The title of Harsch's first novel refers to a demographic theory: small cities lose their most ambitious, talented, and beautiful natives to the lure of larger cities. The "high percentage of misfits, fools, [and] various mediocrities" who remain account for the high per capita incidence of ineptitude, shabby grandiosity, and "enlarged capacity for botching ill-conceived projects." *The Driftless Zone* is a test case for this theory.

The novel's protagonist, a driftless La Crosse down-and-outer named Spleen, unwittingly becomes the target of a notorious contract killer who is in town on a job. A wiser man might leave town under these circumstances, but Spleen is constitutionally unable to operate outside of La Crosse. Therefore, his survival depends on his ability to unravel the mystery in which he is enmeshed while staying a step or two ahead of the killer on his tail. As a local, Spleen would seem to have the advantage of knowing the territory. But familiar surfaces mask unguessed-at secrets, and Spleen's inability to leave town might deny him the perspective he needs to understand

La Crosse the way his would-be killer does. Even Spleen's most worldly acquaintances can do little better than recommend that he model his escape strategy on the plots of old B-movies.

Like Spleen's survival plan, Harsch's novel largely outfits itself from a storehouse of film-noir conventions. In spirit and tone *The Driftless Zone* is an homage to hard-boiled detective fiction (how could it be otherwise in a book whose characters wear names like the Sneering Brunette, the Fag with No Eyebrows, and Billy Verite?). But in its central concept of geography-as-character, its postmodern pastiche of references and sources, and its occasional attempts at Joycean prose, Harsch's novel is more interested in referring to noir than being noir. [Jon D'Errico]

Paul Di Filippo. *Ciphers*. Permeable Press, 1997. 541 pp. Paper: $16.95.

Cyril Prothero, a fragile-minded but really lovable schlemiel and clerk at Planet Records in Boston, comes across a zincless-middled penny minted in Arizona and then a barcode on a CD that invades his body with a flood of unwanted information when he touches it . . . which is the beginning of some High Weirdness, but nothing compared to when poor Cyril returns home and finds his lady love, Ruby Tuesday, suddenly MIA after leaving a cryptic message she's in some kind of major trouble . . . which narrative slowly begins to web with a plethora of even face-slackeningly stranger ones (assault butterflies, bugger-happy holy men, fiendish garden hoses . . .) by means of various spoofy-if-nebulous conspiracies involving snake goddesses, secret gnostic sects, a virus that leads those infected to spiritual enlightenment, and a mysterious international conglomerate called Wu Labs run by a mysterious three-thousand-year-plus-old guy in hot pursuit of immortality and omniscience. The result is a brilliant tour de force for Paul Di Filippo, founder and quite possibly sole member of the ribofunk movement. Nothing works in a straight line in it . . . or, to employ one of the shaping Shannonesque metaphors from it: continual noise has been pumped into this informational system. Consequently, reading *Ciphers* is more like reading the humongous, hyper, freewheeling, encyclopedic-minded and hep-voiced first-and-favorite-phase Pynchon of *V.*, *The Crying*, and *Gravity's Rainbow* than any other writer I know. Its cartoonishly delightful characters, silly lyrics, cockamamie names, hilarious situations, ribald imagination, and breakneck speed add up to a tremendously successful act of literary affirmation. [Lance Olsen]

Ismail Kadare. *The Three-Arched Bridge*. Trans. John Hodgson. Arcade, 1997. 184 pp. $21.95.

The narrator of *The Three-Arched Bridge*, a monk by the name of Gjon, begins his story by writing that he will attempt to tell the "whole truth" and in so doing "record the lie we saw and the truth we did not see." He proceeds to say, "I write this in haste, because times are troubled, and the future looks blacker than ever before." That threatening dark force is the Ottoman Empire, poised to use Arberia (Albania) as a bridge for their advance into Europe. This tale by Albanian writer Ismail Kadare (titles already available in English include *The Concert*, *The General of the Dead Army*, *The Pyramid*, and *The Palace of Dreams*) is set in a small village alongside a river bearing the name Ujana e Keqe ("Wicked Waters") in the year 1377. Up until this time, a ferry has served to transport people and goods across the river. All this changes when strangers speaking a difficult tongue make the local count an irresistible offer in exchange for permission to build a bridge across the river. The local population may privately hold suspicions regarding their motives, but no one speaks out except for an old woman named Ajkuna who continually decries the bridge as the work of the devil. Attempts to sabotage the bridge are subverted by the builders who developd and circulate a myth that the bridge requires a human sacrifice. The monk himself worries that local legends he has shared with a stranger posing as a folklorist have been twisted and perverted for enemy purposes. It is little surprise to the reader when one day a common fellow by the name of Murrash Zenebisha is found immured in the bridge. The monk suspects foul play. This is part of the truth he is trying to uncover. Meantime, the monk and his fellow townsfolk unwittingly, naively watch on as the Ottoman Turks put in place all the machinery for invasion and occupation. Kadare's work has been compared to writers as dissimilar as Kafka and García Márquez. In style and tone, as well as theme, this novel reminds me of Julien Gracq's remarkable *The Opposing Shore*, another powerful parable of the ominous and mysterious operations of opposing systems. [Allen Hibbard]

Cristina Garcia. *The Agüero Sisters.* Knopf, 1997. 300 pp. $23.00.

In Cristina Garcia's second novel history haunts the present, threatening to overwhelm the two Cuban sisters who struggle in different ways to let the past enter their lives in manageable but honest increments. Their stories are told through a complex interweaving of past and present, personal and political, focusing on the everyday lives of Reina and Constancia but never isolating the quotidian details from the politics of Cuba and the Cuban exile community. Perhaps because of this careful adherence to the daily effects of political decisions rather than to governmental proclamations, *The Agüero Sisters* finds a nonjudgmental yet passionate tone in which to tell the painful story of Cuba, Cubans, and Cuban-Americans. Through her description of Reina, a faithful but critical supporter of the revolution, Garcia demonstrates both the harshness and the hope of life in Castro's Cuba. The novel also reveals the hypocrisies of wealthy Cuban exiles such as Constancia and her husband yet refuses to deny the power of their longing for a Cuba that perhaps never existed. Admittedly, the author's sympathies seem to lie with Reina, who embraces whatever sensual pleasures life offers as an alternative to didactic politics: "What she enjoys most is the freedom from a finality of vision, of a definitive version of life's meaning." Constancia, meanwhile, seems caught up in the capitalist/Horatio Alger myth, producing her own line of cosmetics designed to help women stave off the effects of aging. When the two sisters are reunited in Miami, their separate stories and voices merge in an attempt to uncover the truth of their mother's death. The novel does not dissolve the sisters' differences in a false display of resolution, but shows how the very clash produces a passion of remembrance that, finally, writes their family's history. This history stands in contrast to their father's own first-person narrative which is woven throughout the novel and which is discredited for its inability to see its place within a larger context. As such, *The Agüero Sisters* functions as a powerful testament to the importance of recovering history through the telling of women's stories, yet it refuses to place the storytellers on a pedestal, making the act of speaking/writing itself a product of everyday life. [Jane Juffer]

Anne Michaels. *Fugitive Pieces*. Knopf, 1996. 304pp. $23.00.

In *Fugitive Pieces* Anne Michaels offers the story of the poet Jakob Beer, a Jewish survivor of World War II. Instead of exploring the places and routes that have normally come to be associated with the Holocaust, however, she explores the difficulties that Jews experienced in Greece during the occupation, tracing Beer's life from a mud-covered and hiding child, through his rescue by a geologist named Athos, to his transplantation to Toronto, to his final return to Athens with his second wife. In addition to Athos's own story, Michaels offers in the second half of the book the story of Ben a young professor obsessed by Jakob who attempts to use the poet's life and death as a way of figuring out his parents' experience in the war and his own heritage.

The language of *Fugitive Pieces* is often quite lyrical, at times almost revelatory, despite there being a few rare moments which are so lyrical and unrestrained as to seem sentimental or overwritten. Jakob's narrative voice, present for the first two hundred pages of the book, is quite well drawn, at once smart, mildly philosophical, informed by geology, and carefully defined. Michaels's ability to talk about the atrocities Jews experienced is quite impressive, particularly when supported by her ability to speak about geology in a way that seems convincing, original, and carefully researched. The combination of geology, Holocaust, and Greece does much to create an original space for Michaels. Her ability to manipulate and combine aspects of life that most people see as separate is startling and intelligent.

While the second part of the book, Ben's section, is slightly less convincing than the first, and the connections between the halves seem a little too easy at times, *Fugitive Pieces* shows Anne Michaels to be a skilled conflater and gilder of worlds. [Brian Evenson]

Patricia Duncker. *Hallucinating Foucault*. Ecco, 1997. 175 pp. $21.00.

Patricia Duncker's first novel explores the relationship between readers and writers as a love affair, as the unnamed narrator, who seeks to rescue a mad, homosexual French novelist from institutionalized obscurity, finds his intellectual passion for the writer becoming increasingly romantic and, ultimately, sexual. The book is a literary mystery which begins in Cambridge, travels to Paris, then to a French asylum and concludes with a long hot summer of love and doom in the Midi. In a sense, however, the book never really leaves the academy. Pursuing the reclusive object of his desire, the narrating doctoral student indulges in the fetishes of research, fondling his author's manuscripts and literary love letters to Michel

Foucault with even more fascination than he displayed during his voyeuristic peeping into his girlfriend's research notes. Of all the passions explored in this novel, Duncker, herself an academic, writes most convincingly on the titillating trappings of scholarship.

Indeed, the erotics of reading and writing are so clearly brought out in the novel that at first one imagines that Roland Barthes—rather than Foucault—might have been a better choice to preside over the text. However, the ghost of Foucault—severe, transgressive, momumental—implicitly raises the ominous issue of the disappearance or death of the author. The passion shared by the reader-narrator and the French novelist (and the earlier passion the novelist shared with Foucault in their reciprocal reader-writer relationship) challenges Foucault's own theory of authorship: far from allowing the author to recede into oblivion behind his writings, Duncker insists, the reader must love the writer at least as passionately as his texts. And when the death of the author, the Foucauldian (and Bathesian) doom that hangs, unspoken, over this text, comes to pass, its tragedy lies in sundering these lovers, leaving one to grieve alone. [Graham Fraser]

Gerald Vizenor. *Hotline Healers.* Wesleyan Univ. Press, 1997. 172 pp. $21.95.

Casting about to describe *Hotline Healers*, one might say it's a little postmodern, a little magic realist, a little picaresque, a lot parodic, an American Indian trickster story—or "tricky story," as its narrator likes to say as he recounts the exploits of his cousin, Almost Browne, and the rest of the highly extended family who inhabit a fabulous barony on Minnesota's White Earth Reservation. Readers familiar with Vizenor's other fiction, poetry, and essays will recognize and revel in much of this novel's vocabulary—the language of "manifest manners," "cultural dominance," teasing, chance, survivance, motion, and native sovereignty—and not a few of its characters—including mongrels who follow, drive (as in *chauffeur*), and have sex with the human figures. Readers not familiar with Vizenor or with academic Native studies or with the rich diversity of American Indian literatures are in for an often-bewildering, hilarious trip: Almost and his cousin's enterprises selling blank books (which they brazenly autograph: Isaac Bashevis Singer, John Steinbeck, Maxine Hong Kingston); the hero's commencement speech for the University of California's Transethnic Studies Department—an ironic and incendiary performance that throws the audience into "academic hissy fits"; an eighteen-minute taped conference (now lost) in which Richard Nixon offers Almost the vice presidency if he can get the Indians to overthrow Fidel Castro; an Indian princess pageant that the sexily dressed Almost wins by lip-synching Peggy Lee's "Fever"; and an account of the Manabosho Curiosa, an antiquarian manuscript containing stories of sexual conversion of monks with animals. Vizenor's writing is odd and elusive, not merely because it's postmodern or sometimes insiderish (the parades of famous scholars are dizzying). It is elusive also because it is quite pointedly searching for ways to tell Native stories when American audiences are so primed to consume and appropriate all things Indian—when, perhaps like Almost's university audience, readers are "poised to hear the litanies of native creation and victimry" and thus unable to hear anything else, including the humor. Perhaps the narrator's description of that commencement speech best describes Vizenor the author: "he was bound to tease the very sacred denials of transethnic dominance and nationalism. . . . He was timely, and the tone of his voice was rich and dramatic, but he turned and traced words and sentences in such an ironic manner, his tease of survivance, that no one could be sure what he meant." [Siobhan Senier]

Thomas Mallon. *Dewey Defeats Truman*. Pantheon, 1997. 355 pp. $24.00.

Many people remember the hubris of Republicans in the fall of 1948 when they convinced, or thought they convinced, everyone that Thomas E. Dewey, the governor of New York, would be the next president of the United States. The shock of those Republicans—and of the *Chicago Tribune* in particular for printing up the premature headline "Dewey Defeats Truman"—is the impetus for Thomas Mallon's new novel.

Mallon sets his narrative in Owosso, Michigan, Dewey's real hometown, during the 1948 campaign, and uses the town's attempts at capitalizing on this status as a way to explore not only class and political issues but also issues of sexuality and death, including the impact of the recently ended war on those whose lives have been permanently altered by it.

Owosso is a small town in search of a transcendent moment, which the residents assume will come when Dewey is elected president. The town's "biggest industry is death" in the form of a casket manufacturer, and the local boosters would like to change the town's image to something more related to the future. To this end, many of the townspeople feel that Dewey's visiting the town prior to the election would be a sign of great things. The local politicians, including the president of Citizens for the Future, encourage Mrs. Dewey to invite her son back to his hometown, offering to hold a parade in his honor as well as to create a Dewey Walk along the riverbank. The Walk would be a permanent exhibit of the achievements of Dewey's life, including his years as district attorney and governor, soft-pedaling the fact that most of his major activities took place far from his hometown.

The disparate voices of the novel—Republicans, Democrats, union members, disaffected adolescents, women mourning their war dead—are set against each other in such a way that they call into question our notions of history. The characters expect the historical moment of the presidential election to make a difference in their lives and the life of the town and while all of the characters are transformed in some way, neither Dewey's expected win nor his loss has the impact that they anticipated. The townspeople grow and change despite, rather than because of, their brush with history. [Sally E. Parry]

Elizabeth Graver. *Unravelling*. Hyperion, 1997. 346 pp. $22.95.

"Nothing leaves you; things just shake and tumble and return," realizes Aimee Slater, the narrator of Elizabeth Graver's first novel, *Unravelling*. Set in nineteenth-century New England, *Unravelling* chronicles Aimee's journey from her family's small but stifling New Hampshire farm to the City of Spindles—the mill factory town of Lowell, Massachusetts—where the pretty, smart, and willful Aimee succeeds at working the looms, but cannot resist the charms of William Tanning, the factory's mechanic. Aimee's romance with William leaves her pregnant and alone. When her mother forces Aimee to give up the twins to whom she gives birth, Aimee cannot forgive her mother's action nor her mother's shame for her. Aimee nearly starves herself to death before she changes course and begins a life of self-imposed exile. Now thirty-eight, Aimee lives on the edge of a bog in a tiny hunting shack where she raises chickens and rabbits and finds comfort in the arms of Amos, another exile of sorts.

Shifting between Aimee's present and her past, Graver deftly and sensitively outlines the continual clash between what Aimee feels and thinks and does and what Aimee's repressive nineteenth-century New England world tells her she should feel and think and do. Aimee narrates the intricately woven story of her life: "When I look back, I picture the journey marked by a long trail of white thread. It is not fancy thread, but the thinnest, cheapest, factory kind, the sort that breaks if you pull on it too hard." Lucid, unsettling, loving Graver masterly conjures up a beautifully realized tale of one woman's story of loss, love, and redemption. [Jeanne Claire van Ryzin]

Paul West. *Sporting with Amaryllis*. Overlook, 1996. 158 pp. $19.95.

The publication of any new work by Paul West is cause for celebration, and celebrate we should over *Sporting with Amaryllis*. Here West turns his indefatigable imagination to John Milton, and as he did with John Polidori in *Lord Byron's Doctor*, West rewrites history in alarming yet invigorating ways.

The novel opens in 1626 when a seventeen-year-old Milton is banished by his tutor, Chappell, from life at Cambridge. He is to return home to London where he will serve his "rustication." However London is anything but the quiet countryside, and the young man longs "for bustle, sunshine, crowds, a world of unkempt morals, where the will had something to cut its teeth on." It is women, in fact, that he is fascinated by, and his yearning is soon answered by an extraordinary figure.

Although her name is never mentioned, Milton is convinced she is Amaryllis, the shepherdess from Virgil's *Ecologues* and the spirit of pleasure and diversion in "Lycidas." Through her, the novel poses the questions—what is a muse, where does artistic inspiration originate, what are the elements in the strange alchemy of artistic creation? This muse is a source of ambiguity—her age is indeterminate, she both appeals and frightens, she wanders in search of talent which she herself does not possess and to which she can rarely respond with enthusiasm and tenderness.

What she creates for young Milton is nothing less than a liminal retreat. Ironically, through an orgy of the senses, Milton is removed from the quotidian, which for him is university life, classical literature, and a possible career as a clergyman. As is the case for any liminal inductee, Milton's former self is annulled through a series of personally destabilizing rituals.

As is always the case with West, language is foregrounded and offered as a presence as palpable as any character. Each page abounds in delights as West takes nuance and raises it for rapt inspection and consistently manages to make abstractions concrete.

[David Madden]

Frederick Bush. *Girls*. Harmony Books, 1997. 288 pp. $23.00.

"You can't say once upon a time to tell the story of how we got where we are," says Jack, a forty-two-year-old security guard at a tony private college in a small upstate New York town and narrator of *Girls*, Busch's eighteenth work of fiction. "You have to say winter. Once, in winter, you say, because winter was our only season, and it felt like we would live in winter all our lives."

Jack and his wife Fanny are caught in a frozen marriage and wintry emotional life, numbed by the loss of their infant daughter years ago. Emotionally adrift yet also fledgingly pursuing a means to emerge from the iciness that permeates his life, Jack throws himself into the search for a missing fourteen-year-old girl, the seemingly perfect daughter of a minister and his wife from a nearby town. Busch documents his characters' emotional disenfranchisment and at the same time deftly utilizes the details of the harsh upstate winter to echo their dormant lives.

Busch's prose is a masterly combination of intensity, delicacy, and sparseness which, combined, yield an elegant work only a truly estimable writer could produce. By deftly blending characteristics of the hard-boiled detective novel with a powerful intelligence, tenderness, and complexity, Busch renders a novel that is at once something of a literary thriller as well as a cogent and compassionate tale of guilt and the all too human urge to both flee from and resolve the past. [Jeanne Claire van Ryzin]

Mayra Santos-Febres. *Urban Oracles*. Trans. Nathan Budoff and Lydia Platon Lazaro. Brookline Books, 1997. 129 pp. Paper: $15.95.

In her collection of short stories Mayra Santos-Febres distances herself from the power she exercises over her characters and the decisions they make; she doesn't want to be the omniscient narrator playing God. Yet she also wants to acknowledge her own presence in the stories and to show in various strategies of self-revelation the power of narratives to construct reality. True to these conflicting desires, many of the stories seem unfinished; some are almost mystical in their refusal to tie together loose ends. They provide glimpses into characters' lives without offering any resolutions to the often tragic problems presented. The characters are dwarfed by the structural problems of their homeland, Puerto Rico—the racism against darker-skinned people, the legacy of U.S. imperialism, the machismo, and the environmental havoc. At times, Santos-Febres foregrounds the ways in which texts other than her own construct reality, such as beauty ads for straightened hair. Despite the book's emphasis on oppressive structures that seem immutable, the positions characters occupy in relation to these structures is rarely predictable. In "Abnel, Sweet Nightmare," a lonely woman denied love into middle age rushes home from work in order to catch a glimpse of the naked man in the building across from hers as he steps out of the shower at the same time every day; she is a voyeur without any of the power usually accorded that position. Throughout the stories is a careful probing of the materiality of the body—its pleasures and pains—bodies infused with the sweat of labor yet able as well to offer momentary escapes of pure sensuality. [Jane Juffer]

Susan Welch. *Crowning the Queen of Love*. Coffee House Press, 1997. 230 pp. Paper: $13.95.

The connection between needing to find love and identity in a fragmented, disturbing world provides the thematic core of Susan Welch's first collection of short stories. These nine pieces show the dislocation caused by a depersonalized society. They range from a story about a young woman leaving her married lover to wed a young man with mental problems to another about a woman who wonders whether her battle with cancer precludes a romantic involvement with her college instructor.

In many of these stories the protagonists are convinced that some new relationship will create a sense of order and change their lives for the better. However, reality never matches the expectation. In one of the strongest stories, "Stalking Angel Dewayne," a widowed creative writing teacher sees an attractive African-American doctor as an antidote to her joyless existence. She exoticizes him and expects passionate, primitive love; she sends him gifts, waits for him outside the hospital, and virtually forces him to allow her into his life. However he is not the wild lover she wants, but an unhappy middle-aged man with a troubled marriage. Her realization that his affection for her is as dead as the taxidermied animals on the walls of her late husband's study is the first step in being able to create a new reality for herself.

Other stories show love as a compromise amid larger sociohistoric forces. In "Broken Music" a woman escorting her Jewish mother on a tour of the concentration camps feels an attraction for the German tour guide. Her shame is mitigated by finding out how her mother survived the camps. This sense of survival despite serious losses—of spouses, parents, friends—is what makes this collection a fascinating one. [Sally E. Parry]

Philip Roth. *American Pastoral.* Houghton Mifflin, 1997. 423 pp. $26.00.

I have never been a great Roth fan, with the exception of *Portnoy. American Pastoral* contains most of what I don't like in him, but what a dumbbell like Tom Wolfe would like: the big story, the big slice of American life, the panorama, the story, the story, the story, the flesh and blood, a big novel with big themes, the humanness of it all! Four hundred plus pages to explore at leisure the life and times of a high school sports hero from New Jersey, or the decline and fall of same, or whatever, as narrated by Zuckerman himself. Did I mention that this is told to us at a very leisurely pace? A great deal of leisure. If Roth cannot get his Manhattan right, God only knows how he might have butchered Jersey. But why should this matter in a novel of such breadth and depth? And real human feeling? And sophistication? [John O'Brien]

Valerie Miner. *Winter's Edge*. Afterword by Donna Perry. Feminist Press, 1997. 203 pp. Paper: $10.95.

With its new edition of *Winter's Edge* (1984), Feminist Press makes widely available an early and difficult to find novel by Valerie Miner, a writer now well known for her concern with working class women's issues. Set in 1979 and written in the early eighties, her book is still—perhaps even more—relevant.

The novel unfolds around a black woman activist's fight against a moneyed redeveloper for the supervisor position of San Francisco's Tenderloin district. Against this heated political backdrop and a cast of cops, prostitutes, shop owners, gays, straights, Italians, Asians, and Latin Americans, Miner's vibrant heroines, two single seventyish white women, explore their relationship to their community and one another. Chrissie MacInnes is a militant, outspoken waitress who faces threats of violence while working exhaustively for Marissa Washington's election. For the past twenty years, her best friend has been Margaret Sawyer, a shy, "well-behaved," traditionally feminine, long-divorced newstand clerk. While Chrissie places her energy and emotional commitments in political causes, Margaret has difficulty taking stands on "abstract issues," as she understands politics, and instead focuses on "mothering" the people around her. When the election grows ugly and violence becomes a reality, however, both women are forced to rethink their definitions of politics, community, and, finally, their love for each other.

As Donna Perry writes in her informative afterword, Margaret and Chrissie discover the "meaning of their lives at home" amid the "social and political unrest and violence." Can we, Miner seems to ask, look around us and not do the same? [Lisa Logan]

Sharon Solwitz. *Blood and Milk*. Sarabande, 1997. 236 pp. Paper: $13.95.

A rendezvous with the "sense of unresolvable ambiguity of practically everything" is the cornerstone experience for the characters of Sharon Solwitz's first collection of short stories, *Blood and Milk*. Simultaneously sensitive, complex, and darkly comedic, these stories lunge into the labyrinth of relationships between husbands and wives, parents and children, extended families, lovers, friends, Jews and non-Jews. Solwitz's characters often find themselves backed into extreme moments of conflict and confusion in which dramatic and often absurd action seems their only recourse. The result is a boldly honest statement about how we behave and who we are: about the incongruities, discrepancies, and inconsistencies of human behavior. "I am neither saint nor self-protector. My ego refuses either to die or prevail," proclaims the narrator of "Mercy," the chronicle of a rape victim examining her continuously complex and unresolved emotions some fifteen years after the crime.

Rendered in exacting and implosive detail, Solwitz's tales feature characters who exist in some state of emotional extreme, such as Dvora, a schizophrenia-prone Jewish Israeli woman who insists that her husband take a job in Baghdad, only to have her recklessly confrontational behavior eventually drive her mad and endanger the life of her infant son. And in "Milk," Debra is the mother of infant twin boys whose songwriter husband's waffling interest in their children fuels her determination to maintain her family. Taking a job as a stripper in club called Les Girls, Debra's rage against men eventually escalates to a boiling point which prompts her to act out in an almost farcical manner.

Both lyric and forceful, Solwitz's stories employ a precise sense of character and voice to capture vividly that so-common, unfulfilled human wish—to find "a place where there is no contradiction." [Jeanne Claire van Ryzin]

Doris Betts. *The Sharp Teeth of Love.* Knopf, 1997. 336 pp. $24.00.

One might say that Doris Betts's *The Sharp Teeth of Love* shows what can happen to a couple on a cross-country trip if they don't have a car radio that works. On the way from Chapel Hill to her wedding in Nevada, illustrator Luna Stone changes her mind, runs away from her too-beautiful professor fiancé, and hides out in the Sierra Nevadas to take a "vacation from love." While camping and thinking, Luna encounters a strange cast of characters who accompany her through her crisis: a twelve-year-old boy on the run from those who have sold him into the world of child pornography, a deaf preacher from Wisconsin who reads Kafka because he likes the picture on the front of the book, and the ghost of Tamsen Donner, who had stayed with her dying husband rather than try to escape, had died, and was eaten as a member of the famous Donner Party of 1846.

In the mountains Luna reflects on her earlier life in North Carolina, dominated by a military father who feared his daughter might get as "fat as butter." Luna, true to her name, has a nervous breakdown, becomes anorexic, and stops speaking. After her tentative recovery, she begins sketching plants and human organs for pay—because they make "nature hold still"—and meets her future fiancé, a graduate student who eats "her time and her strength" and "her flesh."

Not since her novel *Heading West* (1981) has Betts created such endearing and intriguing characters, with humor—crackling at unexpected moments—so perfectly balanced with tragedy. Luna is a sort of modern-day version of Kafka's "A Hunger Artist," and the novel is about starving people—physically and emotionally—and the extremes they go to in order to feed and nourish their bodies and souls, as well as the silence people adopt when they are malnourished by life. As a character in search of herself, Luna learns in the wide open spaces of the West what she could not have learned in the lush but stifling South about feeding herself, survival, and the kind of sacrifices that real love demands. [Barbara Bennett]

Peter Wolfe. *A Vision of His Own: The Mind and Art of William Gaddis*. Fairleigh Dickinson Univ. Press, 1997. 312 pp. $45.00.

Why, I wonder, has a great, innovative, and influential novelist like William Gaddis inspired comparatively few critical studies? A quick count in the *MLA Bibliography* shows only eighty-eight articles and books on Gaddis published over the last thirty years. Perhaps that explains the need for Peter Wolfe's introduction to Gaddis's career and work. Despite a few annoying mistakes about the novels' characters and incidents and some sloppy psychologizing, Wolfe does a good job of addressing both the narrative techniques that make the novels work and their thematic concerns. He does an especially good job of showing the connections between Gaddis's overwhelming cataloging of the minutiae of his characters' lives and larger, less obvious social, economic, and political forces. An overview of the career is followed by chapters focusing on each of the novels, with most of the attention given, appropriately, to *The Recognitions* and *JR*. This study will be especially helpful for newcomers to Gaddis and graduate students, some of whom, I hope, will go on to make their own contributions to Gaddis studies. [Robert L. McLaughlin]

Frank MacShane, ed. *Ford Madox Ford: The Critical Heritage*. Routledge, 1997. 271 pp. $115.00; Donald Watt, ed. *Aldous Huxley: The Critical Heritage*. Routledge, 1997. 493 pp. $145.00.

Both of these are reprints, making available again these wonderful collections of criticism that shows what the critical reception was for these authors when their books first came out. For Huxley, you have Frank Kermode calling *Island* "one of the worst novels ever written." And the Van Dorens in 1925 praise Lawrence and Huxley because they will carry on the fine tradition of Wells, Galsworthy, and Bennett. Wyndham Lewis attacks Huxley's *Point Counter Point*, but then Lewis attacked everyone. Rebecca West and Theodore Dreiser praise Ford's *The Good Soldier*, but a number of others did not like it at all. Graham Greene gave a good review to *The March of Literature;* Greene's obituary for Ford is also included, as well as one by Sherwood Anderson. These volumes, as well as others that Routledge is reissuing, are invaluable. Their prices will probably restrict them to library purchases, but they should be standard books in any good library. [John O'Brien]

Eric Cassidy and Dan O'Hara, eds. *Thomas Pynchon: Schizophrenia & Social Control: Papers from the Warwick Conference*. Special issue of *Pynchon Notes* 34-35 (Spring-Fall 1994) [1997]. (English Dept., Univ. of Wisconsin—Eau Claire, Ean Claire WI, 54702-4004.) 224 pp. Paper: $10.00.

A few years ago, I had an NEH grant application rejected because, according to the readers' report, there had been so much work done on Pynchon already that there was really nothing new left to be said. I hope those readers see this superb collection of essays, selections from the Pynchon conference held in Warwick, England, in 1994, all proving that there is *much* still to be said about Pynchon. The general focus here is to approach Pynchon's (pre-*Mason & Dixon*) work through cybertheory—cyborg, cyberspace, cyberpunk—and through the theories of Deleuze and Guattari, but the essays represent these approaches and many more: narratology, source studies, cultural studies, intertextual analyses. The most revelatory—for me—of these uniformly strong essays are John Johnston's study of media systems in *Vineland*, Steven Weisenburger's careful analysis of embedded narration in *Gravity's Rainbow*, Bernard Duyfhuizen's exploration of *Gravity's Rainbow*'s Walter Rathenau séance, and Eric Cassidy's fascinating discussion of economic theory in *Gravity's Rainbow*. The issue also presents the abstracts of the remaining conference presentations, plus *Pynchon Note*'s regular review section and invaluable, ongoing Pynchon bibliography. This collection is a must for all who labor in the Pynchon industry; for the avocational enthusiast, it is a good introduction to the latest and most interesting ideas in Pynchon studies. [Robert L. McLaughlin]

Michael P. Spikes. *Understanding Contemporary American Literary Theory*. Univ. of South Carolina Press, 1997. 201 pp. $24.95.

This book fills the gap between a dictionary of theoretical terms and an introductory monograph on a particular theorist. There are short chapters on Paul de Man, Henry Louis Gates, Jr., Elaine Showalter, Stephen Greenblatt, Edward W. Said, and Richard Rorty. For some, this selection might seem narrow: there is no chapter on Frederic Jameson or any other Marxist and no chapter on a psychoanalytic theorist such as Norman Holland or Nancy Chodorow. Also, some will object that Stanley Fish is more important than Rorty. Nonetheless, each chapter should prove valuable not just for advanced students but even for their mentors.

The introduction is particularly useful. It discusses the New Critics and Northrop Frye not as history we have transcended, but as lasting influences on contemporary theory. Most important, it summarizes the contributions of Fish, Jacques Derrida, Michel Foucault, and Harold Bloom so that the reader can understand the chapters that follow. Some will object to the first chapter's defense of de Man's assertion that he is correct even though nobody can be correct. Among the important topics in the chapter on Gates are blackness as absence, Gates's debt to whites and structuralists, and jazz improvisation as a species of Signifyin(g). The overview of Showalter's achievement is especially good in its summary of the cultural work of the quest romance; however, by frequently treating as interchangeable the terms "gender" and "sex," as well as the terms "feminine" and "female," the discussion perpetuates the confusion that bothers many students. The chapter on Greenblatt is a model for showing that a text is the creation not only of an author but also of a culture. The discussion of Said shows his debt to structuralism and points out the problem when Said asserts undecidability and yet also asserts that Eurocentric representations of the Orient are decidedly wrong. The next chapter is more forgiving of Rorty's assertion that we cannot establish facts, but we can establish the fact that we cannot establish facts.

To be clear and concise about a subject that is murky and disparate is difficult, but Spikes succeeds. Moreover, he contributes new ways of looking at central concepts—for example in his explanation that Derridean deconstruction exposes opposite meanings by showing how signifieds contain their opposites. [Darryl Hattenhauer]

Timothy Morris. *Making the Team: The Cultural Work of Baseball Fiction.* Univ. of Illinois Press, 1997. 190 pp. Paper: $13.95.

There is an old saying about sports fiction: the smaller the ball, the better the writing. Timothy Morris's study of baseball fiction is a very good book and for reasons other and more significant than that it is about stories of that small, hard ball. Many academic books in the field of sports-oriented literature are overly descriptive and, at best, offer a taxonomy of such writing. (Perhaps this is so because of the newness of this area of literary studies.) Morris's work, however, is interpretative and theoretically sophisticated. It is as if scholarship in sports literature has now grown up, moved beyond kids' games. Morris argues that "the cultural work and ideological constructions of adult baseball fiction are continuous with those of juvenille baseball fiction" and that "the rhetoric that denies and conceals this continuity can in turn provide a model for insights into the cultural construction of other kinds of literature . . . and into the function of the literary as a cultural value." In chapters on assimilation, heterosexuality, language, and meritocracy, Morris convincingly charts and provocatively analyzes the parallel cultural functions of adult and juvenille baseball fiction. In a final chapter he moves from these functions to a speculation on the larger significance of the literary in a community's self-perpetuation. In the introduction to this book and in the playful language indicative of it (something else that separates it from many previous studies of sports literature), Morris claims that "the instincts of someone born just on the waning edge of the Baby Boom impel me to critique what I have been raised to accept." Morris succeeds in critiquing unexamined assumptions of baseball fiction and the American civilization of which it is a part. [Dennis Barone]

New and Recommended Reprints

• Tibor Fisher. *Under the Frog.* Despite being named by *Granta* as one of the "Best Young British Novelists," Tibor is worth getting to know. Metropolitan, another Henry Holt line, has just issued Tibor's new novel *The Collector Collector.* Owl/Holt, 250 pp. $12.00.

• Michel Tournier. *Friday* and *The Ogre.* Trans. Norman Denny and Barbara Bray, respectively. I don't know what has happened at Johns Hopkins in the last year or so, but it is doing some very interesting literary books, competing with Northwestern and Nebraska as being the best literary university press. Both of these were brought out by Doubleday (hard to imagine now) within three years of each other starting in 1969. In many people's minds Tournier is the major French figure after the nouveau roman figures. Johns Hopkins, 235 pp. $14.95; 372 pp. $15.95.

• Jonathan Franzen. *The Twentieth-Seventh City.* This is a novel, long out of print, that David Foster Wallace has been raving about for years. Franzen is someone else who wound up on that awful *Granta* list. Farrar, Straus, & Giroux, 517 pp. $15.00.

• Alexander Theroux. *The Secondary Colors.* A remarkable sequel to Theroux's remarkable *The Primary Colors.* Owl/Holt, 312 pp. $12.00.

• Rick Moody. *Garden State.* This is Moody's first novel, and for this edition he has written an interesting preface on the origins of the book. Back Bay/Little Brown, 212 pp. $11.95.

• Anthony Burgess. *The Doctor Is Sick.* Reprint of Burgess novel first published in 1960. Norton, 261 pp. $12.00.

• Padgett Powell. *Edisto Revisited.* First paperback edition of this novel, a sequel to *Edisto.* Owl/Holt, 145 pp. $12.00.

Books Received

Arlett, Robert. *Epic Voices*. Susquehanna, 1996. $33.50. (NF)

Askew, Rilla. *The Mercy Seat*. Viking, 1997. $23.95. (F)

Atkinson, Kate. *Behind the Scenes at the Museum*. Picador, 1997. $14.00. (F)

Axelrod, Mark. *Cardboard Castles*. Pacific Writers Press, 1996. No price given. (F)

Barthelme, Donald. *Not-Knowing: The Essays and Interviews of Donald Barthelme*. Random House, 1997. $27.50. (NF)

Barthelme, Fredrick. *Bob the Gambler.* Houghton Mifflin, 1997. $23.00. (F)

Barrett, Eileen, and Patricia Cramer. *Virginia Woolf: Lesbian Readings*. New York, 1997. $18.95. (NF)

Bauchau, Henry. *Oedipus on the Road*. Trans. Anne-Marie Glasheen. Arcade, 1997. $24.95. (F)

Beard, Richard. *X20: A Novel of (Not) Smoking*. Arcade, 1997. $22.95. (F)

Benedetti, Mario. *Blood Pact and Other Stories.* Curbstone, 1997. $13.95. (F)

Bloom, Amy. *Love Invents Us.* Random House, 1997. $21.00. (F)

Bloom, James D. *The Literary Bent.* Pennsylvania, 1997. Paper: No price given. (NF)

Bolker, Joan, ed. *The Writer's Home Companion*. Owl, 1997. Paper: $14.95. (NF)

Bouldrey, Brian, ed. *Best American Gay Fiction 2*. Back Bay, 1997. Paper: $13.95. (F)

Breton, André. *Anthology of Black Humor.* Trans. John Polizzotti. City Lights, 1997. Paper: $18.95. (NF)

Bruns, Gerald L. *Maurice Blanchot: The Refusal of Philosophy*. Johns Hopkins, 1997. $39.95. (NF)

Burgess, Anthony. *Byrne*. Carroll and Graf, 1997. $20.00. (F)

Calisher, Hortense. *In the Slammer with Carol Smith*. Marion Boyars, 1997. $25.95. (F)

Carocci, Giampiero. *The Officers Camp*. Northwestern, 1997. Paper: $15.95. (NF)

Carragher, Michael. *A World Full of Places*. Dufour Editions, 1997. Paper: $15.95. (F)

Chapman, Stepan. *The Troika*. Ministry of Whimsy, 1997. $14.99. (F)

Cherkovski, Neeli. *Bukowski: A Life*. Steerforth, 1997. Paper: $25.00. (NF)

Christy, Jim. *The Buk Book: Musings on Charles Bukowski*. ECW, 1997. $12.95 (NF)

Collins, Warwick. *Gents*. Marion Boylars, 1997. $18.95. (F)

Cooper, Dennis. *Guide*. Grove/Atlantic, 1997. $22.00. (F)

Cronin, Anthony. *The Last Modernist: Samuel Beckett.* Harper Collins, 1997. $30.00. (NF)

Crossley, Robert, ed. *An Olaf Stapledon Reader.* Syracuse, 1997. $45.00. (NF)

Davies, Robertson. *The Merry Heart: Reflections on Reading, Writing, and the World of Books.* Viking, 1997. $27.95. (NF)

Donawerth, Jane. *Frankenstein's Daughters*. Syracuse, 1997. $39.95. (NF)

Donleavy, J. P. *The Lady Who Liked Clean Rest Rooms*. St. Martin's, 1997. $18.95. (F)

Dunant, Sarah. *Transgressions*. Virago, 1997, £15.99. (F)

Edgell, Zee. *The Festival of San Joaquin.* Heinemann, 1997. Paper: $13.95. (F)

Epheron, Amy. *A Cup of Tea*. William Morrow, 1997. $20.00. (F)

Eversz, Robert M. *Gypsy Hearts*. Grove/Atlantic, 1997. $23.00. (F)

Fink, Ida. *Traces*. Metropolitan, 1997. $23.00. (F)

Finkielkraut, Alain. *The Wisdom of Love*. Trans. Kevin O'Neill and David Suchoff. Nebraska, 1997. $25.00. (F)

Ford, Richard. *Women with Men*. Knopf, 1997. $23.00. (F)

Goossen, Theodore W., ed. *The Oxford Book of Japanese Short Stories.* Oxford, 1997. Paper: $18.95. (NF)

Graham, Barry. *Before.* Incommunicado, 1997. Paper: $13.00. (F)

Graver, Elizabeth. *Unravelling*. Hyperion, 1997. $22.95. (F)

Griffin, Brian. *Sparkman in the Sky & Other Stories*. Sarabande, 1997. $21.95. (F)

Griffith, James. *Adaptions as Imitations: Films from Novels*. Delaware Press, 1997. $39.50. (NF)

Hawkes, John. *An Irish Eye*. Viking, 1997. No price given. (F)

Hempel, Amy. *Tumble Home.* Scribner, 1997. $21.00. (F)

J., Angelica. *Fermentation*. Grove/Atlantic, 1997. $20.00. (F)

Jacobsen, Roy. *The New Water*. Trans. William H. Halverson. Peer Gynt, 1997. Paper: $14.00. (F)

Kang, Younghill. *East Goes West: The Making of an Oriental Yankee.* Kaya, 1997. Paper: $16.95. (F)

Kazin, Alfred. *God and the American Writer*. Knopf, 1997. $25.00. (NF)

Kelman, James. *Busted Scotch: Selected Stories.* Norton, 1997. $23.00. (F)

Kerrane, Kevin, and Ben Yagoda, eds. *The Art of Facts: A Historical Anthology of Literary Journalism*. Scribner, 1997. $35.00. (NF)

Kolmar, Gertrud. *A Jewish Mother from Berlin* and *Susanna*. Trans. Brigitte Goldstein. Holmes & Meier, 1997. $24.00. (F)
Köpf, Gerhard. *Innerfar and Bluff: Two Novels*. Trans. Leslie Willson. Camden House, 1997. $26.00. (F)
Lea, Sydney. *A Place in Mind*. Story Line, 1997. Paper: $12.95. (F)
Leontis, Artemis. *Greece: A Literary Companion*. Whereabouts, 1997. Paper:$13.95. (NF)
Levine, Stacey. *Dar—*. Sun and Moon, 1997. Paper: $11.95. (F)
Lévy, Justine. *The Rendezvous*. Scribner, 1997. $22.00. (F)
Linmark, R. Zamora. *Rolling the R's*. Kaya, 1997. $21.00 (F)
Makine, Andrei. *Dreams of My Russian Summers*. Arcade, 1997. $23.95. (F)
Masini, Donna. *About Yvonne*. Norton, 1997. $23.00. (F)
Mathews, Harry, et al. *S.* Brook Line, 1997. Paper: $12.95. (F)
Matson, Suzanne. *The Hunger Moon*. Norton, 1997. $23.00. (F)
McCord, Howard. *The Man Who Walked to The Moon*. McPherson, 1997. $18.00. (F)
McCracken, Elizabeth. *The Giant's House: A Romance*. Avon, 1997. Paper: $12.00. (F)
McGarry, Jean. *Gallagher's Travels*. Johns Hopkins, 1997. $22.95. (F)
McNally, John, ed. *High Infidelity*. Morrow, 1997. $22.00. (F)
Merry, Bruce. *Dacia Maraini and the Written Dream of Women in Italian Literature*. James Cook, 1997. Paper: $14.00. (NF)
Metcalf, Paul. *Collected Works Volume Two: 1976-1986*. Coffee House, 1997. $35.05. (F)
Milligan, Jennifer E. *The Forgotten Generation*. New York, 1997. $46.00. (NF)
Murakami, Haruki. *The Wind-Up Bird Chronicle*. Knopf, 1997. $26.00. (F)
Murray, Les. *Subhuman Redneck Poems*. Farrar, Straus & Giroux, 1997. $18.00. (Poetry)
Myles, Eileen. *School of Fish*. Black Sparrow, 1997. Paper: $14.00. (Poetry)
Nádas, Péter. *A Book of Memories*. Farrar, Straus & Giroux, 1997. $30.00. (F)
Nadolny, Sten. *The God of Impertinence*. Viking, 1997. $23.95. (F)
Nicholson, Geoff. *Bleeding London*. Overlook, 1997. $23.95. (F)
Nyiri, Janos. *Battlefields and Playgrounds*. New England, 1997. Paper: $17.95. (F)
O'Connor, Frank. *An Only Child*. Syracuse, 1997. No price given. (NF)
Onetti, Juan Carlos. *Let the Wind Speak*. Serpent's Tail, 1997. Paper: $15.99. (F)

Phillips, Caryl. *The Nature of Blood*. Knopf, 1997. $23.00. (F)
Powell, Padgett. *Edisto Revisited*. Owl, 1997. Paper: $12.00. (F)
Rabasa, George. *Floating Kingdom*. Coffee House, 1997. $21.95. (F)
Ransom, Jane. *Bye-Bye*. New York, 1997. $17.95. (F)
Ranson, Sadi. *Eels*. Salamanca, 1997. Paper: No price given. (Poetry)
Reynolds, Marjorie. *The Starlite Drive-in*. Morrow, 1997. $23.00. (F)
Reynolds, Michael. *Hemingway: The 1930s*. Norton, 1997. $30.00. (NF)
Rigby, Peter. *African Images*. New York, 1996. $37.00. (NF)
Ritchie, Harry, ed. *Acid Plaid: New Scottish Writing*. Arcade, 1997. $13.95. (F)
Rosen, Norma. *John and Anzia: An American Romance*. Syracuse, 1997. Paper: $16.95. (F)
Sallis, James. *Death Will Have Your Eyes*. St. Martin's, 1997. $21.95. (F)
Sanders, Edward. *1968: A History in Verse*. Black Sparrow, 1997. $14.00. (Poetry)
Sandlin, Lisa. *Message to the Nurse of Dreams*. Cinco Puntos, 1997. $11.95. (F)
Sarraute, Nathalie. *Here*. Trans. Barbara Wright. George Braziller, 1997. $25.00. (F)
Saramago, José. *The History of the Siege of Lisbon*. Harcourt Brace, 1997. $24.00. (F)
Self, Will. *Great Apes*. Grove/Atlantic, 1997. $24.00. (F)
Sharpe, Tom. *The Midden*. Overlook, 1997. $23.95 (F)
Simon, Linda, ed. *Gertrude Stein Remembered*. Nebraska, 1997. Paper: $15.00. (NF)
Smith, Ali. *Like*. Virago, 1997. £12.99. (F)
Sylvester, Janet. *The Mark of Flesh*. Norton, 1997. $19.00. (Poetry)
Taylor, Bruce. *The Final Trick of Funny Man and Other Stories*. Ministry of Whimsy, 1997. Paper: 12.99. (F)
Thames, Susan. *I'll Be Home Late Tonight*. Villard, 1997. $23.00. (F)
Timm, Uwe. *The Invention of Curried Sausage*. New Directions, 1997. Paper: $9.95. (F)
Tóibín, Colm. *The Story of the Night*. Holt, 1997. $23.00. (F)
Tournier, Michel. *Friday*. Trans. Norman Denny. Johns Hopkins, 1997. Paper: $14.95. (F)
———. *The Ogre*. Trans. Barbara Bray. Johns Hopkins, 1997. Paper: $15.95. (F)
Vargas Llosa, Mario. *Making Waves*. Ed. and trans. John King. Farrar, Straus & Giroux, 1997. $27.50. (NF)
Watson, Carl. *Beneath the Empire of the Birds*. Apathy Press Poets, 1997. Paper: $13.00. (F)

Watt, Donald, ed. *Aldous Huxley: The Critical Heritage*. Routledge, 1997. $145.00. (NF)

Weaver, Gordon. *Four Decades*. Missouri, 1997. Paper: $18.95. (NF)

West, Nathanael. *Novels and Other Writings*. Ed. Sacvan Bercovitch. Library of America, 1997. $23.00. (F)

Yoshimoto, Banana. *Amrita*. Grove/Atlantic, 1997. $22.00. (F)

Contributors

ANDRE BLAVIER, librarian, is a co-founder and director of the review *Temps Mêlés,* author of varied books and articles, including an anthology of literary madmen, founder of the original Documentation Center on Raymond Queneau at Verviers, Belgium, and organizer, with Calude Debon, of the first International Colloquia on Raymond Queneau. He is a corresponding member of the Oulipo.

MARY CAMPBELL-SPOSITO is a Research Associate in the University of California at Berkeley's Department of French. She has published severals articles on Queneau.

NICOLE COOLEY is a widely published poet whose poems have appeared in *Poetry, Field Ploughshares,* and the *Nation,* among other publications. In 1994 she was awarded a "Discovery"/the *Nation* Award. *Resurrection* (Louisiana State Univ. Press, 1996) received the 1995 Walt Whitman Award of the Academy of American Poets. She grew up in New Orleans and currently resides in Atlanta.

CLAUDE DEBON, Professor at the Université de la Sorbonne nouvelle (Paris III), teaches contemporary poetry. She was editor of Volume I of Queneau's *Oeuvres completes* in the Pléiade Edition.

LOUISE DeSALVO is Professor of English and Creative Writing at Hunter College. Her eleven books include *Virginia Woolf's First Voyage, Conceived with Malice, Virginia Woolf's Melymbrosia, Virginia Woolf: The Impact of Childhood Sexual Abuse on Her Life and Work,* and the award-winning memior *Vertigo*. Her most recent book, *Breathless,* is a journal about asthma. She is currently writing a book about creativity.

JEFFREY DeSHELL is the author of two novels, *In Heaven Everything is Fine* (1991) and *S&M* (1997), both published by FC2, and a critical book on Edgar Allan Poe, Maurice Blanchot, and Walter Benjamen. He co-edits the series "On the Edge: New Women's Fiction," also from FC2. He currently lives near the ancient walled city of Gazimagusa, in the Turkish Republic of Northern Cyprus, where he teaches English at Eastern Mediterranean University.

CHARLES B. HARRIS has published numerous articles on contemporary American fiction and the profession of English studies. His books include *Contemporary American Novelists of the Absurd* (1971) and *Passionate Virtuosity: The Fiction of John Barth* (1983). He directs the Unit for Contemporary Literature at Illinois State University.

VICTORIA FRENKEL HARRIS is professor of English at Illinois State University. Her articles on literary theory, feminist issues, and such poets as Robert Bly, Adrienne Rich, James Wright, and Denise Levertov have appeared in various scholarly journals and essay collections. Her critical study, *The Incorporative Consciousness of Robert Bly,* was published by Southern Illinois University Press in 1992.

JACQUES JOUET is the author of several books of fiction (novels and novellas), of poetry and of drama, and the 1994 winner of the Société des Gens de Lettres de France's Grand Prix for the novel. He has been a member of the Oulipo since 1983.

HARRY MATHEWS lives in France and the United States. He has written numerous books of poetry, novels, and essays, most recently *A Mid-Season Sky Poems 1954-1991* (1992) and *Immeasurable Distances: The Collected Essays* (1991). He is a member of the Oulipo.

STEVEN MOORE is the author of *A Reader's Guide to William Gaddis's The Recognitions* (1982) and co-editor of *In Recognition of William Gaddis* (1984) and has written many essays about and reviews of contemporary fiction. The former Senior Editor of *Review of Contemporary Fiction,* he now lives in Denver. He wrote the foreword to *The Letters of Wanda Tinasky.*

GILBERT PESTUREAU, Professor of French at Loyola University, Chicago, has published two books on Boris Vian. He is a member of the team of editors for Raymond Queneau's *Oeuvres completes* (II and III) in the Pléiade Editions.

JACQUES ROUBAUD is a poet, a novelist and a professor of mathematics at the University of Paris X (Nanterre). Several of his novels have been translated into English, including *The Great Fire of London, Hortense in Exile, Hortense is Abducted,* and *The Princess Hoppy* (Dalkey Archive Press).

GILBERT SORRENTINO's most recent novel is *Red the Fiend*

(Fromm International). Sun & Moon Press has reissued his 1978 book of poems, *The Orangery.*

BARBARA WRIGHT has translated many French writers, including Raymond Queneau, Robert Pinget, Nathalie Sarraute, and Michel Tournier. Her most recent translation is Jean Rouaud's *Of Illustrious Men* (1995).

Annual Index

References are to issue number and pages, respectively

Contributors

Books Reviewed

Reviewers' names follow in parentheses. Regular reviewers are abbreviated: BE=Brian Evenson; BH=Brooke Horvath; IM=Irving Malin; JB=Jack Byrne; LO=Lance Olsen; PM=Paul L. Maliszewski; Jean Claire va Ryzun=JV; RM=Robert L. McLaughlin; JO=John O'Brien

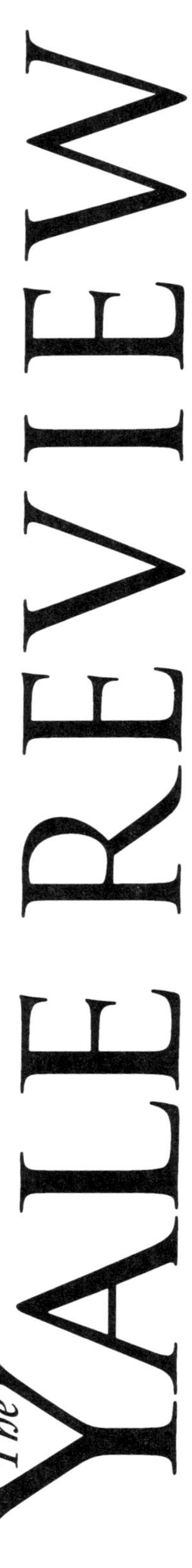
The YALE REVIEW

VQR THE VIRGINIA QUARTERLY REVIEW
A National Journal of Literature and Discussion

SUMMER 1997 *Volume 73, Number 3*

FIVE DOLLARS

The Virginia Quarterly Review
One West Range
Charlottesville, VA 22903

Chartres Cathedral, France

"An extraordinary, visionary book, written out of those edges where madness and poetry meet." —Fay Weldon

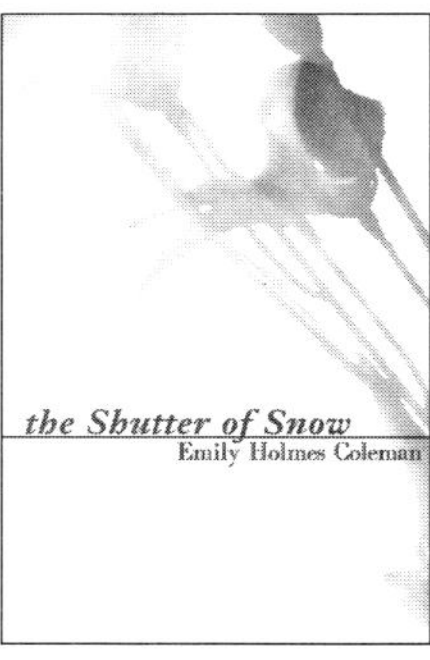

$12.95 pb

1-56478-147-X

The Shutter of Snow

Emily Holmes Coleman

In a prose and form as startling as its content, *The Shutter of Snow* portrays the post-partum psychosis of Marthe Gail, who after giving birth to her son, is committed to an insane asylum. Believing herself to be God, she maneuvers through an institutional world that is both sad and terrifying, echoing the worlds of *One Flew over the Cuckoo's Nest* and *The Snake Pit.*

Based upon the author's own experience after the birth of her son in 1924, *The Shutter of Snow* retains all the energy it had when first published in 1930.

"The book is no less graphic than it is authentic, an extremely rare achievement in the 'firsthand document' school of letters, for usually we have drama at the expense of truth, or bald facts that unwittingly falsify the picture. *The Shutter of Snow* is a profoundly moving book, supplying as it does a glimpse of what a temporary derangement and its consequences may mean to the sufferer." —*Nation*

Dalkey Archive Press

“A stunning paen to the power of the imagination . . . Certainly the work of one of our best writers at the top of his form.” —*San Francisco Chronicle*

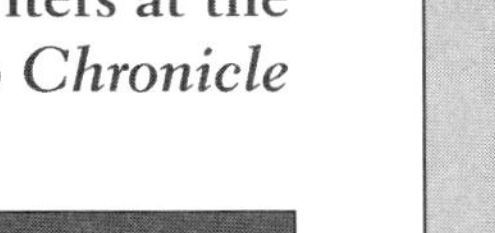

$12.95 pb
1-56478-179-8

The Barnum Museum

Steven Millhauser

The Barnum Museum is a combination waxworks, masked ball, and circus side-show masquerading as a collection of short stories. Within its pages, note such sights as: a study of the motives and strategies used by the participants in the game of Clue, including the seduction of Miss Scarlet by Colonel Mustard; the Barnum Museum, a fantastic, monstrous landmark so compelling that an entire town finds its citizens gradually and inexorably disappearing into it; a bored dilettante who constructs an imaginary woman—and loses her to an imaginary man!—and a legendary magician so skilled at sleight-of-hand that he is pursued by police for the crime of erasing the line between the real and the conjured.

Ingeniously written and orchestrated, each exhibit in *The Barnum Museum* will compel you to continue, each story becoming a lure to the next.

“Stunningly clever and thought-provoking . . . Millhauser is a brilliant stylist who can shift voices like a good ventriloquist.” —*The Milwaukee Journal*

Dalkey
Archive
Press

"America's greatest living writer."—Edmund White

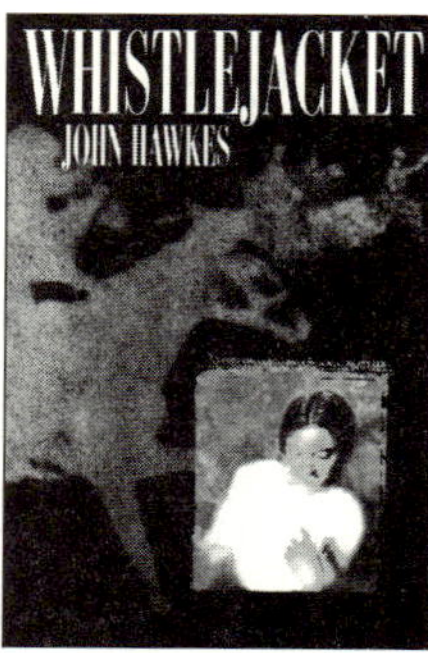

$12.95 pb
1-56478-176-3

Whistlejacket

John Hawkes

While investigating his mentor's life and death, Michael, a voyeuristic fashion photographer, travels through a Dionysian landscape where sex is daydream, women and horses share the same erotic power, and perversity is the rule. In his search, Michael uses photographs and paintings to visualize the past and thereby expose a family's decadent legacy of sex, lies, and betrayal.

An inventive mix of biography, history, erotica, and classic whodunit, *Whistlejacket* is John Hawkes at his best as he blurs the distinction between death and desire, image and language, art and morality.

"From the first, John Hawkes's prose has sounded what Henry James would have said was 'the right note.' . . . His lines are alive as few in our literature."—William Gass

"Outrageous situations and unforgettable scenes refracted through a lens of rhetoric as beautiful as anything I know of in contemporary fiction."
—John Barth

Dalkey
Archive
Press

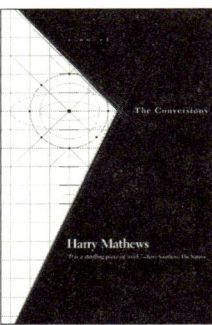

"One of the most remarkable prose stylists presently writing in English."—*San Francisco Chronicle*

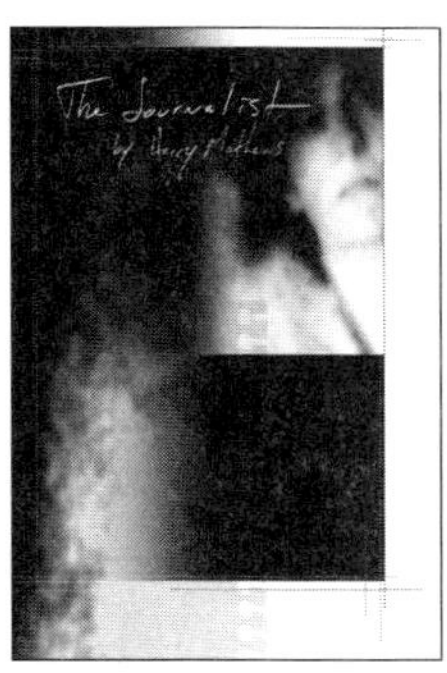

$12.95 pb
1-56478-165-8

The Journalist

Harry Mathews

As an aid to recovering from a nervous breakdown, the narrator of *The Journalist* begins to keep daily records of almost everything that goes on in his life, from how much he has spent on books and movies to what he eats. As the diary progresses, the narrator's entries become more and more detailed and increasingly bizarre, especially as he begins to devise elaborate classification systems for his unwieldy materials. Since these entries require more and more of his time, he begins to withdraw from family and friends, entering a world perfectly ordered, organized, and utterly weird.

"The calm with which Harry Mathews represents the elusiveness of the self in this riveting, masterful novel is like the calm in the eye of a hurricane. *The Journalist* will take your breath away!"—Walter Abish

Dalkey
Archive
Press

Order Form

Individuals may use this form to order Dalkey titles at a 10-20% discount directly from the publisher.

Title	ISBN	Quantity	Price

Subtotal ______________

(10% for one book, 20% for two or more books) Less discount ______________

Subtotal ______________

($3.50 for the first book, $.75 for each additional) Plus domestic postage ________

($4.50 for the first book, $1.00 for each additional) Plus foreign postage ________

Total ______________

Ship to:

____

____

____

____

mail or fax this form to:
Dalkey Archive Press
ISU Campus Box 4241
Normal, IL 61790-4241
fax: 309 438 7422
tel: 309 438 7555

Credit card payment ❑ Visa ❑ Mastercard

Acct # ______________ Exp. Date ________

Name on card ______________

Phone Number ______________

Please make checks (in U. S. dollars only) payable to *Dalkey Archive Press*

Dalkey
Archive
Press